LM Ardor is a former inner city GP

LM Ardor is a former inner city GP

The Practice Baby

LM Ardor

First published by Critical Mass in 2018
This edition published in 2018 by Critical Mass

The Practice Baby

EPUB: 9781925579987
POD: 9781925579994

Cover design by Red Tally Studios

Publishing services provided by Critical Mass
www.critmassconsulting.com

Prologue

The bedroom was neat and still. A double bed was made up with white sheets, an olive-green spread and a single white pillow. In the yellow indirect light that seeped through the heavy curtains it could be a stage set, ready for the call 'Action'.

The corpse was neat too. It was dressed in Tom's clothes: white shirt, beige pants, polished shoes and a brown cord jacket. It was flat on its back, head centred on the pillow, arms by its sides, eyes open and fixed on the ceiling above. A single fly moved across the glazed left eyeball.

Anyone could see it was a dead body, a lump of meat, not a person.

Her job was to declare the body dead, to make it official. She pulled on gloves, knelt on the edge of the bed to reach for the pulse at the angle of the jaw. The mass jiggled as the mattress moved and a strong odour wafted up. Her lower jaw and chest were hollow, empty spaces for tears. But it wasn't the smell or the presence of the body that bothered her—as a GP she had seen and smelt worse—it was the absence of Tom.

The body on the bed wasn't him. The inanimate lump had his shape, his dense black curls and it was dressed in his clothes. But this mass, these seventy kilograms of unrefrigerated flesh, was not Tom. Tom was gone.

Part 1

1.

'Why is my life always less important than some stranger's death?' Beatrice yelled from the top of the walkway to the house.

Dee opened the car door. She put the keys in the ignition but didn't get in. She gave herself a moment to take in the view and resist the urge to respond.

It was a perfect spring morning. Down the slope, between smooth cream and grey eucalypt trunks, patches of harbour flashed deep blue, dotted white with sails. The sun reflected up to spotlight outcrops of golden Sydney sandstone in the bush.

This could go two ways. All the things Dee wanted to say: that she had to work to keep the four of them; that work included care for patients in their last moments; emergencies couldn't be scheduled; that she had needs too, including the need to do her job well, which also provided for them all. The bond she'd formed with Tracy O'Neill through seven years of cancer treatments didn't turn off at 7 pm each day.

None of those arguments would dent Bea's hurt. She was stung by what to her was treacherous neglect by her own mother. Dee's needs were blown away in the maelstrom of teenage injustice. It was best to let the storm run its course.

'Bea, I'm late, I don't have time for this.'

'Just let me drive as far as Sailor's Bay Road.'

'There's no time, and your father doesn't want you to learn to drive from me—he can pay for lessons. Let him sort it out.'

Rob had moved to the inner city two years ago and was a newly minted enviro-moralist. His voice as he pronounced on the virtues of public transport set Dee's teeth on edge.

'Maybe you'd have time for me if I made an appointment at the surgery?'

Dee didn't have the energy for this.

'It's eight minutes till my first patient—we'll talk tonight.'

'You've got your bloody GP meeting tonight,' Beatrice screamed at her.

'Tomorrow then, and calm down. That sort of talk is very unattractive.'

'Fuck you!' Beatrice turned on her heel and went inside. She tried to slam the heavy frameless glass door behind her but it swung gently into place on the hinges Rob had designed.

Rob. Why couldn't he sort it all out? He was the famous architect; designer of 'the Glasshouse' where Dee and the kids still lived after he'd moved to the city with Stephanie, a student thirty years his junior. Now he had babies—twins. It served him right, but it meant less time for his other children. Why did Bea have to suffer for his ridiculous libido?

Six minutes to eight—Dee threw her bag onto the passenger seat and started the car. She was halfway through the three-point turn required to get out of the cul-de-sac when Bea ran out of the house with shoes, socks and backpack in her hands.

'Just as far as Flat Rock Drive?' Bea smiled and buckled herself into the passenger seat.

'I'm late,' Dee protested as they roared off.

'I know. You're always late. Thanks,' Bea said with another smile.

At the lights, Dee looked over at her sixteen-year-old—an early Renaissance beauty with Rob's smooth olive skin and a gentler version of Dee's red hair and green eyes. Bea, in a half put-together school uniform, a slice of Vegemite toast flopping from her hand, had transformed from screaming harridan to loving daughter.

Dee looked again. Was that mascara? Time enough for makeup but not for shoes? She bit her tongue—not now. Maybe the school would sort it out.

'I can skip the meeting if you like.'

'No, tomorrow's okay.'

'You'll have to jump out when I can stop at the turn into Brook Street.'

At the top of the hill, they turned and found the traffic backed up. Each change of traffic lights only let through one or two cars. She was going to be at least fifteen minutes late. Not good for someone who kept people waiting the rest of the day. The morning slots were always snapped up by people who didn't want to wait. It was eight past eight.

'Ring Janelle and let her know I'm late.' Dee fumbled in her handbag and gave Bea her mobile phone 'Put her on speaker.'

'Hi Janelle, I'm late. Be there in—'

Janelle cut her off. 'Well, the first one's not here yet, and it's a double.' She sounded brisk.

'Good, offer them a coffee when they arrive. Who is it?'

'Tom Harris.'

'Tom?' Dee echoed. 'Are you sure he's not there?'

'Unless he's wearing his cloak of invisibility,' said Janelle, sharp now.

'Can you log into my emails and messages and check if he left a message? Oh and ring me if he arrives.'

The phone clicked off. Three cars ahead had made it through the lights. Dee didn't notice. The car behind them tooted.

'Mum, the traffic's moved.'

Dee shook her head and inched the car forward.

'What's wrong?'

'Tom would never be late. Something's happened.' His recent visits had made Dee uneasy.

'Everyone's late sometimes, look at you.'

'I've known this boy since he was born, if he was going to be late he'd let us know. Something is wrong.'

A gap opened up. Dee didn't notice; didn't move.

'Mum, what's wrong with you? Move.'

Dee came back from her anxious thoughts. She put her foot on the accelerator and managed to squeeze past a car turning right with a centimetre to spare on each side. She roared down the hill and got through the next lights on orange.

In Brook Street, she put on her hazard lights and stopped in the clearway.

'Quick, go!'

The lights turned green. The blonde in the huge four-wheel drive behind them blared her horn continuously as Bea gathered bag, blazer, shoes and socks.

'Yeah,' Dee yelled at the blonde, 'why don't you take your off-road vehicle cross-country, fuck features?'

'Very unattractive way to talk, Mum.'

'It's okay, she can't hear me. Come on, out, before she drives over us.'

'Hope your patient's all right. Love you, Mum.' Bea leaned over for a kiss before she opened the door and stumbled over to a low wall to sit and put on her shoes and socks.

At the turn into the expressway, Dee sneaked up the outside lane and forced her way into the line of cars.

'Idiot, for fuck's sake, drive!' she shouted from the safety of closed windows as the silver Range Rover in front of her failed to take advantage of a gap in the traffic.

After twenty-six years she could predict the traffic on the route from Castlecrag to Pyrmont to the second. The turn onto the expressway went smoothly and she sailed across the Harbour Bridge in the middle lane, centimetres from the huge trucks rushing the other way. The speed limit was seventy but she wouldn't get booked if she stayed under seventy-eight.

As they came off the bridge onto the Western Distributor, the driver in front of Dee dithered, straddling two lanes.

'Fucking bloody make up your mind, fart features.'

There was just enough space between him and the guardrail. Dee accelerated and got around him. There wasn't a speed camera in this section. She risked it and sped up to ninety.

With a brief slowdown for the speed camera on Harbour Street, she flashed through an orange light to get across Harris Street, rounded the block to the car park and skidded into the parking spot. Her driver training from the Army Reserve was still useful after all these years.

The surgery car space was the only place in the universe where no one could contact her—no one could ask her to do anything. Nothing worked, wi-fi or phone, and no one could even see someone was in the car without being right up close. Usually she sat for two to three minutes to enjoy no one and nothing: no kids, no staff, no patients, no one else's needs. Today it failed to soothe her. Without the distraction of driving, her thoughts wandered around what might have happened to Tom. Her breakfast became a heavy stone in her gut.

Dee checked the time on her phone. Eight eighteen. Why would Tom not turn up? She got out of the car and went upstairs.

Inside the surgery, Janelle handed her a takeaway coffee. 'Sorry it's cold. Will I get you another one?'

'No, it's fine, as long as it's got caffeine …' Dee paused, not wanting to hear the answer to her next question. 'No message from Tom?'

'Nothing.' Janelle put her hand out to touch Dee's arm. 'Are you okay? You look pale.'

'I feel a bit odd, it'll pass. Tracy died last night and I didn't get home till midnight but now I'm worried about Tom.'

'He probably got confused about the date.' Janelle didn't know Tom as well as Dee. She didn't realise he would never miss an appointment. 'Should I ring him?'

'No, I'll do it.'

Patients missed appointments all the time and, normally, the free time was good. It was a chance to catch up if she was running behind or attack the mountain of report requests and letters in her in-tray. Usually she welcomed a missed appointment.

She rang Tom's mobile and got the 'switched off or not in a mobile service area' message from the phone company. She pushed the coffee aside. She didn't have the stomach for it anymore.

Tom's phone was part of him, an extra hard drive for his brain. There was no way he'd let it run out of battery or switch it off. He was always on time. In the twenty-five years she had known him, he had never been late or missed an appointment, except when he was an infant under the control of Skye.

His obsessiveness made sense as a reaction to life with his disorganised mother. Any inborn predilections for order and routine, any tendency to an obsessional personality style, were amplified by Skye's incapacity to be organised and her reliance on marijuana to deal with stress. There was no order in the world Tom found himself in so he set about creating it. When his younger brother turned out to be severely autistic, Dee wondered if there was a genetic predisposition to Asperger's as well.

She got up and closed the door to her surgery. It gave a solid click. Her room was a safe space: black desk, black leather chairs, grey wool carpet, pale blue walls and a Japanese screen to hide the couch and medical paraphernalia.

She logged in and clicked on his file. Tom's first visit was when notes were handwritten so the computer file had dates but no details. As soon as she saw the date, five days after his birth, Dee remembered the first time she'd seen him. It was for a newborn baby check. He was the first of the 'practice babies'—people she'd looked after from birth. In Tom's case, she had diagnosed his mother's pregnancy, provided antenatal care and listened to his heartbeat in the womb.

On that first visit with him, Skye was frazzled with sore, cracked nipples and fear that she was a failure as a mother. The idea that breastfeeding was a skill to be learned by both mother and baby confronted her worldview that anything natural would come automatically.

Tom was healthy but hungry; three kilos of determination to survive whose only weapon was to cry.

Dee held him while Skye climbed onto the couch. He immediately stopped crying. It was well before Dee had her own children and, with one unfocused look of trust, he tunnelled his way into her heart. It felt like she'd had a part in his production. She and Rob had delayed babies to establish their careers. Maybe she was broody, a hen in need of an egg to sit on, brain primed to squirt oxytocin into her blood and create a bond with this new being. She had never confessed the bond to anyone, not even herself, till now.

Tom's severe childhood asthma meant she'd seen him often. Watched too many times as the little boy in pyjamas perched on the side of his bed, blue and exhausted with the struggle to breathe through bronchial tubes that were spasmed and filled with mucus.

Skye loved her son but was not alert to the warning signs of an asthma attack. She forgot his medication or stopped it for some new miracle anti-asthma diet. Denial was her first line approach to any problem. It made her a hopeless judge of when it was time to call an ambulance to get her son to hospital. As Tom grew older he learned to manage his own medication and had been well, apart from a brief period of teenage rebellion when he was seventeen. In that year he'd come close to death twice. He'd frightened himself and never again allowed his asthma to get out of control.

Once he was put in charge of his own treatment with an asthma management plan he hadn't had a serious attack. The obsessive traits in his personality made him a perfect patient.

Tom made Dee feel unequivocally good. He always had a joke for her and he had a satisfyingly treatable medical condition. He was so much easier to deal with than her own children.

While she looked through her notes from the last few consultations, she saw him, limbs unfurled, in the chair opposite. Tight black curls fell over his impossibly long-lashed eyes. He pushed his fingers through his hair like a comb to flick the curls back. He had no idea he was attractive.

The lights in her surgery were dim. The white and black curtain at the big window next to her desk gave a glow of twilight—a space for patients to bare their bodies and their most intimate fears.

Dee's own fears were the problem this time. A tangle of vague anxieties she'd had for a couple of months coalesced into a web of fear. No—it was calmer, more hopeless than fear. It was grief. Somehow, she knew it was too late already; something had happened to Tom.

2.

Eight weeks earlier, Dee had seen Tom's name on the waiting room list and wondered why he was there. His asthma management plan wasn't due for review yet.

She drained her coffee and ran a hand through her unruly red hair to get it off her face. She walked down the hall. In the waiting room, four heads bobbed up; eight eyes focused on her; four sets of lips parted slightly in anticipation that their turn had come.

'Tom, come in.' Dee beckoned the young man in a corduroy sports jacket.

Tom unfolded his long legs, like a newborn foal surprised at having a body. In the surgery he refolded his limbs into the chair next to her desk.

She waited for him to start. With Tom it was always quicker to do things his way.

'Sorry to bother you, Doc, but the life insurance company want some forms filled in.'

'Life insurance?'

Tom was a child; why would he need life insurance?

'Just in case, you know. If something happened to me ...' Tom paused. He hadn't said why. Was it for his younger brother Charlie; to help Skye with his care?

'I have to pay extra because of the asthma but they still want a report and examination.'

Dee glanced at the form. It was very comprehensive.

'How much are you being insured for?'

'Hopefully five hundred grand if you decide I'll live a few more years.' He pushed at his curls and blinked as if dazzled by headlights.

It was a large amount. With his history of life-threatening asthma attacks he would have to pay a hefty extra premium.

'Tom, are you sure about this? Insurance salesmen can be very pushy. You know they get a commission for life from your premiums?'

'I want to make sure Charlie has security if anything happens to me. Mum's got nothing and she's not going to last forever.'

The form required a thorough exam, referral for respiratory function tests and a summary of his history. That meant trawling through two thick volumes of handwritten notes, which could take hours.

'You haven't had a serious attack since you were seventeen.'

'Yeah, when I finally saw the light and started doing what you told me. But you never know for sure what can happen. You know I'm a belt-and-braces kind of guy.'

Dee nodded. Half an hour wasn't much time for such a detailed report. Everything was to be sent directly to the company. She showed him what she was sending.

It wasn't like Tom to be guarded. Dee was curious. There was something he wasn't telling her.

Vague anxiety gnawed at her as she walked him back down the corridor.

'Bye, Tom. Take care.'

*

It was only a week before she saw him again.

The morning was clear in her memory. As usual she was pleased to see his name pop up, plus it was a chance to find out what was really going on with him. She called his name. He stood up and the woman next to him stood as well.

'Doc, this is Leah. Can she come in too?'

Dee's 'Of course' was automatic. Her flash of disappointment that she didn't have her baby to herself wasn't reasonable. She swallowed it. Tom was a patient. The consultation was for him; not to make her feel good.

The monotone young woman had beige skin the same colour as her dreadlocked hair; even her large eyes were the same dirty sand colour. She held Tom's hand. Her dress was an old heavy satin negligee in a brownish pink that blended into the overall effect. She was almost an apparition, Dee thought. Her natural habitat would be the edge of a forest clearing, ready to escape into the perfect camouflage of tree trunks and bush.

Leah gave a brief shake of her head and looked down at the floor as Dee ushered them into her surgery. She sat in the chair closest to Dee and Tom sat in the second chair beside hers. In the dimmer light of the consulting room, Leah seemed more at ease. Tom did all the talking.

'Leah and I … we want to have a baby.'

'Well that's big news' was all Dee could say for a moment. The insurance application suddenly made sense.

They were both so young. Leah's face had the smooth even fullness of a baby's. Dee resisted the urge to say 'But you're just a baby yourself' like she would have with one of her own kids. Perhaps that's why her relationship with Tom was better than that with her own three?

'Do you mind if I ask how old you are, Leah?'

'Almost twenty,' said Leah simultaneously with Tom's 'She's nineteen'.

'And you've been together for a while?'

'Sort of,' said Tom. 'Leah doesn't believe people should possess each other.'

He touched Leah's arm. His eyes and hands constantly returned to the not-quite-there girl beside him.

Dee left a pause for Leah to respond but she sat, hands folded on her lap, eyes narrowed as though about to dematerialise with a flick of her long, matted dreads.

'Okay, so you're thinking about babies?'

'Yeah, well, maybe; Tom shouldn't be taking all those chemicals.'

Dee decided to pass that over for the moment. 'Leah, are you in good health? Are you taking folate tablets? Are your vaccinations and pap smears up to date?'

Leah raised her eyebrows and gave Tom a look.

Tom spoke. 'I'm worried about autism. I told Leah we had to come because of Charlie. Leah hasn't met him. She doesn't understand how difficult it is to have an autistic child.'

'Nature has its own wisdom,' said Leah. 'Every experience can help us grow. Tom is Aspi and I love him.'

Dee knew Tom referred to himself as 'Aspi' or 'on the spectrum'. It was a popular self-reference for IT workers. His obsessional nature fitted with Asperger's syndrome but his awareness of others and his ability to emotionally connect were not typical.

'Charlie's condition is very different. Perhaps you should meet him, Leah?'

Charlie was fourteen and required full-time supervision. He didn't speak or respond to speech and spent his days in repetitive rocking movements, hitting himself or banging his head against the wall if loud noises or a change in routine stressed him. Skye's whole life was spent caring for her second son.

'We'll see them soon—Mum doesn't know much about Leah yet.'

Yes, Skye and Leah, that could be difficult, thought Dee.

Tom turned back to Leah. 'It does matter. I want us to know what the chances of our baby having autism, or even Asperger's, are before we go ahead.'

'Asperger's is a much broader category,' Dee said, 'which includes people with no serious disability apart from mild obsessiveness and minor social awkwardness. These days it's considered a normal variant. Society functions better with some people who make sure things are done right.'

'Yeah, Doc, I'm okay with it but isn't there an increased risk of autism in children of Aspis?' Tom asked.

'Probably, but my information is from years ago. I usually send people to see Professor Adam Fairborn for this sort of advice. He's Australia's top geneticist—a lot of the original research is his. You need up-to-date information. It's all changing so quickly.'

Dee glanced at Tom and Leah's faces to check they were with her. 'I can give you a referral if you like?'

Leah looked up at Tom. She raised her flattened palms and pursed her lips to fend off Dee's suggestion. Tom laid his hand over hers and settled them back in her lap.

'Yeah—that would make me feel better. The information on the internet is too inaccurate, all biased to prove some point. I just want to know the risk before we go ahead.'

Dee wrote the referral. She asked Leah if she had discussed pregnancy with her own doctor and if it was all right to contact the doctor for her records. The girl did not answer.

'Let me know how it goes,' Dee addressed Tom. 'Professor Fairborn will write to me about it all and I can help if there's anything you don't understand. Let me give you a leaflet about planning for pregnancy. It explains how folate reduces the risk of spina bifida.'

Leah glared at Dee as Tom took the referral and pamphlet.

'I'm vegan so I don't think folate deficiency will be a problem.'

'Good. You're obviously concerned about health. It was good to meet you, Leah.'

Dee stood and opened the door. The three of them stepped into the corridor.

'Do have a talk with your own doctor—sometimes vegans can have B12 deficiency.' Leah scowled and pulled Tom towards the front door. 'But I'm sure you know all about that.'

Dee made herself stop. He'd be a good dad. He had the dad jokes onboard already. His baby would be the first 'practice grandchild'.

She walked back to her room with the next patient, still thinking of Tom. She should have warned him the echinacea in the park were in flower. No, it was okay—he was an adult, about to be a father. He'd remember.

3.

Three weeks after she had given Tom and Leah the referral, Professor Fairborn was the speaker at a medical education meeting at Rozelle Hospital. Dee really wanted to go but it was seven o'clock when she put down the phone after sorting out the last urgent call-back of the day. She would be late. Briefly she considered going home, a surprise for the kids, share their takeaway Thai, but she wouldn't be good company tonight—she'd had to give Tracey O the news that there was only palliative care now for her cervical cancer. Let them have a night without cranky Mum.

She tried to support any educational events, like the ones at Rozelle, that weren't sponsored by drug companies. And it was the last meeting till Feb next year. She wondered if Tom and Leah had had their appointment with Fairborn yet. She hadn't heard from them or the clinic. It would be good to be up with the latest when Tom came back to see her.

She should go.

*

In the park-like grounds of the old hospital there were no streetlights and there was no moon. Dee drove through darkness, the world narrowed down to the intimate tunnel of her headlights. Colonial sandstone buildings were separated by wide lawns nourished by 150 years of history. The delusions, the dramas of the asylum for the insane were over. The sweat-soaked earth was quiet.

She parked away from the big sodium lamp that lit the car park. There wasn't enough time to sit and pack away the day. She got out and let herself in through the back door.

The buzz of voices meant they had broken for dinner. There was probably nothing left now. The light was bright and the crowd were milling around the bain-maries at the side of the large room. Dee dumped her bag on a vacant chair at the back.

The topic for tonight was 'an update on genetics and advances in reproductive technologies'. Cardboard booths in the tasteful grey, light blue and white of GenSafe IVF lined the walls. They held glossy promotional material and pamphlets. Those who arrived early had plastic models of the female reproductive system covered with the GenSafe logo. At the front was Adam, a glamorous star surrounded by dowdy GP fans. It was always easy to pick the speaker at these functions. Their grooming, expensive suits and confident air of superiority stood out. They existed in a higher socio-economic stratum, much more than peers. Dee looked down at her own outfit. Definitely in the GP category.

The GPs wore cheap clothes, pilled cardigans. Their haircuts were cheap and a statistically excessive proportion of the men were bald. Dee knew many of them. They were mostly good doctors who worked long hours for low fees and gave up their evenings to keep up to date.

Adam scanned the room, nodded when his eyes lit on her, then went back to his fans. Involuntarily Dee's hand went to the white streak at the front of her hair. She bent down to her bag to hide her blush. Her time with Adam at university seemed a thousand years ago. Still when he cast his eyes at her she felt a spark. He was handsome, tall with pale olive skin and thick wavy brown hair. He had a trick, a tic almost, of allowing the hair to fall over his face so he could flip it back and come up with a flutter of his lashes to look you in the eye. It was an animal movement, a connection that was fatally effective. Few could resist if he turned it on them.

Dee saw through the illusion now. His sensuality was more self-regard than an indicator of his qualities as a lover. In return for services, such as admiration and practical help with the tasks of daily living that Adam was too busy for, Dee had been allowed to call herself his girlfriend for half a year while they were at university.

He split with her because 'she was genetically unstable' and not suitable as a mother for his children. This came soon after they'd started to study genetics in second year. After three lessons he had decided that the white streak in her flame red hair was evidence of a translocation at the end of her chromosomes for hair colour and an indicator of genetic imperfection.

The hurt had mostly gone now. It had taken some time but eventually she'd realised she'd had a lucky escape. Relating to a narcissist was a spectator sport.

Adam had never married. The girl he had been engaged to in their fourth year at medical school drowned. After that, he never had a long-term partner; although that might have changed in the thirty or so years while Dee had been absorbed in her own life—the practice, babies and a divorce.

The woman manning the booth with handouts had her eyes all over him but he hadn't glanced her way—must be a secretary or nurse—a wannabe, not a lover.

The food was mostly gone. Curling dry crusts of lasagne and three slices of beef rejected for their gristle were all that was left. Dee settled for a bread roll filled with the cherry tomatoes and snow pea sprouts that had garnished the beef. With weak tea in a polystyrene cup, she sat down in the last row. Her mouth was full so she didn't have to talk to anyone.

Adam dimmed the lights for his slides. His work was impressive. His group had pioneered IVF in Australia and they were still the leaders in reproductive technology. It was a field where everything changed so quickly. Dee was glad she'd come. He showed a film of the latest technique, PID, or pre-implantation diagnosis. When an embryo was only eight to twelve cells, hours from fertilisation, a few cells were removed, cultured and their genes analysed in the laboratory. This meant only embryos free of disease or with the desired qualities were selected to be put into a womb to become a baby, a new human being.

The new techniques, especially PID, saved parents from so much distress.

Dee remembered her own distress through the screening tests for chromosome abnormalities when she was pregnant with Oliver. She was late thirties and the risk of Down's syndrome was classified as high. Amniocentesis, taking a sample of cells from the foetus, was an invasive procedure with a significant risk of miscarriage. The wait for results was protracted torture. Oliver was an active baby. His first kicks were before the amniocentesis. With every kick, Dee implored the universe to save her from the decision to terminate.

With Eleanor, she and Rob went ahead without the tests. They couldn't face it a second time.

At the end of Adam's presentation, the usual few had questions. Dee wanted to know more but she knew that if she waited someone else would ask her question.

A hand went up in the front row, Dee recognised the long white blonde hair over an acrylic patterned jumper. Alana, rabidly religious, took over any meeting she attended with long, rambling morally loaded questions about her own practice. A collective sigh went around the room. How long would she go on this time?

'And what's your policy on sex selection? Doesn't this just make it easier? I had a case where an Indian family wanted only boys and I had to tell them that abortion wasn't legal for that reason in Australia. It was very hard … I don't know how many girls they got rid of before—'

Adam interrupted. 'Thank you, an interesting question and a question we need to debate as a society. GenSafe IVF has a policy of service to the community. We provide the technology and it's up to the community to decide how it is used. The technique of preimplantation diagnosis means less trauma and more control for couples wanting to have healthy babies.'

Alana had her hand up, 'But I had a patient who—'

Adam stepped forward so he was directly in front of her. Her words were muffled by his body. He reached above her head to point at a bald scruffy man at the side of the room. 'Dr Prentice, you have a question?'

'How soon can we get appointments?'

Everyone laughed with relief. Alana's rant was averted. There were a few more questions but all were kind. Alana had the effect of galvanising support for whomever she attacked.

'Thanks for giving me your time tonight,' Adam said. 'I'll be here to answer any more questions. My practice manager has referral kits for you all.'

The blonde assistant wasn't what Dee remembered as Adam's type. She was tall and willowy, but nothing stood out. The girls he'd chosen at university, and in the first few years when they were residents at the same hospital, were all striking in some way. Like Dee's red hair and green eyes. She'd so longed to be ordinary then.

The 'referral kits' were showbags with pens, an executive toy, referral forms and anatomical models of the male and female reproductive systems. All labelled GenSafe IVF, of course.

Adam was surrounded by the usual sycophants. There was no chance to ask him about Tom and Leah. Dee grabbed a showbag and headed past the group towards the door but Adam caught her eye. He nodded and moved in her direction.

'Hi Adam. Do you have a moment?'

'Of course. It's been a long time.' He looked directly into her eyes. The spark in Dee flickered again.

'Thanks for the fascinating talk, I'm glad I came.' She put down her bag. 'I sent you a young couple recently for genetic counselling. Have they come in?'

'Yes, interesting, a young man with a hippy girlfriend?'

'That's them, Tom and Leah—why interesting?'

'Well, they wanted to know about the risk of autism. Testing for that is just becoming possible.'

'Tom's brother, Charlie, is autistic and needs full-time care. It's not easy.'

'The boy seemed a bit of an odd bod himself. They've cancelled their follow-up appointment.'

How dare Adam call Tom an odd bod. Dee looked at Adam and saw white teeth, good hair, a few fine wrinkles and an empty smile.

He had no idea he'd upset her. No idea he'd said something offensive. Specialists often referred to patients with casual put-downs as if doctors were all part of some privileged club of superior mortals. Diseases were moral failures, indicators of lower status. Dee didn't want to be part of that club, dependent on others' imperfections to feel superior. Everyone had the right to respect. Even the patients with difficult personalities had medical problems and needed care.

'Tom is probably doing his own research. He is, well— different; on the spectrum as they say. But functional, and smart.' Dee was compelled to defend Tom from Adam's casual put-down. It was useless but she couldn't let it go by. 'The obsessional qualities are an advantage rather than a detraction in his work. He's a "white hacker".'

Adam blinked twice. 'What's a white hacker?' Dee remembered the double blink was a sign that he was disconcerted. It was rare.

'Tom tries to hack into computer systems to check that they're safe. Anyway, he is a true obsessive. I'm sure when they come back he'll know all about what you offer and be ready with lots of smart questions.'

'Good. There's so much we can do for them; we can even check for risk of being on the spectrum. The possibilities are expanding exponentially. It's expensive though. All the tests are offshore. China has the big sophisticated labs—the only place we can get all the information quickly.'

'How about costs? They aren't wealthy. Leah's a student.'

'Somewhere between $10,000 and $20,000 out of pocket per cycle with the extra tests. Not much for the guarantee of a perfect healthy child. We do offer donor insemination if they can't afford PID.'

'Leah loves Tom; she wants his baby, not some donor's. You have no idea how people work, do you?' Dee was tired. It normally wouldn't have popped out.

There was a group gathered around them waiting for a chance to rub shoulders with success.

Adam smiled with brilliant, even teeth. 'It's always refreshing to be reminded that ideals still exist.'

'Good to see you, Adam.' Dee picked up her bag. She left the GenSafe showbag on the floor.

He took her hand, 'Thanks, it's been too long,' and dazzled her with another flashbulb smile. He turned to the group gathered for his attention.

Why was he so sensitive to what she thought? Dee wondered as she headed for her car. And why was he trying to get her attention?

4.

The last time Dee had seen Tom was two weeks before the day of his missed appointment. She'd wondered why he'd come in. According to the most recent peak flow charts he'd sent her, his asthma seemed good and it was too soon for the results of the genetic tests to be through.

Perhaps he was sick? His reaction to echinacea had put him in hospital a few years ago. The cone flowers were in full bloom in the park now and the reaction could start very quickly. Maybe he wanted to talk about the visit to Adam Fairborn—and Leah. If it was just him, she'd find out more about what was going on there.

He was sitting alone in the waiting room. Dee called him into the dim liminal space of the surgery and watched him fold his long limbs to fit the chair beside the desk.

'Morning.'

'Morning, Doc.'

Dee sat facing him across the corner of the desk, her hands open in her lap. Both of them looked at the same spot. Tom jiggled his knee, moments passed; Dee held her tongue. It was good to see him well, but why was he here?

He sat up straight in the chair and opened his briefcase. 'I printed these out for you but you'll also have them in my email to import into the file.'

He handed her his peak flow records for the previous month. The simple test, a measure of how much air he could push out of his lungs, was an objective tool in his own management of his asthma. The sheets were mounted in a manila folder, held in order with binder clips. Every reading for the past three months was meticulously charted. Medications and atmospheric conditions, pollution levels and his activities were entered across the bottom and different coloured highlighters identified days when he had changed his medication in response to a low reading. Ventolin was green, his long-acting bronchodilator was blue and the steroid was orange. The red he used for steroid tablets was absent. He hadn't needed oral medication since winter.

She noticed with satisfaction that he had recorded the flowering of the echinacea in the local park and noted he had changed his route to the bus stop to avoid them. She was glad she didn't warn him—and expose the interfering mother he triggered in her.

'These look perfect, as usual.'

There wasn't much to comment on. Tom hardly needed to see her for these regular reviews but he insisted on his three-monthly visits. She suspected the trauma of his emergency trips to hospital as a child meant he still needed the reassurance of regular check-ups.

'I notice last Friday your peak flow was normal but you started extra steroid then?'

'Yes, Saturday I clean the flat, and the dust stirs up the asthma. You can see I usually need more by Saturday night so I've started anticipating and initiating the extra doses on Friday. See, no dip on Saturday evening.'

If only every patient followed instructions less people would be sick. She might be out of a job.

'Perfect. Tom, you've done well. Just go on as you have been and we'll review you in three months. These charts are great. Would you mind if I used them as examples for other patients, de-identified of course?'

'You've asked me that before. That's why I made paper copies of these; if you want, use them. All the information is in my email to make it easier to put them in my file.'

Something was going on. Tom was excited, smiling, fidgeting with the sleeves of his jacket.

'You will remember to do it though?'

Resistance was useless. Dee made a few keystrokes, found Tom's email, scanned the attachment and imported it into his clinical notes as an excel file.

'So you virus-scanned them first?'

'Of course, that's automatic.' Dee still didn't know why he was really here today but it was always quicker to wait till Tom got to what he wanted. His mental template of the encounter had to be followed or they got nowhere.

'So the security is all okay?'

Dee nodded. Tom had worked for, and recommended, the company she had used for the surgery set-up. Raj, the head of the security company, and formerly Tom's boss, was now a friend.

'Sorry, I know I'm obsessional but I also know that security protocols aren't always followed.'

'Tom, you taught me well. Raj's company did a great job—have you tested us out?'

'Aw, Doc, that was only once and I didn't open any files, you know that.'

Dee waited.

'Okay, okay—I did a test raid and got nowhere … as I expected. The system's good. The only way anyone can get into the files is through a person.' Tom's eyes were fixed intently on her face. 'The most perfect system can't protect you against someone giving away their passwords.'

Was this it? Why did he want to check their security again?

'That's hardly likely. All the staff know how important security is. And I'm the only one with administrator status. How's that?' She turned the screen around so Tom could see his peak flow charts on the screen. 'Now, scripts?'

'I've got four repeats left for everything except the prednisone tablets. They were out of date so I got a new bottle last week. Give me one of those, I always have a spare, like you told me.'

When patients quoted her own words of wisdom back at her she was uncomfortable. It made her remember her own mother's interfering version of caring.

Dee saw from the screen that he was correct. She shouldn't be surprised, Tom remembered everything. It was a good idea to make sure he had a spare. She printed his prescription.

'How did your visit to Professor Fairborn go?' Dee asked.

'Do you know him?'

'Yes, I knew him at university.' She paused to look at him. He was sitting forward, knee jiggling, keen to tell her something. 'Some people find his manner a bit off-putting but he is the top geneticist around. Was he okay?'

'Yeah, he comes across as rather grandiose but he might be useful.'

'The most brilliant scientists aren't always the most skilled in dealing with people.'

There was something different about Tom. He was usually straightforward, concrete in his responses.

He sat on the edge of his seat, head down, both knees jiggling. When he looked at her again it was with sideways eyes.

'But, personally, is he a friend or anything?'

Tom probably already knew the answer to his question. Dee could dismiss it as not his business but there was something odd going on. She wanted to know the reason for the last fifteen minutes of palaver. She needed to answer carefully.

'What's up?'

'You graduated from UNSW in the same year, I thought you might be friends.'

It was so long ago. No one would remember their affair and it wasn't a memory Dee wanted to revisit.

'No, Tom, we aren't friends. Does that matter?'

Dee waited. Eventually Tom spoke.

'There are a couple of things I'm following up.' He smiled, almost a smirk. 'Could be interesting but I don't know yet, I'll keep you informed.'

'Okay.' Dee wanted to know what was going on but she knew there was no use pushing.

'Leah didn't like him.'

Leah didn't like me either, thought Dee. On the one occasion when they'd met she'd barely looked at Dee.

'This is about you and Leah not about me or Adam Fairborn. Say whatever you want. It helps me if I know how the specialists I refer people to perform. I can send you to see someone else, someone with more people skills.'

'I'm the last one who should criticise someone for a lack of people skills.'

'So what is it?' Dee asked.

'Nothing right now—we still have to wait for some results. It's very expensive.'

'I thought you just wanted to know about the risk of autism?'

'He tried to up-sell us on the idea of preimplantation diagnosis.'

'That means IVF though,' said Dee, surprised. 'You're both young—there shouldn't be any trouble conceiving.'

'The prof said that IVF could tell us for sure about autism or asthma. He hinted that there were techniques that could predict height, intelligence, even hair colour—all for a price.'

Dee opened her mouth but closed it again without saying anything.

'Yeah, I was shocked too,' said Tom.

'What do you think about it?' Dee asked.

'The rooms are impressive, discreet. Big tasteful arrangements of leaves with spot lighting on them. It doesn't even smell medical. The computer security at the front desk is totally slack though. You stand right over the receptionists as they're logging in and entering data.'

'Please don't tell me you've been doing anything illegal. You know if there's a danger to others it trumps my obligation to confidentiality.'

'Normal journalistic techniques like research from public records is okay though?'

'You know the law. Anything on the public record is fine but hacking into private medical records is illegal. I can't condone that.'

'Doc, no one does that except in movies and cheap thrillers. All the Wikileaks information was from insiders. The information Bradley Manning copied onto CDs was all stuff he was cleared to access. Edward Snowden's revelations were of info he had security clearance for and took out on portable disc drives.'

'Tom, I've known you since I listened to your heartbeat in the womb. Whatever you're doing, no matter how justified you think it is, if it's illegal, be careful. Anyone you talk to is a security risk and you're putting them at risk from the police and other criminals as well as yourself. Sorry, I know you're a grown-up …'

It was a lie. When she looked at Tom, Dee still saw the little boy with blue lips sitting up on the side of his bed, chest puffed with stale air he couldn't get out of his lungs. His neck muscles like ropes as they strained to force the air past narrowed airways to empty his overinflated lungs.

She shook her head to break up the image. 'Lecture over. Do you have any results yet?'

'But you just said not to tell you.'

Dee tutted loudly.

'Oh you mean the tests. We're still waiting for the full genomes and the sperm freeze tests. I just wanted to get some more background before we went back. There were a couple of things I was worried about. Everyone goes through the same process no matter what they've come in for. The sperm test straight up was a surprise. Now they have my sample it's easy to push us down the high-tech path. The professor does have an impressive record of research. He said he could help but I'd like to do some background research of my own.'

'Tom …'

'No, nothing too illegal but sometimes it's important to have all the information, not just what you're told.' Tom dropped his head and looked at Dee through his long black lashes.

She rolled her eyes.

'Don't worry. I know the company who did their security, on the cheap. It's so full of holes it's practically an invitation to come in and look around. And no one will know I've got in. I'll let you know how it goes. Thanks, Doc.'

'Is everything else all right?' Dee wanted to know what was up with Tom. 'Leah's okay?'

'She's good, not keen on the idea of IVF though.'

'How about Skye and Charlie?'

'The same. Charlie wears Mum down. I try to spend time there but Glen and I don't exactly enjoy each other's company.'

He stood up and was gone. Dee wondered what to write in the notes as the reason for the consultation. She would have to wait till the results came back to see him again and to find out what was going on.

That was the last time she saw him alive.

5.

Dee asked Janelle to send Tom a text; then to try the number of the company she thought he was working for at the moment and to send him an email. Briefly, she considered a call to his mother. Tom was an adult; a call to his mother was an invasion of his privacy. And Skye would be useless, her hysteria a hindrance rather than a help. Dee had enough trouble reining in her own need to interfere in Tom's life.

'Don't say where you're from,' she told Janelle, 'just that you want to speak to him.' Janelle rolled her eyes. 'Sometimes people forget that sort of stuff. I'd rather say it and make sure.'

Dee took in her next patient, an attractive and very fair young woman with a tiny spot on her upper lip. It had been there for a couple of months and was getting bigger. With good light and magnification, Dee knew the spot was a skin cancer, a basal cell carcinoma.

The young woman, Stella, worked in the arts, was in her mid-twenties, stylish with perfect skin and ash-blonde cropped hair. Dee delivered the diagnosis as gently as she could. Stella rocked back and forth between shock and disbelief. Cancer wasn't compatible with her competent in-charge self.

The rest of the consultation was a balancing act for Dee. The cancer wasn't highly malignant but it would continue to grow slowly and relentlessly in the local area unless removed. She tried to reassure Stella that she would be okay without letting her think that the tiny spot could be ignored.

Dee was used to the inevitable reactions: 'I'm too young', 'I haven't done the wrong thing' and 'why me'. Most people, the lucky ones, got to believe in their own invincibility until middle age or longer. Whatever age it came, the first knowledge of one's own vulnerability threw people off any solid foundation onto uncertain ground that could give way with any step. Dee had learned to sit with people when they became irrational or incapable of thought till they had time to process the threat. Stella seemed well balanced. Dee knew she would cope in time.

The lesion needed to be removed by an expert plastic surgeon. Dee could remove it herself but in that position, on the junction of the lip, it would take expert work to avoid a disfiguring scar.

Stella agreed to return once she had thought through the issues. The delicate task took all Dee's concentration.

By the end of thirty minutes she had forgotten about Tom.

Dee walked out to reception thirty-five minutes behind. She couldn't let a beautiful young woman ruin her looks without making her understand the danger.

'Dee, I rang where he was working but he hasn't been in, not yesterday either.' Janelle had followed her to the back room to tell her. The dread flooded back.

'Have you tried the girlfriend?' Dee asked. Her mouth was dry and her chest tight.

'No, no number for her. She wasn't ever officially a patient. Do you want me to check with his mother?'

'Thanks, but no.' Dee knew Skye's reaction would be less than helpful.

6.

Mid-morning and the patient was on the couch in position, legs spread. Dee lubed the speculum and gently put it in place. With her head inches from the vulva she manoeuvred the device until the cervix popped into place between its jaws.

'Good. Everything looks normal. Is that comfortable?'

The phone started to buzz. Why did it always ring when she was in the middle of a pap smear? Janelle knew only emergencies or calls from other doctors should be put through. No matter who it was they would have to wait.

'Do you need to get that?' her postnatal patient asked.

'No, no, it's fine. Relax, we'll be done in a minute.'

'It's fine, the baby's with his father for once—this is the first chance I've had to have a rest for a week.'

'You're sure?'

'Sure, I'll still be here.'

Dee removed the speculum, peeled off her gloves and picked up.

'Sorry,' Janelle said, 'but it's Tom Harris's mother. She's hysterical. I think you need to speak to her.'

Dee's stomach plummeted. Her body knew—something had happened to Tom. She sat down. Then tried to be rational. The phone call didn't have to mean something bad. Skye Harris had only two default moods: blissed out or hysteria.

Skye was probably ringing about an incident between Charlie and her boyfriend.

'Put her through,' Dee told Janelle. 'Hello Skye, can I call you in ten—' Dee didn't get far.

'Oh Dee, thank God it's you. It's Tom, I don't know what's happened, oh please, please, please, … I can't do this, please, Dee, you have to come, you have to talk to the police, oh Dee—' Skye broke off into gasping sobs.

Dee grasped at hope. Police? Maybe Tom had been arrested for hacking and was too embarrassed to call anyone.

'Skye, calm down, take a couple of big breaths for me, that's it, in … out, in … out. Deep breaths, that's good … can you talk now? Tell me what's happened; what is it you're worried about?' Dee looked over to her patient. Her eyes were closed.

'He didn't come over for Charlie's birthday last night. You know he'd never do that—never; and he's not answering his phone; it just goes straight to voicemail. I've been ringing him all night. I went over to his place at six this morning and no answer. Glen tried to get in—our key's disappeared—he tried to force the door—but he just hurt his shoulder and … ' She stopped for several seconds. Dee could hear her swallowed sobs then a big breath in. 'Dee, there's something wrong, I know; a mother knows. Dee, I'm so scared—you have to help me …'

Not turning up for Charlie's birthday was exceptional. Tom was devoted to his autistic younger brother. All Dee's fears from yesterday flooded back.

'Have you been to the police?'

'They're useless, I can't even file a missing person's report for three days. "Don't worry, love, he'll turn up"—that's what they actually said to me. They said I was hysterical.'

They weren't wrong, Dee thought as she tried to calm down herself. Two hysterics were no help.

'What about his girlfriend?'

'Her? She's no good for him. I don't know what he sees in her.'

Dee interrupted. 'Does she know where he is?'

'She didn't see him because he was coming over to our place. I think she knows we don't like her.'

That is so you, Skye, it's always about you—couldn't you give her a chance? Dee bit her tongue.

'She might have a key; did you check?'

'No, how would I know where to find her? She had her own place. Why would he give her a key ...' Skye's words were interrupted by shuddered sobs.

Dee pictured Tom at his last visit. He sat at the end of her desk, left knee jiggling, excited, up to something.

'I'll be there in an hour. Skye, it'll be okay—stop crying—we'll go to the police together.'

Dee turned back to her patient. The exhausted new mother was sound asleep, legs spread.

7.

Dee and Skye were at Glebe Police Station, getting nowhere. The clock behind the counter said 1.45 pm. Thirteen minutes had passed since they had been told to 'wait over there' with a wave towards a wooden bench opposite the desk. The desk sergeant was safe behind an arched opening in the thick wall of the old station building.

Staff came in and out of large swing doors off to their left. The rest of the station, and any possibility of an actual human being with any desire to help, was through those doors. Dee, Skye and Charlie shared the bench with a teenager whose chalky pallor was set off by a blood-soaked T-shirt.

Charlie screamed again. It was a change from the thump of his head against the wall but the desk sergeant was unmoved. When there was no one else at the counter, Dee walked over and stood steadily against it. The name on the desk said Sergeant Joe Duncan. He finished a call and put down the phone. His hands had swollen knuckles and the fingers were flexed and deformed. Her brain, always alert to spot diagnoses, said he had rheumatoid arthritis—his irritability was probably due to inadequate pain relief. She resolved to try to be nicer to him.

'Sergeant Duncan, I'm sorry but I need to get back to my patients. Do you think we can get some help?' She spoke gently and smiled. 'I know this young man and something has to be wrong. He could be unconscious; any delay is dangerous.'

She'd avoided thinking about why Tom wasn't contactable. Nothing made sense. There had to be a simple, rational explanation, she told herself, but nausea and a rumbling in her gut said her body wasn't convinced.

'I understand you're concerned, Dr Flanary, and we have a full report from Mrs Harris.' Somehow, he managed to convey disrespect by the sarcastic emphasis he put on Dee's title.

Skye approached the counter. Charlie was hitting the side of his head with his palm as the pale youth shuffled to the far end of the bench.

'Before you got here, it was "luv" not Mrs Harris,' Skye interrupted with a stage whisper into Dee's ear.

The sergeant spoke louder. 'We'll let you know if anything turns up. Best thing for you is to go home and let us get on with our job. He'll turn up soon enough. Mrs Harris has completed a missing person's report and it will be passed to the appropriate team. They'll contact you if they need any further information. You can go now. Leave this to the professionals.'

'Sergeant, this is serious. We need to get access to his flat.'

Dee knew that she would look a fool if Tom had simply gone away without telling anyone, but she would happily cope with that if only he were okay.

'Thank you, doctor, I'm sure you understand there are policies and procedures to follow. You wouldn't want me coming into your surgery and telling you how to treat patients, would you? I've added your information to the statement and

Mrs Harris looks like she needs to go home and calm down. We can't have the boy disrupting the waiting room,' he said as Charlie grunted and pulled at Skye's skirt then punched her arm.

Skye pushed Charlie away. 'I'm not going home without my son,' she said and sat down. Somehow, she implied that the police were hiding Tom away from her in the bowels of the station. She left Charlie free to roam the area. Dee could see that Joe wasn't impressed but he'd dug his heels in. Any backdown now would mean a total loss of face.

It was lunchtime. A rugby scrum of junior constables entered the station with their hands full of takeaway food and coffee in cardboard cups. As the swing doors opened wide to admit them, Dee spied the tiny figure of Marlena Ng. Her elderly mother was a patient of Dee's and Marlena often came to appointments to translate. Mrs Ng was diabetic and needed lots of care. She preferred to see Dee than the Vietnamese doctor who spoke her language. Dee suspected the mother of eleven enjoyed the extra attention of having a child along as translator.

She stepped outside and dialled Glebe Police Station.

'Marlena Ng, please.'

'Detective Ng isn't available. Can I take a message?' a neutral female voice asked.

'Sorry, this is urgent. It's her doctor and it's personal.' Dee knew playing the doctor card was the only way they'd get anywhere.

There was a short delay then Dee heard Marlena's voice.

A minute later, a neat woman in a maroon stretch blouse and black skirt came through the swing doors.

'Dr Dee, I'm so sorry you've been waiting—come through. Thanks, Joe, I'll handle this one.' It always took Dee a moment to reconcile the voice of a shearers' cook from the back of Bourke coming from the lips of a tiny Vietnamese woman.

As they walked through the magic doors to the police station proper, Joe glared and a sound like steam venting escaped his lips.

'It's okay,' Marlena said. 'He hates anyone younger than him who's the same rank. I'm Asian and a woman to boot. We don't usually let "No go Joe" loose on the public. They say he missed his true calling as a goalkeeper.' Marlena led them to an interview room.

She listened to Dee and Skye without interruption and immediately organised to have police attend Tom's flat.

'If we put out a call saying there's a concern for the welfare of Mr Harris, a patrol car will check it out, even if they have to break in. Do you want to be there?'

Dee and Skye nodded.

'Okay, they'll meet you at the flat.'

Part 2

8.

Dee drove. They dropped Charlie at home on the way for Skye's boyfriend Glen to look after him. Skye sat grim-faced next to her and, as they completed a three-point turn to get out of the narrow street of 1950s housing commission apartments, a skinny man with a straggly ponytail jumped in front of the car. Dee braked. Skye lowered her window to yell at him.

'Stay with Charlie!'

'Jan came up, she'll stay. You don't know what you'll find.'

Skye started to cry. The man opened the door and slipped into the back seat. A strong smell of marijuana came with him. Glen, an ex-junkie, had been around for ten years or so. Tom disapproved of the use of drugs, particularly around Charlie, but he had told Dee he thought having someone around, even someone like Glen, helped Skye cope.

Tom had said Glen occasionally worked as a greyhound walker but Dee suspected he dabbled in minor crime and was sponging off Skye's pension and subsidised housing. Still, he must care for Skye if he had tolerated life with Charlie for so long.

'Oh Dee,' Skye said, 'is it okay if Glen comes with us?'

'Sure,' Dee muttered. Someone to help with Skye would be useful.

'Hi Dee,' said Glen.

'That's Doctor Dee to you,' Skye said.

*

Too soon, they were there. Tom's flat was only a kilometre from his mother's. Built in the 1980s rush to redevelop the inner city, the complex of three hundred apartments occupied a whole city block and was a warren of low-ceilinged, skimpy spaces opening off unventilated stairs.

Glen took the lead as both Skye and Dee held back. The flat was at the rear of the complex. They wound through a series of courtyards sprouting cigarette butts and dusty dead plants. Dee recognised the stairwell. Two of her home-visit patients, Jock and Lil, had the ground floor flat.

Two uniformed policemen were already at the door to the stairwell. They were both well above six foot, rugby solid and blond with their big shiny belts carrying guns and radios. They introduced themselves—Senior Constable Miller and Constable Nilsson. Nilsson looked like a child dressed up in the uniform of a policeman. He had a black cylinder, about a metre long and thick as his upper arm, slung across his back. The strap was pressing into his shoulder. The solid black object sent a shiver through her. Surely they wouldn't need to break down Tom's door?

Miller had his foot wedged in the stairwell door to stop it locking. He pulled it open for them and they passed through.

The smell in the stairwell was familiar: Jock's corned beef and cabbage, she realised, the same meal he'd prepared every week for all the years Dee had been doing home visits to his demented wife. In this mean space, the police were alien giants: Teflon coated; too defined, too clean to be contaminated by the dim and grime. Their perfectly pressed shirts seemed safe, as if no chaos could reach someone whose outer layers were so ordered. The smells of freshly pressed cotton and sports deodorant became a force field around them.

'It's the top floor,' said Glen.

Dee was grateful for the short reprieve.

Keen as nine-year-olds at a school sports carnival, the constables ran up the stairs two at a time with the battering ram. Glen took Skye's arm and propelled her upwards. Dee made herself follow.

Tom's flat was up four flights. As they ascended the smell became worse; mouldy carpet, cigarettes, stale ghee and garlic. Dee tried not to breathe too deeply.

Suddenly, on the first landing, Leah was there beside Dee. A wraith in faded jeans and grey and pink T-shirt, materialised from nowhere. She must have been nearby, waiting for them to arrive. Dee and the girl were behind Skye who, with Glen supporting her, was making slow progress up the stairs. That was okay; none of them wanted to get to the top. They all wanted Tom to be there—carried away with a project, absentmindedly too busy to answer his phone. Dee had pushed the case that something serious was wrong to get the police here. Now she wasn't sure she wanted to know what waited for them upstairs.

A few steps from the top, Dee heard the police bang on the door.

'Mr Harris, open up. Police. Open the door, please.'

She held her breath. There was no response.

Dee turned to Leah and whispered, 'Have you got a key?'

The girl half closed her eyes and shook her head.

They walked up the last few steps.

Once they were all together on the top landing, the slightly older constable looked toward Dee. This had to be done. She nodded and Nilsson swung the battering ram against the door. On the second hit, it splintered and swung open, leaving the closed lock attached to the jamb.

The police went in first. Then Dee and Leah. Together, they filled the living room. It was neat and ordered, no cups or papers or other mess. Skye and Glen hovered in the doorway. An array of winking computers and modems covered most of one wall. The open kitchen was the same—no dirty dishes, nothing on the benches except an open pill bottle on the counter. Dee was about to pick it up but stopped. The policemen had pulled on gloves. Was this a crime scene? She had gloves in her doctor's bag. She sat the bag on the table, put on a pair and picked up the pill bottle. The label read 'Prednisone 25 mg' and gave a date two weeks ago, with her name as prescriber. It looked full. Dee wondered how many Tom had taken.

The police opened the bathroom door. There were towels folded on the rail. Like the rest of the flat, it was perfectly tidy, nothing out of place—no smell—thank god, no smell.

He wasn't here. Of course, he's okay. She began to hope. He must have become excited about some work project and not come home. The police could check his phone records to track his movements. Then she noticed his mobile phone on the computer desk.

Tom would never go anywhere without his phone.

Around to the right and up three stairs there was another door. They all held back. Six pairs of eyes staring didn't make it open. Someone had to look. Dee started towards it but the younger constable moved too. She let him go first.

'In here,' they heard him say a moment later.

No one moved. Let Tom be okay, she thought. He's a child, a baby. He has to be okay.

Dee stood still; her arms were crossed and kneading her left shoulder inside her shirt. She needed something solid, something real, to cling to. Her flesh was warm and smooth, a supple layer above the firmness of muscle and bone. She breathed out, picked up her doctor's bag and made herself follow the child with the peach fuzz cheeks who was supposed to be a policeman.

The blinds were closed: the bedroom hot and still. A large bed almost filled the room. Young Nilsson had to shimmy around the end before Dee could enter.

Tom was on the bed, flat on his back, fully clothed—unmoving. Perhaps he fell asleep without getting undressed? Her brain foundered for an excuse to deny what her eyes told it.

'Tom, Tom ...' Dee said.

There was no answer, no movement. From the end of the bed, she could see his eyes were open, directed at the ceiling. There would never be an answer.

*

Dee's authority as doctor demanded a ritual. No expertise was needed to know Tom was dead, but it still needed to be official.

She got the stethoscope out of her bag and leant over the bed.

A faint overripe odour reached her nostrils. The bed was low so Dee knelt on the edge. It was softer than she expected and the corpse jiggled. A stronger smell, of meat gone off, wafted her way. She didn't want that smell to be her last memory of Tom: sweet, obsessional, generous, lanky, excited, lovely Tom. She allowed herself a muttered entreaty. 'No, God, no. You can't let this be.' Mostly she resisted the idea of a supernatural protector but at times like these a plea to someone in charge welled up from deep inside.

She told herself to concentrate, to get on with it. It was okay. This lump of matter wasn't him. She'd smelt worse. She started breathing again. The smell became a taste.

Tom was dead and it wasn't any good for anyone if Dee let her feelings interfere with doing her job. There was no doubt that this cold stiff mass—whitish grey wax tinged with purple under the arms and neck—was an object rather than a person; the same as any other corpse she needed to assess.

She put her tongue between her teeth and bit firmly, physical pain to stop the tears.

'Can you open the curtains, and the window please?' she asked.

The sudden light gave everything a hard-edged reality. She could see more than she wanted to. A dry film dulled both Tom's open eyes. Above the lower lashes on the left, something moved. Dee leaned closer. A fly rubbed its feelers together as it walked across the glazed eyeball.

The face was sallow, pallid rather than pale, the skin almost transparent to the yellow fat beneath. Dee put two fingers under the angle of the jaw, no pulse, no warmth, just cold and pudgy; slightly greasy too, like meat sweating on a butcher's slab. On the left side, dry yellowish secretions ran down from mouth to ear lobe.

She undid the buttons of his shirt to expose the chest; then unzipped his jeans and folded back the flaps. The skin visible through the hairs on his lower right abdomen had a greenish blush—gut bacteria were taking over. Wafts of the sickly smell grew stronger.

It shouldn't be happening. Corpses were supposed to be old and in hospital gowns or pyjamas. Again, she reminded herself, this wasn't Tom.

Dee switched to automatic. Observe then examine. Tom's right hand clutched a Ventolin inhaler. Dee tried to take it from him. The hand was cold, the fingers tight around the cylinder. She slipped it free and shook it. Empty. She put it down on the bedside table.

Why would he be using an empty inhaler? She touched his arm. When she tried to bend it the whole body moved. The arm was cold and completely rigid. Rigor mortis, how soon did that start and stop? On the underside of the neck there was a dark shadow.

'Can you open the window too?' she asked again. The constable was pale. There were beads of sweat across his forehead.

'Sorry, it seems to be locked,' he said with a grunt as he tried again. The window was stuck fast.

Dee leant across the bed to listen for the sounds of Tom's heart and breathing. It was just ritual, a pointless examination of an undoubtedly dead body but, irrationally, Dee wanted to hear a heartbeat. She listened hard—there was the crackly sound of the stethoscope on the skin, worse because her position on the bed was unstable. Other sounds, her movement on the mattress, the policeman's trousers as he brushed against the bed, were magnified. Those adventitious sounds must also be present when she listened to live people's hearts and breathing but she never heard them. She'd noticed it before with dead bodies. Sounds were magnified by her hope that the person was really just asleep and would take a sudden spluttering breath and be alive again. Of course, there was nothing: no breath sounds, no heartbeat.

Dee moved back to the side of the bed. The dark purple staining she'd noticed on the underside of his neck and arms had formed under his chest too. She wasn't used to seeing bodies so long after death but she knew the discolouration was broken-down blood that leaked from capillaries to settle in the lowest areas of the body once the heart stopped.

That was enough. She'd established he was dead. She climbed off the bed and looked around. The room was neat, the bed made, sheets and blanket tucked in.

'Stay with him, will you?'

Nilsson nodded and continued to fix his gaze out the window.

Miller was guarding the bedroom door. Good. Skye didn't need to see Tom like that. She was slumped against the wall with Glen beside her. Leah sat at the desk with the computers. They all looked towards Dee without speaking.

'It's not good, I'm afraid.' No one reacted. 'He's gone.'

Dee was aware of a fullness behind her eyes, tears had formed ready to roll. She swallowed them away. It wasn't her job to care; her job was to look after Skye. Tom didn't need her anymore. Neither of them would benefit from Dee's grief.

Skye crumpled and slid down the wall to the floor. Dee hesitated then made herself squat down to be level with Tom's mother.

Skye seized Dee's hand. 'He's okay, isn't he? Just asleep. He's always been a good sleeper.'

'No.' Dee held both Skye's hands between her own.

'No,' Dee repeated, 'he's not okay.'

Skye opened her mouth for a moment but no sound came out. Then she shook her head and snatched her hands out of Dee's.

'Don't tell me that. Tom is my son—you can't say that about my son.'

'Do you want to see him?' Glen said as tried to put his arm around her.

'You're in this too, are you?' Skye shoved Glen away.

Dee tried again to hold her hands. Skye flapped them in front of her face and pushed at her hair.

'Stop it—he's not dead—that's ridiculous.'

Dee tried to listen. Her knees were cramped. Skye's denial that Tom was dead grew stronger each time they told her he was gone. After several minutes, it was too much. Dee let go of Skye's hand, stood up and looked around. Constable Miller was talking on his radio. Leah had disappeared.

Skye began to make a strangled sound between a scream and a cry.

'We'll need a death certificate,' said Nilsson, coming out of the bedroom.

'What do you suggest we write in as the cause of death?' Dee's voice was quiet; the unnatural quiet that warns of a cyclone.

She looked at the child masquerading as a policeman. His aliveness affronted her. This great healthy mass—fuzz-covered skin curved over muscle and bone, wrapped in clothes washed and ironed by someone who loved him—stood in front of her ready to tell her how to do her job. What right did he have to exist while the dead flesh that once was Tom lay inert on the bed?

'It's got to be asthma?'

'And tell me, constable, how you've made that diagnosis?'

'Well there's the asthma spray ...' The boy had the grace to stumble over his words.

The other policeman intervened. 'What do you think happened, doctor?'

This one was less offensive—less perfect. He had a few pimples around his chin; a big shiny one ready to burst at the front. He'd squeezed it unsuccessfully. Dee liked him for that. People with perfect skin made her uncomfortable. A lack of blemishes signalled a deficit in self-doubt.

'I don't know. There's no way of knowing without an autopsy. I can declare him dead but I can't certify why he died. That means I can't write a death certificate. You'll need to get in touch with the station.'

Skye's keening in the background grew louder. 'Leave him alone, let him be.'

The constable with the pimple was on his radio to the sergeant. 'No, the doctor says she can't sign one.' It sounded like he was having trouble. No Go Joe must still be on the front desk. He went outside to where it was quieter.

Dee and Glen got Skye up onto a chair. Dee tried to talk to her. Thank goodness Charlie wasn't here, she thought.

Glen drifted over to Tom's desk, sat down and pressed the on button. He wiggled the mouse. 'Nothing happening here,' he said and picked up Tom's phone. 'This is dead too.'

Nilsson looked on obliviously.

'You know there has to be an autopsy? We have to find out what happened,' Dee said. 'This is a crime scene, isn't it?'

The constable got the hint and ushered Glen away from the desk.

'You can't cut up my boy!' Skye screamed. She wouldn't look at Dee and pushed Glen away furiously when he tried to put his arm around her shoulders.

Nilsson approached, squatted in front of Skye and said, 'Mrs Harris, can I help you up? We'll drive you back home.'

Skye didn't acknowledge him; sat, eyes fixed on her lap, and continued to scream the same phrase over and over.

'What about all his stuff?' asked Glen. 'It's not safe here. I can pack up the computers and take them home.'

'We'll take care of things till we get a new door on,' said Constable Miller. 'Please don't touch anything in case we need fingerprints.'

Dee was already late for her afternoon appointments. She assumed one of the policemen had to stay till the forensics team arrived. She was ready to go.

'You can't cut up my boy,' Skye cried.

Dee picked up her bag.

The constables looked at her. 'What about Mrs Harris?'

Dee turned to Glen. 'I'll give you a script for a sedative for her. Make an appointment at the surgery in the next couple of days. Tell reception I said to fit you in.'

Glen nodded and Dee wrote the prescription. She handed it to him and moved towards the door.

Glen sat beside Skye. 'Come on. We have to pick up Charlie; he needs you too,' he said.

Skye blew her nose, got up and followed him down the stairs.

9.

Back at the surgery, Dee debated whether to send Raj, Tom's old boss, a text. Raj was the only person who knew Tom and who wasn't her patient or his relative. The only person she could allow to see her own grief.

Raj's phone had gone straight to voicemail, twice. It wasn't urgent really. Tom would still be dead by the time Raj got back to her. She logged into the computer. Five patients waiting and fifteen messages. Six of them winked urgent at her.

First up was Joy Matthews. Joy refused to see any of the other doctors even when Dee was away. Her last visit had been a thirty-minute monologue about how her daughter-in-law didn't want to see her and had turned the grandchildren against her. She was a sad, lonely old woman. Dee tried to see Joy's nastiness as an expression of her inner pain. It made it easier to listen. Joy had driven away everyone else. Dee usually coped.

'... and then she said Finn couldn't come over—just because I gave the poor starving mite one little biscuit.'

'Joy, you know he's got coeliac disease—you know wheat will make him sick.'

'One little biscuit, he loves Nana Joy's Anzac biscuits. One biscuit never hurt anyone. That mother of his, poor little mite never has any fun. Vindictive minx, she's just using the child to punish me. They all love my cooking and she's jealous—that modern health rubbish she feeds them isn't proper food …'

Dee watched Joy's mean mouth opening and closing like a goldfish in a bowl. The nasty words normally washed over her but didn't stick. Today she couldn't ignore them; they penetrated. She felt contaminated. She cut off into a fantasy of how to get the woman to stop making sounds—a firm hand over Joy's mean mouth perhaps?

The sun had reached the window at the other end of the desk. The curtain, white with bold brushstrokes of black, glowed bright with the summer afternoon outside. Flowers moved in the breeze, young people walked hand in hand, life pulsed and burgeoned. But not for Tom.

Dee turned back to Joy. The only sign that she realised Dee wasn't with her were tiny folds between her eyebrows. Perhaps she had noticed.

Dee moved her phone out of Joy's line of sight and typed a message 'Ring me, urgent' and pressed send.

'Now, scripts?' Dee cut Joy off. 'No, I gave them to you last time so that's it.'

'What about my blood pressure?' Joy sounded surprised.

'We have three perfect readings in the last three months so not necessary.'

'But my back?'

'Did you start the exercises?'

Dee was sure she hadn't. All Joy wanted was an opportunity to complain. Dee knew she wasn't playing along this time, but the mean, self-induced misery was beyond her capacity to absorb today.

'Well, they're not helping.'

'Did you try, at all?'

'Well, not so much. But I know,' Joy sputtered.

Dee's phone rang—Raj.

'I have to take this—just a minute, Raj.' She turned back to Joy and said, 'See you in six months' as she picked up Joy's bag and put it into her hand.

'But what about—'

Her hands were white against Joy's blood-suffused neck. She'd just squeeze till the mouth stopped making sounds ...

Dee shook her head to break up the image then stood up and left the room while Joy sputtered on. It was that or lunge at her throat.

*

Dee walked to the staffroom and closed the door. It was empty, mercifully. Raj was still on the line.

'Raj, thanks. I have to tell you something ... you know Tom Harris?'

'Of course I know Tom; that's how I know you.' Dee heard the smile in his voice.

'Well it's not good news.'

'Okay?' He made it a question.

'Sorry, Raj, but he's dead.'

'What? When? I'm sorry, this isn't making sense—do you know for sure?'

'I declared him dead.'

Dee tried to keep her voice calm as the image of the fly rubbing its legs together on Tom's open eye flashed in front of her. Then she heard someone sobbing; big shuddering sobs. After a moment she realised it was her.

'Dee, where are you? Who's there? I'm coming over.'

'I'm working. I'm okay.' Her voice betrayed her by trembling as she spoke the word 'okay'. She swallowed, pulled herself together. 'It's my job to cope when people die. If I fall apart when something happens I'm not much good to anyone. What about you? Sorry to break the news over the phone but I'll have to go. There are people waiting.'

'Dee, you're not okay. I'm already in the car heading to the surgery,' Raj said and hung up as Dee objected.

She typed 'Raj, too busy to see you. Will ring after work. D' and pressed send.

*

The next patient was calm and undemanding; just a script for psoriasis and a re-referral to his skin specialist for a check-up. She closed the door on him, sat down at her desk and pulled a handful of tissues from the box. She'd allow herself to weep for a minute or two in private. That was her rule: it was okay to cry if no one with a genuine claim to grief was witness. She was careful her own emotions didn't intrude on those of relatives, friends or partners. She worked at not letting her emotions show, at not letting her feelings affect her patients.

Sometimes she felt like a vampire, high on the emotions of others. It all got too complicated as she thought it through.

There was a brief knock. The door opened as she scrambled to throw the damp tissues into the wastepaper basket. Raj walked into the room—a kaleidoscope on legs. Dee had her head down to hide her eyes. She saw his feet first—watermelon-coloured boat shoes with long hairless brown calves sticking out of them, then pistachio green shorts, a lime green T-shirt and a midnight blue canvas jacket with red stitching. He was tall, around two metres, and was one of the most beautiful men she had ever seen—chiselled-from-stone handsome, with glowing chocolate skin, dense black hair and square black glasses to frame his mascara ad eyelashes. His beauty surprised her every time and pressed a reset button on her attention.

When she thought of Tom it seemed wrong to feel anything other than grief but Raj's beauty was irresistible as a tidal surge. She was carried away.

Raj always appeared to be unaware of the shift in people's attention when he entered a room. Perhaps he assumed that people always reacted to others in that way.

'Take off that jacket so I can eat you,' said Dee; the sobs gone.

She processed what she'd said and felt mortally embarrassed. 'Sorry, Raj, that just popped out. You look so gorgeous, almost edible. I didn't mean …' her voice trailed off.

'You're upset,' Raj said and, with his palms towards the floor, flicked his fingers upwards. Neither of them would mention her slip again.

He sat down in the patient chair. They were friends now. Initially Raj had asked her to go with him to *La Traviata* at the Opera House when he had come to the practice to set up their security system. This year he'd given her a subscription for the season. At the opera and fancy restaurants, heads turned towards them. Did people wonder why the beautiful man was with an older woman who was obviously not his mother? Most would assume he was gay and she a convenient non-threatening partner—a reasonable conclusion and one Dee was happy with. Spending time with Raj was comfortable, uncomplicated by the sexual politics that made dating so fraught.

Dee wiped her eyes and nose. Raj pulled his chair around next to hers and sat with his arm around her shoulders.

'Sorry, it's ridiculous. I'm being silly. It was just a shock and I've known him his entire life. He was a great kid.' She stopped so as not to set herself off again.

'What happened?'

Dee told him the story minus the details of the smell and the fly.

'Why's he dead?'

'Everyone seems to assume it's asthma—that does seem the only reasonable possibility … but he was so good at managing it. I can't believe it got out of hand. He's too young for a heart attack or a stroke. There'll have to be a post mortem. I couldn't sign a death certificate—without a death certificate an autopsy is mandatory.'

Raj put his hand on hers as he listened.

'It's complicated. Why did he decide he needed life insurance? And what was the hacking about? He was excited, on to something.' Dee shook her head. 'I just can't believe he wouldn't have started his preventer medication or at least called an ambulance. He's had bad attacks before but he knew what to do now and he was the perfect asthma patient—you know how obsessional he was—none of it fits.'

The bedroom scene was with her as she spoke. She looked down and saw Raj's shoes. His cyclist's hairless legs, smooth dark brown, the perfect colour for his pink suede shoes.

Stop the self-indulgence—Raj knew Tom, he must have some feelings too.

'Are you okay?' Dee asked him.

'Yeah—it doesn't seem real yet. I only knew him for two years. He was one of my best investigators. I was disappointed when he left. But I knew he wouldn't stay. All the qualities that made him brilliant also meant he worked better freelance. That puppy-like enthusiasm and that smile—everyone who knew him fell in love with him, didn't they?' Raj looked at Dee, head tilted to the left. 'Even when he had no idea about other people and got the interpersonal stuff wrong, no one cared. Such a darling.'

'Thanks, Raj, it really helped that you came over. I feel better. I have to get back to work.'

Dee sighed and put her hands on the armrests of her chair. People and their problems were waiting. She clicked waiting room view on her computer—there were no patients on her list.

Raj broke in, 'Janelle and I decided to sort everyone out. They're all happy.'

'But you can't do that.'

'I can and I have. They've all been rescheduled. Grief needs alcohol.'

Dee flirted with being furious. It wasn't Raj's place or Janelle's to send patients off. How was Raj chummy enough with Janelle to sort out the appointments together? Then Dee was too exhausted to think anymore. A rush of relief overtook her. She wasn't fit for caring for others. Poor Joy, she didn't deserve to have her doctor walk out on her. Still, the faint hope Joy would never come back was wonderful—more than adequate relief for Dee's guilt.

'Thanks, Raj,' she said and collapsed back down into her chair.

'Don't sit. We're going out.'

'Okay.'

Dee grabbed her handbag and Raj magicked them away in his yellow Mercedes convertible. In minutes they were on the Harbour Bridge, Raj's low-slung banana yellow boy's toy surrounded by serious working vehicles, vans and trucks or sober sedans. Dee found herself humming 'Yellow Submarine' as the wind tangled her hair and whipped all thoughts out of her brain.

10.

The restaurant next to Raj's office at Milsons Point overlooked an Olympic pool and the harbour. The waiter poured the last of their bottle of an aged Hunter Semillon into their glasses and Raj ordered another.

'More chips too,' said Dee.

'Fried carbs, salt, alcohol, the perfect prescription,' said Raj.

'Raj, you know this isn't real.'

'What's not real? You can feel the sun on your back and the breeze on your cheeks. You can smell the oystery tang of the ocean and all around there's the noise of the traffic on the bridge and your eyes are full of the harbour, of water and breezes and swimmers and blue sky and clouds. What can be more real?' Raj waved his arms about—a conductor bringing each of the elements around them alive to their senses.

'Work is more real. People who have problems; people who are dead and who have no one speaking up for them.'

'Well, why not speak up for them?'

Damn Raj; he could always get her.

'It's too hard and, anyway, it's not my job.'

'Whose job is it?'

'The police, the pathologist, the coroner.'

'That's okay then. I'm sure it'll all get sorted.'

'Stop it, Raj. They don't know Tom like I do. He'd never let his asthma get that bad. He knew what to do. He had all the right medications. Why didn't he take them? Why didn't he ring an ambulance?'

Raj didn't say anything. The ball was still in her court. He sat back, left foot up on his right knee.

'Tom was up to something; I don't think he died of natural causes.'

'Do the police know all that?'

'They'll work it out once there's an autopsy.'

'And what about a crime scene? That's in progress, isn't it?'

'Please, Raj. Let me alone for now. We've just lost a friend.'

'And what about speaking up for those who can't?'

'Yes, yes—I'll go to the police and tell them and make a statement for the coroner.'

Half the second bottle of wine was gone. Her blood alcohol had reached the point where anything was possible. Tomorrow she would go back to the police station and make a statement.

The sun went down in a blaze of pink and purple, a bruise on the edge of the sky. The warmth at her back was gone. Dee shivered, her bare arms covered in goose bumps.

The triumphant sense of possibility, of being able to conquer the world had gone too. Her confidence that the police would take notice of her went with the sun. All she could do was hope for competence.

Raj said he wanted to come with her to inform the police about her suspicions. Dee rolled her eyes.

'They were contemptuous of me before …'

'Men are better with men.'

Dee rolled her eyes again. No Go Joe wouldn't see Raj as the same species let alone a man.

'I'm sure the police are competent. Once there's an autopsy they'll have a proper look at what happened. They'll have to find out what's going on,' Raj said as though it were true. Dee had been there. She had to wait and hope.

Then Dee remembered she had gone to the GP meeting last night. Beatrice would expect a driving lesson tonight. That wasn't possible but she should at least go home to make her excuse.

'I need to go while I can still walk and make dinner. I'll let you know what's happening.'

Raj paid. Since he had drunk too much, he asked Gina from his office to drive Dee home in his car. When they arrived Dee had Gina park at the entrance to the cul-de-sac.

Dee got out and walked up towards the house. She sat out of sight on the top step of a walkway down to the harbour. The trunks of the angophoras and ghost gums glowed orange and silver in the reflected light from the sunset behind her. The harbour was deep blue but for the lights of a ferry beetling its way around Middle Head. Tom would never see this beauty again. It was wrong for the world to just go on.

A white BMW four-wheel drive drove up and stopped outside her house. Eleanor got out and waved goodbye to the passengers with her hockey stick. It must be her friend's mother dropping her home after practice. Dee pushed herself up. It wouldn't do to be seen slumped, drunk in the gutter.

Dee waved as the car went past. A small dark-haired woman was at the wheel. Parvu or something similar, a full-time mother who often drove Ellie to and fro. Dee couldn't keep up. She must ring and thank her.

At the footbridge, Dee paused. She didn't want to go inside but if she waited too long her kids would see her and she'd have to explain herself. She couldn't tell Beatrice she'd been trumped by another patient's death.

Inside, all three of her kids were in their rooms, hopefully getting their homework out of the way. She wasn't any later than normal.

'Mum, you're early,' Beatrice said as she came out of her room and leant against Dee for a cuddle.

'Well yes, I am. And I thought, maybe …'

'A driving lesson?'

'What about a movie and then dinner at the new pizza place?'

Beatrice stood back and scrutinised her.

'Who have you been drinking with? Was it Raj?'

Eleanor and Oliver had appeared at the doors to their rooms. Her three children ready in judgement.

'Does it matter?'

The three of them nodded yes furiously.

'Raj is a friend, it was a nice afternoon and sometimes your mother likes to have a drink, or two.'

'Or three,' they chimed together.

'Do you want to go to the movies or not? 'Cause if you don't I'll have to get dinner on.'

There was a revival of *Casino Royale*, the first of the Bond movies to star Daniel Craig, at the local cinema. Oliver was keen to see it on the big screen. Dee and the girls resisted but there wasn't much else of interest so she gave in. From the stunning start, Dee was gripped and for the next two and a half hours sat suspended a couple of inches above her seat.

11.

A constable from Glebe Police Station wanted to interview her about the death. Dee fitted him in at lunchtime. It was good the police wanted more information, and it saved her dealing with No Go Joe, but a constable? The case wasn't being given much priority.

Dee picked up his card from her pigeonhole: Detective Constable Craig Mason.

There were three men in the waiting room. He was probably the one with the shiny shoulders and scuffed shoes.

'Craig Mason,' she called from the reception counter.

The person who stood up wasn't the one she expected. He could have been an accountant, a young banker or stockbroker; young, late twenties, Dee guessed. Too old to have come straight from school and still be a constable—probably a graduate entrant to the police. And he was too well-dressed—sharp grey suit, ultra-white shirt and lilac silk tie.

She met him in the corridor.

'Thanks for seeing me, Dr Flanary.' He extended a manicured hand.

His palm was soft and moisturised but the grip was too strong. It hurt. She suppressed a wince and gave him a friendly smile.

'Come through.' Dee waved him into her room and shut the door.

Craig headed for the chair at the desk. He was about to sit in her place.

'Have a seat here. I'll need to use the computer.' Dee indicated the patient chair beside the desk. Craig stopped and pulled the chair out from the wall to the corner of the desk and angled it towards Dee so they were directly opposite each other.

Dee sat and swung around to face him. Not tall, he was a natural mesomorph but looked like he kept in shape at the gym. It all said he made an effort, was ambitious and likely to be on the way up. Twenty-five years of experience as a GP also told her he was a candidate for blood pressure and cholesterol problems.

'I'm making a report for the coroner on the death of Tom Harris. I understand you were his doctor?'

'Yes, from when he was born, twenty-five years.' Dee struggled to keep any emotion out of her voice or expression. Emotion wouldn't hold much sway with Craig. Any hint that she cared would discount the value of what she said.

'Yesterday you were unwilling to sign a death certificate. Has that changed?'

'No. A death certificate requires a cause of death and that's not apparent.'

Craig sighed and sat back in the chair. He opened his legs to point his groin at her. Once he was settled he got a small pad out from the inside pocket of his jacket and turned to an empty page ready to take notes.

'Can you tell me Mr Harris's medical history?'

'The only serious illness he had was asthma. He—'

'No other problems, insomnia? Anything requiring sedatives?' Craig interrupted.

'No, Tom hated drugs. His mother had a couple of boyfriends who indulged. Tom worried about his younger brother being affected.'

'So have you ever prescribed any sleeping tablets for him?'

'No, never. The only prescriptions he's had have been for asthma medications.'

'Are sedatives ever used for asthma?'

'No. Absolutely not. Anything to depress brain function could suppress the natural urge to breathe. Why are you asking about sedatives?'

'Sorry, doctor, I can't talk about our findings at this stage.'

Her question at least stopped him harping on about drugs.

'So is there anything more I can tell you?'

'He had bad asthma?'

'As a child he had a lot of severe attacks and ended up in hospital quite a few times. But in the last few years treatments have improved and he was doing well. He managed—'

'When was the last severe attack?' Craig interrupted again.

'He managed it himself and has been stable for years.' Dee completed her sentence in a firm voice.

She turned away from Craig to the computer and made a few keystrokes.

'His last attack was…' She paused to regain her composure as she clicked through the record and her memories of Tom. 'Yes, last time he was in hospital was eight years ago when he was seventeen.'

'And that was asthma?' Dee nodded. 'Would you say he had life-threatening asthma?'

'Certainly in the past, yes, but, lately, essentially no. Tom had an obsessive personality. That meant he followed instructions to the letter, and he was smart. Once he learnt to manage his asthma he never let it get bad enough to be dangerous.'

'He managed it with medication?'

'Yes, several different kinds. I don't know if you know much about asthma?'

Craig looked blank, Dee went on.

'The essential problem is that the air tubes in the lungs get narrowed and blocked so that it's impossible to get enough air out to make space to breathe in fresh air. The state of the airways—that is, the current severity of someone's asthma—can be easily and quickly measured with a peak flow meter.'

Dee picked up a plastic cylinder about fifteen centimetres long and seven centimetres in diameter with a numerical scale on the side.

'You breathe in here.'

She attached a cardboard mouthpiece to one end, demonstrated, put a new mouthpiece on and handed the meter to Craig.

'Have a go if you want, just blow as hard and as quickly as you can into the mouthpiece.'

Craig could not resist. He gave an almighty blow.

Dee looked. 'Mm, 660, that's good, you seem to have good lung capacity.'

Craig smiled.

'Tom was obsessive about measuring and charting his peak flow. Any mild fall to warn of an attack and he would start stronger medications before it got out of hand.'

'So if he was out of medication, if his puffer was empty, he could be in trouble?'

'That would never happen. Tom was obsessive. He had other medications, oral prednisone as emergency backup if the puffers were ineffective, and he was on regular inhaled cortisone to stabilise things.'

'But without medication his asthma was potentially life threatening?'

Dee nodded. Craig scribbled in his notebook.

'Look, constable, you don't understand. Tom Harris looked after his asthma perfectly. It's not possible for him to have neglected it enough to die from it.'

'Is there any other reason he may have let it go?'

'What do you mean?'

'Was he depressed, worried about anything? Could his mental condition have got on top of him, caused him to stop his medication?'

'Tom didn't have a "mental condition". He was obsessive but not to the point of a disorder, not to the point of a diagnosable condition that interfered with his life. His obsessive personality structure was an advantage rather than a hindrance in his life. And he was happy. He had his first long-term girlfriend.' Craig hadn't written anything further while Dee spoke. 'They were planning to have a baby. They went to have genetic counselling about it.'

'Counselling?' Craig sounded interested; had his pen ready to write down her answer.

'Not counselling for a mental health problem, advice about the risk of autism in the baby he was planning. It's evidence of a future plan for his life.'

Craig diligently wrote this down.

'So, doctor, what do you think was the cause of death?' he asked without much enthusiasm.

'The only explanation I can come up with is foul play.'

'In a deadlocked apartment with no evidence of a break-in that's quite a leap.'

There was no question, no request for more information.

She was tired of this game. Craig scribbled on. He hadn't asked anything more about Tom's life.

'Was anything unusual found at the flat?' Dee asked.

'Sorry, any information about an ongoing investigation is confidential.' Craig spoke with obvious satisfaction.

The words 'ongoing investigation' gave Dee some hope.

'There were some other things you need to be aware of.' Dee paused until he looked at her. 'Tom was a cybersecurity analyst; essentially, a hacker. He specialised in medical systems. In the weeks before he died, he was excited about an investigation he was doing—something about designer babies.'

Craig didn't write anything down. His expression was blank. She might have been reciting the times tables. He'd made up his mind. For an ambitious young cop, a quick resolution of a case was a good thing. If something complicated came up, he'd have to give up the case to a senior officer. No credit there.

'And there was the life insurance policy. He took it out three months ago, a $500,000 policy.'

Craig's eyes flickered, betrayed his interest.

'Who was the beneficiary?' he asked.

Dee assumed it was Charlie but the timing suggested the baby plan had something to do with it.

'You must have found the policy in the flat, didn't you?'

Craig pressed his lips together. Was he disconcerted?

'Without a death certificate isn't there an investigation, a crime scene declared?' Dee continued.

What sort of investigation had they done?

'Well, we need to have a crime for a crime scene. It's public money we're throwing around if there's a full crime scene for every sudden death.'

Dee reminded herself that any show of her anger would ramp up the disregard he had for her into contempt.

'So no investigation? Is that what you're saying?'

'Doctor, calm down, that's not it. If there is anything in the autopsy report to suggest the young man didn't die of natural causes then everything will be examined.'

Calm down? Dee didn't trust herself to respond immediately. She stood up. 'Would you like some water?' she asked and left the room.

In the tearoom she splashed water over her cheeks. Tom was dead, a cold lump of meat on a slab in the morgue, and this fool was in charge. She wanted to make him take it seriously, to listen, to care.

Her immediate aversion to Craig wasn't typical. It took extra time to get through the shiny tough shells of patients like him but underneath they were people too.

It was his lack of regard for Tom that made her furious. Yesterday there was the vision of her hands around Joy's miserable neck. Now she wanted to be a bird of prey; she wanted to draw blood from Craig's smooth cheeks with her talons while she pecked out his eyes with her long, hooked beak.

She had to stop this. Tom wasn't her chick and it was too late to protect him.

She took two glasses of water back into her surgery. Craig must get a hard time at the station in that outfit, she reasoned. She tried to feel sorry for him. It helped her rein in her desire to cut him down. Hopefully the autopsy would be ready in a day or two and the police would have to take Tom's death seriously. Someone else would be put in charge. Dee hoped Tom's flat was properly secured.

'So there's not going to be any investigation until the autopsy result?' Dee tried to keep her voice calm.

'That's correct.'

'You might want to check out the insurance policy though?'

'That's of interest, yes.'

'Well I guess there's nothing a constable can do to change that.' She couldn't resist the insult. 'I would be grateful if you could arrange for a copy of the autopsy report to come to me.'

Craig started spluttering about privacy and procedures as she knew he would. Dee cut him off.

'You're right, of course. The request would be more effective if it came from me. Thanks for coming over here to see me.'

Dee got up and left the office. Craig trailed after her.

12.

'Sorry, Joan, for keeping you waiting.'

'No, sister.' Joan Fellows patted Dee on the shoulder and laughed. 'Sorry, I mean doctor. Silly old me. I know you don't mind.'

For Joan, women were nurses, men were doctors. Nothing would change the prejudices of a lifetime. And Dee knew that when Joan called her a nurse it was a signal of inclusion, a connection beyond doctor and patient: *We're part of the same tribe, you understand me and I feel safe you won't use power against me.*

'Nothing I have to do is important and you always take the time when it's my turn.'

So no hurrying you then, Dee thought. It was true though, Dee could never work fast because she couldn't ignore the real problem confessed at the end of a series of time-wasting distractions. To give people the time they needed to confess to what was really troubling them was more effective in the end. She sat facing Joan, resigned to not interrupt even as the message icon on her monitor flashed urgently at her.

It was 11 am. Dee was thirty-five minutes behind. Joan was eighty and had another urinary tract infection. UTIs were a bonus in Dee's day: the toy car in the cereal box, the raisin in the rock cake of appointments. While Joan hobbled to the toilet to provide her specimen, Dee had a minute to check her messages.

The three messages winking urgent were all from Janelle. 'Please do you have an address for Leah Dragic?'

Dee went into the file room behind reception and called quietly to Janelle—better not to let the three patients who were waiting get their hopes up.

'What's this about?'

'We don't seem to have a Leah Dragic.'

'No, she's the girlfriend of Tom who died. She has her own naturopathic doctor.'

'GenSafe IVF have rung three times to get her address. Their practice manager demanded to speak to someone in authority.'

Joan came to the door holding a specimen jar wrapped in half a roll of toilet paper. Dee held open a clip-lock bag for her to put it in. Let the lab deal with the urine-soaked paper.

'Ring and tell them we don't have it. She was never a patient. And buzz the practice manager through to me if she's rude again.'

*

An hour later Dee had caught up a little when Janelle buzzed her. 'Professor Fairborn, he says it's urgent.'

Dee remembered how pompous Adam had been at the medical meeting. He suggested Tom and Leah might want donor sperm because Tom was odd and accused Dee of having 'ideals' as though it were an insult.

'I'll be five minutes if he wants to wait, otherwise get a number where I can reach him around seven.'

Dee finished with Khin Ho, a diabetic who regularly skipped his medications because they were 'too expensive'. His uncontrolled blood pressure had caused a stroke and he'd lost his job. Money was now even more tight. She repeated her spiel about how important it was to take his blood pressure and diabetes tablets otherwise a worse stroke was inevitable. Why he came to see her at all or why he bothered to get new scripts that he didn't fill remained a mystery. She gave him forms for blood tests and scripts and picked up the still buzzing line.

'Adam, what can I do for you?'

'Thanks, Dee. I'm afraid we haven't been able to contact your patient, Leah Dragic—you heard, didn't you, about the young lad's tragic death?'

His concern sounded fake. She wanted to yell at him to stop but she bit her tongue and said, 'Yes, a tragedy; but don't you have the details? She was never on the books here.'

'Ah, well, she's not at the partner's address. We need to get in touch with his next of kin to get disposal instructions for his contributions. We do like to inform people before disposal—especially in such a tragic situation. They did seem to be in love, didn't they?'

Dee was surprised by the idea of Leah as next of kin. It was a grey area but she and Tom had been partners, planned a child together. Contributions must mean sperm samples. She remembered how Tom was upset about the one-size-fits-all approach at the clinic where samples were required at the first visit.

Adam's words about love placated her. Maybe he did have some sensitivity. She was probably a harsh judge when it came to old boyfriends who had dumped her. She relented.

'Adam, sorry. I don't have anything but she's got an appointment with me coming up.'

Dee had been surprised to see the name on her appointment list. She did a quick search for the time.

'Yes, tomorrow at two—we'll get her details and let you know then. Also, can you have a word with your practice manager. She was inappropriately pushy with our receptionist.'

'Of course, that's not acceptable. I'll get on to it. Thanks so much, Dee—it's been too long—we must catch up.'

'Umm, yes.' His insincerity was an insult. How could he think she would be kept sweet by a promise of further contact with him?

'I'll ring you on Friday,' Adam finished.

Dee hung up. Feeling somehow used.

It was the feeling she remembered from the early months after their breakup. It was her first sexual relationship. When their lovemaking didn't make the stars sing the naïve eighteen-year-old she had been thought it was her fault; that she must be frigid. Now she understood, her part in their coupledom was as an aide in Adam's relationship with himself.

All the drawbacks of aging—the loss of physical beauty, the indignity of physical impairments—were worth it, she thought, chiefly because the cringing embarrassments of youth were over. But thinking of her breakup with Adam could still make a cringe creep through her. How desperate had she been to believe her relationship with Adam had any connection to love?

For years after their breakup she'd dyed the white streak in her hair—until Rob.

Rob, another driven high-achiever, loved her hair. He convinced her to let the white streak grow out again. It was probably why she'd chosen him to marry. She thought about their wedding photo. He was stylish in architect black and she in a slinky deep green that reflected off her eyes and showed off her breasts. Her mother cried and revealed a romantic side that was usually locked away, with her gift of the bouquet: tuber roses for their divine smell, peonies, and marigolds; ivory and deep orangey reds. She and Rob looked hot, were hot, even after the kids and after she'd thickened into middle age. They were still hot, if not as often, not as consistently, until his mid-life crisis and the affair with his student, now wife.

Adam was an aberration. His brilliance, the rigor he brought to any scientific enquiry, meant he would be at the forefront of scientific discoveries. Sharing that part of his life was stimulating; it gave her a glimpse of a world beyond. But she was grateful she could put down the phone on that part of her life.

13.

'That Leah is very popular,' Janelle said as she handed Dee a mid-afternoon coffee.

Dee beckoned Janelle into the staff room to find out more.

'I've had three more people asking about her. I put messages on the computer for you about all of them.'

'Have you got a minute to tell me now?'

'Well, first there was GenSafe, you know about that.'

Dee nodded, trying not to show her impatience. 'Tell me about the others.'

'Some insurance company wanted Leah's address, then the detective from yesterday, then Skye. I told them all I'd have to check it out with you before I gave out any information. Is that okay?'

'Yes, that's good.' Dee paused to think. 'And all of them wanted her address?'

Janelle nodded.

'So Skye didn't know it either?'

'Well, it was Glen, her boyfriend. He said he was ringing for Skye but she was too upset to talk so to ring him on his mobile.'

'Did he say why he wanted to know?'

'No, but the others said it was about a life insurance policy.'

'Thanks, I won't have a chance to ring anyone before tonight. Unless there's a cancellation.'

'Not likely. I'll let you know.'

Dee gulped her not-quite-scalding coffee. There wasn't time to think it all through. She would find out more when she rang everyone back.

*

Dee let out her last patient only forty-five minutes late. She was exhausted. Grief lurked at the edges of her consciousness. She wanted to be home.

Tania, the part-time receptionist, buzzed to say there was a detective on the phone. Dee was about to snap at her but it was easier to take the call than to re-explain the protocol about calls. Janelle could deal with Tania tomorrow. Dee didn't trust herself to do it calmly.

'Constable Mason, I understand you're after Leah Dragic's address?'

'No, we have it now, thanks, but the girl hasn't been seen there since Monday. I wondered if you might have any idea of where she is?'

'This is the fourth time someone's asked after her today. What's so desperate?'

'I can't give details …' Craig started with the usual palaver about confidentiality.

'Look, my information is confidential too. It would probably help if we shared what we know and I'd feel happier about revealing confidential medical information if you tell me why it matters that you know.'

Craig sighed. 'Okay, the life insurance company have Leah Dragic as co-beneficiary of the $500,000 policy but they can't find her.'

Dee cut in. 'And the other beneficiary is Tom's brother Charlie?'

'Correct.'

'So why the urgency?'

'In a case like this all the beneficiaries need to be looked at.'

The idea of Leah being involved in Tom's death seemed ridiculous but it was proper procedure to check everyone.

'And of course, if the death wasn't natural causes then Ms Dragic could be in danger too.'

'Why?' Dee wondered what they had found out about Tom's hacking.

'There's a thirty-day rule with insurance. If a beneficiary dies within thirty days of the benefactor then they are disqualified.'

'So Charlie would get all of the money?'

'That's right.'

Dee kept quiet. There must be more. She hoped Craig would fill the silence with the details.

'The mother's partner has a record for minor drug offences and one episode of violence so we just want to be sure.'

'Does he have an alibi for Tom's death?'

'Only from Skye Harris, who also benefits from the insurance.'

'Tom's mother loved him, she's devastated by his death.'

'Even so, she could easily have been asleep and not known where Glen was in the middle of the night. Was she on sleeping pills?'

'Nothing prescribed by me.'

'So?' Craig asked.

'Sorry, so?' Dee was distracted by the realisation that if someone had harmed Tom then they could still be dangerous to Leah.

'So can you tell me what you know about the girlfriend?'

'Yes, sure—Leah has an appointment here tomorrow afternoon. I don't have any contact details but I can ask her what's happening then. She's not likely to want to talk to the police though.'

'It's not a matter of if she wants to talk to us. We want to talk to her. Perhaps she'd be more willing to help if you let her know she might be in danger …' Craig trailed off.

'Yes, I will, of course. I'll let you know what she says. Would the police offer her protection?'

'I'm not sure we'd have the resources for that. If she finds somewhere secure, doesn't stay on her own, she should be okay. There's probably no real danger but we have to go through the motions, wouldn't want to be seen to have done nothing if something happened to her.'

Dee sighed and bit down on her lower lip; too annoyed to respond.

'If, as is likely, the autopsy shows it's asthma then she's all okay,' Craig said.

'Let me know if there are more developments,' Dee said to get him off the line. It would be pointless to explain yet again why Tom didn't die from asthma.

Craig started to speak.

'Thanks, goodbye.' She hung up.

Leah wasn't going to get protection from the police. Dee was comforted by the thought that if they and the insurance company couldn't find her maybe no one else could either.

There were still Glen and the insurance company's calls to deal with. Dee looked at her handbag and at the back door.

She knew the insurance company needed to send a written request for information with a consent form. Janelle could sort that out tomorrow. Glen she could ring from home but it was better to do it here, keep the whole issue here, not let it invade the safe, comforting space where the children and her real life existed.

She found his mobile number. There wasn't any good reason for Glen or Skye to want to be in touch with Leah. They hadn't even acknowledged her at the flat. Dee had the impression that they preferred to ignore her part in Tom's life. Perhaps Skye had decided to be kind; to involve the girl in funeral arrangements. Maybe she wanted to be with someone who had known Tom, to have a part of his life back.

'Hi Glen, it's Doctor Dee. You rang before.'

'Oh, yeah, thanks, Doc,' Glen whispered. There was the sound of a door opening and closing, of footsteps on stairs. 'Sorry, I don't want to disturb Skye. That's better.' His voice was at normal volume now. 'I wondered if you know where Leah's got to?'

'No, I'm afraid I don't. What's up?'

'Skye wanted to talk to her about Tom, I guess. I'm not sure why.'

'So Skye's not too upset about the insurance?' Dee left it vague to find out what he knew.

'Sorry, umm, the insurance? I don't know much about it. I think Skye wants to be in touch with Leah, that's all.'

Glen sounded shifty, evasive. He knew about the insurance policy but wasn't keen to give anything away, Dee thought. Tom had been uneasy about Glen. Dee found she had the same reaction. At least he didn't know Leah was coming in to see her. Even Dee hadn't expected the girl to want to see her. She would tell Leah. The girl could choose for herself whether or not to get in touch.

<h1 style="text-align:center">14.</h1>

Leah was booked for the first appointment after lunch. She didn't arrive.

Dee had been more surprised when she'd first seen the appointment than she was when Leah didn't show. The girl was not a fan of conventional medicine. It must be a terrible time for her. Dee wanted to check how she was going when they were at the flat but Leah had vanished before there was a chance to talk.

There was no address, no other contact details in the file. Adam, Craig and Glen would all be back on the phone for information she didn't have.

Skye might know something more. The thought of facing the anger Skye was using as a stand-in for grief was too much and it seemed unlikely that Skye would be willing to speak to Dee anyway. Perhaps if Janelle rang her? Then Dee wouldn't have to talk to Glen either.

Mid-afternoon, Janelle's message flashed up on Dee's screen.

'Skye doesn't know where Leah is. Apparently she's moved out of the share house she used to be in. I got the impression

Skye didn't want anything to do with Leah. The insurance people told Skye that Leah was a co-beneficiary when they came around looking for her. Skye sounds very angry—with everyone.'

Especially me, Dee guessed.

*

At 7.15 pm Dee slid behind the wheel of her car and put the key into the ignition. She didn't start the engine. The car space was enclosed by metal grilles on both sides and the adjacent spaces were stacked floor to ceiling with boxes and furniture. Yellow biohazard disposal bins lurked in the space's deeper reaches. It was the meanest and darkest space in the large underground lot.

She loved the electronic impregnability of the ugly metal and concrete. Her body relaxed into the car seat, muscles limp; she melted into the blessed dimness. A liminal place to shake off all the emotions that bled onto her from patients in distress, a space to leave behind patients' emotions so she was ready to go home to those of her family.

She stretched her neck and shoulders like a cat, rubbed them against the smooth leather of the seat. This time without obligation to the needs of others was the purest luxury in her life.

A scratchy, scrabbling noise came from the front of the car. Dee opened her eyes and sat up straight. There was nothing for a moment. Maybe she had nodded off and imagined it. Nothing could be here in the car space. Then—scratch, scratch—she heard it again. Her muscles jolted, instantly tense, ready for action. Don't panic. It must be an animal; maybe a stray cat or rats trying to get to the waste. One of the waste bins on the passenger side of the car moved fractionally. Dee turned on the car headlights. The bin jiggled and moved a few inches. Too big for a rat, a cat must be nesting down here.

The passenger-side door opened. The interior light of the car came on above her head. Dee took a gasping breath, her heart banged against the inside of her chest. She was alert. Then nothing happened, the door was open an inch or so. Her mind raced through possible explanations—there weren't any. The door creaked open a fraction more and Dee grabbed her handbag as a shield or a weapon.

'Turn the lights off,' a female voice said from outside the door.

'Who is it?' Dee tried to sound fierce.

'Turn off the light,' the voice was an urgent whisper. 'It's Leah.'

Dee put down the handbag and pressed the switch to turn off the internal light. The door opened further and Leah slipped into the seat beside her. Even in the dim light from outside, Dee saw the girl was pale, trembling, terrified.

'Turn off the lights, quick,' Leah said as she slid down below the level of the windows. 'Can we go somewhere else?'

Dee turned off the headlights and everything went red like a scene from a horror movie.

'Let go of the brake too,' Leah half shouted, half whispered.

Dee realised she had her foot hard on the brake. She moved it and they were in darkness.

'Leah, what's wrong, are you sick? Tell me what's going on.' Dee was sweaty and her heart thumped.

'Please, I want to tell you but can we get away from here first?'

Dee started the car. Leah curled herself into a ball and slid down into the footwell of the passenger seat.

Dee drove to Pyrmont Park, a narrow strip of land along the harbour with a few car spaces on the road and a cliff behind. One other car was already there but the rest of the spaces were empty. She eased the car into a space shadowed by two large date palms.

Dee reached out to put her hand on Leah's arm but the girl was so tense she thought better of it.

'We're here. There's no one around. You can sit up,' Dee said as gently as she could.

'He was watching today when I came for my appointment.'

'You're safe. No one can see us without us seeing them. Tell me who? What is it you're scared of?'

Leah moved her head up to the level of the window. She was edgy, a nocturnal bush creature ready to bolt, faun-like trembling arms and legs, her skin and hair a uniform pale beige.

'What about that car?' Leah asked, looking to their right.

'It was there when we arrived. There's no one in it; probably a jogger.'

Did Leah have a history of mental health problems? Dee wasn't her doctor so had no background to judge her present state. The girl had appeared stable when she'd come to the surgery with Tom. Her current behaviour seemed odd but it was less than a week since Tom's death.

'You don't look well. Can I drive you home? Who are you staying with?'

Dee bit back any other questions. She'd get a better picture of the girl's mental state if she let her talk.

'I'm scared. There was a man watching the front door of the surgery …'

'That's why you didn't come?'

'Yes, he must think I know what Tom found out.'

Who knew about Leah's appointment? Dee pulled herself up. She was assuming that what Leah said had actually happened; participating in the paranoia wasn't going to help.

'Leah, who would know to watch for you there?' As Dee said the words the memory of all the calls wanting to know where Leah was came back to her.

Dee had told Adam and Craig about Leah's appointment, not Glen, not the insurance company. Still, if any of them had spoken to Tania she might have let the information slip. As could Craig, if he thought it would give him information to make him look good.

'He was in a car, all dressed in black with sunglasses on.'

It was summer in the inner city. Hats and sunglasses were not unusual. Black was the colour of choice for local hipsters. How could Leah identify anyone in a car from a distance, with an obscured face? Dee bit back her questions, said nothing. If she disputed any part of the story, Leah would withdraw and she'd never get through to her.

'You know Tom didn't die of natural causes.' Leah said it as a statement rather than a question.

'The coroner will find out what happened. We have to wait for the hearing.'

'Yeah, sure,' Leah said, then muttered so Dee only just heard, 'he could get me by then.'

Dee was torn. She needed to tell Leah about the danger she was in because of the insurance but it was hard to add to her distress. The danger was real though, Dee reminded herself. Tom was dead, and it wasn't asthma. Leah needed to know.

'Did you know Tom took out life insurance a few weeks ago?'

'Sure, you know him, always a plan for everything.'

'You know you get half the money?'

'I don't want money, I want Tom,' Leah spat back at Dee.

Dee tried not to respond to the anger. She wished there was some way to comfort the girl Tom had loved.

'I know but have you thought that if someone harmed Tom, it could be for the insurance?'

'It was the professor who Tom was worried about.'

Dee decided to let that go. She wanted Leah to listen. Any challenge would just drive her to defend her suspicions.

'Leah, there's something you should know. It's important; can you listen to me for a minute?'

Leah, eyes down, sniffed and nodded.

'There's a rule with insurance, if something happens to you within thirty days of Tom's death, all the money, including your half, would go to Charlie. Do you understand what that means?'

'That's ridiculous. Skye wouldn't hurt Tom, she loved him. She was always on the phone, he was always over there visiting Charlie. It makes no sense.'

Leah started to sob. Dee found a mini packet of tissues in her handbag and gave it to her. She wanted to put her arms around Leah, to tell her it would be okay, but she knew the first would be rejected and the second a dangerous lie.

'There's Skye's boyfriend; he could have an interest in Skye getting money …' Dee left the idea in the air between them.

Leah looked up, visibly engaged for the first time. 'Tom said Glen was too stoned to get out of his own way.'

'No one knows what happened to Tom. It wouldn't hurt to be careful, be with other people till thirty days are up.'

'It was the professor. I know, Tom knew.' Leah's voice was strident. She looked at Dee and went on more calmly. 'He had lots of information from GenSafe's accounts but he had other research too. A lot of bad things happened to people close to the professor.'

Dee sighed; let her talk, get out what she had to tell.

'There was something going on with the patients and payments into an overseas bank account. Tom got the names and checked them out.'

It was better not to know the details of how, Dee thought.

'You know Shirley and Ben? They lived near us. Tom helped them set up their wi-fi. He knew their passwords. He checked out stuff from their computers.'

Dee vaguely remembered the couple from some years ago. She had referred them to GenSafe. They'd been trying to conceive for years. Leah must have inside information from Tom if she knew their story.

Lights illuminated the car's back window, the shadows of their two heads flashed across the windscreen. Leah stopped talking and bent down out of sight again. The car passed. Her hands were shaking. When she sat up, Dee saw the throb of her heart in the tender skin at the base of her throat. Leah shook her head and went on.

'They weren't infertile. They just wanted to have a baby who was intelligent. They even got to pick the hair colour and height. That man practically told us we could design whatever baby we wanted if we had enough money. Tom thought it was wrong. And there were other people. Tom doesn't ...' Leah paused and corrected herself, 'He didn't have the medical part of the records but, of the names he looked up, ten couples sent large amounts to the same offshore account. He traced it and it ended up in an account with connections in China.'

'China's a big place. Did he say more than that?'

'Yes but I didn't understand most of it. It was something medical. He kept on about the crisper, saying that must be the key.'

This was all too much. Dee held up a hand for Leah to stop.

'Leah, it's hard to think straight when you're grieving. Everything gets on top of you. Why don't I drive you home? Have you got someone to be with? Can we get you in to see your own doctor tomorrow?'

'Do you think Tom died of asthma?'

'That's what the police think,' Dee said. She decided not to mention the talk of sedatives. That would only feed Leah's paranoia. The knowledge that Dee had talked to the police and had her concerns dismissed wouldn't help either.

'What do you think?' Leah was insistent.

'It doesn't matter what I think. There's nothing we can do. We have to wait for the police and the coroner.' Dee paused, and tried to soften her tone. 'But, just in case, you need to keep safe.'

Leah went on quickly, 'You know someone used Tom's computer after he was gone?'

'What do you mean?'

'The backup drive wasn't in the right place when we were at his flat with the police. When he finished at night he always sat it on top of the keyboard so he knew it had been done.'

Dee sighed. Of course that mattered but who except those who knew Tom would take notice of where a hard drive was put. None of this would be useful as evidence. And he may have been working and not backed up when he got sick ... No, Dee stopped herself, he didn't simply 'get sick'.

'Once the autopsy result is through the police will have a proper look. They'll make a report and the case will go to the coroner. You'll need to give a statement.'

'No way.' Leah shook her head violently. She looked terrified.

Dee let it go, decided to wait till the girl was calmer.

Leah lifted her head and rubbed at her eyes with the back of her hand.

'He was onto something else too. He went to Orange and when he came back he made me stay away. He said it was better if I didn't know what was happening. He said it was too dangerous to know.'

Dee couldn't be sure if Leah knew what had happened, or if she did, if her account was accurate. She was mostly calm and talked without making excuses, without any need to defend herself.

'Tom would never leave his desk out of order. You know him … there's no way he'd leave his backup laying around.'

That was true but Craig Mason wouldn't see the significance of any of this. He'd dismissed Dee's suspicions. The police wouldn't be any help to Leah until the autopsy report proved Tom's death wasn't due to an innocent physical cause.

Dee wrote her mobile and home numbers on a card and gave it to Leah. The girl put the card into her bag. She looked down at her hands, not quite ready to say something that was on her mind. Dee waited.

'Tom said if anything happened I could trust you. And that you had all the information if anything went wrong.'

'Yes, you can trust me, but I'm not sure I have any information. Do you know what he meant?'

Leah didn't answer.

Another car pulled into a parking bay two away from them. Leah slipped back down the seat.

'Can we go? Can you drop me at a train?'

'Where can I find you? Have you got somewhere safe to stay?' Dee backed out of the space.

'It's better if no one knows where I am. I'll call you.'

'That's good. And make sure you're not alone. It's only a few weeks.'

*

At Railway Square, a huge junction of cars and buses near Sydney's major train station, Leah opened the door and jumped out.

Dee called after her. 'Be careful, remember, until January 8th or 9th.'

Leah didn't look back. She ducked between cars and was out of sight in seconds.

The passenger seat was empty but something had been left behind. The car was filled with it. An invisible pressure, a weight pressed down on her shoulders. A duty towards Tom, to find justice for him, and to protect the prickly, difficult Leah, who didn't even like Dee. 'Well, thanks Leah,' Dee muttered. Who else would sort this out?

The traffic in front of her was gone. A bus loomed behind her. Dee put her foot on the accelerator, moved forward and swung left on Quay Street. This was familiar territory. Darling Drive was nearly deserted and led her past Darling Harbour to her normal route home.

It didn't feel normal anymore.

15.

It was quiet at home; the children were at Rob's. She microwaved a bowl of leftovers, ate without tasting and sat on the lounge in the dark with a big glass of red. Her eyes adjusted so she could see the bush outside. The full moon rose huge and yellow over Middle Harbour. The angophora trunks and walkway around the north-east of the house glowed silver. Fairy daylight, she used to call it when the kids were little—would she see Puck and Titania if she watched carefully?

The Glasshouse was famous. All the walls were glass and the house was circled by silvery weathered wooden decks with low stainless steel railings. The walls slid open to make a seamless transition between inside and out. Elegant cream and grey gum trunks seemed part of the living space. Rob had designed all with homage to Danish modern; low wine-dark leather couches and curved teak. The house had made Rob's name as one of the leading young architects in Sydney. They all still cleared out for the Architects Association of Australia's annual open day.

Castlecrag was on a hilly promontory surrounded by Middle Harbour. It was famous for the estate of sandstone houses built by Walter Burley Griffin in the thirties. The streets had names like The Bulwark, The Rampart or The High Tor. Tasteful and expensive houses were nestled in bush and glimpsed the harbour through gums and twisted orange-trunked angophoras.

The Glasshouse backed up a slope with only bush behind. A small wooden bridge connected it to the street about a metre and a half below. Sweet-smelling leaf litter and strips of bark covered the ground on the slopes around them. White flannel flowers and red waratahs glowed bright in season.

After Rob moved out with his student lover, Dee had installed curtains for privacy in the bedrooms and had the walls of the bathrooms made opaque. For a period, when Rob first left, she felt insecure, anxious that bogeymen could be in the bush watching. She tried movement sensors outside the house but they were set off all night by possums, wallabies and other nocturnal creatures. The bush was surprisingly busy after dark. She disabled the sensor lights after only a few days of being startled awake by them all through the night.

In warm weather everything was open and airy, although when it was too cold to open the walls the ventilation was inadequate. Dee loved the seamless transition from inside to outside but Rob didn't believe in flyscreens, so the space was seamless to flies, beetles, mosquitoes, and the odd funnel-web spider as well. Cleaning the acres of glass was never-ending. Now she had cleaners. How did working women manage without cleaners? Life would be so easy if she could have a wife.

It was a wonderful house. The kids had their friends and schools nearby. She was lucky. She should be grateful. So why did she feel as though steely tendrils of Rob's perfectionism had paralysed her brain?

*

Dee opened her eyes. She must have dozed off. Snatches of a dream with Leah and Rob and the house came back to her. There was danger. Rob was there but he couldn't help. He was busy on the toilet. It was important because the toilet had a glass bowl and everyone could see what he produced. Dee was outside the front door. She had to push it hard enough to make a noise, to warn Leah to hide. If she could make a noise with the door she would have solved the mystery of what happened to Tom. The house and Tom and Leah were all part of the same quest. She wondered why she hadn't seen it before.

She tried as hard as she could to push the door but her arms and legs were held tight by a sticky web of grey cords. Each movement was pulled back by a strong rubbery recoil.

She stopped to think. Any movement would draw the attention of the creature who'd built the web. It was a trap. She tried to look around and see what held her and realised her eyes were still closed. She forced them open.

That woke her up properly this time. She looked around. She was in her own lounge room, slumped on the couch. It was only a dream, but the conviction, the absolute certainty, she'd had in the dream state stayed with her. Something had to be done and she was the one who had to do it. The smooth, soft closure of the door had to be overcome. She had to make a noise, make it real.

Leah was clearly disturbed, alone in her grief. The fear was palpably real but how much of it was rational?

What had she said? That people were watching her. That could be true. Even if she was wrong about who it was, it meant she should be careful.

Detective Constable Craig Mason had done nothing apart from alerting Dee to the potential danger to Leah. Did he expect her to do the work of the police? There was no use talking to him. It was best to wait till the autopsy result and then get the information to Craig.

Dee sat up; shook her arms and legs. They moved freely. There was no restriction, no web, no tendrils in her brain. Now it was time for bed. Tomorrow, action. That always made her feel better. She would follow up the autopsy then update Marlena about Leah.

The couple Leah had mentioned hadn't been in for some time. She had a vague recollection they had moved to the Blue Mountains. She could check their notes, see if there was anything to support Leah's assertions about designer babies.

The other person who might be useful was Jock, her client who lived at the bottom of the stairs up to Tom's flat. He probably wouldn't talk to the police but Dee could find out what he knew. She'd seen him last week so he was due a visit early next week. She would have Janelle arrange a time. Jock was a one-man neighbourhood watch team. If anyone had clues about what happened to Tom, Jock would.

Marlena would ensure Craig's report to the coroner had all the evidence. Then the case would go back to the police for a full investigation.

Dee slept soundly for the first night in a week.

16.

Dee arrived at the office, early for once, to find Jean Louis slumped on the railing at the front door, hands clutched across his chest. His face had the grey mud look that said heart attack. She unlocked the door.

'Tell me,' she said as she helped him in.

'Morning, Doc, sorry,' he panted.

'It's okay, just tell me what's wrong.'

'I woke up with a steamroller pressed on my chest at five o'clock and I wanted to see you.'

'What about an ambulance? Did you think of that?'

'I thought you'd know what to do. You'd know if I should be worried.'

Dee rolled her eyes. Jean Louis was only fifty-seven but had smoked till he was fifty. He stopped when his younger brother had dropped dead of a heart attack. Dee had done his first ever cholesterol test and discovered the familial cholesterol problem. Since then he saw her regularly and tried as hard as a French chef running his own restaurant could to look after himself. She took his arm and helped him into the first surgery, pulled out the couch from the wall, to make for easier access if he went into cardiac arrest, and helped him up. The defibrillator they'd bought last year was tested monthly but it was many years since Dee had managed an arrest. Her own heart was pounding in her chest but she kept her voice and manner calm.

A noise from reception meant someone else had arrived.

'Hello, who's that? Can you come in here?' Dee called. 'Bring an aspirin, a glass of water and the ECG trolley.'

'Okay.' It was Janelle, good—she was not likely to show it if she panicked.

'Dissolve the aspirin in water and get Jean to drink it.'

Dee concentrated on getting the ECG connected, then she could see what was happening to his heart if Jean Louis lost consciousness. She took the cover off the defibrillator.

Chris, the registrar, arrived. She set him to insert a cannula, as she did the ECG, which, as she feared, showed a large anterior infarct. The aspirin might help limit the damage.

Janelle hovered at the door. Dee was on automatic now.

'Janelle, ring triple-O. We've got a large anterior infarct, we need a paramedic ambulance with all the sirens, bells and whistles. I'll talk to them if they give you trouble.'

Chris had the cannula in; he was just out of hospital training so he was in better practice at it than her.

'Chris, we need IV morphine. Start with 2.5 milligrams and leave the syringe handy. Get adrenaline and lignocaine ready to go. Then make sure the defib's ready to go.'

An ambulance arrived but it wasn't the paramedics. Should she allow Jean Louis to go with them or wait? She decided to wait. An arrest in a conventional ambulance could be fatal.

The paramedics arrived. They took forever to stabilise him. Finally, they were ready. Dee walked next to the stretcher to the door. Jean Louis held her arm as though physical contact with her would magically protect him.

She closed the door and looked at the time: 9.05 am. The waiting room was full. At least the spectacle with the ambulance, the trolley and the paramedics in their high-vis uniforms demonstrated she had been involved in a major emergency.

All she wanted was to collapse into a chair and let her adrenaline level go back down. Instead she walked around to reception and called up the first file.

'Marilyn, come through,' she called. On with the show.

*

Dee's lunch break had evaporated from ninety minutes down to ten. She remembered her decision to look at the records for Shirley and Ben. That would have to wait.

Janelle came in with a coffee and salad sandwich for her.

'Thanks.' Dee took a sip.

The coffee was still hot. It meant Janelle approved of how Dee had handled the day so far.

'Can you ring the morgue and find out what's happened to the autopsy report for Tom Harris?'

'Isn't it here?'

Janelle walked around to Dee's inbox. She found an envelope marked 'Office of the State Coroner'.

'This is it.'

'Oh.' Dee didn't want to touch the envelope. 'Okay.' She took it and put it back down immediately. 'I'll look at it after I sort out the pathology.'

17.

'Yes, Ken your INR is perfect. Keep on with the current warfarin dose.'

Dee hung up on her last urgent call of the day. She switched off her computer and heard the whirr as the server kicked in to automatically back up once the last user logged off.

Outside it was getting dark. She'd be gone soon. The fading light and the quiet after everyone else was gone were her favourite time of day. The path reports and letters were all checked ready for scanning and disposal. The three referral letters and two scripts she'd promised were done. The medico legal report would take at least an hour. It would have to wait—again. Some things were more important than medico legal reports. It usually gave her a buzz, made her feel in control to say no to more work but today there was no relief to be had from the thing she had to face.

The daylight-saving sun angled in to hit the corner of the desk. The envelope she'd been avoiding all day was there, spotlit, as the sun's last rays focused directly onto it. She hadn't turned the lights on and the white envelope glowed in the gloom of the rest of the room.

It was only the autopsy report, not a sinister portal into another dimension. The glow was the sun, not dangerous radioactivity. Her throat tightened and her stomach churned with grief. She missed Tom. He shouldn't be dead. There was no sense in it. She reconsidered the idea that he had died of asthma and rejected it again. That was impossible.

She wasn't sure she wanted to know the real reason for his death. It was frightening. She was about to open Pandora's box and there'd be no getting the lid back on.

She glanced at the clock. Seven twenty-five. If she opened it her reward would be to go home. Get a grip. She opened it.

> *Well-nourished Caucasian male of twenty-five years. No signs of recent injury or trauma. No surgical scars or tattoos, no external marks. No evidence of violence. Internal organs, apart from the lungs, healthy.*
>
> *Well-established rigor mortis. This together with livedo reticularis, body temperature and the consistent environmental conditions of the corpse, enable an accurate estimate of time of death to within three hours of 11 pm Saturday December 8.*
>
> *Stomach contents: gastric juices only, suggesting subject had not eaten within several hours of death.*

Dee skipped to the conclusion.

> *The absence of any signs of trauma and a finding of hyper-inflated lungs with mucus plugging of bronchioles is consistent with asthma. Rohypnol at 1.5 times the upper limit of the therapeutic range found in the blood with a smaller concentration in the urine suggests ingestion within an hour of death. The concentration is not sufficient to depress respiratory or cardiac function.*
>
> *Cause of death: acute asthma.*

*

Dee pulled up in front of her house. It was 7.47 pm. She couldn't remember leaving the surgery or the drive home. All she wanted was to sit in the car and ignore this world that made no sense but the kids could see her from the lounge. If she didn't go in, they'd be out to get her.

She walked across the footbridge to her front door and failed in her attempt to slam it. The cantilevered glass door opened and closed silently. God save us; she clenched her teeth. The constipated precision of Rob's architecture drove her to blasphemy.

In the lounge, three blobs were sprawled on the couch watching something loud on TV without the lights on. She was wrong to think they'd be aware she was outside. Nothing but the screen in front of them reached consciousness. The coffee table was sticky with takeaway containers, dirty plates and Coke bottles. Their sneaker-clad feet perched amongst the mess.

No one noticed her in the doorway. Laughter erupted. That was the spark. Dee's rage flared like a bush fire in a southerly.

'What happened to the steak I defrosted?'

'Hello Mum, good to see you too.' Ollie was the only one to respond.

After the day's news, she wasn't ready for sarcasm in her own lounge room.

'Move your feet so I can clean up this mess for you.'

'Mum, sit down. There's a plate in the microwave for you. I'll heat it up.' Eleanor got up.

'No, I can't eat in the middle of this mess.'

Beatrice and Oliver looked at each other, nodded and stood up.

'I've got an assignment,' said Beatrice simultaneously with Oliver's 'Yeah, there's a physics test in the morning ...'

Both headed to their rooms. 'What about the Coke?' Dee asked.

'It was free; a special deal. We saved ten dollars. I thought you wanted us to be more careful.'

'And what about the steak we were supposed to have?' Dee yelled.

'Still frozen.'

Then she remembered; she'd been in a rush to get to work early, dinner the last thing on her mind.

'Why's it always me? You lot eat too.'

She stopped herself. They were teenagers; she'd brought them into the world, as they often reminded her. There was no winning this argument. It wasn't even an argument, certainly nothing rational. She was tired and upset. It was just that she didn't want to be responsible for everything and everyone all the time.

Dee slammed the empty containers together, picked up a paper bag off the floor and shoved the mess into them. She marched onto the veranda and slammed the lid of the garbage over the lot.

In the kitchen, Eleanor had set out a napkin, spoon and fork with a plate of green chicken curry and a side plate of fresh rice rolls and peanut sauce.

'Mum, sit down and eat. Please.'

Dee had barely eaten all day—not since Janelle had handed her the autopsy report. She stood at the sink, rinsed the dishcloth and moved dirty glasses and clattered dirty spoons out of the sink into the dishwasher. Halfway through she realised the dishes in it were clean and she slammed the door so hard a glass broke.

'Mum, I'll fix it. You need to eat.' Beatrice was standing in the kitchen door.

Dee took the dishcloth into the lounge and wiped the coffee table. Under her breath she muttered, 'Lazy useless slobs, I should send the lot of them to live with their father, see how he'd cope with this shit cluttering up his precious minimalist existence.'

Out loud she said, 'I can't eat in this mess.'

'Sit down and we'll do it.' Ollie was back. He took the dishcloth from her and led her to the food.

She sat and tried to collect herself. 'The coffee table's a mess …'

'Sorted,' said Ollie and went into the lounge room with a bottle of spray cleaner and a roll of kitchen paper.

Dee looked up. Bea looked anxious and Ellie was ready to cry. She picked up a peanut sauce-covered rice roll and bit it in half. Delicious. The green curry smelt of lime, lemongrass and fish sauce. Dee ate. The girls sat down beside her. Her blood sugar went from 'let's chase down and kill a herd of zebra' to 'civilised, comfortable, time to look around, rest and digest'.

'Who's died then?' asked Ollie from the doorway.

'You don't want to know. No one died, not today anyway. It was just an autopsy report.' Dee stopped and looked at him. He was just fifteen; how did he get to be so wise?

'Do you want to tell us about it?'

'No, sorry, I'm okay now. My work isn't meant to be your problem.' Dee caught Beatrice and Ollie roll their eyes at each other. 'No, I mean you don't need to know the details. It's better if it stays at work. At home, I'm your mother not other people's doctor.'

She reached out and put her arms around the girls.

'Come here, you. You're not too big for a hug,' she called to Ollie and turned to hug him around his waist.

'All right, homework and I'll remember to get the steak out for Monday night. If I'm not here by seven there'll be salad ready to go and potatoes to microwave—and no more Coke even if it saves you money.'

*

In bed, she was wide awake again as soon as she turned off the light. The image of Tom lying on his bed, dead, came to haunt her as soon as her mind was empty. She hadn't rung Raj like she promised. It absolutely couldn't be asthma that had killed Tom. If she rang Raj she would have to tell him all about it. Tell him what she was going to do.

First, she could talk to the pathologist and make sure there wasn't anything he'd missed.

18.

On Tuesday afternoon Dee walked down the ten cracked and steep front steps that kept elderly Thelma Taylor a prisoner in her own home. The state morgue was just around the corner on Parramatta Road. She'd rung this morning to speak to Dr Heinrich Van der Waal who'd performed Tom's autopsy. It was now 3 pm. No one had phoned her back yet. She could spare half an hour. A person at the front desk was more difficult to ignore than a phone message.

Reception was in a large modern foyer, aluminium framed pale glass and terrazzo floors. Dee knew that the double doors off to the left led to the courts. She had appeared once as an expert witness at a coroner's enquiry. Behind the desk, open stairs led up and down. She guessed the morgue and the pathologists' offices would be downstairs, underground in a windowless basement like in all the movies she'd seen.

As she asked for Dr Van der Waal, a pale figure in a washed-out green shirt and lilac tie came through the front door, hands full of coffee and takeaway food.

'Heinrich,' the receptionist called to him. 'This doctor is here to see you.'

Pale eyes blinked through blond lashes at the receptionist as Dr Van der Waal carefully avoided looking at Dee.

'I don't think I've got any appointments?'

'No, I'm Dr Flanary. I left you a message earlier and I was just around the corner so took the chance …' Dee smiled and walked over to put herself between the pathologist and the stairs. 'But I can see you're occupied.'

'Yes, a busy morning.' He gestured with his full hands. 'I've just got to lunch. You're on my list of people to call.'

'If you have a moment now you won't have to ring me later. I just wanted to ask about your report on Tom Harris.'

Van der Waal had the face of a 35-year-old but the posture of someone who'd spent fifty years stooped over a microscope. He gave in and gestured up the stairs. Dee followed him to a messy office with a big window that overlooked Sydney University sports grounds. She sat in a chair opposite his overloaded desk.

'Thanks for making time to see me. I have your report on Tom Harris. He was a patient of mine and I was there when he was found. I wanted to speak to you because I'm concerned that his death may not have been due to natural causes.'

Heinrich looked for a moment at his lunch, sighed, then looked back at Dee.

'There's no doubt, Dr Flanary. As I told the insurance company, who also have an interest in the case, your patient, Tom Harris, died of acute asthma.'

'The insurance company?'

'He had a large and recent policy. It's still in the exclusion period where suicide would mean no payout.'

'There's no way Tom would kill himself. He was planning on having a baby. I saw him just a few weeks ago. He was excited, happy.'

'I agree, there is no evidence for anything other than an acute severe asthma attack. Young people die of asthma all the time. He had a couple of near misses in the past and this one: well, he didn't make it this time.'

'From the literature, I understood that a death due to acute anaphylaxis could be indistinguishable from one due to asthma.' Dee had spent a couple of hours doing research.

A loud sigh came back to her. 'Dr Flanary, I don't know if you noticed in my report that the lungs were hyper-inflated and the bronchioles plugged with mucus. The findings are consistent with acute asthma—end of story.'

'There could be other causes of those findings though, couldn't there?'

'The pathological findings in acute anaphylaxis are sometimes indistinguishable from asthma because death arrives via the same mechanism as an asthma attack. The reaction to the allergen narrows the terminal bronchioles and fills them with mucus. Essentially it doesn't change my report. Your patient died because his lungs could no longer take in oxygen due to asthma. And asthma is commonly caused by allergic reactions.'

'Is it possible to tell if there was an acute reaction to an allergen in this case? I know his family would be comforted to know what triggered this after he'd been well so long.'

'There'd have to be additional tests: histamine levels, although they're unlikely to be reliable when the body was found so late; antigens to specific substances are also possible. I'm sorry though,' he didn't look at all sorry, 'no matter what the result, there's nothing to indicate foul play.'

His eyes flicked towards the white paper bags leaking grease onto his desk.

'Surely the insurance payout provides a motive for the beneficiaries? Tom just wouldn't die of asthma. He was obsessive. He managed it perfectly.'

'Not on this occasion obviously.' Heinrich paused, possibly aware what he'd said was too harsh. 'You're naturally concerned for your patient' seemed to be the best he could think of to soothe it over.

Dee guessed that live human beings rarely crossed his path.

'I find it useful sometimes to talk about how we know things,' he continued. 'My house is in Surry Hills, on a laneway adjoining the police horse stables and training grounds. When I am sitting in my kitchen and I hear the sound of hooves clomping along the laneway I assume there are horses in the laneway.'

Dee knew the argument from medical school. Was it just hypersensitivity and loss of self-esteem after the divorce or was she actually being patronised more since menopause?

'You think I heard the sound of hooves and jumped to the conclusion that there's a herd of zebras passing?' she interrupted.

Dee paused long enough for him to feel pressure to reply, then as he started to open his mouth, she let him off the hook.

'In this case though, I know there's a circus in town and that there are precautions in place to make sure the horses aren't allowed out for the moment. That increases my odds of zebras a little, doesn't it?'

The pathologist screwed up his eyes and rubbed them with his knuckles.

'Dr Flanary, forensic pathology is a science that relies on the balance of probabilities. Many things are possible—a meteor might crash through our roof at any moment but that is so unlikely that it won't make us stop what we are doing to make a final phone call to our loved ones.'

Dee knew anger was useless. Her knowledge of Tom and the circumstances of his death couldn't be seen through a microscope; that meant it didn't exist for Heinrich. The anger faded. She let the pathologist's voice wash over her. What he said about allergy was interesting. The extra tests could help. Maybe he could test for prednisone too. Tom would definitely have taken prednisone if he felt an attack coming on.

She smiled. 'You're right of course. And what you said about anaphylaxis is helpful. I remember Tom had an acute admission due to an allergy to echinacea and they're flowering now.'

'That does fit with my findings.' Van der Waal tented his fingers together to rest his chin on.

'Is there any way we can absolutely prove you're right?'

'I'll order the extra tests. You know it won't change the conclusion though.'

'Just for completeness, can we test to see if he'd taken his prednisone too? His family might be comforted to know that it was inevitable and nothing further could have been done.'

'Okay. I'll let you know. It could take a while.' Heinrich sighed loudly. His eyes were on his lunch. 'I'll try to hurry it up, for the family's sake.'

'Thank you so much. Tom's family will be relieved. I'll ring you in a week to see how it's going.'

The pale lashes fluttered again but Heinrich didn't verbalise any objection. He would do the tests. Anything to get rid of her and get to his lunch.

Dee picked up her bag. 'When will the case come before the coroner?' she asked as she started to get up.

'Well, it won't,' said Heinrich. 'If a death is due to natural causes, which we have no reason to doubt, that's a waste of the court's time.'

No coroner's enquiry—Dee sat back in the chair as though she'd been punched—flattened, all the air gone out of her.

A coroner would consider all the evidence around a death, not only the pathologist's findings. Unless something extraordinary came out of the extra tests, and it wouldn't, this was the end of any hope that Tom's death would be investigated. There was no chance of justice for Tom.

Heinrich looked at her, no doubt expecting a response. Dee had nothing. She sat back up. She had to get out.

'Sorry, I didn't realise that,' Dee said and clutched the desk to haul herself up.

*

She somehow made it back to her car. There was a message from Raj. He was the only person who understood about Tom but she couldn't bear to tell him the news. It was too awful. If she told anyone it would solidify into a fact.

Nothing was going to happen. She felt too hopeless to talk.

She sent a text. 'Sorry, extra busy. Will ring in a day or two.'

19.

Next morning Dee was tired and queasy. Last night's red wine on an empty stomach in front of junk TV wasn't a recipe for bounding out of bed full of energy. The children weren't there to make her put on a show of healthy living. It would be easy to become an alcoholic if she lived alone.

Food didn't appeal but she ate a plate of Oliver's iron man cereal; some sort of pressed cardboard coated in salt and sugar. It did its duty and the queasy feeling receded.

She checked the wine bottle. A little less than half was left. She'd broken her half bottle rule but only by a small amount. In the circumstances, she could forgive herself but she added a new rule: if she drank more than one glass she had to eat.

*

The surgery was quiet. No one in the waiting room. The other doctors on duty, William and Chris, already had their first patients in their rooms with their doors closed. She opened her computer to see who hadn't come. An hour was blocked off, marked SB.

'Janelle?' she asked. 'Who's SB?'

'I don't know. You put it in a couple of days ago, after Jean Louis had his heart attack. I hope it means something. I could have filled it a dozen times.'

Dee remembered. It was the day she'd decided to check out Leah's story then ran out of time when Jean Louis decided she was better than all the resources at the hospital. SB were the couple Leah had told her about. S, it wasn't Samantha, maybe Sheila, something old-fashioned. The B was Ben. The pair used to live near Tom.

They'd had a gorgeous blond two-year-old boy via IVF. She hadn't seen them since they were expecting twins. She couldn't remember their last name. Ben had dark hair and looked southern European. Italian? The easiest way to find them was to search for letters to GenSafe IVF or Adam Fairborn.

The computer produced a list of twelve referrals over the past five years. The last one was Tom Harris. Dee had anticipated he would be there and steeled herself to remember something happy about him. She settled on the pride in his face when he had come in with Leah.

Shirley and Ben were third on the list. Their surname was Albanese. A Maltese name. Once Dee had the file open the details came back to her. The first referral to Adam was five years ago. Shirley came back six months later for a check-up after an abortion because the foetus had 'something wrong'. Shirley was vague and didn't seem as upset as expected. She was calmly determined to try again. Dee didn't know whether to be impressed by Shirley's stoicism or to probe her for repressed emotions.

Dee searched for the pathology results on the foetus. There were none. All she could find was a brief letter from Adam to say he had referred them for the termination after an amniocentesis at fifteen weeks was abnormal. He didn't give any more details. That was odd. To predict risk in future pregnancies it was important to know what abnormality was present. Dee assumed the problem must have been chromosomal because the termination was late, eighteen weeks; after the time it took for chromosomes to be sampled via amniocentesis and cultured.

As she looked through the file she remembered that it had happened twice more. Each time, Shirley was determined to go on and was less distressed than most mothers on the IVF roller-coaster. The thrill of pregnancy then the spill of miscarriage, or in this case deliberate termination, were heart wrenching for those whose life could only be complete if they had a child. Not many couples had the stamina or the funds to do it so many times. Shirley and Ben had multiple tries till they got their perfect boy. She checked the letters from Adam. They were identical: a form letter. Where the word processing program had inserted 'Dear Dr Flanary' Adam had struck out the Dr Flanary and inserted a handwritten 'Dee' to personalise it. It didn't work.

The most recent referral was eighteen months ago. Success came with the first cycle. Shirley was pregnant with twins when she came in to ask Dee to transfer her files to a new doctor in Springwood, in the Blue Mountains.

All the others who she had referred to Adam she remembered. A brief look at the files confirmed there wasn't anything unusual about them.

She checked referrals from the other doctors in the practice. Two had come in for post-termination check-ups after vague abnormalities. Neither case had any pathology results—only the brief identical notes from Adam with the personalised crossing out of Dr and the handwritten first name.

On the letter to William, Adam shortened the name to Bill. William hated his name to be shortened. Dee could imagine the grimace on his face as he read the letter. Adam was hopeless at human relationships—never got the social things right and never paid enough attention to anyone to even notice.

Dee would ask William what he remembered about the case next time they got a moment free together.

The other case was seen by a registrar, Alison, who had been in a training position at Dee's practice for six months. Ali wrote very detailed notes. It was the same story. Two late terminations and eventual success. No pathology results, and the same brief note from Adam. Ali recorded that she had rung Adam's practice twice to get pathology results. Dee searched and found nothing. The last she'd heard of Ali was that she had followed her husband overseas and lived in Malaysia. Dee sent an email to Ali's old email address to ask her to get in touch. It didn't bounce immediately.

The waiting room screen lit up with her first patient, then, as she watched, another three phone messages blinked at her.

*

It was evening before she had time to think about anything but the immediate needs of others.

Dee wanted to tell Raj about what she'd found. There was a message from him on her phone. It was 6.45. The kids deserved to see her too and they would be starving by now. She sent back a text 'Lots to tell you but too busy. Tomorrow? I'm childfree, takeaway at my place?'

If she could make the story more coherent she would approach the police again. Marlena might be able to help. She didn't want to exploit patients for her own needs but Marlena wasn't her patient; only the relative of a patient.

Her phone buzzed with Raj's reply.

'Tomorrow's good. I'll bring food. 7.30?'

'Good. I'll let you know if I'm late. No wine! D'

20.

Raj came in with two large bags trailing a scented cloud of lemongrass, turmeric, coconut and lime. The hopelessness of it all had descended over her again and Dee wondered why she had invited him. He had gone to so much trouble, she had to make an effort.

She set the coffee table with bowls, napkins and water glasses. The lounge had dim light and was less conducive to the detailed formal discussion she wanted to avoid. It was good she'd said no alcohol. Wine wouldn't help them to stay away from the pain and hopelessness around Tom's death.

Raj unpacked salt and pepper eggplant; duck and prawn wrapped in Vietnamese pancake; turmeric chicken curry; wood ear, oyster mushroom and lotus root stir fry and coconut rice. It was too exotic to be from any of the local places. Good food was worth any amount of trouble for Raj.

'I told you it was just us, didn't I?' Dee asked as they sat down.

'Yes, why?'

Dee waved her arm across the array of food. There was far too much for two.

'Oh yes, silly. Back in a minute.' Raj got up and went outside.

In a minute he came in with a six-pack of Coronas and two limes. 'You said no wine.'

For a moment Dee thought she might cry with relief. She so wanted to forget all that happened. Raj could be relied on to make her remember there was a world beyond the one her head was stuck in. He loved excess: in clothes, in entertainment, in food. No matter what happened, Raj had all his senses open to pleasure—or maybe not all his senses—he never admitted to anything sexual. His private life remained a mystery.

He didn't appear to notice that everyone's eyes, male or female, were on him wherever he went. Or perhaps he didn't mind. Constant attention was his norm.

A while later, the coffee table was full of empty plastic containers and dirty plates. They were stretched out at either end of the couch in the semi-recumbent position Rob's low-slung architectural masterpiece forced you into. Raj put a wedge of lime into the necks of two more beers and handed one to Dee. A mild tide of alcohol had comfortably soothed away the need to fix anything.

She'd invited Raj over to tell him what had happened. She levered herself partially upright and gave him a summary. First, Leah and her terror that someone, 'the professor', Adam, was waiting for her outside the surgery, then the autopsy results, which meant there would be no coronial investigation. She filled him in on the insurance payout and the thirty-day rule. Lastly, she told him about Tom's investigations into GenSafe, and Leah's assertion that Shirley and Ben, and others, had bought designer babies from them.

'Okay, why don't we think about this like detectives?' Raj asked.

'Sure.'

She knew her own interest in the victim could impair her judgement. It was the same reason why acting as doctor for one's family was dangerous. It was too easy to take shortcuts due to prior knowledge or avoid proper procedures because of emotional barriers. Logically, it would be the same for a detective with an emotional connection to a victim. The problem was that there was no one official, or emotionally disengaged, willing to do anything for Tom. It was them or nothing.

'Sticking to the facts, what do we have about motive, means and opportunity?' said Raj.

'The police haven't even considered those. They refuse to accept a crime has been committed.'

'Well, if we stick to the facts, do we come to the same conclusion?'

Dee thought for a bit. The central fact was Tom's dead body and the results of the autopsy. His lungs were congested, the same as in death due to asthma. Oxygen couldn't get through the narrowed airways to reach the bloodstream.

'For means we have to have something which causes the same changes as asthma. The killer—' Dee paused; it was the first time she had used that word. '—would have to use something that induced congestion and narrowing of airways. Anaphylaxis causes the same pathological findings in the lungs as asthma.'

'You said before he had allergies.'

'Yes, they're common in people with asthma. Tom had known allergies to a few plants: wattle, plumbago and echinacea. The last time he had a bad attack he was seventeen. Skye gave him "a natural immune system booster" and he was severely ill in minutes. He was old enough to take emergency prednisone and make her call triple-O instead of me. They were in time and he made it, just. The natural remedy contained echinacea, common name, cone flower. They're pretty with purple petals and an orange centre. You see them all over in public parks. The official name is echinacea purpura. Lots of people have severe allergies to them.'

'So the attack that killed him could have been an allergic reaction?'

'It's very likely. There are more results to come that will prove that either way.'

'Doesn't an allergy make the possibility that it was natural causes more, not less, likely?' asked Raj calmly. 'I guess someone who knew he was allergic could administer an allergen.'

'Everyone close to him would know. Certainly his mother and anyone who knew his medical history. But why didn't he take prednisone? And ring an ambulance? It doesn't make sense.'

'Didn't you say he'd taken rohypnol? That could stop him from doing anything.'

'Tom was absolutely against drugs. You knew him. How likely is it that he'd take anything?'

Her plan to stay calm and logical was impossible. Her emotions vacillated between anger and helplessness. Anger took more energy but was easier to bear. How could she get someone to listen?

'Forget that for a minute,' Raj said. 'One step at a time. Let's get all the pieces lined up then look at them. We don't know if he did ring for help.'

She struggled to banish the image of Tom on the bed. Raj was right. She should follow his lead and consider just the facts.

'What about phone records?' she said. 'Can we get those? Surely the police would know if he'd rung an ambulance?'

'But his phone wasn't responding,' Raj said. 'Maybe it was flat or turned off?'

'There's an old couple I see regularly downstairs from Tom's flat. No one can do anything in the vicinity without Jock seeing. I'll get him to let me know if any mail arrives—maybe we can check Tom's phone bill. I don't want to have to ask Skye.'

'I have a contact. It may be possible to get that info without illegally opening Tom's mail, and who gets paper bills anymore. You're supposed to be able to access the metadata the phone company keeps about you. Maybe the next of kin can apply for that.' Raj was excited.

'Next of kin is a touchy subject. I don't see that being sorted out anytime soon. Skye's not likely to be happy about Leah getting half the insurance money or anything else of Tom's. Leah doesn't appear to care, but that could be an act—maybe, I don't think so though. Anyway, she's disappeared.'

To take that request to Skye or Leah would be pointless. Dee sat up and started to put the detritus of dinner into the paper bags it came in.

Raj sat up too.

'Are you okay?' he asked.

Dee had gone back to the image of Tom with Leah, the pride he had in showing her off to Dee. Even the good memories didn't help make it easier. Her eyes were moist.

'This is all wrong. It's not our job to make difficulties for the people who are trying to cope with this loss,' she said.

Raj passed her a pressed handkerchief. She wiped her eyes. He looked concerned.

Raj stood, picked up the rubbish and asked where the bins were. Dee took their bowls and cutlery into the kitchen and stacked the dishwasher. When she came back, Raj was on the walkway looking toward the harbour. Dee stood beside him. The heat of the day was now a cool touch on their skin.

'Do you want to stop?' Raj asked.

'No. Someone has to do this. Let's sit in the kitchen. Brighter light might banish the images lurking in the corners.'

Dee made coffee. They sat on hard chairs in the kitchen with the lights on and the sliding doors open to the green balm of eucalyptus from the bush. The night air was cool and soothed their bare arms.

'Let's stick to how he died. The allergy could kill him?' Raj asked.

'Yes, absolutely.'

It felt okay to talk now, a comfort to share.

Dee had seen near-deaths from allergic reactions. They could be rapidly fatal without medical intervention.

'There are three possible ways he could be in contact with something he was allergic to: accidental, deliberate by Tom, deliberate by someone else.'

'Raj, this is what I've been on about. The first two are impossible. You knew him too. What do you think?'

'There's no way to be sure but I agree the first two are unlikely.'

Dee started to splutter in protest.

Raj talked over her. 'Very unlikely. Which brings us back round to motive.'

'Money or sex are the big hitters as motives for murder, according to my expert knowledge from TV,' Dee said.

'Tom earned around $100,000 salary when he worked for me so possibly double that for freelance; more if he was collecting bug bounties.'

Dee tilted her head and wrinkled her eyebrows together.

'Money professional hackers get for discovering new threats and the way to disable them,' Raj explained.

'He didn't seem to have much money that I knew about. He must have been renting the flat. He gave Skye regular money to help with care for Charlie. I know the bank accounts would help but I can't approach Skye, sorry.'

'It's okay. The insurance is enough of a motive on its own. Five hundred thousand is enough to be murdered for.' Raj paused and looked at Dee to check if she was all right before he went on, 'So Leah and Charlie, the beneficiaries, have to be on our list of suspects.'

'Charlie can't dress himself or speak, and Skye wasn't the most competent parent but she loved Tom. I've been around this family for twenty-five years.'

'Whoever has access to Charlie's money then. What about the boyfriend?'

'Skinny ex-junkie, seems fond of Skye and he tolerates Charlie—which isn't easy. Tom only moved out once Glen was on the scene. He'd probably still be there if Glen wasn't.'

'That doesn't prove Glen didn't see the insurance money as something to make their lives easier.'

'That fits with Leah's story of being watched. Glen has a motive to get rid of Tom, and Leah too.'

'Did Glen know about the insurance? And the thirty-day business?'

'It sounds too complicated—he's not the brightest star in the firmament.'

'The insurance company had to find out about his death somehow. Either Skye told them or the police did. Did Tom tell her before he died though? If not, there's no motive for her and Glen.'

Dee rolled her eyes. 'It's not Skye. Anyway, I told the detective about the insurance policy. He must have checked on it and alerted Skye and the insurance company. Leah said she knew about it so Skye probably did too.'

'So Glen acting without her knowledge is still possible.'

'How can we find out if Tom told them?'

'Could you ask Skye?'

'No, she's still furious with me. Leah might know … that's a dead end though.' Dee paused, realised what she'd said and shivered. 'It's probably a good idea that she's disappeared then—unless of course it's too late …'

They both sat silent for a moment.

'I told her there was a risk but she's so obsessed with GenSafe and the investigation Tom was doing that she didn't seem to believe it was real. I was still hoping for an innocent explanation myself then. I should have made her understand.'

'How? As you said, she's disappeared. Some of the time is gone already. Saturday in two weeks will be twenty-eight days so three days from that and she's safe.'

Even in the brighter light of the kitchen the shadow of murder and murderers contaminated the safety of the space.

'I'm starting to feel a bit spooked. Can we leave it there for tonight?'

'All right, but there are other possibilities to look at. We ought to at least consider them. Another fifteen minutes?' Raj asked.

Dee nodded. 'I suppose we haven't considered the other stuff Tom was onto. Last time I saw him he was excited about what he implied were dodgy practices at GenSafe IVF.'

'Well, if their system had any flaws, Tom could have found a way to hack them. But he knows how not to leave a trace. If there were something criminal going on, that's a motive but only if they know he's onto them. I might be able to find out who set up their computer security.'

Dee hit the heel of her hand against her forehead. 'I saw Professor Fairborn, the head of GenSafe, at a meeting. I was at uni with him. I told him Tom was a hacker.'

'So if Tom was onto something, they could suspect he was into their system and monitor it.'

'Yes, but …'

'I know, you can't imagine the professor as a killer, right?'

'Tom said, well, alleged, they were offering designer babies at the clinic. Is that enough of a motive for murder? The publicity would probably get them lots of customers. But we can't go past the fact that Tom is dead and he didn't die of natural causes …'

'So we have to check out all the possibilities,' Raj completed Dee's sentence.

'There's a major one we're ignoring,' Raj said and waited.

'You can't mean Leah. The girl loved him and she's terrified.'

'All I'm saying is we shouldn't put people in and out of the frame because you "know" it's not them. Leah admits she knew about the insurance and we know nothing of her background. She's disappeared; that could be considered suspicious.'

Raj was right. She'd let her feelings for Tom colour this. If she relied on what she imagined went on in people's heads, no one was a murderer. She couldn't imagine a mental state that would allow the killing of another human being. Yet murders did happen. A step back to consider all the possibilities was the only rational way to proceed.

They agreed that Raj would try to find out more about GenSafe's computer systems and hopefully Tom's phone records. Dee would follow up the pathologist. It was something to do, a plan, a distraction from the fear she felt for Leah. At least the girl had disappeared so no one could find her, unless of course she had already been found by the killer.

As soon as she got the final pathology report, Dee would try again with the police.

Raj went to the fridge and waved another beer in front of Dee. It was 10 pm. She shook her head, got up and put their coffee cups in the dishwasher and turned off the overhead lights.

'Let's leave it now till we get more information from the autopsy,' she said. She couldn't bring herself to make the possibility of Leah being killed real by putting it into words.

Dee wondered if she should offer Raj a bed for the night. What if he thought it was a come-on, which it sort of was. It was much too complicated. If he was gay it would be too embarrassing. Why couldn't she ask him about it?

'I'm okay to drive,' he read her thoughts.

They touched cheeks.

'Thanks, Raj, you're a good friend.'

Dee rinsed the empty beer bottles and put them with the two still full bottles in a plastic bag next to her handbag. Tomorrow she'd dispose of them. No need for the kids to know she'd had Raj over.

21.

The next day, Dee was back downstairs from where Tom had died, an hour and a half late for her home visit. Would Jock let her in? She walked across the same dusty 'garden' of dead bushes and cigarette butts. Jock's flat was on the ground level. She rang and Jock buzzed her through the outer door. Dee stood at the bottom of the same dingy stairwell she'd followed the robot cops up that awful day. The light was poor. She glanced up the stairs and quickly looked away.

The police refused to do anything. Skye had her hands full with Charlie and wanted to believe it was asthma. Leah's suspicions could be paranoia. Dee didn't want to join her in some bizarre folie à deux.

The memory of Tom's last visit to the surgery came back to her. His undefended enthusiasm, his lanky awkwardness—and now her baby hacker was dead. He deserved more.

The door next to her opened. A large unshaven elderly man, flannelette pyjamas stretched across his considerable paunch, glared at her. The smell of stale spices and grease from the stairs was replaced with corned beef and cabbage.

'I suppose you're thinking of coming in sometime. It's one thirty; we should have been in bed half an hour ago.'

Jock hobbled slowly back across the lounge room, his knees held apart by a basketball-size sac of fluid hanging down from his scrotum. He had resisted surgery for the hydrocele till it became too difficult for him to get to the shops. From then it was eighteen months on the waiting list. Now he was finally due for surgery that would allow him to leave the flat again.

'Hello, Jock. I'm sorry. I got held up by someone having an overdose. How's Lil?'

A wrinkled woman with straggly grey hair in a threadbare nightie and adult nappy left the curtains she was fiddling with and came over to take Dee's hands between her own.

'You've come to take us home, dear.' She turned to Jock, 'Get my purse.'

'It's Jenny, love,' said Jock.

Dee extracted her hands. Jock took Lil by the shoulders and sat her down on the lounge. She had no idea who Jenny was but the name always calmed Lil down.

Lil submitted sweetly to having her blood pressure and lungs checked. Her weight was stable and she was no more agitated than normal.

'Have they collected your blood and done the ECG?' Dee asked Jock.

Jock's operation was next week. Dee had arranged home pathology and Lil was booked into respite care for a week so he would have time to recover.

'They said they can't come before three so I cancelled them.'

'But you can't have the operation without the tests and without the operation you won't be able to get to the shops. You told me you'd had enough of being housebound.'

'We go to bed at one o'clock—Lil has to have her routine—I can't upset her for a test. She'll be impossible.'

Jock was implacable. It was hard to disagree with him. Any minor change in routine and calm sweet Lil became a screaming harridan lashing out with fists and fingernails.

The Dentons' extraordinary sleeping schedule was a result of Jock's anxiety. To make sure it was done in time he started each task earlier and earlier. They'd gradually got to the point where he started getting ready for bed at 11 am. At 1 pm they were in bed asleep. They got up to start the day an hour before midnight. In a few more years they would be back to a normal schedule. Dee suspected it made no difference to Lil but if it gave Jock a sense of being on top of his difficult situation then all was well. She rang pathology to arrange a special visit outside the normal hours and Jock calmed down.

'Cup of tea?' he asked. It was a routine and routines were inviolate. The cuppa provided company for Jock and allowed Dee time to assess Lil's mental state and their interactions.

'Had the wallopers here last week asking questions about the lad upstairs—bad business,' Jock said as he dipped a whole shredded wheatmeal biscuit in his tea and successfully conveyed the soggy mess to his mouth.

'What did they want to know?' Dee asked, surprised the police had checked with the neighbours at all.

'Lots of nosy questions. Didn't tell 'em anything.' Jock winked and tapped the side of his nose with his finger.

'Was there anything to tell?'

'Only some bloke watching the front door for a week beforehand.'

'Jock, you have to tell the police.'

'No way. No filth getting anything out of me. I'm no dobber. And whoever did over young Einstein might have a go at us. I couldn't put Lil in danger.'

Dee decided not to push it. He looked bursting to tell but there was no way he would give anyone up to the police.

'What happened?' Dee asked. 'The police say it was an asthma attack.'

'Asthma my arse. Why were they watching the door all week? And who came down the stairs without the lights on the night he died? Poor bugger—seemed a decent sort, he used to collect our scripts from the chemist. Didn't deserve it. At least Bambi wasn't there.'

Bambi had to be Leah. Bambi and young Einstein, perfect names for them.

Dee still wanted to convince Jock to go to the police but if she tried he'd be likely to clam up completely.

'So what happened? There were people watching the house?'

'Not people, one bloke—black clothes and a dark cap pulled down over his face. He was in different cars every day. I got the numbers just in case, and I was right too.'

'You reckon there was foul play?'

Jock gave a shrug but didn't say no. Dee held her breath as she asked, 'You got the numbers of the cars?'

Just then Lil wandered into the kitchen and picked up the kettle. Jock was instantly at her side and gently took it from her. Anyone from any of the flats could come down the stairs late at night but car numbers were real evidence, something Dee could take to the police. But would Jock tell her?

'She's got to go to the toilet now.'

Jock knew the signs that Lil needed a toilet quickly. From the bathroom he called, 'Can we have all our scripts. I'll hunt out those numbers later. Lil's put them away somewhere.'

Dee wrote the scripts. With Lil rocking back and forth on the balls of her feet as she held onto his arm for balance, Jock signed the Medicare forms for both of them. It was 2 pm, a full hour past their bedtime. He was too distracted now for more questions.

Once Lil was in respite, Jock would come into the surgery for his post-operative check-up. Without the stress of keeping a constant watch on Lil he might tell her more.

On the way out, she looked up and remembered the last time she'd seen Tom, the person, not the remnants of him, the corpse. His mix of vulnerability and competence; a grown-up four-year-old with her as the adult looking on, ready for him to fall, ready to catch him, cuddle him and kiss better his injuries—except no one was there to protect him when it happened.

She braced herself to go upstairs.

'Asthma my arse,' she repeated Jock's words as she made one foot follow another to the top of the stairs.

What hope was there that she could get more information from Jock? If there were no hitches with respite for Lil and his operation went ahead maybe he would tell her. The chance of him corroborating any evidence to the police was nil though. Dee would have to see if she could use the information herself to find something the authorities would take seriously.

The door to Tom's flat was new, bare unpainted plasterboard with what looked like the same lock. The handle didn't turn. Skye would have the key.

22.

The key slipped into the lock. It was a week from the funeral. Skye made it plain she didn't want any further enquiry into Tom's death but handed over the key in exchange for Dee's feeble excuse.

Someone had to speak for Tom. And then there was Leah—was she paranoid or was she really in danger?

Dee put the key in the door and heard the tumblers turn in the deadlock. She pushed open the door and noticed the jamb was undamaged metal. When the police broke in, the flimsy material of the door had given way and broken away from the intact lock.

Dee remembered her brief surge of hope that day as they looked at the intact door. All was normal, Tom was fine, this was all an over-dramatisation. Then the police broke it down and the world changed.

Now she stepped inside, closed the door quietly and leaned back against it till her heart stopped thumping. She faced the main room and kitchen. It looked the same as the awful day they found him. On her right, a wall of computer equipment was winking red or green lights at her. It was neat, the cords gathered in bundles and descending through holes in the desk. Tom's chair faced her as though the last time he had got up was to go to the door. What had happened?

She pictured Tom at his desk. A knock on the door and him turning the chair, unfolding those long limbs, getting up, a brief walk across the floor to the door. Surely he would check the peephole? Why would he let someone in—unless it was someone he knew? The other option was someone had a key and had let themselves in without Tom knowing. The last person to sit in the chair could be Tom's killer. Perhaps he sat in the chair to check out the computers then turned to leave, taking Tom's key to lock up.

Dee made herself revise the pronoun to he/she. Killers were mostly men but it was a mistake to make assumptions at this stage. Hadn't Glen sat there when he wanted to take away Tom's computers?

Dee used her phone to take several photos of what she could see from the door. Craig had implied that the police had not taken fingerprints. Their cursory investigation was dropped once they received the pathology report that said he died of asthma.

Dee put the plastic fishing box that served as her doctor's bag on the kitchen table and opened it. She'd stuffed it with crime scene detective tools before she left the surgery. Evidence collected by an amateur would be not accepted by the police but she had to at least try. She pulled on vinyl gloves.

First the bedroom. Her memories of that day all led to the body on the bed and a painful rent in her heart. For Skye it was clearly unbearable to let her thoughts stray near that day. She was willing to believe anything if it let her keep Tom's death out of her mind. It was probably a desire to have the reminder of that day gone that made her hand over the key so easily.

Dee had to put aside her distress, look at everything about the scene and be methodical. For her, the only way to peace was to find out what happened.

The bed was made and there was a slight wrinkle in the quilt in the middle and the pillowslip was creased. Nothing else—no secretions from the corpse. Dee silently thanked a god she didn't believe in.

The Ventolin puffer she had taken from his hand was there on the bedside table. Dee picked it up. It was too light; she puffed it, she'd been right, it was empty. Why would Tom be using an empty puffer? She pulled the empty canister from the plastic holder and noticed something yellow, a fine powder, inside. She pulled a clip-lock bag from her pocket and put in the canister and holder. She climbed onto the bed and looked closely at the pillow. There were fine yellow dots on it too. She took a swab from her bag and rubbed it in the area of the yellow substance. Her grandfather was a policeman, maybe it was in her blood—or maybe it was watching *CSI* with the kids when she was exhausted after work.

Where were the rest of Tom's medications? He was meticulous about use-by dates and always had spares. She walked down the three steps to the bathroom and checked the drawers and cabinet: neat rows of moisturising soap, disposable razors and Band-Aids. There were no medications. That made sense, Tom wouldn't store medications in the heat and steam of a bathroom. She was tempted to go straight to the kitchen but she made herself proceed logically. She turned back to the bedroom and checked the clothes hanging in the built-in wardrobe. Tom had three identical brown corduroy jackets, the kind favoured by academics in the fifties with leather patches to protect the elbows. Half-a-dozen white shirts, gabardine trousers and some jeans. Everything was pressed and on hangers. His socks and underwear were folded and neatly arranged in drawers.

Her eyes moistened. All they were now was used clothes. No one inhabited them to make them matter.

Two drawers were empty and a space to the left in the wardrobe had no hangers. This must be where Leah had kept her things. It hadn't been clear if she lived with Tom or not. Dee didn't know what would happen with Tom's possessions or money. She assumed anyone as obsessive as he was would have some savings. Could Leah have been in to clear out her possessions? She denied having a key. Perhaps she took her things before Tom died?

Dee kept going; she checked all the pockets and pulled out the drawers to see if anything was attached to the backs or under-neath. There was nothing. She bent over to check the shoeboxes on the floor. They were all frustratingly filled with perfectly cleaned shoes, nothing more. Any life must be associated with more detritus than this. Where would someone as obsessive as Tom hide things? The edges of the cheap synthetic carpet in the room were firmly sealed down but an earlier version, dark orange and brown, covered the floor of the wardrobe. It was hard to see in the shadows but the edges looked as though they could be loose.

In the cramped space between the bed and the wardrobe, Dee crouched and twisted to reach the spot where she saw the carpet didn't quite reach the wall. Her fingers struggled to catch the sharp edge of the hard synthetic carpet. Her fingernails couldn't make it move.

'Damn,' she said out loud. As she spoke she heard a tap on the front door.

She froze, instantly guilty; everybody, except of course Leah, wanted all this over with, wanted it to be left at 'natural causes'. Dee felt like an intruder into the grief of others, interfering, making trouble. She was about to be sprung.

The sound came again. Who would be here? Hopefully they didn't have a key. If she stayed still, they'd go away. Who would be interested? Not the killer surely. Why come back after all this time? Gruesome scenes of a killer with a knife flashed through her brain. She decided to be brave and pushed herself up onto her knees. It would be useful to know who was hanging about. Perhaps Leah. Once they stopped knocking, Dee could look out the peephole and see who it was as they went down the stairs.

The sound of the door opening sent a chill through her. Was she about to find out who had caused Tom's death? She dropped back to the floor and wriggled under the bed. It was a squeeze; her bottom only just made it under the low bedrail.

The bedspread reached almost to the floor, it was displaced where she'd slipped under the bed. She kicked it straight with her foot and pulled her skirt away from the edge. The person was opening and closing kitchen cupboards. Then she heard a creak on the stairs; only three stairs up to the bedroom. Her heart made so much noise surely whoever was in the flat would hear it if they came into the bedroom.

Her handbag was slung across her chest and something hard was pressed into her hip—her phone. She stiffened. Don't let me be one of the idiots in the scary movies who dies because their phone rings and gives them away. She flicked the switch to silent. She wanted to swallow but her mouth and tongue were too dry. She was rigid and held her breath. The footsteps were at the bedroom door. How long could she hold her breath or her bladder? Whoever it was must be deaf if they couldn't hear the thump of her heart. They wouldn't look under the bed. Who looks under beds in scary movies? She hadn't looked under the bed. Why would the killer?

A murderer, someone who had already killed one person, was a couple of feet away from her. She heard the drawer of the bedside table opened and then closed. The feet were scratchy on the carpet. They came around the bed towards the wardrobe. At the end of the bed the bedspread was tucked in and a foot came into view. An emerald green boat shoe with a bare black ankle sticking out of it.

Raj. She was about to yell at him for frightening her but had a better idea. She waited till both feet were facing away from her and reached out to grip her fingers around his right ankle.

There was an enormous scream. Raj jumped several inches up in the air and fell down onto the bed. Dee threw the bedspread back and scrambled out as Raj positioned himself Ninja-style against the bedhead, arms up—ready to fight.

'It's okay. It's only me,' Dee said as she knelt against the bed.

'You nearly killed me.' Raj panted with his eyelids pulled back and his mouth open to gulp in air. He was barely able to speak.

'Sorry, oh I'm so sorry, Raj—I thought you were the killer. I was terrified. When I realised it was you I couldn't resist the temptation. Sorry.'

'You don't look sorry. Stop smiling. It's not funny.'

Dee got up onto the bed. Raj's breathing had slowed.

'It was a bit funny,' she said as she leant against him. 'How did you get here?'

'Janelle said you were doing a home visit here. I thought I might catch you. You haven't been easy to get hold of, you know.'

'Yeah, sorry about that. It all seems hopeless and I didn't want to bring you down too. But how'd you find me here?'

'Your car's outside so I waited, then had a wander and recognised the way to Tom's flat. The key was in the lock. You must have left it there.'

23.

Raj found a single bottle of beer in the fridge. He and Dee sat at Tom's kitchen table with half a glass each. All the things—the packet of sugar and the three cans of Rosella tomato soup in the cupboard, the jar of marmalade which Tom had once used—were now just objects. They were second-hand junk, devoid of the purpose infused in them by the needs of a living human. Tom's absence was profound. Neither of them could speak of it.

'Assuming you're right and it was murder, what do we have?' asked Raj after a long empty pause.

'Tom was onto something last time he saw me. And Leah said he'd been to Orange for research in the week before he died.'

'And it couldn't be asthma?'

'There's no way he'd let it get so bad. Tom always had his medications plus backups. He checked and charted his breathing at least three times every day. If there was a problem he knew exactly how to control it with extra medications, inhaled and oral corticosteroids.'

'What about the autopsy report and the sedatives in his blood? Couldn't they make him too sleepy to take his medications?'

'That's one of the things that makes me sure it wasn't asthma. Tom hated drugs. There's no way he'd take anything and he never got a script from me.'

'Dee, they sell that stuff on the street in the Cross—maybe he was depressed and wanted some relief.'

'He was excited. He had a girlfriend who wanted to have his baby and his work was going well. No, I know him—he wouldn't take drugs.' Dee caught herself saying 'know' not 'knew'. If she didn't do something this unbearable grief would be all she had.

Raj, ever logical, went on. 'So we have several mysteries: one, why didn't he take the extra medications; two, why were there sedatives in his system; three, what was he on to; and four, who didn't want that exposed? Five, who would profit by his death or be protected by it?'

Raj typed as he spoke, keeping notes on his iPad.

'And six, how did Tom die?'

'I'll search out his medications,' said Dee, 'see if there are any sedatives; you try to find where there'd be hidden documents.'

'Tom wouldn't have physical documents. They'd be on computer, backed up and encrypted. Encrypted properly—the level of encryption that can't be broken. If there were physical documents the killer would have removed them. I'll check the computers, but I don't think I'll get anywhere.'

Dee checked the fridge. Out-of-date milk with yellow broccoli and mouldy carrots in the crisper were the only perishables. Next to the fridge the bottle of prednisone Dee had seen when they found the body was still on the bench. She tipped out the plain white tablets to count them: sixty, they were all there. She checked the label. These were dispensed the day she'd last seen Tom. Why would they be opened but not used?

'Here's the rest of his medications.' Raj was bent down to the bottom kitchen drawer. Inside Dee could see several boxes of Ventolin with other bottles and packets.

'Why use an empty inhaler when there are three spares here?' asked Dee. 'And the yellow powder on the puffer and the pillow look like pollen. I got a sample.'

'Even if it's something he's allergic to, it doesn't prove how it got here. Tom could have brushed against it, not noticed. There's any number of possible explanations.'

The questions were piling up. Raj sat the drawer on the kitchen bench.

'Stop,' Dee called out and handed him gloves. 'That could be evidence.'

'I don't think what we find will be accepted as evidence.' Raj rolled his eyes.

'Just wear the gloves.'

He put them on. Dee picked up the Ventolin packets. All of them were sealed. Tom had spares. Why didn't he get a full puffer?

Dee took a photo of the sealed boxes and the prednisone with the tablets spread out to show that there was a full complement. There were no rohypnol or empty packets anywhere. No unwashed dishes or glasses on the bench.

'If he took sedatives wouldn't he wash them down with something? I know he was obsessive but ...' Raj said.

'There's a water bottle in the fridge. Even Tom might have drunk straight from that.'

'And it might have been drugged ...'

'In which case whoever drugged the water would have cleaned it out and replaced it.'

'Or removed any other contaminated item.'

'Okay, okay. The possibilities are endless,' Dee said finally. It felt like a dead end.

'What about the computers?' Dee asked. 'Thank goodness Skye was too grief-stricken to turn off the power.'

On Tom's desk was an array of machines, modems, hard drives, a large monitor and two smaller screens all winking with orange, yellow and green lights.

'Tom was a hacker. His passwords would be uncrackable. To even find out if it's crackable could take months. Where's his laptop?'

'Leah probably has it. When we were all at the flat, Leah disappeared while no one was watching. She could easily have slipped a laptop under her arm. Tom might have given it to her. I can't remember if it was here when he …' Dee didn't want to say it again. '… when we found him, but she disappeared from the scene while no one was looking.'

'We should try to find her and it. He'll have left clues.' Raj shook his head. 'No one as obsessive as Tom would let important information be unfindable if something happened to him.'

A bubble of hope lifted Dee. 'You're right! He was obsessive about backups like everything else. He told me he was a "belt and braces type" when he came to get the forms for the insurance.' Dee stopped, felt moist around the eyes.

He'd been so happy that day and later with Leah. He wanted to have a baby—with every precaution of course. Dee swallowed; the picture of him excited when he came to show off Leah was a better one to keep in her head than the not-him-anymore one from the flat. His shy smile as he pushed back his hair to look at his lover—Dee decided to keep that image to block the horrible ones from last week. She was pleased he'd had someone to love him.

'It's hard to get into his head,' Raj said. 'If there was danger, and it seems likely he was concerned there was, then he's not going to put Leah at risk by giving her the key to everything. We don't know though how much danger he thought there was.'

Dee followed on the argument. 'Leah says she doesn't know anything but if they both used the laptop he might have given it to her. Maybe he thought it would be safe with her? Or maybe he thought it was safe because there's nothing on it? She said he wouldn't talk about what he found after he went to Orange. One thing she does remember, because it was odd, was that he talked a few times about the crisper. Said the crisper was the key.'

'Tom wouldn't store passwords anywhere so obvious. Also he'd have off-site backup of any important data,' Raj said as Dee held the door of the fridge open.

Raj pulled out the plastic vegetable drawer.

He picked up the dead broccoli and carrots.

'Put them on the counter,' said Dee. 'Who knows what he might have done.'

Raj rolled his eyes but obeyed.

The crisper was a basic plastic drawer at the bottom of the fridge. Nothing was stuck under the rim. Dee dissected the vegetables into one-millimetre sticks—nothing. Raj looked up the serial number of the part on his iPad and tried the number in the computers but no luck.

Dee checked the time. She'd been at the flat for over an hour. Raj's impatient foot tapping and jiggling was hard to ignore.

'Time to give up,' he said again.

'Okay—if you'll work on the computers?'

'It could take months to crack his passwords. I'd need access to these for a long time.'

'Would you be willing to buy them from Skye? She'd have no use for them. How about I ring her?'

'Sure but isn't she pissed off with you about the autopsy?'

'It's okay, she just needed to be angry with someone on the day. That wasn't really about me. She gave me the key to get in here.'

'I thought no one else had a key. Maybe it's Tom's one?'

Dee walked to the front door and took the key out of the lock.

'This looks old but it's not well used. Maybe it was a spare? I'll ask Skye when I take it back.'

'How did you get her to give it to you?'

'I said I'd lost an earring here.'

'But you never wear earrings.'

'That's why I thought it was fair play. It's such an obvious lie that she must be okay with it.'

'Ahhhh!' said Raj. Then, 'Yes, I'm fine with buying the computers.'

*

'Hello, Skye, you were right. There's nothing here,' said Dee.

'I know.' Skye sniffed.

'I think someone should check out Tom's computer equipment. I've got Raj, his old boss, here. He might be willing to buy it from you. I'll put you on speaker.'

Skye started sobbing in earnest. In broken words she managed to say, 'Well you have to ask Leah.' Skye spat out the name. 'Apparently the girlfriend he's known for five minutes gets half the money from his life insurance. Glen reckons she can claim to be next of kin and get everything else he owns because she lived with him for five minutes.'

Raj raised his eyebrows and Dee shrugged.

It seemed unlikely that Tom had much to leave beyond the insurance. It was typical of Tom to have all eventualities covered. Even the possibility that something could happen to him. Was there a will? Now wasn't the time to ask Skye.

Dee was sure he wouldn't have died without a fail-safe backup plan for someone to have access to his discoveries. Hopefully Leah would have the information. Or would the information put her in danger?

In the background they could hear a regular thump, thump, thump. Dee recognised the sound as Charlie repetitively hitting something solid; possibly his own forehead. The phone was put down. In spite of her scattiness, Skye was committed to her autistic son. Dee had some sympathy for Skye's aversion to the unknown girlfriend who turned up to claim a part in Tom's life. At the flat, Leah had stood alone and made no attempt to talk to Skye or Dee. She wasn't easy to like.

'For God's sake take him into his room and shut the door,' Skye called to someone else. The thumps receded. 'No, you stay in there with him,' she shouted. The phone was picked up again.

'Sorry, Charlie hates me to be on the phone.'

'About Leah—you knew he was close to her, didn't you?'

'Yeah—$250,000 close. Charlie's going to need care for the rest of his life and that new-found friend gets as much as his disabled brother. She had him twisted around her little finger.'

Dee wanted to know when and how Skye found out about the insurance but the subject was too inflammatory.

'Skye, about the computers—is it all right if I get a computer expert to look at them?'

'You can't open them,' Skye said with some satisfaction. Tom was her son and she wasn't about to give away access to him. 'Glen tried to open them but he didn't have the passwords. He reckons they're worth a few thousand.'

Dee looked at Raj. He nodded.

'Yes, it will be difficult without the passwords. Do you want me to have Tom's boss try? Then he could give them back to you to sell.'

Raj typed something on his phone and held the screen up to Dee. She read it aloud. 'It could take weeks, even months to crack the passwords.'

Dee went on, 'But unless it's done no one can use the computers. You wouldn't be able to sell them.'

'Okay,' said Skye finally.

24.

Christmas Eve was frantic. Everyone wanted to sort out medical problems they'd had for weeks before the holidays. Then, from the mid-afternoon, no one came. The shops would be horrible, desperate people trawling through last-minute tat to find presents that no one needed or wanted.

Janelle handed Dee the mail that arrived late at 3 pm. She walked back to her room to process it. She loved Christmas but this year it would be a struggle. It was hard to feel good about anything since she had found Tom dead. No more Christmases for him. No baby, no life or love with Leah, no chance to make sure Charlie was okay.

She had lost the joy of seeing his name in the appointments list, his smile and the toss of his head to move his black curls out of his eyes. The five-day-old baby who looked into her eyes and trusted she would keep him safe was gone.

This year was Rob's turn to host the family Christmas but he wheedled his way into having the celebration at Dee's. The terrace in Chippendale was too small since the twins and he'd promised to do everything and to clean up.

Dee agreed rather than have the kids miss out on their father and half-siblings on Christmas Day. The twins were just six months old and cute as kittens. It would be a fuss but fun. Just the kind of gathering Dee had always wanted when she was growing up.

Once Auntie Alice died, there was just her and Mum at the big dining room table in paper hats from the Christmas crackers, a mass of food spread in front of them. Ham, turkey, homemade Christmas pudding and mince tarts were mandatory. With only two people to eat they were faced with leftovers to New Year and beyond.

Mum was gone too now.

All the griefs Dee had suffered in the past came back: her father, who she barely remembered, stuffy old Auntie Alice, even Mami, her friend from uni who drowned when they were in fourth year, but especially Mum. Mum who had struggled for her daughter's success and then died too young to enjoy it. All the grief was still there strong as when she had first lost them. It felt good to let the pain through—its intensity honoured the importance of the loss.

The death of Tom wasn't the same clear, honourable sorrow. It was messy, wrong, unjust. For the first time she understood the grief of those left behind after a murder, those people who stood outside the court to rail against the limited sentences of the killers. This grief didn't honour Tom's memory.

After five minutes Dee noticed her face was wet. She grabbed a handful of tissues and wiped the tears that had run down her cheeks. Secreting bodily fluids wasn't going to make anyone's life better, nor would it get justice for Tom. Her face must look terrible. She took out two eye pads, wet them and sat, head back against the chair, to let the cool water soothe her eyelids.

The head of a black-haired bear was mounted on the wall above her like a trophy. Between his huge white boar-like teeth, he held a small mammal. He snarled and tossed his head about as the creature tried to escape. Saliva splattered from his mouth. Dee realised the animal in his jaws was her childhood pet Tigger. It was her task to rescue him.

The eye pads fell onto her lap as she tried to stand up. How long had she been asleep? The dream was ridiculous. Last night she'd given into relentless nagging by Oliver and allowed the kids to watch *Borat*. The image from the movie of a bear's head on a plate in the fridge had stuck in her head. The urge to rescue Tigger stayed with her.

She checked the computer. The last two patients had cancelled. All she had to do was the mail and she could go home for four full days.

The pile of specialist letters, drug company advertising and requests for reports was about half as big as normal. Everyone else, specialists and lawyers, even drug companies, had extended holidays over Christmas.

She stopped. What a bitter, boring person she'd been lately. She'd tried hard not to let the Tom stuff get to her but everything was tainted by the injustice of it. How could she turn less paperwork and a four-day holiday coming up into something to be resentful about?

She had to be more positive. The living—her kids, her patients and even herself—would be better off if she found a way to get over it, to get on with the living world. She stretched her slumped shoulders and looked at the photo of the kids on the desk. That always cheered her up. The snapshot was taken at Dee Why the last time they all went out on a family outing—before Rob lobbed the hand grenade of Stephanie into their lives almost three years ago. Dee hadn't been to the beach with the children since.

It was almost Christmas. She had a whole four days off. It was time she made time for fun with the soon-to-be grown-up people who were still her children.

She returned to the correspondence. The promotional material for drugs went straight into the recycling. A couple of letters went to the pile to scan into patient files. The last was a plain hand-addressed envelope. Janelle hadn't opened it. Anything that could be personal she left intact for Dee.

Dee was cautious. Personal mail was uncommon. It carried an emotional charge—sometimes good; often if it had been sent to her at work, bad. She took a deep breath and inserted the letter opener into the slot under the flap.

She unfolded several sheets of paper printed on pathology letterhead. There was a handwritten note from Heinrich clipped to the front.

'Final results for Tom Harris. The conclusion, death from asthma, is unchanged. I'll add them to my report on my return in January. Thought you'd like to know. Heinrich.'

The supplementary pathology was complete. Dee scanned to the end.

> *High levels of acute phase antibodies to echinacea, other acute inflammatory mediators including eosinophils and histamines were found. Death was due to asthma secondary to a massive allergic reaction to echinacea purpura, the common purple cone flower—currently in bloom locally.*

The yellow powder from the flat had been confirmed as echinacea by the Sydney University Department of Plant Biology. It fitted.

Dee went back and read carefully through the whole document. The test for prednisone was negative. That wasn't possible. Tom knew what to do. He'd have rung triple-O and started prednisone immediately.

No coroner's enquiry. No further investigation by the police. No one to stand up for Tom.

Now she had to go home and trim the Christmas tree with the kids. She had to be happy.

25.

On Christmas morning Dee woke up with Tom still in her mind. Voices came from the lounge room. Oliver and Eleanor sounded as though they were arguing about how to wrap a present but then the sounds changed to laughter. She could smell coffee and something frying.

Seven o'clock. It was time to get up, put a brave face on. Today she owed to the living. She rummaged around in her drawers for eyeliner and lipstick and put on her slinky green opera dress with red mirror-ball earrings from the two-dollar shop. There was an old eye shadow in bright green she added at the last minute.

Beatrice had French toast and blueberries ready on the table when she walked into the kitchen. Oliver handed her an espresso.

'Happy Christmas.'

*

Rob and Stephanie arrived around mid-morning. The Glass-house was still Rob's home—every annoying part of it an expression of his design aesthetic but the promise that he and Stephanie would do everything today helped her focus on the better parts of him.

The new wife worked at pleasing Dee. Dee was host but free of cooking and serving. Stephanie was probably happy to be relieved of the twins for a few hours. All three children were willing assistants. Dee was slightly jealous.

Raj arrived at eleven.

It was the first family gathering he was invited to, the first time he had spent time with her children. Dee had negotiated strict instructions that he could bring champagne and chocolates and a small present each for the children—nothing else. He made several trips from a taxi to the front door with a large esky and three cardboard boxes.

'Hi Raj,' Dee said as she brushed his cheek with her lips. 'I thought we agreed only champagne and chocolates?'

'Yes?' he said and carried more cargo in from the front door.

He opened the esky to reveal a dozen bottles of Veuve Clicquot on ice. From the boxes he produced two silver ice buckets, champagne flutes, two platters of Belle Fleur chocolates and armfuls of Christmas bush.

'Thanks,' said Dee, 'how could I doubt you?'

'Thank you for inviting me.' He stopped to gaze at her. 'You look beautiful.'

'Um, thanks' was all she could manage.

She looked around. No one was close enough to hear. She bustled off to get vases for the flowers so he couldn't see the flush at the base of her neck.

The turkey still had a couple of hours to cook when Raj arrived so he and Rob and Dee sat together on the deck with the six-month-old twins. Raj poured champagne, and produced a bowl of Balmain bugs and melted garlic butter for dipping.

He cracked and peeled a bug for her and presented it on a Chinese spoon. She frowned, ready to say 'Didn't I say nothing else?' but instead opened her mouth to accept the bug. It was perfect, sweet tender meat, salty and garlicy.

'Delicious.'

Raj kept their glasses topped up. Dee switched to mineral water after her first glass disappeared in a couple of gulps. Any more and all the emotions she was hiding might flood out through her eyes.

Raj made it harder to forget about Tom. She wanted to tell him about the final results but there wasn't much point. No one else deserved to suffer because of her misery.

The children were mostly with Stephanie in the kitchen. She was breastfeeding so no booze but she seemed relaxed. Rob was good with the babies, better than with his first brood. With twins there was little choice. Stephanie breastfed one while Rob topped up the other with solids. They swapped babies for a repeat performance then Stephanie escaped back to the kitchen.

Rob was left with a baby on each knee.

Dee was tempted to help but she didn't want to fuss over the babies, didn't want to rescue Rob. Her own children needed more than they got of her. How often did they have a full day together without all sorts of busyness?

She got up and went to the kitchen. Stephanie was carving while Beatrice set the table. Oliver had his head in a cupboard in search of a gravy boat. The children treated Stephanie like a friend. There weren't so many years between them.

No Eleanor though. Dee walked to the back of the house. Eleanor's door was open. Her room was empty. No one was in the bathroom.

Dee went outside onto the back walkway. No one was there but the last of the three garbage bins was askew.

She looked closer. The toes of pink sneakers projected between the bins.

Ellie was in her favourite childhood hiding place, headphones on and her elderly teddy bear, Growly, on her lap. Dee moved the last bin and sat beside her.

Eleanor didn't respond. Dee gently took the headphones off her ears.

'What are you doing out here? Are you okay?'

Ellie shook her head no.

'Are you going to tell me what's up?' Dee said as she cuddled her sensitive third child.

'Is Raj your boyfriend?'

'No. He's just a friend. Is that all right?'

'Are you going to get a boyfriend?'

'I might one day. What do you think about that?'

'What happens to us then?'

'Nothing happens to you. I'm your mother and I always will be. Do you think I'll run off with someone and not care about you?'

Ellie nodded. 'Dad did.'

Dee waited a few beats.

'I won't. I promise. And your dad still loves you.'

'He left though.'

There wasn't much Dee could say to argue with that. Those were her own thoughts, when she let them into consciousness. It would be so easy to be bitter, to hate Rob for his betrayal. Out here next to the bins with Eleanor she had the luxury of unfiltered feelings. Why did she have to go in and be a grown-up?

There was an urgent cry from a baby, then two together. She turned her head. Rob was up, a twin in each arm, both screaming at him. She smiled; it served him right. She turned back to Eleanor.

'Dad knew I'd be here. And I always will be. You'll have to leave me.'

Dee pulled Eleanor up with her and assembled her social face. They went inside. Stephanie roped in Ellie to finish decorating the table.

When she returned to the deck, Rob and Raj had a baby each. Raj held the girl expertly in the crook of his arm. She was sound asleep. Where had he learnt that?

26.

Work was quieter than usual between Christmas and New Year. Dee rang Glebe Police Station to speak to Marlena.

'Yes, I remember,' Marlena said, 'but isn't the case closed? Hang on a minute.' Dee could hear a keyboard clacking. 'Yes, it says here no suspicious circumstances, death due to acute asthma, case closed.'

'Marlena, I know the boy. He wouldn't let himself die of asthma. I'd stake my life on it, and not suicide either. There's something going on here. Is there anything you can do to find out more?'

'Not easily. No one can trawl through other cases without a reason. It's difficult enough being a woman, not to mention an Asian woman, in the force. There are plenty of blokes who'd be happy to report me if I get something wrong,' Marlena said quietly.

Dee waited.

Finally Marlena sighed. 'Okay, I'll talk to whoever's working on it and I'll get back to you.'

They exchanged mobile numbers.

*

Marlena rang the following afternoon while Dee was busy. Dee rang back later but got Marlena's voicemail. To cut through the telephone tag, Dee sent a text. 'Can we meet at Gallon after work? I'm flexible, any time from 6.30 on.'

Dee walked the 750 metres to the Pyrmont end of Harris street, not sure if she really wanted to hear what Marlena had for her.

What appeared to be a tiny bar with sandstone walls expanded Tardis-like as you entered. There was a general convivial buzz from the several saloons at the front but, beyond the big open courtyard, the back bar was quieter. The detective wasn't there yet so Dee sent her a text. 'Out the back. Red, white or beer?'

By the time Marlena arrived two generous glasses of Swan Bay Shiraz were lined up and plates of crushed and fried potatoes and a Caprese salad had just landed on the table.

'Thanks, Marlena. I thought it was better to be away from the station, and you do live near here, don't you?'

'Yeah, next block, 205. You've got a good memory.'

'Well I knew it was somewhere near your mum ... but first things first, we probably both could do with a drink.' Dee picked up her glass. The diminutive Marlena managed to climb up onto the stool and clinked glasses with her.

'I'm sorry—' Dee started but Marlena interrupted.

'Don't apologise, I understand; it does all sound dodgy but there are procedures and, no matter how much I want to help, there's some stuff I can't do.'

'I know but I don't know where else to turn. Please forget I know your mother, you know this makes no difference to that relationship. It's not only about justice for Tom; I'm worried about his girlfriend. She could be in real danger.'

Dee hated the feeling that she was exploiting her connection with Marlena's mother.

Marlena reached over to pat Dee across the shoulders. Dee must have sounded on the edge of panic. All she could think of to say was sorry but she didn't want to start apologising again and sound even more out of control.

'Thanks.' Dee tried to sound matter-of-fact. 'How's the investigation going?'

Surely if there was real news Marlena would have come out with it straight away? All the same Dee could feel her heart bashing against the inside of her chest.

'The final pathology report is in so it's case closed.'

'But what about the sedatives? That's absolutely out of character for Tom. And the finding that there was no prednisone in his blood. The first thing Tom would do in an asthma attack would be to take prednisone. It doesn't make sense.'

'Half of our overdose cases have relatives claiming there was no way they'd take drugs. The sedatives could explain why he didn't try to help himself. There's not enough to build a case on in the face of a finding of natural causes. The detective handling the case is a Constable—'

'Craig? Looks like a real estate agent?' Dee asked.

'That's the one, Craig Mason. Not a font of sympathy or understanding—doesn't notice women unless they're potential conquests. He's a bit green but keen for promotion. For him it's all wrapped up, cut and dried. It wouldn't do him any good to keep the case open. A closed case is a result, a success for him.' Marlena paused.

'Craig said he checked on the mother's partner and that he had some past convictions,' Dee said. 'He's got a motive and a record.'

'There's no crime though, we've got no reason to follow up anything now.'

Marlena sounded gentle but Dee couldn't let it go. She pushed on.

'What about the girlfriend? What about the insurance? What about Tom's investigation? He hacked GenSafe and claimed to have evidence their clients were being charged tens of thousands of dollars and the payments were being sent offshore. He told his girlfriend it was too dangerous to stay at his flat and now he's dead and no one knows where the girlfriend is. Isn't anyone worried about what's happened to her? If there's foul play she could be the next victim. Did you find out about Glen's record?'

Marlena looked around them. 'You didn't hear this from me. Glen Sturrock has several convictions for possession of marijuana and one for heroin, all personal use quantities. Only one conviction for violence. Glen attacked his half-brother. Got a community service order and suspended twelve-month sentence for assault. That's all Craig had recorded. I can't access anymore.'

'Maybe there's some public record I can access?'

'Local court records or newspapers if it got that much attention. I can sneak a look again to find the place and date. I'll text you the info.' Marlena picked up her glass and took a long sip. 'Shame he's not a terror suspect, no holds barred then.'

They both laughed. Dee wasn't ready to let it go though.

'What about the clinic? Can the police check that out?'

Marlena put down her drink and raised both palms. 'Dee, it's over. The official position is that the death was natural causes. That makes it easier for everyone. I don't think it's likely that anything else happened but I do know you and I trust you, and you knew the vic so I have some sympathy. You have to accept that nothing more's going to happen though unless some other evidence comes up. Every query in the computer is logged so there would have to be a reason to justify my looking up anything more.'

Dee knew she couldn't ask Marlena for more. It would probably have been better to go straight to Craig and leave Marlena as someone she could approach if it all went wrong. Too late now. Their wine glasses were empty and the potatoes cold, the salad untouched.

'I'm going to have a coffee. You can drink; what about another one of these?' Dee held the stem of the empty glass of red with two fingers.

'No. Thanks though. I've got an Asian capacity for alcohol. More than one drink and I'll be joining you in an investigation to right all the wrongs of the world.' Marlena stood up. She was even shorter when she was standing.

'The kids are at their father's. I'm going to stay and make this dinner,' Dee said.

The truth was Dee wasn't ready to go. Going felt like giving up.

Marlena put her hand on Dee's shoulder. 'You know we don't win every time. Sometimes we have to let go and get on with the possible.'

Dee watched as Marlena wriggled through the courtyard between suits with blonde girlfriends. She was the only person on her own in the bar; alone with the problem of justice for Tom.

Marlena had said they would only look into it if there was more evidence. Where was that going to come from? Dee wasn't a detective. There didn't appear to be any way forward. Any sensible person would give up.

But Leah was so frightened and so sure she was being watched, Dee thought. How did the person watching the surgery, if there was one, know when Leah was due for an appointment? Why did Adam need her address so urgently? The 'if' was an important qualification in assessing Leah's story, she reminded herself.

Dee remembered the sneering tone Adam had used about Tom at the medical meeting. She went over it in her mind. She had defended Tom; told Adam he was a hacker. Could that have meant Adam detected Tom's raid on GenSafe's computers? The logical thing to do about that would be to report it, to prosecute Tom rather than murder him.

Unless Adam had something major to hide? She knew Adam was totally single-minded. He never allowed anything to come between him and what he wanted. But what could he want? Everything – success, wealth and academic respect were already in his hands. He had no need for illegal or illicit activity. She reminded herself that her inability to imagine how or why someone would commit murder didn't exclude the possibility. Murders happened every day.

With that logic, she had to admit Leah was also a suspect. She had a clear and sufficient motive and she was missing. Her allegations about Adam could be a ploy to deflect attention from the insurance as a motive.

She should find out more about Glen. Check up on his record. If it was him, Charlie and Skye were at risk in the future, once they had the insurance money.

The police were no help.

Raj was the only person who would listen. She didn't want to ring while she felt so hopeless. They had a date for the opera on Sunday night. The kids would be home tomorrow. They always brought perspective when she was down. It would be better to wait till she felt better before she inflicted herself on anyone else.

Home was the answer. At home she could drink herself to forgetfulness and fall into a dreamless slumber. She bought a bottle of the Swan Bay Shiraz she'd been enjoying with Marlena and drove home with it for company.

27

On Saturday morning Dee drove into her car space relieved nothing happened on the way. She probably should have taken a taxi. She'd woken early with a dry mouth. After several glasses of water and two paracetamol, she left home early and drove carefully within the speed limit. A whole bottle of red at home plus a glass at Gallon was bad. It was possible she was still over the limit. Janelle was on duty. There were just the two of them and it was only till midday. Dee ordered a sausage roll with tomato sauce as well as her usual double shot latte. Janelle offered her a strong mint. Did her breath smell of alcohol?

Roger lay on the couch in the spare surgery ready for his regular bloodletting for polycythaemia. There was only one other patient to see.

Dee had made it. Soon she could go home and nurse her headache, have a quiet afternoon and recover ready for the children to be back that night.

She sat her phone on the trolley, wheeled it over to Roger and pulled on gloves. She fastened the tourniquet on his arm and unsheathed a cannula. Her phone beeped, she glanced at it. There was a text message from an unknown number—Glen S. Blayney May 2007. Marlena had delivered on her promise.

'Shit,' she said to herself as the blood welled up from her gloved finger.

Roger hated blood. He kept his eyes closed through the process and hadn't noticed. It was one small mercy.

'Sorry, just a minute,' she said, disposed of the cannula and went to the next surgery to wash her hands and apply a Band-Aid.

It was years since she'd had a needle-stick. This time it was with an uncontaminated needle but that was only luck. If the needle had had Roger's blood on it they would be into the whole PCP prophylaxis protocol. That required permission from Roger for blood-borne virus testing, bloods from her and follow-ups for both of them. The whole fuss would go on for months.

Tom was still there in the back of her mind. Alcohol was an unreliable friend. This time it inhibited the brain cells for physical coordination rather than those that felt grief.

28.

Raj was due in five minutes. Dee checked the mirror on her wardrobe door. The deep-green silk jersey dress draped around her breasts to emphasise her waist. It skimmed discreetly over her hips and thighs. With the updated shoes and handbag, the outfit had cost more than she usually spent in a year on clothes. The feel of the fabric, the designer labels, made her feel safe in the first-night crowd.

The front doorbell rang. Dee listened. Ollie got to the door first. He took Raj into the lounge. She couldn't quite hear what they were talking about. Probably sport. Beatrice came out of her room and Dee heard her compliment Raj on his tux. It was a step forward. Raj didn't seem out of place. Christmas had broken the ice.

Dee gave them a few moments together. She went into Eleanor's room, held out her arm and whispered, 'Come on.'

'Do I have to?' Ellie said but got up and took her mother's hand. Dee nodded. Ellie leaned in so she was enclosed by Dee's arms. They walked together into the lounge.

'Hi Raj,' Ellie said politely.

'Hello Eleanor.' He stepped back half a pace to look at Ellie. 'Wow. What a stunning pink. Where did you get it?'

The hoodie, which Dee thought ridiculously girlie, was in a hot candy pink. Ellie had worn it every day for a week. As Dee watched, her daughter's face almost broke into a grin.

*

'Thanks for being nice to Ellie. She's shy,' Dee said when they were in the hire car.

'She's very sweet. She reminds me of girls in India. They're not as grown-up as here.'

Raj was excited. Mozart's *The Magic Flute* was his favourite opera. The exotic costumes and frivolous plot might have been created for him. In his midnight blue tuxedo with scarlet bow tie, cummerbund and socks and with deep blue patent leather shoes he wouldn't be out of place if he walked onstage.

Talk of past productions bubbled up from him with the enthusiasm of a four-year-old who'd just caught his first tadpoles. The ultimate was at the Met in New York in 2007.

'Diana Damrau is the ultimate Queen of the Night. I'll never see another performance to top that,' he said.

Tonight was the gala opening of the season; they would be pulling out all the stops, including fireworks over the harbour at interval.

His enthusiasm should have been infectious but it wasn't. Dee smiled and responded as required. She had to tell someone about her meeting with Marlena but it seemed wrong to contaminate Raj's excitement.

By the time their limo sailed through the security gate at the entrance to the Opera House, Dee wondered if Raj had completely forgotten about Tom. They walked up the long low stairs to the level of the iconic sails. As usual, heads swivelled as they caught sight of Raj. They emerged into the glass-walled foyer surrounded by the harbour. The sunset still glowed in the sky off to the west, silhouetting the Harbour Bridge and the city skyline.

Everyone glowed and glittered in evening dress. A yellow arc of the full moon pushed up from the water off to the east. The moonrise was a welcome distraction from Raj as the focal point of everyone's attention.

Dee stood in the faint breeze from the open doorway and watched as Raj got drinks. He towered over others in the crush at the bar.

He was a good friend. When he'd first asked her to go with him to the opera he said he had a spare ticket because a friend was ill.

The first night after *La Traviata* they talked for two hours. It was easy. They were instantly comfortable with each other. Dee guessed Raj was lonely; in need of uncomplicated adult company, like her.

She had never asked how rich he was, his lifestyle told the story. Oliver had googled him. Dee made a fuss but was pleased to have the information without stooping to snooping herself. The IT start-up he created in India had sold for $10 million dollars before the GFC. In Australia his computer security firm was reported to have more than sixty percent of the medical market, from government to individual practices like Dee's. Money wasn't an issue. He was a generous friend.

Last year he presented her with a premium reserve season ticket to the opera. The year's subscription prompted her to buy the new outfit. In it she was less like the dowdy mate of a magnificently plumed bird, or looking as though she was accidentally standing next to Raj and they weren't connected at all.

Dee loved the music, the singing, the costumes and the over-the-top drama of it all. Raj's gift opened a world she would otherwise have missed. The pleasure was complicated by memories of her mother; tinged with sadness and the notion of sacrifice.

As a child Dee occasionally came home to find Puccini or Verdi arias floating through the house but her mum would turn the music off when anyone else was around—as though opera were something shameful or self-indulgent. Her mother died not long after Dee's graduation as a doctor. At the funeral, she found out that her mother gave up training as a soprano when she married.

Mum's vinyl records were still around somewhere. Probably in the storage basement at Rob's office; unless he'd thrown them out. Surely he wouldn't though without telling her?

Dee used to play them on the turntable Rob had bought in his jazz period. As work grew busier and the weekends were filled with ferrying three children to endless activities, she played the records less and less. She couldn't remember the last time.

The Magic Flute was Dee's favourite too. She never knew the words but its lightness made it easy to play without sinking into sorrow that Mum was gone. She hoped her mother would be happy her daughter had discovered the magic of her world.

'I've booked supper at the Bennelong. Is that okay?'

Raj was back. He handed her a glass. She didn't want to let go of a tender sadness for Tom and for her mother. Neither of them would ever feel the breeze of a midsummer night, be in a crowd in the myriad colours of their best outfits, marvel at the birth of a full moon, taste champagne. The only place they existed was in the memories of those who knew them. If she stopped thinking about them they didn't exist anymore. She wanted them to be here to enjoy the world too.

Dee held the glass up to her face so she wouldn't need to talk. She took a sip. Delicious—icy, yeasty bubbles brought her out of her head and into the sensations filling her mouth and nose. She came back to the present. For tonight she should be here for Raj and herself. She should let go of those who were gone and be with the living.

The bells rang. The multicoloured flock startled and took off up the stairs to their seats. Raj stayed put as usual. He sipped the rest of his drink. It was the same every time. Dee worried they would be locked out. Several minutes after everyone else was gone they moved to the door. He took her elbow on the stairs. It was an old-fashioned gesture of courtesy—useful with the unaccustomed heels. The rest of the audience watched as they squeezed past those already seated to get to the middle of their row.

As they sat down, Raj whispered, 'There's some news about Tom's computer. I didn't want to spoil the opera. I thought it'd be better if we talked about it properly later. I want you to see this first.'

The lights dimmed, the conductor walked on and the crowd applauded.

Dee couldn't say anything. Raj's love of the dramatic moment was one of his most endearing qualities but sometimes she wished for less of it. At interval she would protest and get the story.

She gave herself up to Mozart. The plot was ridiculous but it had an emotional logic. It provided an excuse for the costumes, the sets and the characters' overwrought outpourings.

The Queen of the Night emerged from vapours at the back of the stage. Dee opened and closed her eyes to check what she saw. She held her breath—stunned. The soprano had flaming red hair with a white flash at the front. Her dress was green.

Raj whispered, 'It's you,' and it was.

Dee slid down in her seat. It felt weird; as though she had deliberately drawn attention to herself as an imitation of a character on the stage. She looked around. Everyone's eyes were fixed on the stage. No one would remember her except while they filed slowly along the row to their seats, even then it was Raj they were looking at.

*

At interval Dee made Raj wait till the others had left the auditorium before they got up. She hurried down the stairs and went outside to the relative darkness of moonlight. Raj picked up their drinks. Embarrassment and curiosity vied for top billing in her emotions.

'Please, Raj, what's happened? Tell me,' Dee asked when he returned from the bar.

'Not yet. I want you to see the Queen of the Night aria before we talk about it. It's important.'

Dee sighed. 'Yes, about that too. Did you know? You could have warned me.'

'The Queen of the Night is usually in black. The only time I've seen her with red hair was Vienna in 2005, or maybe 2006. I'm not sure.'

'Stop it, Raj! That doesn't matter. I feel like a complete idiot. Let's go back in now. I want to be sitting down before everyone else comes in.'

'Of course. What's wrong?' Raj looked mystified.

'No, you wouldn't understand, would you?' Sometimes the baby-fresh innocence of his own peculiarity was too much.

In the second act the queen appeared with a dagger. She implored her daughter to take vengeance on the evil sorcerer

Sarastro. It was the most wondrous coloratura overture, dubbed unsingable due to the stretch to high Fs —the highest notes in opera. It was Mozart's challenge to sopranos.

'This is it—this is the bit that made me think of you.' Raj put his hand over Dee's.

Dee had heard the aria before but with the surtitles she understood the words for the first time. The queen was a powerful figure in an otherwise frivolous story.

> *The vengeance of Hell boils in my heart,*
> *Death and despair flame about me!*
> *If Sarastro does not through you feel*
> *The pain of death,*
> *Then you will be my daughter nevermore.*
> *Disowned may you be forever,*
> *Abandoned may you be forever,*
> *Destroyed be forever*
> *All the bonds of nature,*
> *If not through you*
> *Sarastro becomes pale! (as death)*
> *Hear, Gods of Revenge,*
> *Hear a mother's oath!*

By the end of the final act, the moon was full over the Opera House and Harbour Bridge. The Bennelong restaurant bar sat at the top of the plinth under its own mini version of the famous sails.

'What's up?' Dee asked as they settled into swan chairs at the bar.

'You know I've always thought the Queen of the Night was the best character in *The Magic Flute* and now I know why.' Dee started to object but Raj was too excited. 'She's so fierce, and so determined, what about "the vengeance of hell boils in my heart". And the singing ...'

'Well I could have done with some warning.'

'Believe me, I had no idea about the costume. But it's so perfect. She's always reminded me of you.'

'You think I'm a mad woman intent on revenge by getting my child to commit murder? Don't be ridiculous.'

'No, no—sorry. That's not it at all. It's just the power, the determination … all that's there in you too.'

Their order arrived. Neither of them spoke as the waiter arranged margaritas and mini lobster rolls in front of them.

Raj was perched on the edge of his seat. Once they were alone he leaned forward conspiratorially. 'Well, it wasn't easy, but I have a contact at the ISP we use; we're a major customer for them so they try to help out when they can. Tom's computer was in use for about three hours on the night he died. There was minimal activity but it was used to connect to the cloud and search for data around the estimated time of death.'

Dee felt dizzy. She put down her glass. This was proof— someone was in the flat when Tom died. Who and why? It fitted with what Jock said about someone sneaking down the stairs in the early hours. There was no break-in. Who had keys? Only Skye, who claimed to have lost hers, and Leah, who said she had given them back to Tom. Dee didn't want to go there. Both of them loved Tom. Perhaps it was someone Tom had let in himself?

'You've gone pale.' Raj looked expectantly at her.

'Leah said the backup drive wasn't in the right place. I thought she was just paranoid.'

Raj waited then spoke again softly.

'Yes, well that fits. I'm still working on one of the backup drives, all the computers were shut down so I still need Tom's password to access them. But, interestingly, one of the backup drives had a protection against accidental cut-off. The mystery user didn't shut down in the correct order so we may be able to get in and get more.'

'Raj, we have to go back to the police. This proves it's murder.'

'My contact is not going to risk his career by admitting he gave out data. And just because someone was there doesn't mean they murdered Tom. He could still have died from asthma and then someone took advantage of his death to search his computer files. Let's leave the police until I see if I get somewhere with Tom's computer.'

Dee needed fresh air. The glamorous bar with Swedish designer chairs and artichoke lights was suddenly oppressive.

Raj left his liquid-light jacket over his chair so the staff wouldn't think they'd done a runner and they went outside onto the upper concourse, between the restaurant and the foyer of the opera theatre. Cleaners and catering staff were clearing the foyer.

Dee took deep gulps of the cool fresh air from the harbour. Raj held her arm. He had his hand at the small of her back. Each point of contact was alert, electric with the physical presence of Raj. She lifted her head. His face, as he gazed across the water in the moonlight, was a modern sculpture composed of silver and navy planes. He was the most beautiful man she had ever seen.

'What about the clinic?' Raj said. 'Tom's hacking? I looked up Adam Fairborn. There's a lot out there about him. I watched his TED talk about new reproductive technologies—impressive but I didn't warm to him. Everything he said was so cold, so clinical. There was something missing. He didn't seem quite human. You were at uni with him. What did you think?'

Dee felt a blush start on her chest. She turned to the railing overlooking the harbour before Raj could see the blotchy redness progress up to her face.

'He's a genius, won the university medal, not really socially adept but that's not an essential skill for a brilliant researcher.'

Dee hoped the pause before her reply hadn't betrayed her embarrassment about her past history with Adam.

'What about him as a suspect?'

Raj sounded matter-of-fact. He didn't appear to have noticed her awkwardness.

'Adam is rich, successful, respected. He hardly knew Tom. There's no motive unless Tom found out much more than we know. And let's not forget Glen. He's capable of using a computer if it was open.'

'Tom talked to Leah about the clinic. He didn't say anything about Glen.'

'Yes, it's odd,' said Dee. Raj raised an eyebrow. 'He knew something might happen. Why else send Leah away? He could have been wrong and it was Glen who was the danger. It explains why he let the killer into the flat.'

Raj nodded; ready to consider the proposition.

'So why wouldn't he leave some way to get the information he had collected? If we find that we'll know who had a strong enough motive to get rid of him. You worked with him. There's no way he'd let all that data get lost if something happened to him.'

'Sure but it has to be somewhere we can access. He has to have given someone a clue.'

The two of them said it together.

'Leah must know.'

29.

Dee knocked on Skye's door. It opened the couple of inches the security chain allowed. Skye's face appeared in the crack.

'Skye. How are you?'

There was no answer. The door closed.

'I've brought back Tom's key,' Dee spoke louder.

Skye undid the chain and opened the door fully.

'Come in,' she said, her voice without colour.

The place was a mess. Skye usually kept things under control but there were dirty dishes and clothes and piles of papers strewn everywhere. Charlie was on the floor under the table hitting his head against its leg. All around him were envelopes with readdressed mail stickers on them. Some were torn, some chewed; none had been properly opened. That must be why there was no mail for Tom at the flat.

Dee stood in the middle of the room and repeated her question.

'How do you think I am?' Skye snapped back.

'Sorry—you'll let me know if I can help, won't you?' Dee handed the key to Tom's flat back to Skye.

Skye's face crumpled and she sat down on the couch to sob.

'Sorry, I'll go.' Dee put the key on the table. 'And sorry it took so long to get this back to you.'

'It's okay, Glen found the other one in Charlie's room.' Skye stopped crying. 'Don't go—I can't stand it here on my own.' She shoved a pile of rubbish off the chair next to hers. 'Sit down, please.'

Dee sat and put her hand on Skye's shoulder.

'Where's Glen?'

'Who knows, he's gone off for a few days. Some urgent greyhound business down the coast or so he says.'

Dee's felt a chill. Thirty days would be up next week. What was Glen up to? She couldn't bring up her fears with Skye.

'It's tough. I wish there was something I could do. Do you want me to see if we can get some respite care for Charlie?'

'No, thanks. He's upset too. I don't think he could cope if I sent him away. It keeps me sane to have to look after him. When Glen's here it helps.'

Dee found some tissues in her bag. Skye grabbed a handful, wiped her eyes and blew her nose. Dee spied the edge of a photo album under rubbish on the coffee table.

'You've been looking through old photos?'

'I don't know if it helps. Glen told me to stop but I can't.'

Skye picked up the album and put it on Dee's lap. Dee turned the pages.

It was devastating but compulsive. Skye cried gently as they looked through the pages together. The collection stopped when Tom was about seventeen. Probably when he started storing photos on his computer.

At the end there were several loose photos of him older. Nothing of Leah.

'Tom printed them for me.'

As they sat to look at the photos the pain of Tom no longer being real pierced Dee all over again. Skye became calmer. She touched the face of each print lovingly as though she were stroking her son. Dee looked up. Charlie was quiet; still under the table but no longer hitting his head.

'No photos of his girlfriend?' asked Dee.

'Why would there be?' Skye's mouth curled with contempt.

'Do you know where she's disappeared to?'

'Why would I? Little gold-digger. She manipulated Tom into giving her the insurance money that was supposed to be for Charlie. You're the third person who's asked me where she is. Off with some other prospect I guess.'

Dee wanted to know where Skye got the key and who'd been asking after Leah but couldn't ask.

She put her hand on Skye's but Skye became more agitated.

'You can tell her from me she's not going to get his money, or the flat. I've got Charlie to think of. What's going to happen to him when I'm gone?'

'I know it's hard with Charlie but Leah doesn't seem interested in money. I doubt she would fight you for Tom's property.'

Skye wasn't comforted. She pulled her hand away from Dee's.

'Why can't you all leave him in peace?' she shouted.

Loud noise was intolerable to Charlie. He stood up, rocked back and forth in the centre of the room and started to hit his forehead with the heel of his hand. A horrible thump each time his hand connected with his head made conversation impossible.

'Sorry, I'll go. Let me know if I can do anything to help.' Dee headed to the door.

Skye let her out. Her shouts were over; replaced by defeated pleas.

'Just leave him in peace, please, Dee. Just leave my boy in peace.'

*

Early the next day, Dee called in at Tom's apartment block. Several of the letterboxes under the stairs were full to overflowing with advertising flyers and other junk mail. Tom's and Jock's were empty. Someone must be collecting the non-addressed items. They wouldn't be redirected. Skye wouldn't come here regularly.

Dee shone the torch on her phone to see inside the box. It looked empty.

The door behind her creaked open.

'Morning, Doc,' said Jock, 'can I help you?'

'Not unless you can tell me where Bambi lives.'

'She lived here for a while but I think she had another place down on Wattle Street. That row of terraces that's falling down.'

'How do you know?' Dee asked. She needed to be sure.

'Well, that's what her mail says. You'd better come in.'

Inside, Jock scrabbled through a mass of papers in a cupboard too high for Lil to reach.

'The car numbers aren't up there, are they?' Dee asked without much hope.

'No, Lil couldn't have put them all the way up here. Don't you worry, once the operation is out of the way I'll be onto it.'

Dee knew the numbers would only be found when Jock made time to find them. She moved on to the possible. 'And do you know if Tom owned his flat?'

'Yes, he bought it ages ago. He must have been saving since he was a kid. Had it rented out at first. It's worth two or three times what he paid for it now.'

Jock handed her three letters originally addressed to Ms Leah Dragic, 437 Wattle Street, Ultimo, 2007. They had been redirected to Tom's flat.

Dee knew the row. Unrenovated and unmaintained they were the only houses left in the street that was now a one-way multi-lane link road from the eastern suburbs to the north and west. Only students or derelicts would tolerate the noise, the dirt, the outdoor bathrooms and toilets.

*

The door was opened by a bearded male. Dee introduced herself as Leah's doctor and asked if he knew where she was. He looked Dee up and down and then stepped back to let her inside.

'Another one. You might as well have the tour. And, no, I don't know where she is. I don't know any relatives or other friends. You could try the School of Natural Therapies but I think the others did that and the school didn't know where she was either.'

He showed Dee the room that once was Leah's. There were cardboard boxes in the corner stuffed with clothes, books and a guitar.

'So other people have been looking for her?'

'Yes, the insurance and someone from a clinic. We even had a break-in. What idiot would want to rob this place? They only went through Leah's stuff anyway.'

'Did they take anything?'

The boy looked at her, raised a studded eyebrow and waved his arm at the mess.

'Not that we could tell. There wasn't anything in here about where she might be. I looked pretty hard myself. She still owes her share of the rent. If you find her, get her to call me. Tell her we're going to rent out the room. You couldn't take her boxes, could you?'

The flatmate seemed grateful when Dee agreed.

'She's okay, isn't she?' he asked once he knew Leah's belongings would be gone.

'I'm not sure. I hope she's just hiding out.'

'You probably should have this.' He held up his mobile with Leah's number displayed on it. 'The others seemed dodgy so I didn't give it to them. It might not be much use though. It's a prepaid and I can't get an answer.'

The door slammed behind her. Dee was glad to escape without a fall through the rotten floorboards and to get away from the stink of tomcat.

*

She looked through the boxes then stacked them in the car space at work. There was nothing useful, no address books or letters or mobile numbers.

She tried the number for Leah's mobile but there was no connection, nothing, no message.

The search for Leah was at a dead end. It would be easier on everyone if she gave up. The children were upset when she was home late. Janelle would be annoyed because Leah's boxes made it hard to get to the waste bins. She'd already accused her of being distracted. Marlena didn't want to hear from her. Skye had lost her son and wanted him left in peace. Dee was keeping the grief stirred up. Everyone wanted her to stop.

Except Raj. He understood but she wondered if it was all a game to him; a real-life detective story to be solved by clever deduction.

She went upstairs to the surgery and looked at the appointment list. Her next patient was Joy. Dee had been horrible to the poor woman last time. She was probably still angling for Dee to do some useless test. That wasn't a helpful thought. She walked to the waiting room and called Joy in with a smile.

'Oh, doctor,' Joy was distraught, 'what can I do? She won't let the grandchildren come to see me anymore.' She started to sob with great heaving movements of her shoulders.

The nasty old woman had no one else in her life. Dee was the only person willing to comfort her. Last time, even she, a professional who should know better, had responded to the nastiness rather than the underlying hurt.

Dee moved the tissue box so it was closer then put her arm around Joy's shoulders.

30.

Dee unlocked the front door to let out Josephine, a last-minute fit-in. No one who had ever suffered a urinary tract infection could say no to providing treatment to a sufferer. It had taken Josie seventy-two straight hours at the casino to plough back the $10,000 win she'd had on the pokies. In that time, she'd hardly eaten or drunk or gone to the toilet. Strangely, Josie had seemed relieved to have lost it all, as though the process of putting all the winnings back through the machines was a tough task she'd succeeded in conquering.

Everyone else was gone. The light through the curtains next to her desk had been gone for an hour now.

It must be after eight. Shit—what's for dinner? Oh, and the driving lesson. What would Beatrice say? 'Josephine's UTI is more important than my whole life' with dramatic shoulder-shrugging and eye-rolling. She might even squeeze out a tear.

But no, Dee remembered, they'd changed plans. For some reason she couldn't remember they were at Rob's.

Relief and disappointment came together. It was a chance to catch up on paperwork but a takeaway in front of the TV with a glass of red was too miserable. How could she miss her children and be grateful for time to herself at the same time?

Her in-tray was full, mostly with the pre-computer paper files for two medico legal reports. They could wait. The reports from specialists and advertising, she checked or chucked. At the bottom of the pile was a plastic sleeve of photocopies from old newspapers.

She tipped them out onto her desk.

There was an A3 size copy of the front page from the *Central Western Daily* from 11 August 1989. The headline read 'FAIRBORN CURSE CONTINUES' with subheadings 'Double suicide leaves son alone' and 'Son, last of dynasty'.

Wade and June Fairborn of Fairborn Downs were found dead at the family homestead late yesterday. Local cleaner Maria Portello made the grisly find when she arrived after a week away. 'They must have planned it for just after my last visit,' Mrs Portello said.

The couple cancelled their milk and newspapers telling local newsagent Jon Garson they would be away for several weeks. Superintendent Doyle of Orange Police said that the double suicide had been planned for months with Mrs Fairborn stockpiling medications for her back pain.

The wealthy pastoral family have been dogged by tragedy since the death of four-year-old Evie from snake bite. The infant was found with multiple snake bites to her right arm. Police believe the girl was trying to retrieve a teddy bear from a crevice in rocks behind the hay store. Just two months later, eldest son Wade, eleven, was found dead in a dam on the property.

Their sole surviving child, Dr Adam Fairborn, was visibly distressed as he read a brief statement.

*'My parents never got over the loss of two children,'
he said. 'I tried to be everything for them but it wasn't
enough.'*

There were two other pages.

A clipping in stark black and white had a picture of a pretty
four-year-old with hair in blonde plaits nursing a teddy bear.

*Evelyn Fairborn, age four, died on Thursday of multiple
tiger snake bites. The child was in the care of a nanny
when she wandered off to find her lost teddy bear. Her
brother Adam, eight, found her lifeless on a rocky
outcrop behind the farmhouse.*

Another from two months later, October 1968, reported the
death of young Wade Fairborn in a dam. The copy was less
clear, taken from a discoloured original, a lot of black and
words here and there becoming black blobs. Dee could make
out most of it though.

*The coroner has found the death of eleven-year-old
Wade Fairborn to be misadventure. The boy was found
floating face down in a dam by his younger brother,
Adam. Wade, who had developmental difficulties, could
not swim. An autopsy found a large indent in the back of
his skull. It is believed he slipped on rocks, hit his head
and stumbled semi-conscious into the dam.*

Dee reread the pages and checked her in-tray again. That was
it, no more documents and no indication of how they got
there.

Where did the clippings come from? Not a letter—there
was no note attached—just the date and source written on

each page in a neat regular straight-up-and-down hand. The hairs on Dee's forearms sat up. It was the precise handwriting of Tom—a ghostly reach from the grave. Sweet, excited Tom who should be alive, who would be alive if he hadn't been murdered. He had made these copies but who had sent them? Possibly, probably, Leah. If Dee could find out where they were sent from she had a chance of finding Leah.

Dee got up to search the wastepaper baskets—they were all empty. She sat down to reread the newspaper clippings about Adam's family tragedies. Why would Tom go to so much trouble to delve into Adam's childhood?

Only Leah would know. No one had seen her since the night she'd climbed into Dee's car. She wasn't at the funeral. Was she in danger?

Dee had to know.

Janelle picked up after eight rings.

'Sorry, I know you're putting the kids to bed but I need to know where those photocopies came from.'

'Photocopies?'

'You know, in the mail today.'

'Tania did the mail and she's gone out dancing tonight.'

'Oh.'

The tiny hope of a lead was doused by the knowledge that Tania was uncontactable. Even so, Tania's head was in a different universe most of the time. The chance of her recalling a task like opening the mail was minuscule.

'Like her brain,' Dee added silently.

'Are you okay? You're not still at work at nine o'clock are you?' asked Janelle.

The automatic mother-guilt jabbed Dee before she could block it with the thought, *They're at Rob's.*

'Yes, at work and no, not really okay.'

Janelle made a noise of concern as Dee caught up with what she had said.

'Sorry, that came out wrong. It's okay, I'm just worried about Tom Harris's girlfriend. No one's seen her but I think she sent me some newspaper clippings and I thought the envelope might give me a clue about where she is.'

'Did you try the recycling?'

'Good idea, thanks.' Dee hung up.

Downstairs, the big commercial recycling bin was full to overflowing. Dee looked hopelessly at all the junk mail and paper waste for a hundred apartments and six businesses. She moved a pile of cartons from the top but it was impossible to identify which waste was from the surgery. All sensitive or identifiable material was shredded anyway. Dee had checked already; the bin for material awaiting shredding was empty.

Time to go home. Straight to bed—she was too disappointed to eat or ring Raj with the news.

*

As she let herself in with the usual curse to Rob about the pretentious heavy front door design, her mobile rang. It was Janelle.

'Tania's just got back to me.'

'Thanks, but I've given up. It's impossible to find anything.'

'No, listen. Tania does the mail because she saves the stamps for her nephew. She's still got today's in her purse and—' Janelle paused, 'there's one from an A4 manila envelope that was handwritten. She's got the stamp but she said she can't make out where it's from.'

'When's the recycling collected?' Dee asked.

'Why?'

'I've got to get that envelope.'

'It's in the morning, early. Dee, you'll never find it.'

'I might now I know what I'm looking for. Thanks.' Dee hung up and picked up her bag and keys and headed out again. The door didn't seem as heavy anymore.

<h1 style="text-align:center">31.</h1>

Raj answered on the first ring. She spoke to him on speaker phone as she left the cul-de-sac. When she pulled up at the door of the car park there was his tall figure, sitting on top of a small ladder with aprons and heavy-duty gloves ready.

Once again, she found herself staring at his hairless brown calves. This time the top half of Raj's body was immersed in the pile of recycling. They were sexy legs. Dee pushed the thought down. Raj was a good friend. Who else would come out at a moment's notice and volunteer to be the dumpster diver in a situation like this? Friends were precious. She didn't need any more complications in her life.

And how could he not be gay with those clothes? Homosexuality was illegal, and prosecuted, in India. It would be understandable to cover it up.

Ten minutes later, they had it. A manila A4 envelope addressed to Dr Dee in a distinctive uneven scrawl. There was no surname and no street number. It didn't quite look as if it had been written by a young person. Even so, Leah was the most likely sender.

*

Dee and Raj were installed at a laminex table in the Super Bowl restaurant in Chinatown. The place was a favourite late-night haunt of top chefs coming off duty. Raj ordered Peking duck and rice to share.

The whole restaurant seemed to be obsessed with him. Thirsty eyes everywhere slaked themselves on his chiselled features, his smooth skin and jet-black hair. His black chunky glasses echoed his square features and exactly matched his hair colour. The eccentricity of his clothes gave permission for blatant stares—no need to be furtive when what he wore said 'look at me'.

Dee found the stares difficult to ignore. Raj seemed not to notice. She tried to concentrate on the food. The BBQ duck was crisp and juicy—with the exotic taste of star anise. She hadn't realised how hungry she was till the food was in front of them. They ate without talking till their plates were empty.

Dee pulled the envelope out of her bag. There was no return address, no sender's name. The corner with the stamp was missing. She checked inside again. Nothing.

The waiter cleared their plates. Dee ordered more tea to buy some more time.

She got out the photocopies. Raj read through them.

'How well did you know this Adam? Did you know any of this stuff from his past?' Raj asked.

Dee picked up her water glass to hide her face.

'No. I thought Adam was an only child. I guess losing two siblings could explain why he comes across as cold. The parents' suicides were later. After uni I sent him patients but that was our only contact.'

'If Adam had anything to do with these deaths it makes it more certain that Leah is in danger,' he said.

'I don't see how this connects to Tom's death.'

'Leah says Tom was worried about the professor. We can't ignore possible evidence because of your relationship with Adam at uni.'

Dee couldn't cope with what Raj meant by relationship. She changed the subject, told Raj what Skye and Jock said about Tom owning the flat.

'That adds to the motive for Glen,' she said.

'Didn't you say Leah's not interested in the money for the insurance?'

'Skye doesn't think that. She expects the worst from "the little gold-digger".'

'We still need to know what Tom was working on and find out if Leah is okay. She's the only person who could have sent this stuff.'

'I have to find her,' said Dee.

'You decided that before.'

'I know, I know, I know.' Dee held up her palms to ward off Raj's observation. 'But it seemed so impossible. When I got this I thought there was a chance … but it isn't enough. Sorry. It's all a bit of an anti-climax tonight. I hope I didn't take you away from anything important.'

'At least I got to have dinner with you.'

Dee felt a flush start its creep up her neck. Compliments felt insincere; made her feel distanced; patronised.

'Oh, Raj, don't carry on.'

She told herself to lighten up. Raj was a good, strong friend. No one else had supported her over Tom's murder. It wasn't insincere. Compliments from a gorgeous man should feel good. He had to be gay. That made it easy—no complications.

32.

Jake, Dee's first patient, was a newly sexually active nineteen-year-old concerned he had genital warts. Her head was bent over his penis to gently examine the area through a magnifying light when she heard raised voices from reception.

'Sorry, I'd better see if they're okay out there,' she said.

As she passed the boy a disposable sheet to cover himself, Glen burst through the door, closely followed by Janelle, William and a man in a suit who she didn't know.

Glen paused to take in the situation. 'Sorry, mate, but this doctor is an interfering busybody who needs to learn to keep out of other people's affairs.'

William pulled the screen in front of the examination couch across then stood beside Dee. Glen's eyes were red, his face greasy and his hair uncombed. He stood, shoulders raised, skinny chest puffed out and arms out from his sides like a gorilla. This could be nasty. Dee hoped he was not on ice and was rational enough not to mount a physical attack. His hands looked ready for action. They were empty but he could have a weapon concealed inside his jacket. Dee was grateful William and the man in the suit were there.

'Janelle, go to the front desk, ring 000, get the police here now. Then get yourself and everyone out of the surgery.' She turned to Glen. 'What's this about?'

'How dare you come round upsetting Skye. She's got enough to cope with, can't you let her alone? She's lost her son.' Glen's voice had calmed to a wheedling, resentful tone.

'How about we get you to sit outside and I'll see you in a few minutes.' Dee tried to communicate calm. There was the sound of sirens in the distance.

'Yeah, while you wait for the coppers to come and grab me. I'm not an idiot.' Glen brought his face close to Dee's. 'Leave Skye alone, bitch.' He turned on his heel and left.

The police arrived some twenty minutes later and promised to have an 'unofficial word' to Glen.

*

Tania hadn't arrived by the time Dee took in her 10 o'clock at 10.10 am. She had to force herself to concentrate. Fortunately it was a simple tetanus booster after a minor home renovation mishap. She finished and let the patient out. Where was Tania?

As Dee called for her next patient Tania rushed through the back door.

'Sorry, the bus broke down,' she panted.

'I don't suppose you could phone to tell us? You've got the stamp from yesterday?'

'It's here somewhere.' Tania rooted around in the bottom of her oversized bag.

Dee's next patient was already in the surgery. She couldn't wait for the search.

'Just put it in my pigeonhole. I haven't got time for this now.'

*

Dee dragged her attention away from the problem of finding Leah. The new patient was anxious. He had never had his own doctor and his girlfriend, a long-term patient, had made him come in for a check-up. Check-up was often code for something the person was too scared to talk about so Dee had to make an effort; listen properly. After twenty minutes he confessed to rectal bleeding. The bleeding was significant and there was no apparent cause on examination so Dee referred him for a colonoscopy. She was now running late but he might have bowel cancer; the extra minutes she took may have saved his life.

The torn corner of the envelope and its franked stamp were in her pigeonhole. She had a quick look at the stamp but couldn't make out what it said. She put it down on her desk. There were three people waiting. Leah would have to wait till lunchtime.

*

Dee shone the torch from her phone on the stamp as Tania looked over her shoulder. She couldn't make it out. She took the fragment over to the magnifying light she used for skin examinations.

'The name of the town's all smudged—something Creek, postcode 262, something illegible.'

They looked up all the postcodes starting with 262. The only 'creek' was Majors Creek. It was a tiny settlement in the far south of the state, in the foothills of the Great Dividing Range.

The envelope was franked at 2.13 pm the previous Friday. Whoever posted it might have gone to the counter to buy stamps—someone may remember.

*

Dee was busy for the next hour till someone had to go to the loo to give a urine specimen. Tania brought in a printout of a satellite view of Majors Creek from Google maps. Dee searched on her own computer. It was a tiny settlement in a valley on the far south coast of New South Wales between Canberra and the coast.

Satellite view showed only six or seven buildings scattered over a couple of hectares. Dee 'drove' around the settlement using street view. Half the buildings were derelict. The pub was still operational and a couple of houses looked like they could be occupied. The only access was via unsealed roads. It was set in a small flat area in the middle of rugged mountainous country and was mostly undeveloped bush. There wasn't another town for miles.

If Leah was there someone might know her.

33.

Dee made copies of the papers from Majors Creek, put them in a manila envelope and addressed it to Detective Sergeant Marlena Ng at Glebe Police Station. She put it in the outgoing mail tray in reception.

If Dee went to Majors Creek she wanted someone official to know why.

After the next patient, Dee went to retrieve the letter. It could mean trouble for Marlena at the station. She had tried to help and didn't deserve to be compromised by material about the closed case.

The mail tray was empty.

'Tania's taken it to post on her way home,' said Janelle. 'If there's more I can take it later, not sure if it'll make the six o'clock pick-up though.'

Dee tutted in frustration. She took out her mobile and rang Tania. No answer of course.

'That girl never answers her phone,' she muttered to Janelle.

As she walked back down the corridor to her room, Dee wondered if she should send Marlena a text to warn her to intercept the letter. Tania emerged from the toilet.

'Oh! You're here. Where's the mail?' Dee couldn't keep the anger out of her voice.

'In my bag. What's wrong?' Tania stood frozen, a rabbit in the spotlight waiting to be shot.

'Can you get it? I need something back.'

'Sure,' said Tania, still stuck to the spot.

'Now, come on; not next month.'

*

For the rest of the day Janelle was restrained, efficient as always but there were no jokes or banter in between patients.

When Dee asked her to get Marlena's address she nodded as though that explained everything—and it probably did. She stepped from reception back to where Dee stood in the file room.

'Tania's young and a bit ditzy but she's always cheerful, always has a smile even for the difficult people. All the patients like her. And so do I. She does what she's asked and she's usually spot on time.'

Not today—but it was no use saying that. Janelle was fiercely fair. Dee felt better now she had the letter back. Janelle was right; she had gone too far with Tania.

'All right, I'm sorry. I'll fix it next time she's here.'

*

Dee drove past to check she could find Marlena's house, then parked the car out of sight around the corner. The letterbox was a slot in the door. Dee opened the gate onto the street as quietly as she could and climbed the steep stairs to the tiny terrace house. The envelope was in her hands. As she pushed it through Marlena's front door an explosion of barks erupted and the paws of several dogs clattered towards her.

Please don't let her be there. Dee turned and skittered down the stairs without looking back. It would be easier to bother Marlena if she were an anonymous police officer, if Dee didn't know her because she was the relative of a patient. But if she didn't know her outside official channels there was no reasonable—reasonable to the police that is—excuse to contact her. And Dee certainly wouldn't have the poor woman's home address.

Dee kept her head down and walked quickly back to her car.

34.

Through the whole four-hour drive from Sydney, Beatrice, Oliver and Eleanor complained as though their own mother were a kidnapper. School holidays and all they wanted was to sit indoors on their phones. Or go to parties because 'everyone was going'.

'What about nature? Don't you want to lay with the sun on your back to watch a seagull hover inches above a crest of sand? There's an ocean pool enclosed by breakwaters and a long wild beach to walk along.'

'There's a party at Sam's—everyone will be there,' from Beatrice.

Ollie had a sudden spasm. 'This place has got wi-fi? Mum, please tell us that this place has got wi-fi.'

Dee pressed her lips together then forced herself to take a deep breath. Her favourite memory of childhood was looking up at seagulls hovering just above the sand dune that separated the rocky pool from the long wild beach.

What kind of unnatural creatures had she brought into the world?

She could cancel their mobile phone contracts. She pictured their reactions, slugs shrivelled up in a pool of their own juices when salt was poured on them. There'd be noises too—loud squeaky screams of existential angst. The images gave her the forbearance to keep driving rather than stop the car and leave the three of them on the side of the road.

Family holidays as a child meant camping at Moruya Heads with Mum and their cousins. There was one shop and cold-water showers but Uncle Bill took them fishing and there was a safe place to swim between the breakwaters. There were bush tracks and lizards and birds' nests and rock pools and crabs. All the kids left the tent in the morning and, apart from quick raids for peanut butter sandwiches, came back only when it was too dark to see. Did kids these days ever escape supervision for a moment?

At night they lit kerosene lanterns and played Ludo or Monopoly. As they got older they were called in to make a fourth for 500 or Gin Rummy with the grown-ups. No phones, no TV, no internet, no electricity. The holidays at Moruya were the high points of Dee's childhood. Her three would never experience nature without the protective filter of technology.

*

They arrived at twelve. The Dolphin Motel was on the beach and had a pool. Dee checked in to a two-bedroom 'family unit' with a balcony overlooking the sea. Praise the Lord, there was wi-fi. There was an argument over beds. Ollie was the only one who'd brought a phone charger. He drove a tough bargain to get the big bed to himself while the girls had a double bunk.

Shortly after they arrived, Dee picked up her handbag, ready to take off again. It would be easier to check out Leah on her own and she wasn't sure if she could cope with any more time in the car with three teenagers suffering withdrawals from the city.

'But what will we do?' asked Beatrice.

'Yes, what about us?' said Oliver with exaggerated tones of resentment and incredulity.

'There's no food. I'm hungry,' said Eleanor.

'You're on holidays. And it's a beautiful day. Go outside.'

Dee picked up a plastic information folder.

'Look, this has lots of stuff. Here's a list of places to eat that you can walk to. And a local map. What about fish and chips? There's picnic tables near the river.'

No reaction.

'The beach is just here. You could swim in the pool or go for a walk to the end where the lifesavers are.' She pulled a fifty-dollar note for each of them out of her wallet. 'Here's some cash and my Visa card. Don't leave Ellie on her own …'

When she left, all three of them were sitting inside with their phones. They would have to go out eventually to get food.

On the way out, Dee went to the office. She let Andy the manager know that the teenagers would be home alone.

'No worries, love. I'll send my young fellas across to say hello. We'll see if they want to have a fish later.'

Fishing didn't sound like a sufficiently cool activity for urban teens.

*

Majors Creek was eighty kilometres away. On a decent road it would take less than an hour. Dee checked the time. It was almost two hours since she'd left the motel. The unsealed road wound upwards in a series of hairpin bends. It was only a narrow ledge etched out of the side of a steep mountain. Signs warned that timber trucks used the road. She hoped they wouldn't be about over the holidays. She'd passed only one other car. Fortunately, when they met she was on the side closest to the hill not at the edge of the precipitous drop.

Maybe she'd missed the town.

When the road widened a little she pulled over to check Google maps. There was no phone reception. She was getting as technology-dependent as the kids. She checked the odometer. There were another six kilometres to go.

In ten minutes the terrain flattened out and the forest was replaced by scrub. She overshot a turn to the left, then noticed a stone chimney half overgrown with lantana. This must be the place. She turned around. The side road was signposted 'The Eldrich Historic Pub'.

Dee drove around the several blocks of what may once have been a town. There were half-a-dozen old stone buildings still standing and more that were just a chimney or a wall in an overgrown garden.

The pub was a traditional building surrounded by a veranda. There were tables and chairs and a sign that advertised live music on Saturday night. A car and motorcycle were parked outside. It was the only place that looked occupied.

Halfway along the veranda there was a sign 'Post Office', a bank of PO boxes and a half fly-screen door. She had arrived at Majors Creek Post Office.

35.

The rickety screen door slammed behind her and a bell tinkled. She had stepped back forty years. There was a high counter, brass scales and a rack of ink stamps. The wooden pigeonholes behind the counter had six letters scattered among them. The floor was dusty and the light that entered through a torn holland blind gave the whole space the sepia tone of an old photograph. A pile of cartons sat in the corner and several addressed boxes on the floor. On her right, a rack of prepaid envelopes and express post satchels reassured her that this was a current post office but there was no sign of an official or service person.

Dee perused the framed 'paintings by a local artist'—lurid sunsets over the valley and a pretty drawing of the old hotel she was standing in.

After several minutes she opened and closed the door—the faint tinkle didn't summon any of the spirits who inhabited the place.

The bar next door had a dartboard hung underneath a large TV broadcasting cricket to two elderly men perched on stools. Both had a schooner of beer in front of them and appeared balanced by elbows resting on towelling strips along the edge of the bar.

A woman with a face like crushed tissue paper and hair dyed an unnatural black greeted Dee.

'You're too late for the counter lunches but there's two pies left. Beer?'

'No thanks. I'm here for the post office.'

'I'll meet you there.' The woman stepped through a door at the end of the bar and waved Dee towards the veranda.

Inside the post office, the woman wiped her hands on her apron and pushed at a loose strand of hair at her neck.

'Yes, love?'

Dee could see that a direct request for information was not likely to succeed. Why did she think she could just come and expect people in this remote area to trust her?

'Yes. Can I buy three envelopes and stamps. And I'd like to have them franked as coming from here. Is that okay?'

'Post them here and they'll be franked from here,' the woman said as she handed over the goods.

'Okay, I'll have these postcards too then.'

'The stamps are cheaper if you just put them on the postcard without envelopes,' the woman said with a shake of her head.

'Good idea.' Dee handed back the envelopes. 'I might take you up on that pie and a middy too.'

'Veranda?'

'Inside maybe, it's a bit cooler.'

Dee sat at a round laminex table in the corner of the bar and ate her pie. Fat, meat, carbs and salt uncontaminated by anything healthy. The beer was perfect with it and washed away the dust of the seventy kilometres of dirt road.

She addressed the postcards to the kids and Raj, and sent one to Rob as well, let him wonder what she was doing away in the country. The old men at the counter talked about the cricket, old games and old players but with sideways glances at Dee.

On the screen a century was scored by a young player, his first.

'You must have seen plenty of those?' said Dee.

'You're not wrong there, love. What'ya say, Eddie?' The man closest to her had silver hair combed straight back from the top of his head and a generous dusting of dandruff on the waistcoat he was wearing in spite of the temperature.

Eddie was more casually dressed in a cotton shirt, braces and jeans with a pale corduroy cap pulled down over his forehead. He nodded and pushed out his lower lip.

'Eddie knows all the scores from Australia's first test on. Ask him anything.' This brought another nod from Eddie who was now staring at Dee rather than the TV.

Dee had some knowledge of cricket, mostly from James, an elderly test player who was a patient. He always had to go through all the latest cricket news before he'd let her deal with his multiple illnesses.

It was enough. By the time she'd finished her beer Eddie was talking to her too.

*

When the cricketers broke for tea, Cedric, the older and more sociable of the two, asked, 'And what's a young lass like yourself doing all the way out here?'

'Ah, I just brought the kids down to the coast for the holidays and I heard a friend was staying up here somewhere and thought I'd look her up.'

'Staying around here, you say? This is it for places to stay, ain't it, Eddie?'

'I'm not sure where she's at though. She sent a letter from here last week, Friday around two in the afternoon.'

Cedric climbed down from his bar stool and sat next to Dee. He made Eddie come over too. 'C'mon, you old sourpuss. How often do you have an attractive young woman wanting to talk to you?'

The smell of ingrained beer and sweat when Eddie sat down were strong enough to make Dee's eyes water. Cedric appeared not to notice.

'Another beer?' Dee asked.

She bought a round and switched to the draft brew the old men favoured.

'And what's your friend's name then?'

'Leah.' Cedric and Eddie shook their heads. Dee pressed on. 'She's young, about twenty and a bit of a hippy. Probably doesn't drink either.' Dee bit her tongue. She didn't want to give away that she wasn't Leah's best friend, but Eddie and Cedric didn't react.

'Know anyone called Leah, Misty?' Cedric called to the barmaid. Misty was a ridiculous name for a woman of seventy.

'Posted a letter last Friday?' Cedric continued.

'Joe was working Friday; he'll be in later. Don't know any Leah,' said Misty. 'No one new around here; no young girls are going to get away unnoticed.'

Dee shuddered as she wondered what that might mean. The beer had gone to her head. She and 'the boys', as Misty referred to them, were on their third schooner. Dee had to keep up or they'd clam up. She hoped for an introduction to Joe later if she could still speak. There was no way she'd make it back to Moruya tonight. She found her mobile in her purse but there was no signal.

Eddie smiled. 'No service on that up here,' he said with some pride. 'You're not in the city anymore.'

On the veranda there was a public telephone in working order. She hadn't seen one for years. With her credit card, she called the kids. None of them picked up. She left a message that she would have to stay overnight.

*

The bedroom was taller than it was wide. There was a narrow bed against each of the side walls and a window opening onto a shed housing a generator. Each was covered with a dusty brown bedspread from the fifties. The bathroom was down the hall. It had an ancient bath with a handheld shower. The linoleum on the floor was cracked and sticky with a crusty bloodstain on the floor next to the toilet. Dee decided to stop drinking beer to avoid having to use the facilities too often.

Around sunset the oldsters toddled off in opposite directions towards what looked like abandoned houses. Misty had disappeared into the warren of tumbledown, tin-roofed lean-tos attached to the back of the pub. Dee moved onto the veranda to watch the sun go down over the paddock opposite. In the slanted evening light, the bramble-covered ruins of a stone house and the silver grey fencing of the paddock softened to romantic ruins.

The sun went down leaving only reflected light above the hills to the east. An intense buzzing sound from the south gradually grew louder. After some minutes a huge motorcycle pulled up with a growling purr. The rider, a tall stringy man, took off a black full-face helmet to reveal a weather-beaten face and straggly blond hair in a ponytail. His black leathers were scratched and worn. He took off his gloves and Dee noticed that his nails were kept long and filed at an angle—a guitarist. His eyes, protected by his brows, were less damaged, not as old, as the rest of his skin. He was lithe and easy in his movements without the stiffness of even a forty-year-old, she thought. He might be anywhere from twenty-five to thirty-five, a country boy, weather-beaten before his time. His eyes flicked quickly past the older woman sitting alone on the veranda. He walked straight into the bar.

*

Mosquitoes appeared with the twilight. Once they started to attack, Dee had an excuse to retreat inside. The bikie was behind the bar. He must be Joe.

She sat on a stool at the bar.

'You've got some enthusiastic mozzies up here,' she said to cover the embarrassment of following him inside.

He nodded.

'Drink? Or something to eat?' he asked and handed her a menu and drinks list.

Dinner was steak or burgers with chips or mash. Misty reappeared. She offered to defrost some sausages or a veggie burger if Dee wanted them.

Joe said he'd have a steak with the lot and a glass of red wine. He probably got free meals in return for manning the pub when Misty was away.

Dee took the lead from Joe and chose steak and chips. It would be cooked fresh and hard to get completely wrong.

'This is Joe,' said Misty after she had poured him a glass of red from a two-litre cask from the fridge. 'This lady wants to know about last Friday.'

Joe grunted noncommittally. It was hard to tell if he was shy or surly.

Misty disappeared into the mysterious rear of the hotel.

'How's the red?' Dee asked.

'Drinkable.' He looked at her for the first time.

'Do you have anything that's more than drinkable?' Dee asked with her best smile.

Their meals arrived together. Misty set one table for both of them. Dee poured a second glass of red for Joe from the bottle she'd bought. She asked if he knew Leah. He didn't deny knowledge of her. That was as good as an admission that he knew the girl. He didn't give much away but wasn't hostile to Dee's questions.

She didn't have to drive anywhere. Another glass or two of wine and he would hopefully trust her.

36.

As promised, Joe was outside with his bike at first light. There was no sign of Misty and the kitchen and bar were locked. Dee mixed the instant coffee with long-life milk from her room and swallowed it straight down while he waited. Their quest was to reach Bendethra, a remote valley accessible only by high-level four-wheel drive.

At first Dee sat back. She balanced with a light touch at Joe's waist. As they turned onto the old fire trail she slid her arms further around his sides and clung to him like a limpet. The gravel road sloped steeply downwards towards a sheer drop on the right. Dee hung on, arms linked around Joe's skinny torso.

She could see where his leathers got their scratches and scrapes. She was wearing trousers but the thin fabric, and her skin, would be shredded by the gravel if Joe misjudged a turn. Already he tilted the bike close to horizontal on the corners. Her leg was only centimetres from the rough surface. If they came off, she'd be crushed by the heavy bike—she stayed tense ready to fling herself backwards if Joe lost control. It could be days before anyone found them.

Would Misty sound the alarm? Or was her old hippy brain damaged by too many drugs? Dee couldn't think of her as a competent person. Misty wasn't someone to rely on.

According to Joe the letter was brought in by a mountain man, Jim Davies, who had come to set up a retreat from civilisation in the seventies. His followers had come and gone for a few years but now there was just the old man, living self-sufficiently in the remoter reaches of the already remote Bendethra National Park.

The trip went on and on. Dee wanted to ask how much further it was but she knew Joe wouldn't be able to hear her. After an hour of relentless ups and downs, clinging to the sides of jagged hills, they came to a green flat clearing with a river meandering over flat rocks. Shadows still ruled the depths of the valley but it would be idyllic once the sun was overhead.

Joe slowed and Dee let go with one hand to rap on his helmet.

'How much further?'

Joe took off his helmet and got off the bike. Dee did too. She stretched her arms and legs to unlock them. He set the bike on its stand.

'Who knows. Jimmy moves about a bit; and he ain't keen on visitors, especially unannounced visitors.'

'Well if I knew how to announce myself then I wouldn't need to risk my life on the back of your bike,' Dee said with more spirit than she meant to reveal.

'Don't worry. It'll be okay,' he said kindly without any reaction to her criticism. 'I'll have a bit of a scout around. You stay here.'

The bike roared off and Dee was alone. Would he ever come back? Would anyone find her down here? Would they think to look?

Her throat was dry and her head was stuffed with cotton wool that was expanding and contracting in rhythm with her breath. The helmet and the dust from the road? More likely the beers and red wine yesterday. Why hadn't she brought water?

The sun slowly crept onto a patch of dark green grass right at the edge of the stream. The sparkle of light from the water triggered jagged lines across the vision of her right eye. She hadn't had a bad migraine since menopause. It wouldn't be good on the back of a bike. There were aspirin at the bottom of her handbag. She'd have to drink unboiled water from the stream. How many diseases could she get? Hepatitis A she'd been vaccinated against; what about giardia?

A clip-lock bag she still had from playing detective at Tom's flat served as a cup. The water was fresh, delicious, like no water she'd ever drunk. She drank several bagfuls and washed cool water over her throbbing head and face. She took off her shoes then waded to ankle depth to wash her dusty feet in the stream. There was nowhere to sit comfortably so she lay on the soft cushiony grass face down with her back in the sun. She was a kid with no cares, the child she'd been on summer holidays in Moruya.

*

The wet sound of chewing woke her and she opened her eyes to see a wallaby nibbling the grass inches from her face. Slowly she moved her head to look around. There was a smaller animal next to the dark-faced creature near her. Both looked suddenly towards the bush off to the right and the joey leapt headfirst into its mother's pouch then the mother bounded away with a pair of spindly legs sticking out from her middle.

As she lifted her head Dee couldn't see or hear anything that might have spooked them. Then a movement came from where the wallaby had looked. Dee gasped, then realised it couldn't be anything dangerous—it was probably only a bird or a possum. Still she stayed still and stared at the spot. The red new tips of the saplings quivered for a moment and all at once the figure of Leah differentiated itself from the bush.

'Dr Dee,' she shouted, 'are you okay?' She ran through a few metres of low saplings and strands of bark that covered the forest floor, across the grass and threw herself onto the ground to embrace Dee.

The girl was trembling and held hard onto Dee. Her face was wet and smeared with dirt. She was wearing the same clothes Dee last saw her in. Leaves and twigs clung to her dreadlocks. The soles of her bare feet were cracked with deep dirt-filled crevices around the heels.

When the faun-like girl had stopped shivering, Dee moved a little. Still holding the girl's hand, she asked, 'What's wrong? Are you frightened of something?'

'I thought he'd got you.' Leah's voice shuddered and she took several gasping breaths. Dee waited and held her till the girl was ready to talk. 'You were laying on the grass and you didn't move. I thought he'd killed you too.'

'I'm fine. No one even knows where I am,' Dee said although she realised as she said it that no one knowing where she was could be a problem.

Slowly, Leah told her bits of what was happening. Her flat in Sydney had been ransacked and she'd fled to Jimmy, an old guru her mother had known in the valley in the seventies. Now she was staying with him in caves in the hills. Two weeks ago the police had been asking her flatmates questions about Tom.

'They wanted to know about the insurance policy. The life insurance Tom took out. It was lots of money, $250,000. They say I have to come back to claim it. But they're suss, I reckon it's some sort of trick.'

'Do you think Tom told Skye about it?'

'How would I know?'

Dee waited.

Eventually Leah said, 'I think so. She was angry with him because of me. The insurance was part of why she was upset.'

'At least the thirty days are up soon.'

'So?'

'So you can stop hiding out down here after that.'

Leah shook her head. 'What about the professor?'

'Why would Professor Fairborn murder Tom, let alone want to follow you?'

'I told you. Tom found out he was into bad stuff. Tom thought he was dangerous. Dangerous enough to force me to stay away. Tom said I could trust you. You have to believe me.'

'There are things you don't know about Glen. He could easily have been the man you saw in the car.'

'It wasn't,' Leah said feebly.

All her aggression was gone. She was terrified of Adam. Dee had to accept her on her own terms. There was no way to get through to her otherwise. She put her hand on Leah's.

'It's okay. Don't worry. Let me see what I can do to find out what's happening.'

They sat quietly for a while.

Dee wondered how Leah knew what was going on in Sydney.

As if she had read Dee's mind, Leah explained how she hadn't left the camp since she'd arrived but sometimes Jimmy got lifts into town from National Parks workers who maintained the fire trails or he cadged lifts from four-wheel drivers in exchange for dried kangaroo meat and skins. He brought occasional news and luxuries like vegetables. It was lonely but she felt safe. The insurance company had been around to her flat but the flatmates told them she was gone with no forwarding address. No more had happened with the insurance but somehow she knew about the break-in and that whoever it was had turned over her room. She seemed grateful that Dee had stored her boxes but wouldn't give any details of with whom or how she was communicating with the outside world.

Life in a bush cave without modern communications would be tough. For a vegan, the diet of freshly killed bush animals must be a shock. That Leah tolerated it was testament to her fear.

'What do you want me to do?' Dee asked. 'You can't live like this the rest of your life. Why don't you come back with me and we'll go to the police together?'

Leah dropped Dee's hands and jumped up. 'If I go back he'll get me too. Don't you believe me?'

The girl turned and moved back towards the trees. She stepped into the scrub.

'Leah, wait! What if I go to the police? I'll tell them what's happened and you can stay here till we know it's safe. I won't tell anyone where you are till I know.'

Leah didn't say anything but she stopped at the edge of the clearing.

'Tom said you could trust me. You can. Besides, who else is there? Unless you want to spend the rest of your life in hiding.'

'I know.' Leah's voice was small.

'I'll talk to the police. I know a woman who works at the Glebe station. How can I get in touch to tell you what happens?' There were so many things she needed to know. Leah was almost invisible already.

Leah stepped further into the trees. Dee stood up from the ground and stumbled towards the creek.

'Bugger,' she said and grabbed at a low hanging branch. The branch broke free to show its bright pink and cream centre. Dee managed to regain her balance.

'Are you okay?' Dee heard from where the girl had disappeared.

'Yes, I guess my leg went to sleep. But no, I'm not really okay. I need to find out what's going on. Can't you stay and talk? Please, Leah, don't you want to find out what happened to Tom?'

'I already know what happened to Tom. I don't want it to happen to me or to you either,' Leah said with a tone of exasperation. Dee could also hear a tremble in her voice. She was frightened and she was right to be.

'Come back, please. I'll listen and do what you want but you have to explain it to me.'

Leah emerged. Dee walked over and took her hand like a child and led her back into the sun. They sat together on the cushiony grass. The sun was overhead and patches of light made the clearing seem less remote, more normal, like any safe and sunny place. Leah had her back in the sun, her face was in dappled shade. It was hard to read.

'If I go to the police,' Dee began, 'I have to tell them all of what's happened if I want to convince them to do anything. Can't you tell me?'

'Okay.' Leah sighed. 'But you have to promise you won't say anything to let them know where I am.'

Dee nodded. Leah sat, mute. She wanted more. Dee said it aloud. 'I promise, nothing that will give a clue about where you are.'

'All right—you know Tom. He was really excited about a baby. When we went to GenSafe we got there as they opened.

He looked over the counter and saw the receptionist enter the password for the appointment database—that included billing details. Of course he had "a bit of a look" at the records. Lots of patients were paying money into an overseas account; big money. Minimum payments of $10,000; some up to $40,000. Tom was suspicious. When he checked the couples out, they weren't the right age range for IVF. Not enough older couples and not enough with long medical histories. Then all the information from Orange made him more suspicious that something was going on.' Leah paused.

She had more to say. Dee held her breath and waited.

Leah looked around; she moved closer to Dee and whispered, 'The professor rang Tom on the Friday before he died. He knew about the hacking. He was trying to find out how much information Tom had. Tom was worried. He said the professor was dangerous and made me stay at my grandmother's. He told me to take his laptop.'

'There might be some clues about what happened on the laptop. Do you think you could let a friend of mine look at it?'

Leah looked down. 'I don't know,' she said in a way that sounded like no. 'Anyway, Tom found more information about the professor after that.'

'Have you thought the laptop might be a danger to have around?' Dee said. 'It might be safer if you don't have it.'

Somehow she needed to get Leah to trust her with the laptop. If Tom thought someone was after him he might have passed the files over to Leah on the laptop and wiped them from his own system.

Surely he would have had some other backup too? Dee remembered how excited he had been when he last saw her. When she was back in Sydney she'd look again at her notes, go over the consultation. What was she missing?

'Leah, if you want I'll have the computer copied and sent back to you.' Leah raised her head. She seemed interested. 'That can't happen here though. If I can take it, I'll have it back to you in a few days.'

'No one else can have it.' Leah was emphatic. 'You have to promise you'll have it with you the whole time.'

'I have a good friend …' Dee started to say.

'No!' Leah started to get up again.

'Okay, no one else. I'll keep it with me the whole time,' said Dee. 'Do you have a password?'

It was like pulling teeth.

'Once you're back at the pub I'll get it to you. Once you're safe.'

The wind picked up. There was a sharp crash from the bush behind them. Both of them jumped.

Dee said, 'Shit, what's that?'

Together they turned their heads to discover a small branch had snapped and fallen a few feet away. They both laughed.

'Aren't you scared out here in the bush?'

Leah shook her head. 'It's safer than the city. No one comes down into the valley without us knowing.' She paused and in a quiet voice said, 'I know he's looking for me.'

Even if misguided, Leah's fear was useful in keeping her out of danger. It was pointless to reason with her, to reassure her about one danger and then tell her to fear another. Raj hadn't discounted Adam and perhaps Dee needed to be open to the possibility that a person she knew could be a killer. She couldn't promise Leah any long-term security in Sydney. It was important to use logic not emotion when someone else's life was at stake.

Dee wanted to put her arms around the girl but that would spook her. Like a bush creature, she had a safety distance and retreated if Dee came closer than her escape zone.

'Okay, I'll keep it with me all the time and bring it back next weekend. How will I find you?'

'If you come back someone might follow you.'

'That's unlikely.'

'No, don't come back. There's no internet out here so it's no use to me. Can you find somewhere safe to keep it? Not with you or at the surgery.' Dee nodded. 'I'll get in touch if I need you.'

It was easiest to agree. The girl had a point. Any contact with Dee could mean others would find Leah.

'How do I get the laptop?'

'Be on the veranda of the pub after five today. If there's no one else there it'll be delivered to you. If anyone else is around you'll have to wait.'

37.

Dee sat with her back to the wall and one glass of red in front of her at the small metal table on the veranda of the pub. The view was of a dense green picnic ground fenced with rough wooden posts. A few she-oaks and a row of weeping willows shaded a concrete picnic table. An ancient stone fireplace served as a BBQ.

At 4 pm a VW campervan pulled up with a pair of grey nomads who slowly unpacked an awning, then a folding table and chairs and made themselves a cup of tea in the fireplace. Dee's phone was on the table. Even with no signal it felt a comfort, a connection to her life outside this valley. She checked the time again.

Twenty minutes to drink one cup of tea. How long would they stay? She could befriend them and warn of the dangerous axe murderer in the parts to move them along. Maybe she could pretend to be crazy and move them along that way. That could backfire; she was already behaving like a crazy woman, disagreeing with the pathologist's report and running around like an amateur sleuth.

She went inside. Her credit card worked in the public phone at the bar. Finally, Eleanor answered her mobile. The others were all outside with Jim, the motel owner's son. They were cleaning the fish that they'd caught for dinner tonight. They'd had a great day. Eleanor wanted Dee to look at her picture with a three-kilo snapper on Facebook and didn't comprehend that there was no internet, not even 3G.

'Jake and Shane are having a barbie with all the fish we caught.'

'How old are Jake and Shane? Will there be alcohol?'

Dee made Ellie promise to be in by 10 pm and told them she'd try to be home tonight. Eleanor didn't seem to be missing her. How much parental supervision would there be at the BBQ?

'Put your sister on the phone.'

'But she's already over there.'

'Tell her I said she's in charge. She needs to be the responsible adult.'

'Mum, we can look after ourselves. I'm nearly fourteen!' Dee could hear the eye-rolling in her voice. She thought Eleanor would be the easy one, the one to do teens without the extremes. Everyone who had grown-up children told her she was wrong. Bugger; sweet Ellie was morphing into a teenager too.

Outside, the old codgers continued to flutter around unpacking milk crates. The billy can they'd boiled water in for tea went back on the fire. It boiled and the woman tipped in a packet of pasta. Fifteen minutes went by. Dee wanted to tell them to check the pasta packet; ten to twelve minutes was enough. Another five minutes, far too long for pasta, and the man painfully drained the water off. He was plump and the first few steps when he moved were stiff and flexed. Some form of arthritis, probably osteo, Dee diagnosed automatically. She judged by his slight limp he had a left hip problem.

A snail would have beaten him at setting up the table. The female partner was quicker, positively buzzy next to the tortoise, but handicapped by an obsessive need to repack every item she took out of a crate in exactly the correct place. While the pasta cooked she hung her washed underwear on a small line inside the van. Inside, rather than under the awning. Dee could hope it meant they were going to move on, that they didn't intend to stay the night. If the force of her silent entreaties could make them move they'd be long gone by now.

Eventually, after packing and repacking four milk crates, Buzzy pulled out a can and tipped beige sludge from it into the pasta. The mush they'd produced could have been consumed through a straw but the pair ate slowly, no doubt observing the mantra to chew each mouthful a hundred times. Maybe all the chewing was an attempt to wrest flavour from the stodge.

As the sun went down behind the hotel the mosquitoes descended. Dee was equipped with repellent, tropical strength. The tortoise was swatting away at his bare arms and legs. At 6.45 pm he stood and tottered across the road to the hotel carrying a toilet bag and towel. Please don't let him stay, Dee begged the gods.

Dee understood Leah was frightened but the melodrama of waiting till no one was around was surely unnecessary. The nomads couldn't be any danger, except perhaps to human tastebuds.

The tortoise ordered a middy of beer and a gin and tonic for his partner. Then he left her to drink alone as he headed for the 'for customers use only' bathroom. Twenty minutes later, he emerged. The woman had her shower while he sipped on a single beer. Dee noticed he had clubbed fingers, a sign of heart or lung insufficiency.

Joe was on his third glass of red and sat next to Dee on the veranda.

Somehow the nomads got underway, no doubt to find a free camping spot off on a bush trail. Toilet and shower access was cheap at the price of two drinks.

Dee waited another half-hour. Joe produced toasted ham and cheese sandwiches. Could she tolerate another night in the saggy bed? After the dusty ride she'd have to brave the dirty shower before bed. And Joe was hanging around; he'd given up his day to help her. Did he expect some payback for the ride?

The last of the brief twilight had passed. There was no moon and beyond the six feet or so of the veranda lights was total blackness. Joe came out and walked over to her. The barmaid from the afternoon shift had disappeared.

Under his arm he had a cloth bag. He sat down and chatted briefly leaving the flat object in the bag on the table. It must be. Dee felt it. Yes, it was a computer.

'Did Leah say anything else?' Dee asked.

'No. She said you'll know.'

'Thanks, Joe. It's good to know Leah has a friend.'

Joe mumbled something Dee couldn't hear and got up. She'd embarrassed him. She felt relieved he didn't try anything on and simultaneously ridiculous that she'd assumed someone twenty years her junior would be interested in her.

<h1 style="text-align:center">38.</h1>

The events of the day had spooked her. It was eight o'clock. Her choices were a two-hour-plus drive along a precipitous winding dirt road down the mountain or another night in the hotel. Joe had primed the jukebox with eighties country and western tracks and had opened another bottle of wine. They were the only two people at the hotel. Smoke came from the chimney of a stone cottage two hundred metres up the road and at 8.30 the lights in the windows were extinguished. There were only three other houses in the town that weren't derelict but no lights or smoke betrayed any sign of human occupants.

Exhaustion dragged at her eyelids. She looked across the table at Joe. The alcohol had loosened him up. His eyes were wide. He leaned forward, forearms on the table. She let his stories of motorcycle rides through the mountains of Columbia flow over her with an occasional 'Umm' or 'Really?'. Dee was on mineral water. She could smell the alcohol on his breath.

Her thoughts were of a real bed, a decent shower in a clean bathroom. Most of all she wanted her innocent baby Eleanor, her half independent, half vulnerable Oliver and her beautiful sweet and sour Beatrice. When she tuned back in, Joe was in Nepal crossing a rope bridge in the foothills of the Himalayas.

Dee shrugged and stretched her arms. 'Well time for me to get moving.'

'You know there's wild pigs and roos all over that road at night. If you hit a pig or blow a tyre there won't be another car till tomorrow.'

Was it self-interest or chivalry? He was a good bloke, must be bored out of his brain here.

'I'll be careful. My children will be expecting me. Any chance of a coffee?'

The decision was easy. Joe boiled the kettle. Dee kept the computer in its cloth bag over her shoulder as she gathered her things from the room and paid for the accommodation. If she thought like Leah then she'd believe anyone could be hiding in the shadows, watching for their moment to snatch the bag. Her world had opened up with Tom's death. So many things she'd once thought ridiculous now were within the realm of possibility—including a murderer out of sight in any shadow. She shook her head and told herself to get a grip, to stop being silly. The advice was no longer convincing.

After another dose of instant coffee, Joe walked across the road with her to her car.

'Take it slow, use low gear for braking, don't swerve to avoid an animal on the curves.'

It was good advice. Dee knew the perils of driving on winding narrow dirt roads were multiplied at night in the bush. A spooked kangaroo or wild boar could wipe out a car.

He'd made her a coffee for the road in a takeaway cup. Dee stowed the computer in the footwell on the passenger's side seat and hid it with her bag. It would take about two hours to go less than eighty kilometres; then she would be with the kids.

*

A kilometre down the road at the edge of the abandoned town she saw the campervan pulled over next to the lantana-draped ruins of a cottage. In a hundred metres the bitumen stopped and the road started down the mountain. The taller trees met above the narrow road. The road was a ribbon of red dirt and stones etched out of the side of the steep hill. On her left the ground had been cut away and raw earth formed a wall; on the right the hill fell away as steeply as it rose above her on the other side. The car headlights barely penetrated the dense, dusty undergrowth. Dee plunged downwards in a tunnel defined by the car's headlights.

The local ABC radio station had an earnest American woman spruiking a way to make funerals more participatory. Dee had an image of the corpse being exhorted to say a few words and laughed, although she agreed that the funerals she'd been to where friends and family took an active part were better. After twenty minutes, the reception faded to static. Dee scanned for other channels. These hills were remote and unpopulated—no phone coverage, no radio.

There was another hour and forty minutes to go. Roadkill every hundred metres or so reminded her to keep her speed down. The curves in the road were hypnotic. She yawned. The single glass of wine wasn't helping her alertness. The sensible thing would be to stop the car for a nap. After several kilometres, the road widened briefly after a small bridge. Dee pulled over. She turned off the headlights, put her seat back and closed her eyes. The bush was loud. Behind her, water splashed on rocks. There was a sudden loud rustling about a metre away on her left. Her heart leapt up in her chest. She quickly reached to check the doors. They were locked. When she braved a look there was nothing; but her eyes weren't adapted to the dark yet. She must have spooked some creature at the creek.

The fright woke her completely. There were podcasts on her phone of a science show she enjoyed. They were from a couple of years ago but she'd never got around to listening. They might help her stay awake as she drove. She drank Joe's coffee and used the empty cup to prop up her phone so she could hear the talks.

As she was about to take off, lights flashed in the bush opposite; another vehicle was driving down the mountain. Better to let them pass than have them behind her. She waited. Thirty seconds later a campervan beetled down the hill. They slowed then stopped twenty metres in front of her. It had to be the grey nomads from the pub. Why stop? Both front doors opened.

Dee decided not to find out. She started the car and drove off. As she got to the tortoise she slowed briefly to give him a thumbs up as she passed. They were probably just being kind but there was no way she wanted to find out for sure. As she got past them she felt her heart thumping. In the mirror she saw the van door slam shut and the lights come on. Lights flashed onto the bush on the cliff side of the road as she drove; occasionally, on a straighter stretch, she saw the van's weak narrow beams behind her. They were driving safely, but didn't fall far behind. Dee was fine with that. There was nothing they could do unless she stopped. The only reason she would stop would be if she hit something.

The adrenaline kept her thoroughly awake but she drove cautiously. By the time the bitumen started she saw their lights only on long straight stretches of road.

At the highway she paused until she saw the VW's yellowish beams in the rear-vision mirror. A row of cars appeared going north. She was in luck. Dee turned left to follow them. Dense tall forest lined both sides of the road. She passed two small tracks, probably fire trails. Just around a curve, she slowed, turned off her lights, drove up a service road then quickly turned into a small cleared space between the trees. It was a gamble but she was more at risk if she was followed to the motel.

It was only seconds until lights flashed past on the road— weak, yellow lights—it had to be them. She checked the time on her phone. Would it be best to wait to be sure they were gone? No, if they caught up with the other cars they would turn back straight away.

Dee backed up and carefully, without headlights, turned south onto the highway. Moruya was only a few kilometres away. Once she saw houses she turned on her headlights and turned off the main road. She used her phone to navigate to the Dolphin Motel via back roads then parked out of sight of the road. Once she arrived, she waited in the car for fifteen minutes. No other cars were about. She wondered if she had over-dramatised the situation. The couple probably just stopped to check she was okay.

All the lights were out. Everyone at the motel was asleep. She knocked on the door of their room, no answer. She rang Bea.

Inside, three teenagers, tousle-haired and smelling of sleep, all talked at once, each demanding she pay attention to their story and their photos. It was still hundreds of miles from Sydney but she had made it. This, these three, were her home.

39.

Monday was busy. Dee barely had time to scratch her mosquito bites from the pub veranda. It was a merciful respite from the worry about Tom and Leah. Weekends and holidays provided extra time for people to examine the minutiae of their bodily sensations and discover brain tumours or other exotic illness. Dee gave everyone a through hearing and examination. Sometimes they were right. Even rampant hypochondriacs get real illnesses at the same rate as the rest of the population. Most she encouraged to wait before she ordered intrusive or expensive tests. The majority of odd, isolated symptoms disappeared by themselves within a week or two.

She lugged the laptop around with her and locked it in the surgery safe while she was at work. It was heavy, a weight in her bag as she climbed the stairs to and from the car park.

On Wednesday in the middle of home visits she noticed its absence. She was tempted to ring Janelle to check it was still okay but knew she had simply forgotten to take it with her. It was safer at the surgery than with her as she trailed about the housing commission flats in Glebe. A heavy bag carried by a doctor was an easy target for a snatch and run attack.

She wanted to know what was on it—to hand it over to Raj. Leah had said she would give her the password. It was better to wait.

*

On Thursday around 11 am Janelle came into Dee's surgery with the mail instead of leaving it in her pigeonhole. She looked excited.

'There's another one,' she said, holding an unopened envelope postmarked Majors Creek.

'Thanks.' Dee put it in her pocket.

Janelle looked disappointed.

'Thanks, that's great,' Dee said again, 'I was waiting for that.'

Dee waited till she was home and dumped her bag on the coffee table in the lounge. She ripped open the envelope. The only content was 'TomJimmyJoe' written in careful separate letters on a piece of scrap paper. She fired up the laptop and typed the words into the password field. The screen sprang to life with a picture of Tom's face in extreme close-up.

Raj arrived within ten minutes of her call to say she had the laptop. He was on the lounge at the Glasshouse, fingers flying over the keyboard. After half an hour, Dee was sick of the suspense.

She stood at his side for a while to get his attention.

When 'How's it going?' got no response she said, 'Ground control to Major Tom.'

He looked up. She handed him a beer. He took it and put it down without taking a sip.

'Raj.' Dee waved her hand between his eyes and the screen. 'Tell me what's there.'

'Oh, sorry, nothing—but there may be a partition and hidden files. Another twenty minutes and I might be able to get in. You really need to get better wi-fi.'

'Why wi-fi? I told Leah we wouldn't do anything to the computer.'

'It's okay. I'm running some online diagnostics; they won't leave any trace.'

Dee went to the kitchen and opened a second beer for herself. It was good of Raj to do all this but the female thing, the bored wait while the important competent male person got his thing done, was painful. After the divorce she thought all that was over.

Do something useful, she told herself. All the useful tasks were female domestic chores: sort out the washing, organise a menu and shopping list for next week, make dinner. None would relieve the 'waiting for some important male outcome' distress.

She rang for pizza and made a list of what they had so far about Tom.

Written down it didn't amount to much. Her knowledge that Tom would not let his asthma get out of hand wasn't evidence to anyone other than her. They had to find out more.

*

The pizza arrived as Raj was ready to quit.

'There's nothing useful. It's all been cleaned up recently. The hard drive has been reformatted and personal stuff of Leah's reinstalled,' Raj said.

He looked disappointed.

'You didn't really expect Tom to leave anything easy to find, did you?' Dee asked.

'No, not really, but whatever Tom found in Orange was significant. That's when he asked Leah to stay away.'

'Raj, I don't know. If it's all about Adam, it could be a big distraction. It probably has no connection to how Tom died.'

Raj interrupted. 'I know you've got an emotional attachment to it not being your old buddy but that's when Tom reformatted the laptop. There must be more. We need to know what he found in Orange.'

Raj's repeated insinuations about her and Adam were difficult to ignore.

'How?' she snapped.

Raj couldn't possibly know about her history with Adam. Why was he so sensitive to the issue? He was right though, they should pursue all the clues; not rely on gut instinct.

'We need to go there.'

Her anger was gone. 'Okay, when?'

40.

Friday evening, as Dee cleared her desk, Raj rang for the third time. He had a list of restaurants in Orange for Saturday night. Dee had no idea why he was so excited. She couldn't see anything useful coming out of it.

The days were up and Leah was out of danger. That didn't put Glen out of the frame. He might have been unable to find Leah. Or she could be dead at the bottom of a waterfall in the Araluen Valley. Goose bumps raised the hairs on Dee's arms. A killer was still out there.

'Raj, why don't we just go by car? It's only four and a half hours. It's nearly six on the train.'

'It's an adventure. I'll bring tiffin and we'll get rooms somewhere glamorous.'

'Tiffin.' Dee sighed and wondered, not for the first time, if it was all a game to him.

Her plan to drive up and back in a day had turned into a circus. Now they were spending the whole weekend. And they'd be noticed.

'Don't forget; it's the country. They don't do exotic. Your inner maharajah has to go incognito for people in Orange to talk to us,' Dee warned.

*

On Saturday morning at Central Railway Station the teenage girls on the seat next to Dee pointed to a figure striding towards them and asked each other, 'Who's that? Isn't he in a movie?'

Dee looked along the platform to see six foot five Raj in a slim-cut suit with a shirt the same shade of not-quite-navy and a narrow charcoal tie. The contrast to the worn detritus of humanity's rejects who were gathered for the early XPT train to Orange could not have been more obvious. He glowed with the aura of the famous or mega-rich or beautiful. She looked down; please don't be wearing watermelon or lime shoes—mercifully they were plain black although polished to an eye-damaging shine.

'Do you like it?' He sat down. The girls giggled and stared.

'Raj, you look like a movie star. James Bond.'

'Thanks.'

'No, that wasn't what I meant. The aim was to look ordinary, harmless—forgettable. No one's going to think you're harmless in that. We'll get some jeans and a T-shirt when we get there.'

Raj emitted a noise of protest but didn't verbalise it. He would comply.

On the train, first class was unoccupied except for them. Raj was miffed about Dee's lack of appreciation of his dressed-down outfit. For the first ten minutes of the trip he looked at his phone and didn't talk.

But he was too excited about their adventure to be quiet for long. His idea to take the train was to be exploited to the full. He was equipped for a safari. His wicker picnic basket had china cups for the espresso he decanted from a thermos to accompany spiced peaches with buffalo yoghurt and chocolate croissants.

His PA had also packed lunch. Chicken sandwiches on fresh sourdough and a crisp green salad. The poor assistant must have been up before 6 am to get the fresh bread and prepare everything—all on china plates with proper cutlery.

Raj had gin, tonic and fresh limes. All on ice. It was tempting but Dee said no.

They needed to be sharp.

*

The journey was slow. Dee wondered what the X in XPT meant. It couldn't be for Express. Over the mountains they emerged onto the western plains, wheat farming country, wide, flat and fertile; vast fields of ripening crops, green wheat stalks rippling with promise.

Bathurst was the last major town before Orange, their objective. Dee was surprised when the train stopped fifteen minutes out of Bathurst at a small town called Blayney.

She pointed out the window for Raj to look. 'This is Blayney, this is where Glen was charged with attempted murder.'

'But didn't you say he wasn't convicted, he pleaded to a minor charge of assault? It doesn't get us anywhere.'

'Yes, but when I looked it up I had no idea where Blayney was. It's here near Orange. Tom could have been researching Glen too.'

'Did he have any reason to look?'

'How do we know? The only way to find out is to check it out for ourselves.'

<h1 style="text-align:center">41.</h1>

Dee expected the offices of the *Central Western Daily* to be old and dusty with a big wooden counter manned by men in navy blue dust coats. Instead it was like any open-plan modern office. There was none of the smell of newsprint or clang of presses and no elderly editor ready to tell her the local gossip from thirty years ago over a pint at the pub.

At the counter a twenty-something woman with cropped black hair couldn't take her eyes off Raj in spite of the brown slacks and navy T-shirt they'd bought at Target. Dee might as well have been invisible.

'What's youse looking for? Got a story? I could get youse in the paper if there's a story,' said the girl to Raj, who stood silent, apparently stunned by the Aussie country slang. Dee tapped his ankle with her foot.

'We're doing some historical research and wanted a look at your archives,' said Raj.

The girl looked disappointed. 'There's no archives here since we got the new building.'

Dee gave him another tap with her foot. It was no use her trying to speak.

'Oh—a friend of ours got some photocopies of old news articles here a few weeks ago. That wasn't here?'

'Youse could try the lib'ry. All the old stuff's over there now. Mr Fielding, he's the editor, won't be in till Monday. He's been here forever; he might know.'

'We have to leave tomorrow. Is there any way to contact him?' Dee piped up. Raj was useless.

'No,' the girl reverted to the default position of the resentful receptionist: obstruction.

Dee kicked Raj's ankle harder this time. Raj finally got it and turned his best smile on the girl.

'I'd be so grateful if you could get a message to him. My name's Raj. This is my card.' His hand brushed the girl's as he handed it to her. 'I don't know what we'll do if we can't get information while we're here. Perhaps I can check in with you later to see how it goes? How can I get in touch with you?'

'I'm Lois.'

The girl wrote her mobile number on a generic card and put it into Raj's hand.

'Thanks so much, we're at the Duntryleague Hotel. Please ring anytime.' Raj reached across the counter to shake her hand.

*

'Microfilm, it's like when I was in high school,' Dee said.

Her eyes were dry, irritated by the blotchy black and white images flashing by. If she read the label for each it would take forever to find anything but if she didn't there was no way of knowing what was significant. There were no indexes beyond the date of publication of the paper. The dates from Tom's copies were all they had to orient them.

'This isn't civilised. A proper IT consultant would have this indexed in hours. Don't they know there are programs that search text and organise it?' Raj complained for the fourth or fifth time since they had been there.

'We've come all this way. We can't go home empty-handed,' Dee said. What she thought was *this would have been much easier without Raj along.*

'It's hopeless. We could be here for days.' Raj took off his glasses and rubbed his eyes. 'How about a break, a walk in the Botanic Gardens?'

'How did Tom do it? He can't have stumbled over the articles he found unless he was here for weeks.' Dee ignored the call to have a break. Sometimes she wondered about Raj's motivation. He didn't have the fire inside that drove her on to find justice for Tom. Perhaps it was that he didn't believe they would succeed. She worried about that herself.

'A bit of shush please. This is a library!' the woman with helmet hair at the front desk announced at top volume.

Dee felt like a naughty schoolgirl. At that moment Raj's phone vibrated. He held up the screen for Dee to see the message.

'Hi Raj, Mr Fielding will be in at 7 am tomorrow if you want to talk to him. Let me know if you need any other help. Lois.'

'Thank goodness. Good you switched it off too,' Dee whispered. 'Let's get out of here.'

42.

The waiter unfurled the starched napkin onto Dee's lap with a near miss between his hand and her breasts. The whole lap, breast, napkin thing was one part of why Dee felt uncomfortable with the 'fine dining' experience. Raj loved it. His research determined this to be the finest restaurant in the foodie destination of Orange and that meant the full silver service catastrophe. Dee wanted takeaway in their hotel rooms and an early night so they could get up early to meet the editor.

Raj wanted a big night out. It felt right to let him have his way after all he'd done to help.

The restaurant was in the nineteenth-century post office with sandstone walls and several small rooms. There were four tables in their room including a family with a teenage boy and young girl. All eyes were on Raj, who seemed oblivious.

'Let's not discuss the Tom thing here. It's too quiet,' Dee urged Raj.

'And sad,' said Raj.

It was good to hear Raj say he was sad; to know their quest wasn't only a puzzle or a game for him.

'Yes, I know. Thanks, Raj. The other thing is—we need to be careful we're not overheard. Adam is liable to react badly to people asking questions about his past.'

Their order was placed and the amuse-bouche of parsnip soup with flakes of scallop tartare cleared away. Raj had impressed the waiter with his order of an expensive local sparkling wine to start. Dee looked across the silver and linen and polished glassware at Raj. The deep brown of his skin toned perfectly with the dark blue of his suit. His cufflinks were acorn-sized pieces of onyx set in silver that drew her eyes to his beautiful, long smooth hands. He had to be gay.

The absence of Tom as a topic left a hole in their conversation. Since his death he'd been the major focus their time together. This was their first time away with each other too. Dee tried not to think about what she and Raj meant to each other. Her inclination was to avoid classification of relationships and let them develop without restraint or guidance. Sometimes she considered that cowardice and sometimes she saw it as wisdom.

Their friendship was due to Tom. Another reminder of him; a good one and one that hadn't faded into the past like her dimming memories of his presence. Raj was charming and, importantly, not sick or dependent but she knew nothing about the rest of his life. There was no evidence of partners, either male or female. He never mentioned the wife and daughters in India that Tom had told her about, although that could have been a cover story. Maybe this was the weekend to find out.

'What can we talk about then? Nothing to do with work either,' said Raj.

'What about you tell me the story of your life?' Dee was emboldened to ask. The bubbles had gone straight to her head—exactly the right place for them to be.

Raj's skin was too dark to blush. He ran a finger along the inside of the collar of his shirt as though it had suddenly become tight.

'Okay, why not? There's very little to tell. Poor little rich boy—not really though—more poor little middle-class boy in a family who used to be rich and still told themselves they were important. My father built bridges so he was away a lot. Mama had staff so she got dressed up every day and we went out. One of her favourite places to take me was the library. We looked at pictures of Rajasthani princes and she told me stories of her ancestors, princes and maharajahs.

'Mama was glamorous but always feared people would think she was lower caste because her skin was dark. I think the stories were to make sure those accusations were squashed before they had a chance to be expressed. Both my sisters were lighter skinned and the big refrain of our childhood was how lucky it was that it was the boy who was dark.'

'Oh Raj; that's awful.' Dee reached across the table to put her hand over his. She was shocked—what a terrible burden for a child. Dee knew about the prejudice in favour of lighter skin tones but hadn't connected that with the shame a growing child would feel.

Raj looked at her hand on his. She pulled it away. She'd violated a taboo.

With patients she was always aware of the power of touch. It needed to be restricted when people had bared their intimate parts, bodily or emotional. It was too powerful to be used spontaneously.

'Sorry,' she said and looked down.

'No, don't be sorry. I'm sorry to talk about ancient history. I wasn't asking for pity but it's nice when someone understands.' Raj reached across to grip her hand with both of his—a sort of handshake passed between them.

They'd each finished a second glass of sparkling before their entrees arrived. Raj chose another local wine to go with the rest of their meal. It seemed churlish to reject his generosity.

The other tables and conversations disappeared into a space made of candlelight, crystal, sandstone and starched white linen. The light was soft and somehow without shadows. The room gave sounds a ring of crystal clarity. Both of them were smart and glamorous. The sadness she'd felt since the horrible find of Tom's body was still there in the moisture she felt in her own eyes and the way the light reflected in Raj's.

Alcohol rendered their sadness heroic. Together they would solve this, get justice for Tom.

'Is it painful to remember this stuff?' Dee asked.

'No, it's nothing. I've had an easy life, I'm smart, my business is going well. I'm out to dinner with a beautiful woman. What more could anyone want?'

Raj had referred to her as beautiful before. Occasionally, if the light was right, Dee saw a hint of beauty in her own face. Her red hair at least was striking. Her breasts and waist were okay for a middle-aged woman and her bottom and thighs, well there wasn't anything she could do about those. The traditional Indian depiction of the female form matched her own, she thought.

'Raj, I know you mean well but when you say things like being out with a beautiful woman, it makes me embarrassed.'

Raj pursed his lips and put his head to one side. 'Why would you be embarrassed?'

'Sorry, I shouldn't have said anything. Let's forget it.' Dee realised she sounded as though she was fishing for compliments. 'Finish telling me your story.'

'I'll tell you the rest but I'm not going to stop telling you that you're beautiful, because you are.' He ignored Dee's raised palms and went on. 'I came to Australia to study because my sister couldn't get into school in the US and my parents wanted us to be together. At the end of university I spent a few years establishing a business. By chance, basically because my father's business was hacked, I started in internet security when there weren't many people doing it. The system I created was bought out for six million dollars US. That was a fortune then. In India, I could live the rest of my life in luxury on six million.'

'It's not too bad in Australia either,' Dee said.

Raj was dismissive. 'Internet start-ups sell for hundreds of millions now,' he said, as though selling his company for six million represented a failure.

Two waiters arrived to simultaneously place a plate in front of each of them—gnocchi with shrimp in brown butter for Raj and double-cooked quail with a lime, salt and pepper dipping sauce for Dee. The table was quiet for some minutes.

'But you didn't live in luxury on the money?' Dee prompted once the plates were empty.

'No, a life of idleness wasn't in my parents' plans. Grandchildren were important and as the only boy I was to carry on the family name. Money helped offset the skin colour handicap but it was still more difficult than we thought. The right girls seemed to get close to commitment then drop out at the last moment.'

'That's ridiculous. Why wouldn't they want you?' said Dee and immediately blushed with what she'd revealed of her own feelings.

Raj rolled his eyes. 'You must have guessed.'

So he was gay. A little bit of her had hoped it was just a cultural difference so she didn't have to believe it. Was his sexuality so shameful that it had to be hidden in Australia in the twenty-first century?

It was a relief this had come up before they got back to the hotel tonight. With all the alcohol, there was a danger they could fall into bed together. A disastrous humiliation that would threaten their friendship.

Every waiter and the manager of the restaurant appeared together at their table as if summoned by Raj's scandalous revelation. It only signalled the main course: Murray cod roasted whole in orange butter and black olives, filleted silver-service style and accompanied by Paris mash and shaved fennel. A salad of green leaves was dressed with local olive oil and aged balsamic and their glasses topped up. Only a third of the second bottle of wine remained.

They were alone again.

The flurry gave Dee a chance to collect her wits. Raj hadn't said anything definite. Did he expect them to talk about his sexuality without putting a name on it?

'Is being gay that big an issue in India? There must be traditional ways it's dealt with.' She was over pussy-footing around, pretending things were okay if no one said the big bad G word.

Neither of them had touched the food in front of them. Raj had his eyes on the fish and reached for his fork.

'Tell me. Why can't we talk about this?'

He put down the fork.

'It isn't easy when everyone assumes you're gay—just because I like to dress well?' Raj smiled to make it a joke.

His eyes sparkled in the candlelight. Dee's moistened too.

'Did the Mogul emperors have to dress down to prove their manhood? There's a rajah trapped inside this humble body and he needs to dress appropriately.'

She pursed her lips and pulled her eyebrows into a semblance of serious support for his statement. She nodded. Raj seemed appeased.

'I'm getting confused. So you're not gay?'

'No,' he paused. 'Well, I'm not totally averse to men. They're so easy for sex. But my real interest is in women. I love women. How could anyone not? I'm always surprised all women aren't lesbians.'

'Yes, well, a wife would certainly make my life easier.' Dee stopped. If she allowed Raj to divert her now she'd never get the story. 'Hang on, can we go back a bit? What happened with the potential brides?'

'The families all assumed I was gay.'

Dee squirmed—she had jumped to the same conclusion.

'These days that's a problem. Women expect a husband who can do his duty.'

Whether sexual needs were met or not in a marriage affected people's lives profoundly. Talking about those needs, though, felt old-fashioned, contaminated with practicalities. The realities of the meshing of bodies, all without the sexual feelings of the moment, were awkward, almost sordid. Images of medical instruments to insert into people, corsets with pink elastic, surgical trusses, lubricants and rubber sex toys came to Dee's mind.

She wanted a veil drawn across the details. She moved the onus of explanation onto Raj to talk about just what he was comfortable with.

'So …?'

'Then Marina came along. She was smart, and beautiful and determined to have me so we married when I was thirty-five and she was twenty-three. It didn't turn out to be what either of us wanted. Things were difficult from the start. I thought it was just that she was shy, over-protected, you know, but I could see the disgust in her eyes if I touched her. When we'd been married five months, Priya, her best friend, moved in and Marina slept most nights in Priya's bed. Once a month she'd come to bed with me for a few nights and a kind of sex would happen. It wasn't comfortable. She'd just lie still and I felt horrible. She wanted it to happen though. She wanted children, and I did too.'

'Sounds like as reasonable a basis for marriage as many.'

'Yes, except that she chose me because she thought I was gay and that I'd be cover for her and Priya. Oh, and I'd supply them with children of course.'

'Oh Raj, that's terrible,' Dee spluttered. The maître d' who was hovering nearby took the opportunity to interrupt.

'Excuse me. Sir, Madam. Is anything wrong?' he said as he indicated their untouched plates with an open palm.

Raj and Dee looked up at him as though he were from another planet. Raj collected himself first.

'Oh yes,' he said as he picked up his fork again, 'it smells delicious.'

'Yes, just carried away with talking,' Dee said as she lifted a forkful of fish to her mouth. 'Mm, it's very good.'

The two of them kept their mouths full until he went away.

'This is good, if a bit cold. Can we eat and get back to the tragedy later? I don't know if I'm up to reminding myself of what a disaster I've made of my life,' said Raj.

Dee finished her fish in silence although the urge to comment on Raj's revelation was torturing her. As soon as their plates were cleared she burst out.

'But you mean she thought you were safe to marry because you were gay?'

Raj raised an eyebrow and twitched his eyes towards the only other occupied table in the room over his shoulder.

'Raj, they're too busy playing with each other's laps under the table. They're not listening to us. Tell me what happened.'

'Nothing much. It went on like that till Marina had a baby girl. Marika, she's eleven now. That made us talk about it. We had to be better parents, get on with each other once there was another being, an innocent baby, involved.'

'You never told me you had a child.'

'It's difficult to explain without the whole story. Anyway, I've got two daughters. Abbi is nine. Priya is her mother—by artificial insemination. I felt like the stud bull—valued for about two minutes and then irrelevant forever.'

Behind Raj the other customers were paying their bill. The waiter was lurking again, dessert menus in hand. Dee called him over and ordered the dessert platter to share and a Pedro Ximénez sherry each.

'Bring the bill and two short blacks, all at the same time as the dessert too.'

Someone had to take care or they'd still be here in the morning when it was time to see Mr Fielding. Raj looked wrung out. Dee could see that there was more he hadn't got out yet.

'So what's the rest?'

'Nothing, that's it.'

'No, it's not,' Dee said gently. 'Remember my profession is helping people confess their deepest secrets.'

'I haven't seen them for a while.'

'How long?'

'Three years.' Tears welled up in Raj's eyes. 'Priya is a bit neurotic. She worries Marina will leave her for me, which is ridiculous, but they both think it will be better for the girls if I'm not around to confuse them.'

Dessert and coffee and sherry arrived with the bill. Dee handed her credit card to the waiter.

'Add fifteen percent for a tip and I'll sign as we leave.' She dismissed the waiter with a curt thank you.

'But this weekend was my treat,' Raj tried to object.

'You're looking far too silly to be taken seriously—and you need to tell me why you think being with their father will confuse your children.'

Dee put a mini brandy snap filled with chestnut crème into her mouth to give Raj time to ponder what she'd said. The clarity of being moderately affected by alcohol made it easy to be sure he would see reason. Soon enough he did.

'I know that really but I don't know how to go about seeing them without causing a fight with their mothers. That wouldn't be good for anyone.'

'Three years is a very long time for a nine-year-old, or an eleven-year-old. Something has to happen soon. You need a good lawyer and a good relationship counsellor with experience in custody issues.'

Dee knew alcohol made her dogmatic. Sometimes that was a good thing. 'Monday. We'll make appointments to see the right people straight away. You must know lawyers here with connections in India. Now don't waste this dessert.'

Across the table Dee linked the fingers of her right hand into his. He looked up at her. Without further words an agreement was forged to move on, to fix the situation.

43.

A warm light penetrated Dee's eyelids. Her limbs were stiff. It felt as though she hadn't moved all night. She allowed her eyelids to open a millimetre. She was in a big white room under a white doona. Heavy curtains covered the windows except for one crack which admitted a beam from the morning sun straight onto her face. Movement was painful but she turned over out of the sun. Her lips were dry and her mouth parched to the point where her tongue was stuck to her lower lip. A sickening smell of dusty potpourri motivated her to get up and open the window. Standing up suddenly wasn't a good idea. She crept back under the covers.

Her phone was on the bedside table. It read 5.57 am. Her alarm was set for six. Last night came back in fragments. How many standard drinks had she had? A bottle of wine each plus the dessert wine—better not add it up; by any measure it was too much. The automatic accompaniment to a hangover was self-recrimination. What had she said, was she out of control, loud, silly, pushy? The next step was to scan for any embarrassing things she may have said or done. Then she could replay them in her head all day as the nausea and fogginess kept her brain from anything more useful.

She sat up. The world was steady. The walk home and the three large glasses of water she'd drunk must have had some effect; either that or she was still drunk. As a precaution she took two paracetamol and drank a further two glasses of water.

The shower was strong and hot. The stinging jets on her skin let her drift through the events of the night. She and Raj had enjoyed each other's company. The attention she received as partner of the handsomest man in the restaurant was flattering; reflected glory was almost as sweet as the real thing. And Raj had finally told her the story of his marriage; the tragedy of his forced alienation from his daughters. And they'd agreed to fix it. The walk home took more than an hour, through dark streets with moonlit gardens and not a soul or a car about. They were magic creatures, gods roaming another world, immune to the daylight cares of the everyday.

Halfway back, Raj had asked, 'Can we hold hands?' Dee took his without saying anything and they walked the rest of the way like lovers. On the landing outside their rooms they kissed and pressed their bodies together.

'Not now. We need to be up early,' Dee said as she broke away—even when significantly affected by alcohol she was too cowardly to deal with any more intimacy. No, not cowardly: cautious, sensible. Raj had just confessed that he was hetero-sexual. She was attracted to him but not safe enough yet to take off her clothes, to reveal her 52-year-old physical self. She'd said no to something she'd fantasised about since she'd met Raj. The walk must have sobered her up.

Oh, God, had she really said, 'Not now'?

Stop, stop, stop! It was a wonderful night. She refused to spoil it with recrimination. To banish the embarrassment, she turned her body to and fro in the shower, recalling the sensation of being pressed against Raj. That alone made the evening worthwhile.

44.

The editor, Mr Fielding, was in his sixties, wiry with lots of silver hair and bright blue eyes. In between the wrinkles on his face, an inquisitive ten-year-old peeked out. He took Raj and Dee across the newsroom into his glass-walled office. They sat several feet from him at his huge desk. He leaned back in a brown leather executive chair that made him appear several inches taller. A faint scent of cigars gave him away as a smoker.

'Mmm, Adam Fairborn. Had a young lad here a few weeks ago wanting information about him. Anything going on?'

'It might not come to anything—it's better if we don't say at the moment,' said Dee.

Fielding was silent. The empty space forced Dee or Raj to reveal more.

'Of course if it does turn out to lead somewhere anyone who helped with information would be first to know,' added Raj.

The older man sat forward and put an elbow on each knee. 'So there might be a story in it? And we'd get first crack at it?'

'Of course, we're a way off at the moment but the story might turn out to be important,' added Raj.

'Adam is one of our local boys made good; a famous son of Orange. You know he won the Eureka prize for innovation in genetics research in 2014? Is it something like that again?'

Dee didn't know where to go with this. Faced with questioning, their motives and the story they had worked out—that they were nominating him for an Australia Day honour—seemed both tacky and feeble. She nodded, hoping Fielding imagined something of interest and that Raj would go with the flow.

'Adam, or Professor Fairborn, wasn't giving anything away,' said Fielding.

'You spoke to him?' asked Dee.

'Information straight from the horse's mouth always hits home with readers. Plus it seems fair for the subject of a story to put their side.' He paused, looked them up and down. 'And what's your interest in all this? Are you journalists?'

'No. Not journalists—researchers. I'm afraid confidentiality is a priority at this stage but we're happy for you to have first access to any story.'

Raj handed Fielding a card with his name, a mobile number and nothing else. Fielding sat back and massaged his jaw with his left hand. 'And you're not private detectives? Look, I didn't know Adam well. My son was at school with him. I asked him what he remembered last time he was visiting.'

'Any background at all would be helpful,' said Dee.

Fielding sat back, opened his legs so his genitals pointed at them. Dee forced herself to relax, settle in for a story.

'The family were squattocracy, here from first settlement. Big spread out of Molong, Fairborn Downs merinos, stud rams, that sort of thing. Wade Fairborn married a local girl, beautiful, but not the same social class. There were rumours that the marriage wasn't happy, especially when Wade Junior, the oldest boy, grew up a bit and wasn't the full quid. They said Wade blamed his wife for the boy's problems, and himself, you know, because he'd married beneath him. Took to the drink, fancy stuff, single malts, big reds. Big parties, chefs from Sydney. I was younger than the father and older than Adam but once I got the job as boss here I'd get invites to the bigger dos. The wife was always dressed up, designer clothes, high heels, but she was a mouse. They say he used to beat her.

'All the socialising stopped once the little girl died. That was in the late sixties. I wrote the story. The details were hushed up. I always thought there was more to it but Wade was mates with the magistrate and police commissioner and everyone else in town, no point in raking through the muck when nothing could be proved and the child was dead.'

Dee was torn between the need to know more and the danger that Fielding would stop talking if his flow was interrupted. She could sense Raj wanted to know more too but she held her palm towards him below the desk to say keep quiet.

'After that they brought in a full-time tutor and Wade Junior didn't leave the property. No one thought he could do any more harm.

'It wasn't much later that the boy died too. Drowned in the dam, slipped and hit his head on rocks. Adam was an only child after that. Things didn't sound too happy out at the property. No more parties. The patriarch was drunk most of the time and, according to the housekeeper, the mother spent her days in bed with migraines.'

'The girl was bitten by a snake, wasn't she?' asked Dee.

'Yes, well, that's how she died. No one knows how her doll got dropped down between boulders out in the paddock.

The children were forbidden to go near the area because of the snakes. But Wade Junior was uncontrollable—aggressive, especially towards Evie, and she was a sweet little thing who didn't fight back. Word was he used to hit her when no one was looking and used to take her toys. Theory is she followed him out to the boulders to get the doll back while the housekeeper was busy.

'If you had time you could take a run out there. Bob Collins owns the place now. He should be able to show you around. I'll give him a ring.'

Fielding must have believed there was a story and decided to be helpful. He organised the visit and directed them to a car hire place.

As they left, Dee asked him about Glen.

'Sturrock, you say? And in Blayney? Nothing comes to mind. But the *Blayney Advocate* is stored at the State Library of New South Wales. Shouldn't be too hard to find the case.'

45.

The row of poplars leading up the hill to the homestead and faded 'Fairborn Downs' sign arched over the gate were easy to find. The house was an imposing homestead with wide verandas overlooking acres of rolling paddocks, grassy and golden at the height of summer.

Bob Collins, a big man of about forty-five, met them at the gate. They got out to shake hands and then transferred to Bob's Landcruiser to 'take a turn around the place before it gets too hot'. Their hire car was left at the gate.

He was friendly and not inquisitive about why they wanted to know more. Fielding must have given them a good report.

They drove past the house. On one side brown cattle with white faces stood like great slabs of meat chewing the lush feed.

'Simmentals,' said Bob. 'The old man was one of the pioneers of the breed in Australia. Did well out of them. Things were a bit rundown by the time I came along, but the blood lines were still here.'

The dam was large, in a natural basin formed by an outcrop of white boulders at one side, and overhung with eucalypts on the other. A jetty of old grey timbers was collapsing into the water. There were ducks and reeds. A fascinating place for children to play and, Dee noticed, out of sight of the house.

'Didn't expect it to be full at this time,' said Raj.

'A freshwater spring bubbles up over there from the rocks. Means this property can survive much longer in the droughts than anywhere else in the district.'

Raj nodded as though he was a farmer born and bred.

'That's where it happened—the older boy, found drowned. Slipped on the rocks and hit his head apparently.'

'Apparently?' asked Raj. Bob looked them up and down and moved into the shade.

'Well, there were rumours—everyone blamed the boy for the little girl's death. And the body had been dragged out of the water before the police got here and the tracks into the water obscured by other footprints. No one could explain how he hit his head and then ended up face-first in the water.'

Dee widened her eyes and raised her eyebrows; an invitation for Bob to continue.

'You know about the eldest boy?' Bob asked. 'Not normal, couldn't speak more than a few words, always screaming and hitting himself. These days they call it autistic but then it was just retarded. Everyone was relieved when Adam was born and grew up normal and then Evie, a gorgeous little thing. She and Adam were inseparable. He used to protect her from Wade Junior.'

'She needed protection?' asked Dee.

'My mother worked as housekeeper here for a while. She tells some tales about how Adam would refuse to go to school until there was someone to protect Evie from Wade Junior. Wade was nasty, a big brute of a kid, didn't go to school. The teachers couldn't handle him so he was kept at home—quite a handful. He'd steal the girl's toys and hit her if she tried to get them back. That's how they think she got out to the rocks where the snakes were. The gate was open and her doll was dropped down between the rocks. Evie wouldn't go on her own—couldn't open the gate herself. There was talk of charging the nanny with manslaughter for letting the children out of her sight but old Wade wanted it hushed up—so it was. Verdict of accidental death. Same for the older boy. And that's how it used to work in the country. Still does really. All the top people know each other and protect each other, think there's no point in displaying the dirty linen; they know what's best.'

Dee nodded but didn't interrupt the flow.

'According to Mum, life was miserable out here after that. Wade Senior drank all the time and his wife took to her bed with some imaginary illness. Adam was always an odd one. The housekeepers were his only company. None of them lasted long enough to have a relationship with him but he didn't seem to care. Kept his room immaculate, no one was allowed in there even to clean or change the bed. He spent all his time studying, gathering specimens from around the farm to dissect for his science projects.

'The house was empty, cold. In the daytime Wade would be out on the farm, baling hay, dealing with the cattle, fixing fences, supervising old Matthew who did most of the heavier work. Lunch was a tray in her room for the wife and Wade took a lunch pack out each day. On weekends, lunch was just the housekeeper and Adam, who'd take off to his room as he was swallowing the last mouthful. Mum got orders from Wade and money for supplies. Her job was to leave dinner served up on a plate for each of them and wash up the dishes in the morning. The big formal dining room was never used; Wade ate in his study, the wife in her room and Adam who knows where. It was weird, three people living separately in the one house. There was never any sound, no radio, no TV. Even when all three of them were there. Mum didn't like it, she left after a few months. They had a lot of housekeepers over the years, no one could cope. My brother replaced Matthew as general roustabout when he died. He reckoned the old couple mellowed after Adam went off to university. Wade cut down his drinking and the two of them started eating meals together.'

'Tragic story,' said Dee. 'And in the end the parents suicided, didn't they?'

'Yes, sad after things seemed to be going better between them. They'd taken a trip to South Africa where Wade's grandmother had come from and June had started to come back to church. Wade Senior went to AA, a big step in a country town. It was quite a shock when they were found dead.

'After that there was nothing for Adam out here. He sold the place. Got a good price. I should know; I'm still working for the bank.'

46.

On Monday night Dee looked at her unpacked bag from the weekend. It could wait. Mondays were the busiest day of the week. After a long day and a dramatic weekend she needed sleep. As she shifted the bag out of the way, Raj rang.

'Hi Raj.' Dee heard the sleepiness in her own voice.

'Did I wake you?'

'No, no, it's only nine thirty—but I was about to go to bed. I'm worn out. You must be too.'

'No, I'm good. I've got news.' He sounded excited.

'Okay.' Dee tried to sound enthusiastic but wasn't sure she was ready for more news.

'Glen tried to kill his half-brother over a will. I had someone search the Blayney local newspaper. There was a front-page spread when it first happened. Glen was charged with attempted murder at first. But here's the thing, the brother said he'd been drugged and then woke up with Glen strangling him. Thank goodness it's past the thirty days. At least Leah's safe,' said Raj.

'You said a will was involved?' Dee was fully awake now.

They both paused. It was evidence that Glen knew about inheritance rights and was willing to take action, including the sedation of a victim.

'The half-brother, who'd looked after their mother for the last fourteen years of her life, threatened to dispute the will so Glen wouldn't get a share of the house.'

Dee didn't say anything.

Raj said, 'Are you there?'

'Yes but I've just had a thought. What if Glen thinks Leah is going to claim Tom's flat?'

'Is that likely?'

'If you had Glen's mentality you might think it was likely.'

'So Leah is still in danger?'

Dee sat down on the bed. 'Maybe, but it doesn't matter in a way. The poor girl is so obsessed about "the professor", she won't come out of hiding any time soon. And Tom was still murdered and whoever did it thinks they got away with it. There's a killer on the loose. Once all this fuss has blown over, the next danger is to Skye and to Charlie. Someone has to do something.'

47.

Craig Mason, the junior detective who'd interviewed Dee and prepared the report for the coroner, and Marlena, were already at the Social Brew Cafe as Dee approached. Dee hadn't been sure if Marlena would even answer when she'd sent a message that there was more evidence about the case but she had agreed, and even suggested she bring Craig along. Could Dee's urgent after-hours visit to her mother for a UTI a week ago be weighing on Marlena's mind?

'Sorry I'm late.' Dee hoped her sweaty face told them she had practically run the distance to make up time.

Craig stood up. His expensive suit, gym-toned body and what the kids called 'man scent' said high-flyer sales executive, not police constable.

'Thanks for seeing me, I really appreciate it,' Dee said.

'You know there's not much scope to do anymore now we have the official finding by the coroner,' Marlena said as Craig nodded. 'There would have to be some strong new evidence for any further investigation.'

Their coffees arrived. Craig jiggled his leg as he sat forward in his chair, ready for a quick exit.

'You told me Glen Sturrock had a record for assault,' Dee said and unfolded a copy of the front page of the *Blayney Advocate* on the table. 'This is the original story.'

'Did you know this?' Marlena asked Craig.

'No, the charge was assault. He got a suspended sentence. It couldn't have been serious.'

'Or the victim was too intimidated to say what really happened,' Marlena interrupted.

Dee and Marlena both stared at Craig as he read the article. He sat back in the chair. Dee had a chance to convince him.

'Tom was worried. He made his girlfriend stay away from the flat. Someone was watching the flat for a week before Tom's death and someone came down the stairs at 3.15 am the night he died without putting on the lights.'

'That's not what our enquiries with the neighbours found.'

You wouldn't get any information from Jock, thought Dee. His generation of wharfies saw the police as the enemy, 'the wallopers'.

'It's complicated—the man I spoke to, a patient of mine, isn't going to talk to police. He probably didn't even open the door when you came around. But I believe him—he's got no reason to lie.'

'Dr Flanary.' Marlena usually called her Dee—this felt official. 'The insurance company is doing its own investigation. The beneficiaries are the ones with a motive. That includes Mrs Harris and her partner plus the girlfriend, Lee isn't it?'

'Leah,' Dee corrected.

'And the girl's disappeared, as has his laptop,' Craig interrupted.

'She's terrified the killer is after her too. She's convinced Tom was murdered because of his hacking. He discovered designer babies were being offered at GenSafe, the clinic I sent them to. She maintains someone was watching her when she came for an appointment at the surgery. People have been asking after her at her share house and there was a break-in there a few days after the death.'

'The insurance investigator has understandably been trying to find her. Of course they've been to her house.'

'And the break-in?'

'Doctor,' Craig's use of her title was a formality to permit him to patronise her, 'this is the inner city. How many break-ins do you think we have each week?'

Marlena was still on side. 'You know the danger if this is looked at too closely?'

Dee shook her head no.

'If the insurance company decides it's a suicide there won't be any payout. If the boy was besotted by the girlfriend, do you think he could kill himself to guarantee her future?'

Don't be ridiculous sprung to Dee's lips but she said, 'No, he was in love and they were planning a life together. Everything was going well for them. Neither of them would want him to die.'

The coffees were empty. Craig had his hand on his phone and car keys, his right leg jiggling again as he sat on the edge of his chair.

Marlena was one rank and twenty years of experience above Craig but in spite of all the 'equal opportunity political correctness' it wouldn't be long before he was promoted. Men, especially young fit white men with a degree, were meant to be in charge. Meantime he'd have to toe the line and pretend to take notice of Marlena.

Marlena wasn't yet ready to lie down and let him walk over her.

'Leave it with us; we might be able to nose around a bit, put you at ease. Our job isn't just to keep the public safe, they have to know they're safe,' she said with a nod towards her junior officer.

Dee knew that giving advice to Craig was hard to resist for Marlena.

'This is on me,' Dee said as Marlena fumbled for her purse. She picked up their bill and handed a fifty-dollar note to the waitress.

'Craig, I've got to check on a case up the road. I'll see you back at the station.' Marlena stood up and turned to Dee. 'You walking along Harris Street?'

'Sure.' Dee exchanged smiles with Marlena over Craig's head.

A few yards away from the cafe Marlena turned to Dee and said, 'Sorry it's so hopeless. I might be able to get the lad to have a go at finding alibis if I imply it'll be a coup if he uncovered more to the case. It could backfire though. Are you certain about all this?'

'Marlena, I know Tom didn't die of natural causes. And I think his girlfriend is in danger. It's too late for Tom but what if we can stop another murder? That's enough, isn't it?' Dee heard the earnest pleading in her own voice.

'Leave it with me. I'll let you know if we get anywhere—but no amateur sleuthing—if this is real you could be in danger too.'

'Okay, thanks Marlena.'

'And Dee, can you do me a big favour?' Marlena paused.

'Of course, anything.'

'Don't ring me. I'll let you know what's happening. I've applied for a promotion and I don't need any complications at work.'

48.

Dee stretched her arm to grab her ringing mobile. The program she was watching had ended. She must have dozed off. 'Unknown number.' She usually let them go to voicemail but it could be Leah. She picked up.

'Hi Dee, Marlena. I hope it's not too late.' Her accent was unmistakeable; almost a caricature.

'No, of course not. Is there news?'

'Sort of but not what you want to hear I guess.'

'Anything is better than what I've got now.'

'Maybe not.' Marlena paused, then said, 'Sorry. No luck with permission to access mobile phone locations. Craig did question Glen and Skye. She says he was there all night when Tom was killed although she does admit she'd been stressed out and took "something natural" to sleep.'

'I guess an alibi from someone you're sleeping with isn't always ironclad. Anyway, Tom was drugged, Skye could have been too.'

'Or they could both be involved.'

Dee made a noise of protest. Marlena kept talking. 'Craig also went to GenSafe to check out Professor Fairborn. Apparently he was with the practice manager for dinner and she stayed over at his apartment for the night. The woman confirmed the story.'

'Yes, I've seen her. She's in love with him. She'd say anything,' Dee muttered. 'Sorry, Marlena. I'm surprised Craig bothered.'

'He did get a bee in his bonnet about it all. He checked bank records for Leah. Nothing at all since she withdrew $600 from her bank account on the Friday after your patient died.'

That was the night Leah had jumped into Dee's car, terrified she was being watched by Adam.

'That was all she had. No credit cards or other accounts we could find. Her student allowance has gone into the account since but it hasn't been touched.'

'Leah could already be dead.'

'Or hiding out until all the fuss is over and she can get $250,000 without anyone asking questions.' Marlena went on more gently. 'Sorry, Dee, everyone has an alibi except Leah and I agree it doesn't seem like it was her, that is, assuming a crime was committed at all.'

Dee wanted to say again that Tom didn't die of natural causes. She bit her tongue. Marlena had put herself out already. Saying the same thing over and over wouldn't make Dee sound more rational.

'And there's something else,' Marlena said. 'The boss found out Craig went to see Professor Fairborn and went ballistic. Craig's in trouble and of course he dobbed me in so both of us are in the shit.'

Dee knew where the boss found out what was going on. A complaint from Adam through his networks. Probably plays golf with the police commissioner or her husband, the top politicians too. He always knew the value of the right connections.

'Marlena, I'm sorry if I've caused you trouble—I didn't know where to turn.'

'I'll cope. It's not so bad to see the young Turk set back on his arse but it does mean we can't do more digging.'

49.

Dee was behind by ninety minutes from mid-morning. There were two emergencies.

First there was an eight-year-old close to coma with the onset of diabetes. The previously healthy child was hours from death. It took fifty minutes to make the diagnosis, get a paramedic ambulance, stabilise the girl for transfer and to get through to the registrar at the hospital so the critically ill child would not be kept waiting at the front desk.

The parents were too terrified to be functional but somehow Dee got them all safely to the children's hospital.

The next patient was new, a young man of thirty-five, who hadn't seen a doctor since he was a teenager. He came in concerned about a spot on his back which had started to bleed. The diagnosis was obvious: an advanced melanoma. After thirty seconds for the diagnosis, Dee spent fifteen minutes on explanation of what a melanoma was and why he needed to put off his proposed overseas holiday to have it treated. It took another twenty-five minutes to get him an urgent appointment with a specialist melanoma unit. Dee was now an hour and a half late.

'Perhaps you need to plan for emergencies?' said Heather, a lawyer in her thirties with a perfect ash blonde bob and an outfit that would cost what Dee spent on clothes for several years.

Last time she was in, Heather had lectured Dee about time management and how much she charged clients for ninety minutes of her time. Dee resisted asking if she was to be billed for the waiting time: not a good idea to suggest even in jest to a person without any apparent sense of humour. Her perfect grooming and mask-like makeup were beyond possibility for Dee. The all-in-control types always made her feel inadequate.

Dee had tried for twenty years to smooth out the ups and downs of urgent problems. The solution was to be strict about time and make people come back to deal with the unexpected. She knew no matter how many times she resolved to do it, the urgent problem always took priority. She couldn't do it.

Dee steeled herself to not be angry. It only made things worse.

'You're right, we'll try harder. Now, what can I do for you?'

The patients after that were okay with the wait. They knew she would take the time required if it were them who needed extra time in an emergency. Why was it always the ones like Heather who stayed in her thoughts and ruined her evening?

*

By eight o'clock that night she was exhausted but satisfied. The things she'd done in the long day mattered, they were important in people's lives.

Janelle had left a note: 'You need to call Adam Fairborn when you finish. He's very insistent and says it doesn't matter what time.'

Could she put it off? Just not ring or leave it till later; ring him from home after a meal and with a big glass of red at her elbow. Her stomach jangled as though she'd drunk too much coffee. Why did she feel anxious? It was only a phone call. Maybe he wanted to explain what was going on.

She sent a text to Raj. 'Just about to talk to AF, will ring you later. D'

Her hands trembled as she dialled Adam's mobile from the surgery phone.

'Adam. You rang?'

'Dee. Thanks for calling back.'

There was a pause. Dee waited till he filled it.

'Are you all right?' The voice was conciliatory, concerned; as though he was talking to a child about a lost teddy bear.

'What's this about Adam?' Dee expected him to be angry. What was his angle?

'Dee, I'm concerned—you seem stressed. I hear you've been poking around in my childhood in Orange. What happened there isn't something I want to think about too much but I'd hope that as old friends you could ask me about it rather than …' He broke off, hurt in his voice. 'My early life wasn't easy, I never talked about it.' Another pause then a soft voice, 'It's hard—I find sympathy demeaning.'

'How did you know?' His quiet tone, the talk of sympathy, made Dee uneasy.

'That hair of yours does make you recognisable. The librarian there is my mother's cousin. We keep in touch.' Adam left a long pause. 'I can't imagine what's going on unless you're having some sort of breakdown. I know it was hard on you when we broke up and I guess you must be menopausal now.'

Dee's jaw dropped open.

'What?' She extended the word over several seconds. The delay saved her from yelling at him—maniacal anger wouldn't add to her credibility as a non-crazy person.

'Please, I'd like to help,' he said. 'I've never felt I handled our history together with enough care and I'm sorry if that's left you with any lingering distress, any bad feelings about yourself.'

'Adam, stop there. Our breakup at uni is ancient history. It has nothing to do with what's happening now.'

'What is the problem then? There's no reason for your behaviour—how would you feel if someone started digging around in your past, suggesting the police check your alibi for a death that was due to natural causes?'

'It wasn't natural causes.' Her words slipped out, 'My patient was murdered. And the police aren't at my command. Did they have reason to question you?' Dee had moved from shock to anger. How dare Adam think their breakup still affected her after all these years.

Adam sighed. 'Can't you see that this is ridiculous? Everyone—the pathologist, the police—all agree the lad died of asthma. Are you the only person in the world who has a magical hotline to the truth? You've got everything all out of proportion. And what's it got to do with me?'

'I don't know. Tom's girlfriend is frightened and thinks his death is connected to their visit to GenSafe. I had to tell the police what she told me and what I knew about Tom's last weeks. I certainly didn't suggest they ask you for an alibi.'

'Don't deny it. My sources confirm you have been asking questions about me and tossing wild accusations all over the place. The kindest interpretation is that it makes sense in terms of your delusion about the boy's death being murder. It needs to stop. You need treatment. I've got standing in the medical community. If you keep this up it will damage your reputation more than mine.' He paused, his voice became softer. 'What we had in the past did mean something to me and I can't stand by while you're ill like this. I hoped we could settle this between us but I can see you're beyond being able to listen to reason. You know there's a statutory obligation to report impaired practitioners?'

He waited. Dee didn't say anything. What was there to say?

'The public needs to be protected. We need to be sure that your mental state isn't affecting your capacity to practise medicine.'

'Are you saying you're going to report me to the medical board?' Dee's face was burning.

'I'm only concerned you get some treatment so you can get well. There may be a better outcome if you self-notify.'

Dee stood up and paced around the room as she tried to get control.

'Self-notify? You want me to go to the medical board and tell them I'm nuts? You're being ridiculous, Adam. All I want is to ensure justice for my patient. A young man of twenty-five has been murdered.'

'Dee, I only want to help. We were close once. Believe it or not, I do care and I feel some responsibility for you. As a doctor, I have to protect the public and report any practitioner who needs help.'

Adam was not going to change his mind whatever she said. Was the purpose of the call to freak her out? He could put a tick next to that one. Not enough though to induce her to report herself to the medical board—to agree her suspicions about Tom's death were crazy.

'Thank you for your concern. You'll do what you think best without input from me so let's end this conversation now. Goodbye, Adam.'

She hung up and collapsed in her chair. The trembling was worse now. She wanted to cry. A report to the medical board meant she could be banned from practice. Medicine was her life; all she had ever wanted to do. She loved her work, her patients needed her and she didn't want to admit it, but she probably needed them too. To be useful, to be needed, to help people deal with the most personal moments of their lives was a great privilege.

Her mobile was on silent but it vibrated and lit up. Raj—there were three messages and three missed calls from him. Dee picked up.

'I'm okay, sort of.' Dee felt ashamed as she burst into tears. 'Please, you'd tell me wouldn't you? I'm not crazy, am I?'

'What's going on? I'm worried.'

'Adam knows we were in Orange. He called me; said I was delusional.'

'You're not crazy. You know that. Don't let him get to you.'

'The police have been warned off anything to do with the case. That would be Adam's doing. And Marlena said Glen's away. It feels like something's going on.'

'It's too late. Glen's got no reason to hurt Leah now.'

'Yes, but I'm still uneasy about him. What about the rest of what Tom left? If Leah's out of the way there's no one to dispute Skye's claim for the estate.'

'You're right. Glen's already proven himself capable of violence over property. But we can't forget Adam. He's the one Tom was worried about. There's something going on, maybe Tom found out something worse. Leah's terrified of him. The designer babies business on the side—is that enough of a motive for murder? I don't like Adam. He's creepy.'

Dee was rattled too. Adam's cold determination on the phone took her back to the time he dumped her. His coldness then was implacable, a solid wall of indifference. It sent an icy dagger down her spine.

Raj hadn't met Adam, hadn't seen that side of him. His antipathy to him was curious. Did he know or have an instinct about her uni relationship? Could he be jealous?

She should tell him about the past and about the medical board threat but she couldn't. She was too ashamed. What if Adam was right and she really was delusional?

She pulled herself together, told Raj not to worry and said her dinner was ready.

50.

Dee arrived home to an empty letterbox. It was two weeks since Adam's threat about the medical board. Perhaps he hadn't gone through with it? Her appetite was back after weeks of looking at food as though it were a plastic model in the window of a Japanese restaurant; unrelated to anything one would put in one's mouth. It was only seven o'clock and she was alone. The kids were at Rob's. She could watch whatever she wanted on TV. The Bengali vegetable curry she'd made on the weekend smelt delicious as it reheated in the microwave. The cleaners had been in; everything was clean and uncluttered, peace.

As she set up glass, wine, napkin and cutlery on the coffee table she passed through the hall. A glance at the hall table was a mistake. There'd been no mail in the box but she saw the usual daily heap of magazines, bills and other rubbish had been brought in by the cleaners. On top there was an A4-sized envelope with a handwritten address and 'Personal: to be opened by the addressee only' stamped in big red letters across the front.

Instinct told her not to touch it. She considered having dinner first but her appetite had disappeared again. Her stomach turned over even at the thought of wine. Best to get it over with.

With the tips of her fingers she carried the horrid object into the lounge and sat down. It wasn't easy to open but she ripped it with the aid of the fork she had set out for dinner. The letterhead said 'Medical Board of NSW'. After that there were words she couldn't differentiate into any meaning. At the bottom of the page was the name and address of someone she knew to be a psychiatrist with a time and date. Next Wednesday at 8 to 10 am. There was a thick wad of accompanying documents.

She dropped everything and sat back against the lounge as though winded by a punch to the gut. The curry smell from the kitchen made her nauseous. She was going to vomit. She stood up, started towards the bathroom but it was too late. The contents of her stomach were dripping through the fingers clutched over her mouth as she got there.

She sat slumped against the wall next to the toilet. How could they? How could they? All she wanted was to care for her patients. They knew she put all she could into their care.

The shower. She had to wash it all away. She undressed and cleaned up the front of her top then hopped under the steaming hot water.

'You can't do this!' she shouted over and over. Then, 'I'm a good doctor. I put everything into looking after my patients and I'm good at it.'

She wasn't sure who she meant by 'you'. Gradually the water did its work. She started to focus.

Her plan to get the police to investigate had gone nowhere. Now she was under threat herself. For the first time she felt personally vulnerable.

Sleep would be impossible. She wrapped herself in a towel and rang Raj.

'Please be there,' she said to the phone as it rang out.

The lounge was in semi-darkness with only the blue flickering of the TV screen but the kitchen and the hall next to the front door were lit. Damn Rob and his famous Glasshouse. Why did she still live here? What stopped her letting it go? The kudos of living in one of Sydney's most iconic houses wore thin at night when she was home alone and anyone could watch every move she made.

Dee systematically turned off all the lights, including the TV. The night was cloudless with a half moon. After a few minutes the walkway and the vertical bars of tree trunks in monotone silvers and sooty greys were clearly visible. There was no one in sight but there were blind spots where the walls were opaque. Someone could hide on the walkway only inches from her if she was in the bathroom or bedrooms.

She sat down and realised she was still only dressed in a towel. In the dark she went to the bedroom and got dressed in a T-shirt and loose pants; then she changed to pants that had pockets so she could carry her phone and car keys with her. In case she needed to run she put on socks and proper walking shoes.

All the while she told herself to get a grip. It didn't work.

The lounge room was in the middle of the house, farthest from access points. Dee sat there. She was fully clothed and it was only eight thirty. If she turned on the TV or looked at her phone she could be seen from the outside.

The bottle of red was still there on the table. The grip of her palm around the metal cap on the bottle, its resistance and the perfect moment when the screw cap gave, brought relief, calm and the promise of the perfect blood alcohol level—a place somewhere into the second glass when the immediacies of the world shrank and everything that mattered, family, love, friends, her physical presence, assumed their proper places in her consciousness. She poured a large glassful. As she sipped, the arguments she'd made for calm started to convince her. The bush in the moonlight was still. There were no serial killers in sight.

The letter was still there on the table. There were pages of explanatory notes. She should turn on the light and look at it. As she got up to go to the light switch there was an eruption of high-pitched screams then a crash above her. Heavy footsteps ran across the roof from north to south.

Dee jumped and gasped. Her heart thumped in her chest. It kept on thumping. It was only a possum who'd lost a territorial fight making his escape across her roof. Most nights there was possum action. After years of coexistence she usually didn't even wake when it happened. Tonight, she was terrified.

Alone wasn't going to work. She went to the bathroom and tried Raj again.

No answer but a few seconds after she hung up he rang her. The relief was wonderful. She let go and slumped down onto the floor and leant against the toilet.

'Oh Raj, thank goodness. What are you doing tonight?'

51.

'Dee, I'm so glad you rang. I thought you might be in bed but I wanted to talk to you.'

Raj sounded worried. How could he know what was going on? Maybe he'd guessed from the missed call.

'Me too, thanks. You've been off the air—busy?'

'I've been Skyping India. Abbi's sick. They think it could be measles.'

'Oh, Raj ...'

'They weren't going to tell me. I only heard second-hand that there's been an outbreak at the school they go to. Marina said it didn't matter. I've been looking it up—children die of measles.'

There was no way Dee could bring up the medical board letter. How could a threat like that compare to a threat to your child? She had three healthy children, thank God. She needed to get a grip.

'That's true. Most children get through it but there is a significant risk of complications. So I guess you're going to India?'

'Do you think I should?'

'Of course you should.'

'Priya says I'll embarrass them and they aren't ready for someone so "unusual".'

'Isn't Priya gay?'

'Yes but not publicly.'

'Raj, you know that's just internalised homophobia. Priya doesn't sound too together. The kids could do with some alternative role models. What about Marina?'

'They're both devoted to the girls but scared of the consequences if anything came out about their lesbianism.'

'What do the girls think is going on? That their father doesn't care enough to see them?'

'Please, Dee, don't you think I've tortured myself enough with that? No one's said anything to them—it's not spoken.'

Dee had to try to understand. India wasn't like the West where the battles for gay liberation had been fought since the seventies. To be gay in India was a criminal offence. But she had also seen the harm that came from hiding. Her mother's brother was gay. Lovely, funny, smart Uncle Frank, who'd killed himself before being sacked from his job as a university lecturer. He was outed by a student who had seen him on a beat. Her mum never spoke about the details but it sounded as though he might have weathered the storm if he hadn't felt such deep shame about what he called his compulsion. Life was much easier now for those who were different; still not a piece of cake but easier and that ease had been won by being open, 'out and proud' rather than ashamed.

'Raj, you need to go back and see the girls, especially Abbi. Marina has no right, legal or moral, to prevent you seeing them.'

'We've been talking about that and she seems to be coming round to a short visit—I don't want to push it in case she backtracks.'

'Stop being ridiculous. Your daughters need you. Take charge; ruffle some feathers. Measles is a serious disease and highly contagious; chances are Marika will get it too. They were vaccinated, weren't they?'

'Yes, of course, but epidemics pop up all the time in India. The gardener's son had it and it swept through the school. The annual death rate from measles in India—' Raj's voice broke; he couldn't go on.

'Raj, just go.'

'Okay, thanks.' Dee heard tears in his voice.

*

The possum territorial dispute continued across the roof for a couple of hours. Dee reasoned that no one had a reason to attack her physically. The threat to her career and reputation was enough.

Raj's news put things in perspective. She didn't have a sick child.

52.

On the weekend, the kids were officially back with Dee, although their many extra-curricular activities meant her main contact was while ferrying them to and from soccer, drama, and parties. Beatrice did a lot of the driving. She would soon be ready for her test.

Ollie had a meltdown about where his socks for soccer were. Dee didn't rescue him. It was his job to wash the uniform and he had to deal with it. She watched as he ranted and slammed things about. He was so much like her. Once she detached and let him be responsible for the socks she even loved him for his bad temper. Like hers it happened when he was stressed, when something simple, like food, or a sleep, or even a cuddle, was missing. Then once the basic need was supplied he'd calm down, show his vulnerability.

This wasn't a serious episode, only an attempt to get her to sort it out. When she didn't, he found some dirty socks in the washing basket and wore those.

'Ollie, Ollie,' Dee called as he got out of the car. 'Come here.'

'What do you want? I'm in a hurry,' her son called back in a mildly exasperated tone.

'Come here.'

He came. Dee got out of the car and gave him a full body hug.

'I love you and I'll never stop.' His body submitted and Dee felt him melt into her.

'I know,' he said quietly then stiffened. 'Let me go, I'm late.'

He wasn't late but she let him go. Beatrice, who was driving, rolled her eyes as Dee got back in the car.

'Watch out; you're not too old either,' Dee said.

'Mum, what's got into you?' Beatrice smiled.

*

That afternoon Dee took the medical board letter outside and sat with her legs in the sun to read the rest of it. The general preamble described the duty of the medical board to protect the public from practitioners who were dangerous due to a physical or mental impairment. That was reasonable, but the presumption of innocence was different from that of a court. The protection of the public was paramount; the rights of the practitioner less significant.

Dee had to tell someone what was going on.

The children were too young. Their role wasn't to care for her. It was better if they found out once it was done—whatever the outcome they wouldn't have this agonising wait; they could get on with it; deal with the actual situation—that was always easier.

At work she should give William and Chris some warning that their workload was about to double. The reception staff would need to know what to say to her patients. Janelle was a great sounding board. Dee felt bad about not giving her some idea of what was happening.

Raj was the person she was closest to now but he was away with his children for the first time in years. This news would be too much.

She considered other friends. There was no one she wanted to know while there was the slimmest hope that she would be allowed to continue in practice. The thought of the conversation was too much.

Rob was her last resort. If pushed, she might have to tell him, ask for his help. Dreadful as their breakup had been, the years they were together meant something. She trusted him as a friend. To tell him made it real though, and Rob would tell Stephanie. Dee was uncomfortable with that. They were all civil, it was the only way, but there was still a power play between the old and the new wives. To be in need of help undermined her as independent, happy with life, free of the encumbrance of a husband. It made her vulnerable. She decided to wait till after she saw the psychiatrist.

53.

The psychiatrist's rooms in Neutral Bay were in a restored terrace house in a residential street. The suburb was on the opposite side of the harbour from her practice, away from any place she usually referred patients and not close to her home. A painted glass plaque next to the door said 'Mayfield'. There was no sign that the place was anything other than a domestic dwelling. Was it his home? She checked the address on the letter again. This was it.

The discrete entrance intensified her shame. No one knew about the medical board enquiry, not even Raj. She had told Janelle and the others that she had a dental appointment.

The door was opened by a man around Dee's age dressed in a conservative tie and white handmade shirt ironed to a perfection that said stay-at-home wife.

'Dr Flanary?'

Dee nodded.

'I'm John Jamison. Please come in.'

As he shook her hand he gave her a big smile, one that almost reached his eyes. His teeth were white but slightly irregular. She got a glimpse of sharp canines.

The empathic, respectful tone and the faux-real smile were techniques used to disarm patients who were used to being in control; the ones who didn't usually see doctors, who were too busy and self-important; or the bullies: the ones whose fear was managed by domination of others.

She hesitated at the door, then sighed and stepped into his domain. She followed him through a reception/waiting room area that was unmanned to a room with a couch, armchairs and a desk with a phone and a file with her name on it. The furniture was Ikea, decent quality but not recent and there was the faint musty odour of a place closed up most of the time—not his house. The large window opened onto a narrow side passage and had a wooden slat blind to allow in some light while still maintaining privacy.

Her head fizzed with flippant irrelevancies. Was he teased with his initials, JJ, at school? It was a name for a pet or a hooker. She had a pun on the word 'neutral' in Neutral Bay on the tip of her tongue. She bit the inside of her lips. She had to sound reasonable and concerned; not trivialise the situation with jokes.

Try to be positive, this was a chance to put her side of the story.

He gestured towards an armchair and asked if she wanted coffee or tea.

'No, thanks,' said Dee.

'How would you like to be addressed?' JJ asked as he sat down.

'This is a formal situation with major consequences for me, so let's stick with professor and doctor.'

No JJ jokes.

'Good.' He smiled again.

Dee was faintly resentful. He appropriated her protest by agreeing with her suggestion of formality—as though it was his idea to acknowledge the threat rather than hers.

'You are aware of the purpose of this meeting,' he asked and immediately continued, 'I have been asked by the medical board for an assessment of your mental state after concern from another practitioner.'

Dee nodded.

'It's easiest if we sort out the basics first. My usual practice is to record all interviews so I can listen properly without taking notes. They're for my private use of course. Is that okay with you?'

What could she say? If she refused she sounded paranoid, but the idea of a recording made her uneasy. A subpoena could release any notes, written or recorded. Her words could be taken out of context and used in evidence against her. Still if, she corrected herself, *as* she had done nothing wrong, it couldn't harm her, could it? And it meant he couldn't twist or misrepresent what she said. Her head was spinning before they'd started the interview.

'No, I'd be more comfortable with you taking written notes. And a copy for me would be helpful.'

At least that meant he'd have to take his eyes off her now and again. She couldn't see any recording device. Was it hidden under the desk with a remote switch? Her mind was racing. She was doing herself in with these fears. If she didn't get control she'd come across as a total nutter.

Her thoughts spun off onto the observer effect—being examined by a psychiatrist made her have crazy thoughts and be paranoid. The other explanation was that she was clinically insane. People who were psychotic had no idea they were irrational. Why couldn't that be what was going on with her? She didn't seriously believe that but had to admit it was possible. Still if she were truly psychotic she wouldn't have any doubts, everything would have the absolute certainty of psychosis.

Without Raj, no one, except old Jock the eccentric neighbour, and Leah, whose sanity she herself had doubted, believed her. This was probably exactly how someone who was delusional would feel.

How much did the observer effect come into play in her interviews with patients? She resolved to be more careful, not to be too quick to come to a judgement about a patient's sanity.

For now she needed to get a grip, pay attention, be in the moment—use mindfulness techniques to get control. She concentrated on his hairline. There were two-millimetre clumps of hair in a line across his forehead: a hair transplant.

His vanity on display cheered her up. Evidence of vulnerability, a flaw in his personality, made him less threatening, just a man, not a brilliant analyst who could see into her thoughts.

It might be better for their relationship if he didn't see her looking at his hairline.

'Of course,' he said. This time the smile showed his gums. Dee wanted to bare hers in response but didn't. He got up and took a clipboard and pen from his desk drawer.

'Let's start with your background first and leave the current situation till we know each other better.'

You already have Adam's version of the current situation in your head, she thought.

'Tell me about your early life.'

Dee was an only child and for most of her childhood her mother was a single parent. So many clichés were associated with both those situations. The professor would categorise her and her mother as in some way damaged, impaired by poverty and isolation. Her mother was a schoolteacher, and headmistress by the time she retired. After her father's early death, Dee was cared for by a neighbour who was a full-time carer for a son with cerebral palsy.

'Mum was a schoolteacher and Dad died when I was five. She never remarried.'

'Siblings?'

'No, but I spent a lot of time with a neighbour who had four children.'

'Tell me more about your mother.'

'She was a good person. Kind and affectionate.' He wouldn't understand that kind and affectionate could be expressed through a close, obsessive control of her daughter's activities. 'Before my father died she was an opera singer but she gave that up and worked as a teacher to support us. It was hard but she gave us a good life. She was a headmistress by the time she retired.'

'Any mental health problems, alcohol, drug use?'

'No.' Dee wasn't willing to go there. She'd often wondered why her mother didn't go out with other men. Why she gave up opera, wouldn't let it be played in the house. This man wouldn't understand.

'And your father?'

'He was a surveyor. He taught at the university at night. He drowned. I only have a few memories of him.'

'Did your father have any history of depression?'

'No.'

'Any other family history of depression or suicides?'

Are you trying to suggest …? Again, Dee stopped herself from vocalising the thought. She would come across as angry and defensive. Her parents were good people—how could this brief interview get any idea of their complexity. The psychiatrist was just doing his job. She needed him to think she was reasonable, sane.

'No. Dad was killed by a freak wave when he was fishing on the rocks—Mum said he kept us fed by fishing.'

JJ didn't write that down.

'You spent time with neighbours. Any issues there?'

'It was fun. Like having a family.'

That made it sound like her mother was inadequate. She was just busy, getting on with the challenges of single parenthood.

'Did you ever experience abuse?'

'No. Never.'

JJ looked down to make a note. Each time he wrote she assumed a judgement like 'denies abuse' or some equally prejudiced interpretation of what she had said.

'Any other major traumas in your life?'

'No, no major traumas. I was probably too young to understand what happened to Dad. Mum was strong. She protected me from her grief.'

Dee was surprised at how combative her thoughts were. This man and the medical board were supposed to be benign, disinterested, wanting to find out the facts, their only purpose to protect the public. It didn't feel like that.

His questions about her childhood and time at medical school picked away at what she had done to cope with having to move away from home, with a mother who sacrificed, scrimped and saved to keep her there. Coping seemed like a failure to recognise the difficulties. At the same time any signs she wasn't coping indicated failure.

She was in a lose–lose situation.

She didn't mention her relationship with Adam although she knew JJ would have Adam's account of it.

He wanted to know about her alcohol intake.

'Two to three standard drinks once or twice a week.' No one tells the truth to that question. 'And no other substances. I don't gamble.' Dee answered all the questions she knew would follow. It saved the insult of being asked.

Another smile with a slight twist to his mouth this time.

'You are divorced. Your husband has remarried. How did you find that?'

'I think we managed better than most. We made an effort to be friends for the sake of the children. We have family times, like Christmas, together.'

'The children live with you. Is it stressful to be a single parent?'

'No more than being married to a husband who was always at work.'

'Is there anyone in the picture for you?'

'No.' Who could explain what was going on between her and Raj? She kept talking, 'But I have several close friends. No close family. I still see the neighbour who minded me when I was little.'

'How is your physical health? You have a GP, I assume?'

'Good and yes.'

'Are you taking any regular medication?'

'Perindopril for mild hypertension.'

'How is menopause treating you?'

'Gently.' A ridiculous question didn't deserve a serious answer.

The questions and their order were familiar. She had taken many basic psychiatric histories.

They came to the current situation. She couldn't deny the facts.

She had questioned the autopsy findings. She had approached the pathologist to question his conclusions on the cause of Tom's death. She had told the police about Tom's and Leah's concerns about Adam. There was no mention of Glen. Dee didn't bring him up.

She hadn't accepted the authority of the police on the law or of the pathologist on the medical findings.

'I understand you and Adam Fairborn ...' JJ paused and looked up at her as if looking for the right word, 'had a liaison, when you were at university?'

'Yes, for a couple of semesters. It ended early in second year. We didn't live together but we were lovers.'

'Can you tell me about it?'

The open-ended question was a deep pit hidden under a flimsy roof of twigs and leaves on the jungle path JJ led her along. He wanted her to reveal evidence of an obsession with Adam.

'Adam was my first lover and, yes, splitting up was difficult at first. I soon had another boyfriend and Adam had other girlfriends. We were in the same classes a lot of the time so we had to be civilised about it.

'After university Adam went into genetics so we lost touch until he opened a private practice. I sent him patients. He is the top specialist in his field. I hadn't seen him for years until a medical education meeting last year where he was the speaker. I haven't had any personal contact with him for many years.'

Dee stopped talking. JJ stared at her expectantly.

'That's it, until my patient, Tom, who died, went to see him and died shortly after. Adam rang me to find Tom's girlfriend's address.'

'I understand the young man was somewhat of an eccentric. In his history to Professor Fairborn he confessed to being obsessive, quote, "an Aspi". His brother is autistic. He saw Professor Fairborn because of concerns that his own child might be at risk of autism?' JJ made it a question.

Dee nodded.

'Then, when your patient was found dead, you told the police Professor Fairborn was implicated in his death?'

'No, not implicated, connected. The police had to know all the circumstances. I knew Tom his whole life. I know he didn't die of asthma. It was murder.'

Dee felt the drop as strongly as if the floor had given way beneath her. She had fallen into JJ's pit.

'Have there been other times in your life when people didn't understand things you've experienced? Times when you have understood things beyond what others believe?'

He was asking if she had delusions or hallucinations. No, his words were 'have you had *other*' delusions or hallucinations.

His mind was made up before she walked through the door. Medicine was full of authority and hierarchies. Pathologists did not make mistakes. GPs could not question their competence. It was how the system worked. Dee didn't stand a chance. If she persisted in questioning the autopsy she was delusional. She was delusional so anything she said about Tom's death was a product of her psychosis.

'No.'

Dee was done. She wouldn't argue or protest, wouldn't flail about in the pit.

She stumbled through the rest of his questions.

The issue was not if she had a mental illness but whether her mental illness interfered with her competence to practice. He seemed satisfied. There weren't many other questions.

'Thank you, Dr Flanary, for coming to see me,' JJ said, gums bared, canines ready to tear apart flesh.

'Can I get a copy of your report?'

'My brief is from the medical board so any release of the report will need to be through them.'

'What will you recommend?'

'Dr Flanary, I cannot pre-empt the board. They will have a range of information to help them make a recommendation. Any opinion I gave now could be misleading.

'The Impaired Registrants Committee meets next week. You will be informed of their decision within a week after that. I don't believe there are grounds to ask for an urgent suspension before that meeting.'

One last glance at his hair transplant and Dee was out the door.

54.

CSI was on TV. Beatrice and Eleanor watched all the crime shows. Dee was drifting in and out of sleep on the lounge. It seemed to be the only place she did sleep lately.

In bed, as soon as she turned out the light, the psychiatrist and the medical board's upcoming decision would jolt her awake till the early hours. She'd read for distraction with exhausted eyes closing repeatedly till she dropped her book. That would wake her again till she fell into proper sleep for an hour from 4 to 5 am.

*

Remotely, she was conscious of the 'yee-aw' of a Skype call.

'Mum. Mum.' It was Ollie with her phone. He put it in her hand. 'You've got a Skype call.'

As she woke, the sound stopped. She was alone on the lounge with a rug over her.

'Ollie, what's happening? What's the time?'

'We didn't want to wake you up. It's ten thirty.'

'Thanks.' She held his hand to her cheek.

She must have slept for two and a half hours, her longest, soundest sleep since the medical board letter. It was wonderful. She could almost cry with relief.

The phone showed two missed Skype calls from Raj. Abbi was her first thought. He would be with her by now. Please let her be okay. Dee climbed into bed with her laptop and Skyped him back.

'Dee,' he answered straight away. She saw he was happy.

'So she's okay?'

'Recovering, yes. And so far Marika hasn't got it. We're all so relieved.'

'I'm so happy for you. A sick child puts everything else in perspective, doesn't it?'

'Yeah, even Priya is being nice to me. I can sort of see what Marina sees in her. It's not quite happy families yet but we're all working on it.' Raj paused and went on in a more formal voice, 'And I want to thank you for making me come.'

'It was your decision.'

'Yes, but if you hadn't told me I had the right I might have stayed helpless. I told them when I got here that I wasn't going to stay away after this and they both folded. It was so easy; once I'd made up my mind, they accepted it—a total surprise.'

A pang went through Dee. Raj would move back to India. She realised how much she had started to depend on his support. She switched off the camera.

'That's lovely, I'm so happy for you.' She tried to stop her selfish need for Raj to be in Australia from creeping into her voice.

'Are you there? Your picture's gone.'

'The wi-fi slows down sometimes. It'll be back soon. So you'll stay for a while?'

'Till the incubation period is over for Marika, another four days. Then I'll be back more often till I get things organised. I'm so lucky.' He stopped. 'Dee, how are you?'

Dee's brain focused on 'I'll be back more often'.

'Fine, nothing happening, kids are well, work's work. The usual,' Dee managed to say.

She needed Raj to stay away from the Adam stuff. It was too raw to talk about. She was alone with the medical board worry. Ashamed. She knew she hadn't done anything wrong but it felt shameful. Then the doubt overtook her again. If she actually was crazy and obsessed with an ex-partner, wasn't this exactly how it would feel?

'Tell me about where you are. It all sounds so exotic.' It was easier now Raj couldn't see her face.

As they talked Dee went into the bathroom to wash her eyes before she turned the camera back on. Any mention of her problems she deflected with questions about India and the girls.

At the end of the call, Raj said, 'I know what you're doing and thanks. There's no progress yet with the passwords. Once I'm home I can research Adam myself. If Tom got information I can too.'

'And Glen. He could still be dangerous.'

'Please, Dee, you have to consider them both to be dangerous until we know what happened. Tell me you'll be careful.'

'Okay.'

'What about Leah? No word?'

'Nothing. I'm worried about her.'

'Me too,' said Raj. 'I'll be back soon. Please remember to keep safe.'

'I'm okay.'

Dee couldn't tell him that she was safe now because she was about to be discredited by the medical board. Any hope that Tom's death would be recognised as murder was gone. She was now no threat to whoever had killed Tom. She hoped the murderer knew that.

'You won't do anything till I'm back, will you? Please promise me.'

'Bye, Raj. Thanks for caring.'

55.

The children had started to worry about her, to check up on how much she slept and ate. She'd negotiated with them that she would stay late at work to finish some medico legal reports. The real reason was to write summaries for some of her more complex patients, the ones it would be difficult for another doctor to take over.

She picked up a letter from her in-tray with 'To be opened by the addressee only' handwritten in bold capitals across the front. It was as though she had stepped on a landmine. Once seen, her peace was destroyed. She couldn't put it down; couldn't step away. She had to open the letter; let it detonate to blow apart her life.

It had been sent to the surgery. The medical board correspondence had been sent to her home, and they didn't meet for another week. It wasn't them.

It could be innocent, a note from a patient, an invitation to a wedding, some trick from a drug company to get her to read their advertising. The writing was somehow familiar, in blue ink from a fountain pen. She picked up her letter opener and considered that at least it was handy to plunge into her heart if …

If what? She was at the edge of tears. In a weird self-fulfilling prophecy, the inquiry into her sanity was making her insane.

That was stupid. It was only a letter. She ripped it open.

My Dear Dee

I am sorry!

I was shocked to hear the medical board has taken this heavy-handed approach. My expectation was an informal discussion and for them to encourage you to see a therapist.

Please, as you probably know, I was a member of the board for some years and still provide expert opinions from time to time. I think my connections mean something.

I would be happy to get in touch before their next meeting and suggest a gentler way forward. You are a good GP. We can't let this aberration ruin your career.

Please let's talk about how to proceed. I do want to help.

Can we meet, soon?

Once again, I am so terribly sorry. Please let me help.

Your friend

Adam

She put the paper down, sat back in her chair and picked it up again. Adam said he was sorry and wanted to help. Was that possible? She didn't want to be deregistered. Was this a chance to avoid it? But to accept help from Adam and to agree that she was deluded about Tom being murdered was difficult to swallow.

So far nothing she had done about bringing Tom's murderer to justice had got anywhere. Should she give in and pretend to accept the autopsy? Maybe her reaction really was a product of her overstressed, grief-stricken imagination?

Was she really crazy?

Perhaps she should find out what Adam had to offer. She picked up her phone to ring him. His number was on the letter in front of her. She entered the numbers and sat with the phone in her hand. She let her thoughts wander over Tom's life; from the baby she'd bonded with when he was five days old to the excited adult who was planning a baby of his own. Raj and Leah, the other people who really knew Tom, both believed he had been killed. Both of them were suspicious of Adam.

The green call symbol and Adam were a finger's length away. Raj words, 'be careful', came back to her. He was right. She couldn't be sure about Adam, or Glen. She didn't press the button. Relief flooded through her. She deleted the numbers and sent a text to Beatrice.

'On my way. What's for dinner? Mum xxx'

56.

Dee grabbed her bag for an emergency home visit to Lil, whose behaviour had deteriorated due to severe constipation. A manual evacuation was unpleasant but more effective and quicker than massive doses of laxatives. Jock was grateful. He promised, as he did at every visit, to 'do a good clean-up to find those car numbers'.

Who would take over Dee's housebound and nursing-home patients if she was banned from practice? No one was indispensable but the home visits were difficult. They cost more than they paid—a courtesy to people she had seen for years until they deteriorated; a long-term relationship. To ask another doctor to take on a home-visit patient they had never seen, and at a financial loss, was difficult. The other doctors at the practice would be stretched to see her regular patients without an extra half-day or more for the housebound.

Had the others at the practice guessed something was wrong? There were no signs. She'd have to tell them soon, give them some warning. And tell the rest of the staff and the kids. She dreaded those conversations. How long would the medical board give her to sort out her patients once they made their decision?

She headed to reception to pick up some more Medicare slips for her bag. Her pigeonhole was stuffed full with old paper files. She looked; it was the two thick volumes of Tom Harris's pre-computer notes. She felt dizzy; put her arm against the wall. A ghost had appeared. There was so much of him in those thick tomes.

A couple of deep breaths and she could stay up without support. She told herself to get on with it. Life was for the living. Nothing would be achieved by being upset. That was a useless indulgence.

Being struck off might even be a relief. She could get some sleep. She wouldn't have to come to work and face these reminders of her failure.

Did her disability insurance cover being struck off? She hadn't checked yet. She should do it but the thought of it made her feel nauseous.

If only Raj were here.

The two files, each the size of a ream of paper, were piled on top of each other. She put down her doctor's bag and picked up the top one. Attached to the front was a request for a copy of the records from the insurance company.

'Do you know what's happening with this?' she asked Janelle.

'That's what I want to ask you,' said Janelle. 'It'll take at least a day for one person to copy all that. What do you want us to do?'

'Print out the computer file— it goes back nine years—and send that with a note about the cost of copying the rest. If they're willing to pay we can give Helen some extra hours to do it.'

Dee thought the insurance company wouldn't need or want all the old paper file, but for a payout of $500,000—maybe it was worth their while trawling through Tom's childhood?

*

Dee arrived back at the surgery at five thirty. There was only one emergency call to handle before she went home. Home to spend the next fifteen hours on useless rumination.

Adam's letter was still there in her in-tray—a potential way out. She opened her phone and saved Adam's phone numbers to her contacts. She could ring him before she left. Meet somewhere public on the way home from work. What harm could he do?

Dee was still slumped in her chair when Janelle put her head around the door. Dee wished her away. She needed to be alone to gather the courage to speak to Adam.

'Yes?' She said with a tired sigh.

'Sorry but I didn't know what to do, even the computer file for Tom Harris is enormous. Is the insurance company willing to pay for everything, or just the clinical notes?'

Dee forced herself to concentrate. An idea triggered in her brain. She sat up.

'Hang on, give me a minute. Don't do anything yet. And can you get William or Chris to sort out the INR for Harry? I have to check something else.'

Dee logged back into her computer and opened Tom's notes. Her hands shook and her lips were dry. She almost didn't want to know if she was right or not.

No—this had to be done. She took a breath and clicked through the headings until she found what she was searching for.

'Peak Flow Charts'. She opened them. Tom's precise charts went back years. They were scans of the paper charts he brought in. She looked for the date of his last visit, the day two weeks before his death, the day he'd insisted she import his peak flows as an excel spreadsheet.

At first glance they were the same as the photocopied versions but at the bottom of the screen were tabs for extra sheets.

She moved her mouse down and clicked the first tab.

At the top of several lines of text there was a date and a name and a link.

She copied and pasted the link into Google. It was a newspaper article in a foreign language.

The next link was to a translation, incomplete but enough to establish that the article reported the death in a car crash of a scientist, Erik Lindquist, during a conference in Istanbul in 2003. Then several pages of information about the conference Lindquist was attending. An obituary from the *Journal of Molecular Genetics* talked of the great loss to genetics and of his future as a Nobel laureate for his research in gene splicing. The conference program had photos and profiles of the keynote speakers. Immediately below that of Lindquist was a face that startled Dee. Adam Fairborn, MD, PhD.

Dee flicked open the six tabs. Each was about the death of one individual, with stories from several sources and a note about how the person was connected to Adam Fairborn. This was the proof she needed for the psychiatrist and the medical board.

As she looked the screen became blurry. She put up her hand to check she had her reading glasses on then realised why she couldn't see—her eyes were wet with tears. For a minute she thought she was about to faint then realised she was hyperventilating. She concentrated on slow breaths, did the exercises she gave patients with panic attacks. It was difficult to keep up. She resolved to be more understanding with people who couldn't do it.

Slowly she felt better, wiped her eyes and buzzed Janelle.

'I need some help—can you come in?'

'You're all pale. What's wrong? I'll get William.'

'No, I found something in Tom's file. It's important. I need to…' Dee paused.

Janelle was standing in the doorway with half an eye on the front desk.

'Come in, leave the desk for a minute. Tom Harris sent these to me so they'd be safe. Any other copies have probably been destroyed. This is important, write it down. Can you print out more copies, send hard copies by post to me at home, to Marlena Ng, to Glebe Police Station, Attention Craig Mason and to Rob's office? Then scan and email them to me and to Raj as well.'

'I finish at six. Can it wait till morning?'

'Janelle, if there's any way you can do it now I'll be forever grateful.' Dee held out her trembling hands. 'I'd do it but I don't think I'm capable.'

Janelle looked at Dee silently for a moment.

'Okay, but you need to tell me what's going on.'

'Thanks. I will, but not right now. Is that okay?'

Janelle put her hand on Dee's shoulder. 'All right. Will you be okay getting home?'

'Yes, and thanks again. I wouldn't ask if—'

Janelle interrupted. 'Shush; go home. It'll be done. We'll talk tomorrow.'

'Don't say anything to anyone, please. It's important.'

Janelle handed Dee her bag and opened the back door for her. Dee gathered the printed pages, went down to her car and drove home.

*

'Mum,' Eleanor came out of her room, with a big smile, surprised to see her mother so early. She held out her arms, 'Cuddle?'

'Do I deserve this?' Dee said as her youngest held her tight.

'Yeah you do. I love you, we all do.'

Dee thought of the horrors waiting for her in her email and she thought of her family.

'Do you want a roast chicken?' she asked. There was time to get to the supermarket for a chicken. She'd make a bread and butter pudding for dessert.

*

The smell of the chicken roasting with rosemary filled the house. The warm sweet perfume of vanilla and raisins added a complex dimension of comfort. Like music playing, an orchestra of smells; the bread and butter pudding was the viola—a sweet note of complexity.

The girls were in their rooms with homework and Ollie was practising a piece on the oboe. The smells and sounds made it easier to print out the material from Tom's file. Dee sat on the floor at the foot of her bed and spread out the pages.

First she sorted them into individual stories and ordered them by date. There were six. Most recently, a year earlier, a medical technician from GenSafe had drowned while snorkelling at Clovelly. The police found traces of party drugs in his system and the conclusion was accidental death due to swimming while intoxicated. The body was bashed around a bit by the swell but police declared 'no suspicious circumstances'. The obituary in the local paper mentioned his job. Tom must have searched extraordinarily widely, or possibly had inside help, to make the connection to GenSafe.

Another employee of GenSafe had died only a year earlier. The woman was forty and had come off a motorbike in Bali while on holiday with girlfriends. The inquest report addressed her husband's claims that his wife would never ride a motorbike. Her friends told a different story. The woman had run into a male friend in Bali and didn't stay with the group at the hotel they were all booked into. The man was not traced although the woman's travelling companions thought he was someone she had known from Australia. Conclusion: accidental death secondary to riding a motorcycle while drunk.

A later article reported that Lindquist had died because he was driving while intoxicated with rohypnol. The translation of the article mentioned that he was a promising researcher. A year before that was an Australian PhD student in genetics, also found dead with a massive dose of rohypnol in his blood while overseas for a conference—this time in Bangkok. One of his supervisors was Adam Fairborn. Both the dead were working on gene shears although at different universities. Adam had several papers with Lindquist as co-author. Tom had made a note that he was searching for a list of attendees at the conference in Helsinki. Apart from an article in the English-language *Bangkok Post* no investigation details were given.

The stove timer beeped. Time to turn the chicken breast up for ten minutes to brown and to organise someone to set the table. She briefly checked the other stories. She already knew about these. Adam's Japanese girlfriend who died when they were all in fourth year at uni. The autopsy report was there. Dee was surprised that Mami had been five months pregnant when she died. Mami's death was ruled accidental. She drowned after diving and hitting her head on a submerged rock at Lane Cove River Park. No one at uni had known about the pregnancy except, Dee guessed, Adam.

'Mum, what's happening? Do you want me to turn the chicken?' Beatrice called.

'Yes, thanks. Put the timer on for ten minutes more. Take out the pudding and get your brother to set the table.'

Oliver called out, 'Done, done, done, done' in imitation of a clock chime.

Dee looked at the last group of papers. In their final year Ly, Adam's only competition for the University Medal, killed himself by electrocution in the electrophysiology lab late one night. No suspicious circumstances were found. Ly was known to be grieving a relationship breakup and although there was no note, the careful set-up of the wires was so deliberate that a finding of suicide was made.

Ly was a hard-working boy from Singapore with an unexpected, quirky sense of humour. His old-fashioned chivalrousness had intrigued Dee. They had become friends. Their contact was only occasional. They had different friendship networks but when they did have a chance to talk they understood each other. She was shocked by his death, everyone was, but no one had questioned the suicide. Dee remembered the gracious reference Adam made to Ly in his acceptance speech for the University Medal at their graduation. She shivered and gathered the papers into one pile.

As she looked at the wad of papers, the horror overcame her again. Her blood turned to icy coolant in her veins, flowing but no longer human. No human heart could deal with what this meant. Adam simply killed anyone who got in his way, including his own parents and brother. So far, with Tom, the count was up to ten. How many others could there be?

What could have happened if she had agreed to meet him? A middle-aged doctor certified as insane who was about to be deregistered. An overdose, driving her car off a cliff while drugged—no one would question suicide. Except Raj, who would be dismissed as a victim of folie à deux.

More terror hit her as she remembered her breakup with Adam. How fortunate that she had accepted it quietly. Poor Mami.

The timer beeped again.

In a few seconds she would take the dinner out of the oven and pour boiling water over broccoli to go with it; for the sane, lovely people who were her children. How could someone like Adam exist on the same planet?

The articles weren't proof but there were too many accidental deaths and suicides around Adam to be coincidence. The police had to investigate.

So far Adam had removed the threat from her by discrediting her. She was about to be officially crazy, obsessed about an ex-lover. He didn't know she had the files Tom had collected, the evidence of long-term connection to all the deaths. The fact she and Adam were in open conflict might provide her some protection. Surely the police would investigate if she were found dead. Although suicide was plausible.

Leah was more at risk. She couldn't live forever in the bush waiting for Adam to forget. Clearly Adam would not forget.

Dee put the papers in her bag—she didn't want anyone else to come across them. She walked into the kitchen. She had to tell the children something; give them some warning that their lives were about to be turned upside down.

The table was set and the chicken on the carving plate. Eleanor turned off the kettle and poured it over the broccoli.

'Who wants to carve the chicken?'

Oliver was first up and grabbed the knife.

'You never let me do it,' Beatrice objected.

'Your turn next time,' Dee said. 'You get the vegetables out of the pan and onto a serving plate.'

The three of them looked at each other with raised eyebrows. Dee didn't usually let them handle hot baking dishes or carving.

They sat down and filled their plates and ate silently, intent on the first few mouthfuls.

'You're all growing up. Beatrice has her driving test soon,' Dee said once the urgency of starvation was over.

'You didn't forget it's on Friday, did you?' Beatrice asked. 'Indira's mother's taking me but I'll need the car. You said you'd get the train to work.'

'Yes. I'll catch the train.' Dee avoided admitting she had forgotten. 'It won't be long before all of you will have licences. Time for some changes. You want to be treated more like adults, don't you?'

They all nodded but they looked wary. They knew she was stressed out. Who knew what they imagined was wrong with her? Doubts about her sanity? She'd had those herself.

Her nerve failed. She couldn't spoil their dinner. They didn't need to know till the medical board decision was handed down.

57.

It was 6.30 pm; five hours since she'd had Janelle ring Marlena. Dee sent newly married Emily to the toilet to get a specimen for a pregnancy test and went through to reception.

'Nothing?' she asked Janelle.

'No, sorry.'

'And the others knew to put her through?'

'Dee, they all knew. No one has called you from the police.' Janelle sounded impatient. 'Should I call them again?'

'No, it's too late. What about my mobile?'

'Nothing—only a wrong number. Half an hour ago. They wanted a George. Hung up when I said I didn't know him.'

'Was it a woman? Aussie accent?'

Janelle nodded.

Dee grabbed for the phone. There was a mobile number she didn't know. Emily walked back into the surgery with her specimen. Dee put on gloves and took the jar of urine. Emily and Joshua had come in together two months ago for a pre-pregnancy check. This wouldn't take long to sort out.

'Okay, do you want to watch?' Dee asked.

Emily was quiet but nodded her head. Dee sat down and held the test stick over the desk between them. Within seconds a strong plus sign appeared.

Dee was ready with a smile.

Emily burst into tears.

It was a trap Dee hadn't fallen into for years now. She told the registrars, 'Always know before you do a pregnancy test how the person feels about being pregnant.'

Dee sighed quietly and asked, 'How do you feel about that?'

*

Forty-five minutes later, Dee was at her desk alone. She had arranged an ultrasound, referral for termination of pregnancy, information about emergency accommodation and a referral for domestic violence counselling.

Janelle had gone. All the lights were out apart from her room. Dee closed her computer. The backup kicked in automatically. The routine, things proceeding as they were meant to, was usually a comfort. Tonight, it reminded her of how out of control the rest of her life was.

Her phone was still on her desk. She picked it up and rang the unknown number.

'Hello?'

The voice was male. Dee's heart sank. To hope it was Marlena was a fantasy born of desperation. She had to get the new evidence to someone official.

'Oh, sorry, I had a call from this number, I thought it was from someone I knew. Sorry, I'll let you go.' As she spoke there were muffled sounds from the other end. The man's voice came back.

'Hang on a minute, a person here says they rang someone on my phone.' The voice changed to Marlena's unmistakably flat Aussie vowels.

'Dee?'

'Marlena, you got my message.' Relief. 'There's new evidence, I sent copies to you.'

'No, please no.' Her voice was high, anxious. 'Where'd you send it?'

'To your house, I think. Janelle sent it yesterday. It should be there now.'

'Shit, thank goodness.' The relief was clear in Marlena's voice. 'This has all blown up. I can't talk to you. No one from the station can. The commissioner's warned us off. My promotion's probably off.'

'But this new information links Adam to multiple suspicious deaths over years—'

Marlena cut her off. 'Dee, if he's committed genocide we still can't go after him. That's it.'

'Can you at least read what I sent?' Dee heard the desperation in her own voice.

'Dee, you have to forget it. Please stay away from this. Your professor's got some friends in very high places. If work even knew I've spoken to you I could lose my job. I have to go.'

'How can I get in touch with you?'

'You can't. Please, Dee, I can't do anything about this. No one can. Leave it alone.'

Marlena hung up.

58.

Dee drove home and parked outside the house. The children were with Rob. That felt safer. He wanted to know why they had to change their night but was okay when she said she couldn't tell him. Her heroic struggle to be civilised and accept his new life/wife had paid off.

Would she need to move them all to somewhere with proper security?

The house was completely dark, the glass walls opaque and reflecting the street. She was safe in the confined space of the car: the doors were locked; she could see all around, and she was in view of neighbours. Anyone could be lurking in the dark spaces of the house. Once she turned on the lights inside, her vision of the surrounds would be gone. She would be visible to anyone in the bush.

She looked around. There was no one about. No unknown cars were parked in the cul-de-sac. Nothing was out of order but the darkness spread out into horrible possibilities. It no longer felt safe to go home.

When the kids were home their noise and enthusiasm banished the blackness. She could ring them at Rob's. They'd think she was pathetic. She was pathetic.

Where was Raj? With him she was comfortable. He was the only person who knew about all this and who didn't think she was crazy. Once he read the emails he'd surely ring.

A night alone exposed by her transparent house was too much. She started the car and drove to work. She parked in her car space and waited till she saw a couple get out of their car. She walked up the stairs with them.

Once she was on the street it was busy, people talked, ate, lived, had ordinary lives while in her head she was in a thriller. Her anxiety seemed overwrought in the midst of normal life around her. Why would Adam do anything more to her when she was totally discredited?

She walked to Darling Harbour and checked into the Ibis Hotel because she knew it had secure lifts. The receptionist gave her an upgrade to an executive room with full-length glass windows overlooking the harbour and the city. The sheets were crisp and smooth. The smell and smoothness of freshly made white ironed linen was luxurious. After dinner she would have a bath, a full hot tub with jasmine bath salts.

It was silly to be frightened. She was hungry. She wouldn't let this stop her from having a life. She picked up her wallet and went downstairs. The hotel food was boring and expensive so she went next door to the pub for a bottle of Shaw and Smith Sauvignon Blanc then across the road for a bento box of prawn and vegetable tempura from the local Japanese. It was fine. No one sinister was following her.

*

Back at the hotel an Asian man in a suit got into the lift with her. He used his key card to go to floor seventeen. She got out there too. He turned left along the corridor while she walked slowly to the right. She glanced back. He was still walking; his room must be at the far end. She stood at a doorway without a light under it and opened her wallet as if to search for a key card. She didn't have to pretend to fumble with it, her hands were shaking.

It was ridiculous. The man had a key card for the lift. Why was her heart thumping? She heard a door close and looked again. He was gone.

She walked back to the lift. It was empty. She found her card and went up to twenty.

Back in the room she dimmed the lights and changed into the hotel's white robe. The city and the harbour were laid out for her. She ate without regard for crumbs or who would have to clean up. In the morning she could sleep in. There were no worries about traffic or what to wear.

In the bath she was half asleep in a cloud of scented steam. There was a knock at the door.

'Turndown service,' said a male voice with an Asian accent.

'Not tonight. I'm okay, thanks,' she called back.

Then she heard the door handle turn. She sat up. There was a wine glass on her chest. She moved it onto the floor and stood up. She stepped out of the bath and grabbed a towel.

The door to her room was open. Her thoughts sped up. The best move was to get out to the corridor and scream. But he must know where she was. She'd go along with it till she could see where he was and then run.

'Hey, I'm in the bath. Can you come back ...' Dee said loudly as she peeked into the room.

A small Asian man stood next to the bed. He was the same build and age as the man who had got into the lift with her but was in a hotel uniform. He looked startled.

'Sorry, sorry. Turndown service.' He held a Lindt Lindor Ball out towards her as evidence.

Dee had to get her breath back. She muttered, 'Okay, leave it and go,' and retreated to sit on the side of the bath.

'Sorry,' the man repeated as he left and closed the door.

Dee locked the door and put on the chain then opened it again and put her head out. There was a trolley parked opposite and the door three along was open. The same man came out of the room. She closed her door and chained it.

Nothing was disturbed. Her chocolate was on the bedside table. It was a pretty elaborate charade if someone was after her. She threw the chocolate in the bin. No need to be foolhardy.

Fried food and alcohol stunned her into a semblance of sleep. She woke at 3 am with her tongue stuck to the roof of her mouth. There was less than a third of a bottle of wine left. She'd have a hangover in the morning. She drank three glasses of water and cleaned her teeth. She needed to cut down. Once the medical board fuss was over she would do an alcohol-free month.

Her phone had ten percent battery. She checked her emails and messages: nothing from Marlena. That was as she expected, but there was still nothing from Raj.

The rest of the night she dozed, anxious, her thoughts tumbling over and over her fear for Leah, doubts about her own sanity, the shame once she was officially deemed crazy, and fear for her life. The lovely bed had become a place of torture.

Once it was light she got up and dressed. Her phone was flat. Reception charged it for her while she had a breakfast of coffee and fruit. She couldn't face the buffet.

The phone pinged as she went back up to the room. It was Raj. She sat on the bed that now looked as if a wildebeest migration had passed through overnight.

Dee, got your email. This stuff is awful. The police have to do something. Sorry for the delay. Abbi's improving so we're at the country house and the internet and phones are unreliable.

You should stay at my apartment. It's got secure entry and my security patrol monitor it. I told my PA to get an entry beeper and alarm codes sent over to you today. The security guys will be on alert. I've got someone watching the entries, the car park, the lifts and the stairwells 24/7.

This is dangerous. Be safe. Let me know what the police are doing.

I miss you.

Raj

Someone knew and believed her. She could have kissed the phone.

Beatrice had her driving test tomorrow. Rob had even agreed to pick up the car and get her there. Their lives went on. It wasn't fair to ask them to pack up their lives to camp out in Raj's two-bedroom flat. She might take up his offer herself though.

$$59.$$

Janelle buzzed. 'It's Beatrice. You need to take it,' she said and hung up.

It was 3.23. Beatrice wouldn't normally ask for her to be interrupted. Dee hoped she hadn't failed the test.

'Mum, did you have Telstra coming today?' Beatrice sounded tense.

'What do you mean? Are you okay?'

'I'm okay. Did you have Telstra coming today—at home?'

'No, why? What's going on.'

Beatrice started to cry. 'Mum, there was a guy in the house when I got home. He said he was from Telstra—I don't think he was.'

'Where are you? Why did you go home? Has he gone? What did he look like?'

'I'm next door, at Nola's. He's gone. Nola wants to ring the police.'

'Do that. I'll be there soon. Stay with Nola till I get there.'

The patient Dee was with worked out what was going on and told her he would come back tomorrow. She ran down the stairs to the car. The space was empty. Her car was gone. It took an anxious moment before she remembered Bea had it for the driving test. She hadn't even asked Beatrice how she went with the test.

She raced back upstairs out of breath.

'I tried to grab you before you ran out. The taxi will be here in a minute,' Janelle said.

'Thanks. I thought my car had been stolen. Sorry. Bea's okay but I should go.'

Janelle nodded.

The taxi pulled up and honked its horn. Dee ran out the front door. Janelle knocked on the car window as she buckled herself in.

'You might need this,' she said and opened the door to give her her handbag.

*

Nola made them tea while Bea told her story. She had driven home on her own with red P-plates proudly displayed on the front and back of the car. She didn't ring Dee in case she told her to go back to school. She was going to the supermarket to get something for dinner, a celebration dinner for her P-plates but she needed money and came home to get Dee's credit card.

There was a white van in front of the house, in their unofficial parking space. Everyone in the cul-de-sac was terribly polite about parking in front of their own place. The van obviously belonged to a tradie. Beatrice parked carefully in front of it. Etiquette said the van should be parked in front of the house he was working at.

Inside, Bea noticed the lounge room door was open. It was hot but they never left doors open. Dee was obsessive about closing doors and windows. She thought Eleanor or Ollie must have opened it before they left to go to Rob's.

Beatrice walked across the lounge, slid the door closed and turned towards the study.

As she turned, a movement caught her eye. A figure in black came out of the study. Her body jumped several inches into the air as she gasped involuntarily.

'Who—?' she started to say.

'Telstra. Just fixing the wi-fi,' the man interrupted. Beatrice said nothing but kept her eyes fixed on him as she stepped backwards towards the door. The man came towards her. Her first thought was to duck, to headbutt him in the balls but he pushed past her to the front door. He was gone before she had her breath back. Her memory was of dark overalls with a black cap pulled down to his eyes. His white hands were the only light thing about him—gloves, the white vinyl type.

In the seconds it took her to get to the front door, the van had turned around. The tyres screeched as it sped away. She could just make out the numberplate. It might have started with WX and ended in a 5?

Her hands were shaking but the man was gone. After tea and Nola's fruitcake, Dee and Beatrice inspected the house together. Nothing in the lounge was disturbed. In the study Dee's laptop was on and an external disc was connected to it via a USB port. Otherwise it looked as though no one had been there. The only thing Dee noticed was the bottom drawer of the filing cabinet was out by a few millimetres. It was prone to stick and she'd cut her shin on its sharp edge more than once. Now she always gave it an extra push in. Someone had looked through it.

She didn't touch anything. When the police came they would be able to find out what was going on with the computer. She switched off the wi-fi in case it was transmitting remotely.

'Mum, what's going on?'

60.

The police arrived at 8 pm: two plain clothes officers, a woman and a lumpen man. They flashed their badges at the door as they mumbled unintelligible names and ranks. As Dee showed them around, they scoffed at the locks on the veranda doors and told her she needed to install an alarm system.

Beatrice gave her statement. The woman took notes.

In the study, the man looked at the computer with the external hard drive attached, put on gloves and was about to pull it out.

'Hang on. The disc needs to be ejected first. There could be evidence lost if you do that,' Dee said as she reached towards his arm.

'Look, love.' Dee felt her hackles rise as he spoke. 'The only reason we're here is because it's a quiet night. No one is going to investigate a burglary in this area. The rate of solved B&Es is close to nil. If your daughter was injured it might be a different matter but she's okay. Don't get too excited. Be thankful nothing's gone and the place isn't wrecked.'

'Officer, thank you.' Dee made an effort to control her voice; to sound calm and reasonable. 'But this isn't a simple break-in. It's part of a bigger case; part of a murder being investigated by Glebe detectives. You can ring them. I have the number of one of the detectives on the case.'

He hesitated, confused about his next move.

Dee got out her phone and wrote down Marlena's number and put it into his hand.

'Okay, wait.' He went into the lounge and whispered into the ear of his mate. She stood up, went onto the veranda and made a call. The big lump still had Marlena's number in his hand. The woman spoke for a couple of minutes and then came back inside.

'Yes, Dr Flanary, Glebe Police confirm there was a case involving one of your patients but that is now closed.' The woman spoke slowly and deliberately as though to someone with little English or to a small child. 'We have your daughter's statement and fortunately she's unharmed.'

She probably spoke to Craig. Dee bit her tongue. Anything she said would only reinforce their view of her as crazy.

A little later, she walked the pair to the door. It was all over. There was no hope that they would investigate. The external drive was still in her computer. Raj would be able to tell what was on it and if anything had been transmitted. That was better than the police taking it and doing nothing.

'Love, you'll save yourself a lot of worry with an alarm system. Make sure the kids are safe, hey? I've got a couple of contacts who'll look after you if you mention my name,' the man said.

He was about to pat her on the shoulder. She scowled and moved out of reach. He handed Dee his card.

No one had been hurt. The break-in would have gone unnoticed if Bea hadn't come home unexpectedly.

With a chill Dee knew: Adam was still looking for something. They were all in danger—especially Leah.

If only the girl wasn't so hard to contact. What sort of a life could she have in the bush? Still, she was right about Adam being dangerous. It was wise to disappear. It was 9 pm. Dee looked up the number of Majors Creek pub. If she was lucky there would be customers and Misty would still be open.

'Eldrich Pub.' It was Joe.

'Joe, it's Dee. You remember, I'm a friend of Leah's.'

'How could I forget!' He sounded as though he'd had a few. There was the buzz of intoxicated chatter in the background.

'Do you know how she is?'

She heard footsteps. The background noises faded. Joe's voice came back.

'Funny you should ask. There's been an old couple here asking if we knew her. I didn't say anything but Misty might have given the game away when she told them to talk to me.'

Dee's stomach clenched. 'Who was it? What did they look like?'

'I told them she used to be here but she'd gone away. I said I'd let her know they were asking if she came back. Did I do the right thing?'

'I don't know. Sounds like they knew she was somewhere in the area already. Where are they now?'

'Don't know. They had a campervan. Probably camped in the bush somewhere.'

'Was it an old VW? Did the man have a limp?'

'Gee, sorry. I didn't take much notice. Could have been a VW, I suppose—don't know about a limp. One thing though, the bloke had these funny fingers, knobbly on the ends, like drumsticks.'

It had to be the couple who had followed her down the mountain. Could Adam have employed them to track Leah down?

'Leah could be in danger. Can you get word to her?'

Someone called out 'Joe' in the background.

'Okay, give me a minute, mate,' Joe said. 'Sorry, there's a biker booze-up on here. I'm glad you rang; I don't feel good about Leah all alone out there.'

'I thought she was staying with Jimmy?'

'Yeah, she was—'

He was interrupted by a chant of 'Beer, beer, beer!'

'Okay, I'm coming,' he shouted. 'Can I call you back after eleven when I've got rid of this rabble?'

There was no benign explanation for anyone enquiring for Leah. If Adam found her in the bush she could disappear without a trace, another missing person. An old couple didn't sound like Adam but Joe was young. Who knew what he considered old? Could the campervan couple be the ones who'd followed her?

She had to get to Leah before Adam did. The decision was made before she called Joe back. She would drive down tonight. Leah could stay at Raj's till they sorted something out. Beyond that, she didn't have a plan but if Adam got to Leah first any plan would be too late.

Her children had to be out of the way first though. They deserved an explanation of why their mother was so erratic lately. And they needed to understand the situation was dangerous. Adam wasn't going to give up. Dee sat the three of them down on the lounge.

'The break-in today wasn't a random burglary. One of my patients, Tom Harris, was murdered a while back and I think the killer is looking for information. Tom uncovered incriminating stuff about him.' Oliver waved his arms to interrupt but Dee shushed him. 'Let me tell you the rest first. I want you to concentrate, then questions.

'This killer is a man, slim, tall, around six foot two, dark hair and well dressed. He's in his early fifties. There's no reason for him to have any interest in you but he thinks I might have information. There's someone else in danger too—a young woman who is on her own down the coast. I'm going to warn her the killer is active again and find her somewhere safe to stay.'

Beatrice looked pale. 'So that bloke today could have been him?'

'I'm afraid so. But he had no reason to do anything to you and he didn't.'

Oliver was the most vocal. 'What about you though? Is he going to do something to you?'

'Probably not,' Dee said, determined not to lie to them. 'If anything happened to me it would make the police look at him again and he doesn't want that.'

She couldn't tell them that he had her under control by other means. To add that their mother was about to be deemed officially crazy was too much for one night.

It was hard to explain why the police were no use and how she knew all this but eventually her kids agreed to accept what she said. The example of the police inaction on the intruder backed up her argument.

'So you all need to pack enough for a few days at Dad's and Beatrice will drive you there after she's dropped me at the airport to pick up a hire car. You'll have the car if you need it for the weekend but you have to promise me not to come back here without Dad.

'Now, hippity hop, let's get moving. I want to leave in ten minutes.'

Everyone rallied for the emergency, no complaints from the children and even Rob, when she told him, was cooperative; probably too stunned to ask questions.

Part 3

61.

Joe kept driving down the mountain. Dee could smell salt on the breeze; they must be nearly at Moruya. If only she'd known, she could have started in Moruya instead of driving to the highlands and all the way down the mountain.

Soon after the road flattened out and the first cleared paddock appeared, he turned the bike into a narrow track off to the right and ascended again to a badlands of small rocky hills, a mini mountain range where the valley petered out.

The shed was on a rise so it was safe from flooding in the summer downpours. It was constructed of double-storey corrugated iron on three sides. The northern side was open. The iron roof looked sound and the concrete slab floor solid. Leah had assembled a partial wall of hay bales across the open area to protect the makeshift bed and table she'd made from wooden pallets. A cloud of eucalypt-scented smoke from a rough stone fireplace filled the rafters. It looked cosy and romantic but the nights would be long, cold and lonely.

Joe had dropped Dee at a creek about a kilometre away. The water was too deep for the bike. She'd followed instructions to keep the marshy low-lying ground to her right then follow the twisting track to a second creek crossing where she saw the smoke from the shed. It was difficult to walk and her city sandals were wrecked in the water. At least they stopped her slipping on the mossy rocks.

As she walked up to the shed, Leah ran down the open paddock in front to greet her. She grabbed Dee. Leah's ribs were sharp as Dee put her arms around her chest. How much weight could she lose without getting sick? The normally reserved girl clung to Dee as though to life itself. She pulled herself together and offered Dee tea.

The kitchen was made of milk crates stacked on top of each other and a board with a heavy rock on top of that.

'Possums,' Leah said as she moved the rock. Half-a-dozen glass storage jars sat along a horizontal section of the shed's wooden frame. One had rolled oats, there were a few lentils and the rest were empty—no fridge or running water. Leah tipped water from a plastic can balanced on the edge of the slab and balanced a saucepan of it in the fire. Two plates, two knives and forks and two mugs sat in an enamel bowl on the floor.

She pulled up a milk crate for Dee to sit on. The tea jar had one teabag, peppermint. Leah made tea for both of them from it.

'Sorry, no sugar. Joe'll get more provisions soon.'

'Leah, you can't live here. What happened to the other place?'

'Jimmy's on a bender. He found some gold-tops, you know, magic mushrooms,' she explained as though Dee hadn't been around in the seventies. 'It'll be all right in a couple of days. Anyway, Joe's been staying with me.'

Leah's voice was carefully neutral when she mentioned Joe.

'How's Joe been?'

'He's lonely, I think. Wants a girlfriend.'

'And you don't want a boyfriend?'

'No.' Leah's bottom lip trembled. 'It's okay when Jimmy's around. Joe's a good bloke and he's done a lot for me. I couldn't survive here without him. It's hard to make him understand that I don't want him ... or anyone, except Tom.' Leah looked down into the fire.

'You can't stay down here forever. This isn't a life. Look how much weight you've lost.' Dee took Leah's arm. It was bony, pale and as thin as a ten-year-old's.

Leah didn't reply nor move her arm away from Dee's touch. Just kept her fingers clasped around her mug and looked into the fire.

Dee sipped the tea. She looked over at Leah. After the terrified opening up when Dee arrived, Leah had closed down. As she released Leah's arm she feared the fragile creature beside her might slip away.

'It's not safe, he knows I know.' Leah didn't use Adam's name—didn't bring that evil into the space.

'But it's okay now. I found the other information Tom had about Professor Fairborn. There's a whole pattern of deaths around him. None of them officially murder but there are far too many to be coincidental. The police have all the evidence they need now. The information is out there already so there's no reason for the professor to come after you.'

Leah kept her eyes on the fire. She didn't say no.

'It's too dangerous for him to attack you. Why don't you come back with me? You can stay with us till you get somewhere. Why don't I ring Joe and get him to come back?'

'The only signal is from the top of that hill.' Leah pointed to a scrub-covered steep track starting from the east side of the paddock. 'It's about twenty minutes, just keep going up. You'll need boots.'

Leah took off her Blundstones. They were too small but without socks Dee squeezed them on. Her open sandals were wrecked from the creek.

'Tell him to bring the Jeep.'

*

Dee got to the top of the third rise and discovered another.

'Just keep going up,' Leah had said.

It was a long way. She checked her phone again. Fifteen minutes gone and still no signal. Now as she was facing east the shed was in the sun around to her left. From the hill she could see where Joe had dropped her. The track to the shed snaked around the base of the hill. From where she was it wasn't far if she went directly down.

The top of the hill finally came into view and she scrambled up the rocky last section of the track and collapsed breathing heavily at the top. The whole valley was laid out below. She could see why Leah had chosen it. There was only one way in and that was across two creeks. From the main road the shed was well hidden behind the hill Dee was now at the top of. Even the smoke from the fire dispersed before it could betray her presence from the road.

Joe didn't answer his mobile so she sent a message. He was unlikely to be in mobile range. She rang the pub landline.

Misty answered. Joe wasn't there but he'd be back soon. Dee wondered how sure Misty was and asked her to give him her message.

'We're ready and Leah wants to come too so he'll need to bring the Jeep.'

'You'll be right, darl. I'll let him know. He'll be there.'

'In the jeep?'

'Yeah, right, um—in the Jeep.'

Misty sounded like she had forgotten the details already. What was the chance she'd remember anything at all if Joe didn't arrive back soon? It wasn't reassuring. Dee didn't fancy another trek up this hill if he didn't come. She'd wait and try the pub again in twenty minutes.

62.

Dee settled in the only shade, a scrubby tea tree that grew out of the granite knob that formed the top of the hill. The sun was at an angle and the valley floor and shed were in shade. The grassy open area directly in front was lit in patches and the fence and gate glinted silver grey. The buzz of insects, sheep moving about and butting one another, the faint trickle of water from the creeks she had crossed, details she'd normally miss, filled time and space.

The valley was surprisingly noisy. This wasn't as isolated as the national park where she'd last seen Leah. Farmers had trucks and generators that could be heard from miles away. The road was about five kilometres off to the left and Dee heard an occasional car and the brakes of timber trucks as they wound down the mountain on the gravel road from the highlands to the coast. Crows' calls dominated the soundscape with a persistent 'Caw, caw'—sounds that were more drawn out and eerie as the shadows got longer.

As she waited, Dee opened Google maps and the blue dot showed her that she was right. The property was at the bottom of the mountain, only a few kilometres from where the road became bitumen. Maybe twenty to thirty minutes from Moruya.

The treetops shifted in the wind and the shadows changed. Different spots were highlighted as the angle of the sun changed. A dozen sheep moved into view in front of the shed. A pair of lambs played at headbutting each other and Dee saw Leah come out to watch them.

A foot from her left elbow there was scuttling in the grass. Dee jumped up. She couldn't see anything. Let it be a lizard. When she clomped about in the heavy boots the scuttle moved away. Snakes avoided people if they could, except for tigers or if they were protecting their young. Leah's shed with the woodpile and the bales of straw would be highly desirable accommodation for breeding snakes. It was dangerous out here. Dee had to get Tom's girlfriend back to her life.

The sun glinted off the second creek crossing and Dee was surprised to see a patch of uniform colour, a square of silver, at the edge of the track just past the last gate. She looked harder. It was a big four-wheel drive, parked off the track in the bushes. Was it Joe? It didn't look like a Jeep but from so far away it was impossible to tell. There wouldn't have been time for him to have received the message from Misty and get down the mountain though. Must have done it off his own bat. Funny place to park too. Why didn't he just drive up to the shed?

Dee didn't want to think who it could be if not Joe.

Leah stood at the front of the shed watching the bucolic scene. The vehicle couldn't be seen from where she was. The girl walked about thirty metres, looked around and then turned back towards the shed.

There was a flash of movement from the bush behind Leah. Dee wanted to yell but from this distance it was useless.

Suddenly Leah looked towards the trees behind the shed. The sheep startled and ran in the opposite direction. Then Leah started to run. A black-clad figure came into view only ten metres behind her. Dee was too far away to tell who it was. A tiny pang triggered in her heart. All dressed in black in the country—who else but Adam? It had to be him. Someone she'd had feelings for was a murderer. All those deaths—she shivered—how lucky she was to have escaped from their relationship alive.

Had Dee led him to Leah? There'd been no sound of a car. He must have been here already. The grey nomads were working for him—she had been right to be frightened when she was pursued down the mountain. It didn't make any difference now though.

Leah stumbled and Adam threw himself on top of her. She was face down; so thin and weak that she had no hope of shifting under his weight. Adam held both her arms as she scrabbled with her legs to get traction to turn over. He twisted till he sat on the small of her back as he held her arms stretched up towards her head. Several times he held both her hands with his left as he reached to his belt but her struggles forced him to use both hands again. Next time she struggled he punched her in the ribs, hard. Dee saw the fragile girl go limp.

Dee shouted. Her instinct was to run down the hill and pull him off. That was useless. Adam was strong and smart, there was no way she could deal with him alone. The police were her only hope. She had to stop him before he got away with Leah or the girl would never be seen again, a suicide, a runaway, a crazy girl who'd thrown herself over some cliff in these remote mountains. Nothing to do with the respected Professor Fairborn who would have his love-struck practice manager as an alibi.

Dee took a series of photos. You couldn't make out who the people were but it was clear something bad was going on. This time he got a roll of tape from his belt and wound it around her arms. Then he tore off a piece to cover her mouth. He tied her arms to the lower rail of the fence and went back to the shed.

He's looking for me, that gives us time, Dee told herself.

She rang 000. There were three rings before they answered.

'Police, Fire or Ambulance?'

'Police.'

'Police emergency service,' a young woman answered in a singsong voice.

'Please, there's a woman being abducted. I need police. I'm near Moruya. I'm not sure where.'

'Okay, slow down, I understand you've got an emergency, but first we need to know your name and where to find you.'

'I don't know where I am, somewhere up a hill near Moruya, I think. Can't you find me from the phone tower?'

'Settle down, first tell me your name.'

'Look,' Dee wanted to shout but tried to speak calmly, 'this is Dr Dee Flanary and a woman is going to die if you don't get someone out here.'

'D, is that your initial? You'll need to spell the name for me.'

'Listen, the property where I am is about five kilometres off the Araluen Road on the south side, the only building is a shed and there are two creek crossings on the track close to the shed. The turnoff is about 500 metres beyond the first cleared land at the bottom of the mountain. That's the best I can do with location. The local police might recognise where I am.'

Adam was nowhere in sight. Leah half stood, twisted and turned to free her arms at the fence.

'I didn't get the spelling of your name.'

'It's D-e-e F-l-a-n-a-r-y. Please just listen,' she said slowly and deliberately. 'I'm a doctor and I need police now. And an ambulance. This is not a hoax. Get someone here.' She hung up.

The recent case of a boy who had died in the Blue Mountains because triple-O had to have a street address was fresh in her mind. The passive aggressive nonsense from the operator was a waste of time she didn't have. The operator had the information, she needed to do something. It was either going to happen or not—probably not.

Marlena's mobile number went straight to voicemail. 'This is Dee. Adam Fairborn has Leah. We're near Moruya. He'll kill her if the police don't get here soon. Triple-O has the details recorded but I don't think they're going to do anything. I'll give Raj the details and he'll get back to you. I have to—'

The voicemail dropped out. The main message had gone through.

Raj had to be there. There was the noise of an international call then silence. At last the phone rang. He picked up straight away.

'Dee, where are you? The kids said you'd gone away. Are you—' His voice was panicky.

'Stop, Raj. I need you to listen. Adam has Leah. I haven't got much time. Once Adam gets away I'll be just another crazy menopausal woman accusing him. We're down the south coast. You have to get the police here.'

'Okay, keep talking. What should I do?' Raj's instant unconditional support was like a mother's embrace. There was hope.

'Try Marlena first, then the Moruya police. Marlena said if you use the words "concern for the welfare of ..." the police will take it seriously.'

'Okay,' Raj said. 'I need to know where you are. Take the phone and open the compass, I'll wait.'

He had a task and was focused, cool and deliberate. Dee tried to be the same. Her fingers trembled. She fumbled till she found the compass app. She reconnected the call.

'I need to get down to them.' Her voice was sharp.

'You've got the compass? Follow the instructions to calibrate it and then take a screenshot. It's got your latitude and longitude. Send it to me. And a photo of any landmarks.'

Dee took a slow breath. If Leah was to survive, Dee had to calm down. Her hands were clumsy as she rolled the phone to calibrate the compass. The concentration helped her into a zone where all that mattered was the most efficient way to rescue Leah.

'There's no mobile signal except at the top of this hill. I'll send you the photos and screenshot then I've got to get back down to delay him.'

'Dee, there's no use both of you being killed—'

She hung up. There was no time to talk about anything except rescuing Leah. If Adam got away the girl would be dead and no body would ever be found. Dee's pictures were too distant to identify him, and who knew what a clever defence barrister could do with evidence from someone under investigation by the medical board? The only chance for Leah was to get her away from him. Dee had to delay Adam until help arrived.

The screen shot of the compass, a shot of the valley and shed and the photo that best showed Adam dragging Leah by the hair went quickly by SMS. There were others of Adam and Leah together—evidence but low resolution, not enough to definitively prove it was him. Dee's brain had switched to emergency mode—narrowed focus, no emotion—the task to rescue Leah became a logical puzzle.

She had to choose. Keep the phone or risk Adam getting it off her.

The pictures were too far away. She had to get more. The phone could be useful as a distraction.

Dee had done all she could to get help. The rescue was up to Raj. There was no one she trusted more.

The quickest way down the hill came out near the second creek. Halfway down she saw Adam in the shed. He had her handbag in his hands and was sitting on the edge of the slab tipping it out beside him.

The rest of the way, Dee mostly slid on her bottom. In the glimpses she had of the shed and paddock, Adam wasn't in sight anymore.

'Keep on looking for me,' she urged.

63.

She was quiet through the creek and kept to the scrub on the side of the track. As she came up the rise, Adam had his full attention on Leah. Dee watched him detach Leah from the fence, grab her by her dreads and force her along the track towards the car. Their progress was slow as Leah stumbled and resisted but she was no match for Adam's strength.

Near the gate, Leah made a huge effort and twisted suddenly to knee Adam in the balls. The full weight of her skinny body wasn't enough. He stiffened but didn't let go of her hair. Another punch to the ribs. Dee saw the force as Leah was lifted off the ground. She must have broken ribs by now, possibly a punctured lung. A punch from the right was marginally less dangerous. A ruptured spleen was possible but less likely than a ruptured liver if he was left-handed. Dee stopped the medical analysis and made herself concentrate on what to do.

They were at the car. All Dee could do was hope Raj had got help while she delayed Adam's escape. If Adam knew she'd seen him with Leah he'd take the time to get her too. Or maybe not. She needed to get close enough to show him she had photos—dangle the bait to hold him here till help arrived. If help arrived? There were too many ifs to waste time on. The only hope was to act on the assumption that help was on its way.

The back doors of the big four-wheel drive were open. Dee could see it perfectly from the creek side of the gate. She waited till Adam bent down to tape Leah's feet.

'Adam, hello,' Dee said as he turned full face into the photo she took.

'Dee, what a pleasure. I hoped I might find both of you here. Lovely place, so peaceful and remote.' He was perfectly calm; didn't miss a beat.

'Might not be such a clear-cut outcome once they see these.' Dee held up the phone. 'I've got a few now.'

This time there was a pause. For a second Adam hesitated, blinked his eyes as if the scene in front of him was out of focus. But the smooth, in-charge professor took over again in a moment. A switch was thrown from sarcasm to concern.

'Dee, this doesn't have to happen like this. All I want is to talk. No one likes their reputation trashed by insane accusations. Once we're somewhere safe, I can untie Leah and we'll sort it all out. It's not a decent life for a young girl out here; and all for nothing.'

He started to move towards Dee but as his grip loosened, Leah bent her head down then jerked it back up. There was a sickening thud as the full force of her skull connected with the tip of his chin. He stumbled back against the open boot of the car. There was blood on his chin. Please let it be his not Leah's, Dee prayed.

'The police know about all the other deaths too,' Dee shouted but it was useless. Adam was totally focused on Leah. Dee fumbled with her phone and started to video the scene.

Leah tried to run but Adam's right hand was still tangled in her dreads.

'Enough. Stay still or I'll make you still!' he shouted.

Leah continued to struggle. Adam turned her around, changed hands on her hair and stepped back. He swung his right fist upwards and the uppercut connected with her chin. Leah's head jerked sharply back. Her eyes were half open but blank as she slumped against the back of the car.

Dee gasped as if she had felt the blow herself. She waited, breath held, for movement from Leah. There was none. Was she dead?

Adam hoisted her backwards into the car and slammed the doors closed onto her thighs. He used his weight against the almost closed doors to pin her inside. That gave him two hands free to tape her legs together.

Dee videoed it all. As he got Leah under control, Dee gradually moved in a circle till she was at the open gate. There wasn't much time. She was sure he was fitter than her and could run faster. She closed and latched the gate.

Adam pushed Leah's taped legs into the boot and closed the doors. He turned around and saw Dee on the other side of the gate. He stopped.

'Dee, it's okay, come and get in the car so we can get the girl to a hospital.'

His calm and reasonable tone sent a shiver through Dee. Only a monster could sound like that after what he had just done to Leah.

'You've probably killed her. This time you're not getting away with it. It's all on video.' Dee held up her phone.

Adam started to move towards her. Dee backtracked.

Adam stopped and held up his hands. 'It's okay, I'll stay here. Just listen. The child is psychotic. For her own sake,

I had to subdue her till we reached help. You should be thanking me. Look, once we get her safe I can help with the medical board. You've been under a lot of strain. Some time off and a counsellor for a few months and everything will be back to normal.'

'That's not going to wash anymore. I've got the video.' Dee waved the phone at him.

Adam hesitated then turned back to the car. Dee ran. In the time it took him to get through the gate she'd be at the first creek crossing. The water would slow him down but would it be long enough? All the photos in the world wouldn't bring Leah back to life once Adam got away with her in the boot. Dee had to believe that help was on its way.

She got across the creek easily in the Blundstones and clumped up the narrow mud slope between the steep sandy banks on the other side. The boots were full of water and left obvious deep muddy prints. The bush rose steeply to the right, up the hill to where she'd been. If she went back up she could check if help was on its way as well as send the video. At least then the world would know what had happened to her and Leah. Up the hill she'd be visible for some of the way. Adam was fitter, he'd easily catch up with her before she could get a message out.

If Leah was dead already she should save herself, get away as far as she could. The chances of Adam finding her in the bush were minimal.

But if Leah was alive Dee had to stall longer. Adam didn't need to hurt her. His complaint to the medical board was going to destroy her credibility. He thought there was no mobile coverage and would realise she hadn't got the video out yet. He didn't know about the pictures from the top of the hill or that help was—might be—on its way. The phone was the only thing that could be used against him. If she gave him hope he could catch her and get the incriminating evidence, he might hang around longer and help might arrive in time.

She took off the boots, dried her feet on her shirt and crossed to the other side of the path in bare feet as the four-wheel drive churned through the slippery round stones of the riverbed. At the top of the rise out of the creek crossing, Adam stopped. Dee could see him looking at her footprints. Her breath was loud in her ears; she opened her mouth to minimise the noise. Her heart thumped so loudly she was sure he'd hear it if he got close.

A dense thicket of she-oaks grew where the stream meandered through low ground to make a marsh. Joe had warned her not to deviate from the track even though the grassy cover looked solid in places. She shuffled under the low branches. The ground was covered in a cushion of the long soft needles of the she-oaks.

Adam opened the door and got out. He paused to look around then moved up the hill in the direction of her footprints. He disappeared quickly. Dee wriggled back under the low branches of she-oaks. She moved slowly to warn off any snakes, although Adam was more dangerous than any of the creatures in the bush.

Go on, go up, go after me. She willed him to pursue her as she calculated how far to let him get till she could get to Leah.

There was no sign of him further up the hill. This was a game to him. How long would he fall for her trick? She felt sure his eyes were scanning the bush right now. How close was he? How long would he wait?

She wanted to run to Leah—and do what? Yell through the door, smash a window and drag her out into the bush? None of those options would be any use. A rock would smash the car window but how would she move with or hide an unconscious body? Any noise would bring Adam right to them.

Keep your nerve, wait, she told herself. She slipped the phone out of her pocket and switched it to silent.

She scanned upwards. He could be up there waiting for her to move or he could have crossed back to her side of the track further round the hill and be creeping up behind her.

She needed him to be out in the open so she could keep a safe distance between them.

As she watched the hill she realised Adam could be anywhere. If he stepped carefully he could be only a few metres behind her before she noticed him. She slowly scrabbled across the ground till she was closer to the creek where he could not sneak up on her. In between sustained attention to the hill, and any birds that might be disturbed and break cover above the canopy, she tried to scan 360 degrees every minute or so. The bush was eerily still. No birds or scuttling small mammals or reptiles anywhere near. It was probably just her presence that had silenced the normal activity. Don't let it be Adam.

On the day she'd found Leah in the national park the girl had appeared as if from nowhere. She was no colour, a beige blankness that blended perfectly with the bush. Dee could do with some camouflage.

She-oaks grew in wet places, the edges of streams and marshes. Dee dug down under the bed of dry needles and found damp mud. It smelt of rotten egg gas but she rubbed it all over her arms, face and neck. She looked down at herself, the boots were already satisfactorily filthy. Her jeans were handy for the back of Joe's bike and sliding down the hill on her bottom but denim navy wasn't a bush colour. She scrabbled for more mud but the first hole was now just water. For a while she used her left hand till that was just water too. Slowly she wriggled backwards. Her T-shirt was beige, it needed patchy dirt to break up the uniformity. Her jacket had been pinched from Eleanor. A zippered hoodie in a light pinky-orange cotton knit. The wind protection of the zip and the hood to cover her hair were useful on the bike but in the bush it was totally high-vis. She quickly slipped it off and rubbed it with clods of thick blackish mud from close to the edge of the creek.

She had no idea how much time had passed. Her bottom was the only thing that wasn't muddy so she wiped her hands clean on it and slipped the phone out of her pocket.

Shit. She remembered her hair, bright red with a white streak. You could probably see it from outer space. She slathered more clods of smelly mud all over her hair too. Her Army Reserve training was coming back. A weapon would be good but for now she needed to rely on her wits and what she knew of her opponent. He was fit but it was gym fitness not bush fitness. Adam had no respect for her capacity to fight back. Both were flaws she could exploit. And he really hated to get dirty.

It was fourteen minutes since the last message to Raj. No chance of help yet.

She opened the hoodie and used her teeth to tear off a pocket from the inside. She tore off some smaller shreds of fabric and stuffed them into her jeans. She broke off small branches and stuck them through her hair and into her top. *Monty Python and the Holy Grail* popped into her head. She didn't want to be the knight who thought he could fight on after all his limbs were cut off. No, she was disguised as a 'shrubbery'.

She looked at the phone again but she couldn't remember what time it had shown before. She went back to the message time. Another five minutes gone. Her brain was on overdrive and she couldn't trust it to judge how long had passed. She turned down the light on the phone and started the stopwatch. They had to be somewhere between twenty to forty minutes from Moruya. No chance of help for another ten minutes at the earliest. She silently willed Leah to keep breathing.

In a short time, a minute or possibly seconds, three crows rose cawing loudly from about a third of the way to the summit. It had to be Adam. Let it be Adam. She needed to know for sure. If he was up the hill she had a good five or ten minutes till he got back. There were some small rocks in the mud. They were the only things she could fling any distance. She found one she could throw. She tossed it at a hollow tree trunk across the creek. No reaction. Further away on her side of the creek she'd spied some blue objects gathered together, a bowerbird nest. Hopefully the nest owner was waiting for a female to be attracted by his display. This time she chose a bigger rock and lobbed it right into the middle of the blue collection. The male came out fighting, wings extended, feathers fluffed and screeched blue murder. That was enough. If Adam was close she would hear him move.

Dee counted to sixty, probably around thirty seconds. No Adam, so she got up and went to the creek where she stepped carefully across leaving a trail of muddy footprints from her boots on the other side. She laid her trail of a torn fragment of orange hoodie and some broken branches. Her heart was thudding. It must be strong or she'd have dropped dead of a heart attack by now.

She told herself to pay attention. She couldn't afford to waste a second.

She let her bright red phone case slide down the slope above the creek so it came to rest on a rocky ledge out of reach of the path and of the creek. The cover landed on its side. From above you couldn't tell it was empty but from below you could possibly see it was just a cover. If Adam wanted it he'd have to scramble down the mossy bank and hopefully fall into the sucking mud. Dee broke off a sapling and managed to reach far enough to push the cover back from the edge. There was no way to tell now if it was only the cover or the real thing.

No time to dry her shoes again so she walked backwards, carefully putting each foot on a previous footprint. It was good; it made the prints look fresher. She needed to be quick. She snuck back under the low branches just as there was a noise above the car. Adam crashed through the spindly undergrowth of juvenile gum trees. He stood on the track in front of the car about 100 metres from her and scanned the bush. His eyes passed right past her without a flicker. Apparently he didn't see her but who knew how that machine brain of his worked. Maybe he had seen her? He started to walk into the bush at a slight angle to where she was. He'd pass within a few metres of her. If he had seen her she'd be too close to escape when he pounced. Her legs twitched with the need to run. It was almost impossible to lie still with him so close. She had to hold her nerve and hope he'd see the fragment of hoodie.

His hair was ruffled, and there was dirt on his trousers. Dee had never seen him with a hair out of place before. He stopped just five metres away. His back was to her.

'Dee, this is silly. If you want Leah to get help we have to hurry, come on out. You know it's the only way.'

The idiot was looking right at the creek and a torn patch of her jacket. Dee waited, she took tiny breaths to keep quiet.

Look, look! she urged silently.

Adam walked a few metres on; too close to the bowerbird's exclusive domain. The brave bird charged him. Adam jumped but recovered quickly. He looked around and spied the orange patch. He walked to the creek but hesitated at the edge, dirt and mud were not his style.

'Dee, you know this is going nowhere. Leah needs medical attention. Is her life worth these idiotic games? Come out and we'll go straight to the hospital.'

Just look harder, she mouthed.

Adam reached down and undid his shoelaces and put his socks and shoes neatly together. Then he undid his pants, stepped out of them, folded them neatly and sat them on top of the shoes.

Yes, yes, you idiot. Bare feet would give him no grip. He was in the water, up to his ankles, slipping on the mossy rocks. He almost fell before he took the sensible course and followed Dee's footprints across the larger rocks that were mostly out of the water. He scrabbled to get up the bank and walked the few yards to the torn orange patch.

He squatted and looked down. Yes! He must see the muddy handprints she'd made on the rock above the phone case. He had to guess she'd leant down to try to retrieve the phone. Even if he was suspicious he couldn't afford to ignore it. If he had the phone all his troubles were over.

Adam stood and walked away along the path. Dee's heart sank. Was he blind or so focused on her that he would leave the phone? She calculated the distance to the car. Would the keys be in the ignition or his pants? Neither scenario fitted but he hadn't taken them out of the trouser pocket when he took them off.

She was about to make a run for the car when Adam reappeared on the track above the creek. He had a long straight gum branch in his hand. He lay down on the rock and used the branch to try to pull the phone case up. Maybe he was onto her and wanted to see if it was the phone or only the case. The branch wasn't quite long enough and he wriggled further out over the rock. This time he seemed to have connected and pulled the branch back up towards him. It was almost right up, near his other hand when something red clattered down the slope into the creek. Dee heard Adam mutter an expletive. He never swore.

She checked the time—another eighteen minutes. That made thirty-two minutes since Raj called for help. Were the police on their way? Leah's brain could be compressed from a haemorrhage. The lower part of the brain, the part that controlled the vital functions, would be squashed down through the hole for the spinal cord at the base of the skull. As the delicate tissue was compressed Leah's heartbeat would fail, her breathing falter then stop. Every minute counted. The girl needed medical attention. Dee had to make sure Leah was still alive when help arrived.

Adam had retraced his steps, this time across the higher, safer rocks. He looked upstream. It was about ten metres to where the phone case had fallen, across large slippery boulders and some dark pools. It was impossible to tell how deep they were.

He jumped in. For the first few metres the rocks on her side of the bank blocked his line of sight. Dee moved quickly. She was tempted to check his trousers. She hadn't seen him take the keys out of the pockets. But she knew him. He wouldn't leave them. It was too risky. It could even be a trap to get her out in the open.

Once he saw the empty case he'd be back. As he walked up from the creek bed he would be eye level with her hiding spot. She needed to be ahead of him. The rational thing for him to do was to get rid of Leah and then organise help to deal with her and the video.

The only place to stop him was the next creek crossing.

The boulders blocked Adam's view and the water cascading between them was noisy enough, Dee hoped, so he couldn't hear her. Her body was stiff as she wriggled out of hiding. The boots were stiff too but had stretched a little across the toes. Her instinct was to run to Leah. Instead she ran to the track, too scared to look back. Her footsteps sounded thunderous. At the bend she snuck a look. There was no sign Adam was out of the creek. Relieved, she sucked in desperate lungfuls of air. Her breathing wouldn't be heard over the sounds of the water. But she was uneasy, the picture in her head was wrong, she looked again—where were his shoes and trousers?

Suddenly her left leg was gone from under her. She fell face first onto the edge of the track. Her foot was held fast. Adam was below her using her ankle as leverage to pull himself up the short steep bank of the road. His grip was steel. This was it, if Adam got hold of her she was dead. A sudden force of hatred filled her, how dare this murderous iceman touch her again. Her brain was instantly clear—be quick, get him while he's off balance. She shot her right boot out in his direction and connected hard with something flat. Simultaneously she grabbed handfuls of pebbles and dirt. The grip on her ankle was gone. She used the force of her kick to turn herself over and jump up to her feet.

Adam was on his back two metres below her, one hand scrabbling to get upright and the other palpating his bloodied nose.

'Never, ever, touch me again,' Dee screamed at him as she flung a sharp rock right into the middle of his forehead. He stopped and looked up. She threw the rest of the dirt and pebbles in his face then ran for the creek faster than she had ever run in her life.

*

At the crossing she went slightly upstream, hid behind a rock and stopped to catch her breath. Her hands were shaking. As she gulped air, she shook her head in wonder at how she had managed to get away. Keep going, she reminded herself. Adam wouldn't be far behind her and she doubted if she could summon the adrenaline to fight him off a second time.

She scrambled up the bank under the cover of shrubs without leaving obvious footprints. Fifty metres on and she was now on the coast side of the hill. There was a vibration in her pocket. A message from Raj: 'Help on way'. She held the phone up at all angles. The signal was gone. The main road was within view. The distance was a kilometre or more and was all paddocks, open country with straw-coloured grass that offered no shelter or camouflage. If she went towards the main road she'd get reception but also be a sitting duck for Adam once he got past the second crossing. He'd be gone before help arrived. Leah would never be seen again. It all depended on how long it took him to recover from her attack. No, she couldn't risk open ground.

She found a spot in a grove of gum saplings about fifty metres upstream from the crossing.

The sound of the four-wheel drive came first then she saw it approach slowly, very slowly. Adam's rage at being beaten would fuel his need to get her; would drive him to make mistakes. Perhaps his slow speed was to keep down the noise of the engine or to look for footprints. There was still a chance; she had to wait till he was in the right spot.

The big four-wheel drive bumped down the side of the creek. This was the more challenging crossing. The bed of the creek was made of round river stones slippery with moss. It was more than five metres wide and deep enough to reach the car doors. Adam would hate to get his shoes wet.

As soon as he was into the tricky bit of the crossing Dee jumped out and waved the phone.

'Stop!' she shouted.

Adam didn't see her in the shadows. She screamed at him but he drove on. He'd be across in a minute. Dee pushed at the big flat rock beside her. It was too heavy to topple to make a splash. She had to make him notice her. She tucked the phone into her bra and squatted down close to the water. She hit the surface as hard as she could with the full length of both arms and hands to make a splash. It was a risk—the phone was her only evidence. She couldn't get it wet.

Adam turned his head. He'd seen the splash. Dee stood up and waved the phone. He stopped. She didn't have long before he would come after her. She relied on him to not get out straight away in the middle of the stream. Sure enough, he hesitated. When he accelerated to drive out of the water the car shuddered, and he accelerated more. The tyres dug deeper. Dee moved upstream. There was a pause and she heard the engine tone lower. He'd worked out to engage the lowest gears. The sound of the engine became a high-pitched whine as the tyres dug deeper down into the smooth round river pebbles.

Once again, Dee had a choice, go uphill or across open ground. Uphill, Adam had the advantage because of his fitness but she'd also find more reliable phone reception. She turned upwards and was fifty metres up when the engine shriek stopped. In another few seconds she heard the car door. She hoped he'd taken his shoes off. Bare feet would make the mossy rocks more difficult. With luck he'd fall; maybe break an ankle.

A long stretch of main road was visible from the side of the hill. She saw a disturbance in the air, a plume of dust coming up the valley. She prayed it was the police.

Light was low on this side of the hill. She could see the elongated shadows of the fence in the paddocks between her and the main road. In another half-hour the sun would be gone completely. A night in the bush would be dangerous, Leah would die of her injuries or Adam would finish her off, hide the body in the bush. Please let it be the police.

She kept running. Her phone buzzed in her bra. Reception. She stopped in a dense thicket of low scrub with saplings above her head and pulled it out. It was slightly damp, perhaps she'd gotten it wet in the stream. Her top was dry, it must just be perspiration. She pressed the button and it woke; she almost cried with relief till she noticed the battery was down to five percent. The video was the last thing she'd taken. She pressed share and then Raj's email. As she pressed send she caught a sound below her. She froze. It was close, too close. She pressed the phone with its light against her chest. She allowed her eyes to move. She couldn't see him so he hadn't seen her, she hoped. Quietly, with her breath held she lowered herself back under the bushes.

Adam appeared on the kangaroo trail going up to the open grass at the top of the hill. He was just ten metres away. He stopped and scanned. Dee was rigid. His eyes passed straight over her wedged between a boulder and a sarsaparilla vine.

The sound of sirens was suddenly loud. A police paddy wagon and an ambulance were at the gate off the main road. Adam must be able to see them from where he was. He turned and went back the way he came picking his way carefully on bare feet. Once he was out of sight, Dee considered what to do. She didn't trust him. He could be waiting down the path. She had to wait till the police were at the creek.

She shuffled backward towards the gully above the creek. Adam wouldn't walk there with his tender feet. A large boulder overhung the water. Dee slithered over it and then, in a partially controlled slide, she moved down about five feet. As she stood up she slipped and went down further. She couldn't get the phone wet. She flailed with her left arm, grabbed a bunch of fern. Her fall slowed. She got her boots into a groove. Her footing held.

The crossing was thirty metres away. The police and ambulance were at the open back doors of the four-wheel drive. Adam splashed across to them.

64.

'I'm a doctor,' he called out. The paramedics were intent on their task. They ignored him. This was their turf. They were the experts at on-the-scene resuscitation.

Adam started to argue with them. A police sergeant came out into the creek to intervene. Dee splashed and stumbled down the creek. They all looked up at her.

'Thank God. Dee, you're okay,' said Adam.

He turned to the policeman and spoke in a low voice. She caught the words 'careful' and 'dangerous'. The sergeant, an older man with a red face, nodded and called to a young constable at the edge of the stream.

'Help the lady out of the water, son; sit her in the van. Careful.'

The boy in his perfect uniform picked his way over to her and took her filthy arm. Dee realised she was exhausted. As soon as she was at the bank she collapsed flat out on her back. The young man wanted her to move, to get into the car. She pulled out the phone from the bra and handed it to him.

'That's evidence, keep it safe,' she said. He took the sweaty phone between two fingers. 'Careful!' Dee said more sharply than she intended but he took it to the car and put it in an evidence bag.

'Lock the car,' she shouted at him. He clicked the key. 'Now I need to talk to the sergeant.'

The constable did what she asked. Dee sat up, moved to the edge of the stream and leaned down to wash the mud off her face.

The young policeman came back with the sergeant and Adam. Dee was sitting with her feet in a pool at the edge of the track. She bent forward to splash the cool clean water over her scratched, filthy face. Her hair was still full of dried mud but she figured it wouldn't get clean without full immersion. Better dried dirt than wet mud streaming down her face.

The three men bent over her with concerned looks. The constable had his hand on his gun.

'This man abducted and assaulted the woman in the car. He's dangerous. You have to protect her from him. If you let him near her he'll finish her off so she can't give evidence against him.'

'Dee, settle down. We'll get you to help. The paramedics can get you some medication,' Adam said with a tone of concern. He turned his head to the constable, 'Tell them to draw up an injection of Midazolam, or whatever sedation they carry. Maximum dose—she's psychotic and quite large. I'll give it to her IV. She'll be calmer and it's safer for everyone if she's sedated.'

'This is not how it seems,' Dee protested as the young man set off towards the stranded car where the ambos were still working on Leah. At least that meant she was alive.

'Constable, stay here,' the sergeant said. 'Professor, nothing's happening till I get a story from this woman and from you. You're not in charge here.'

Adam went quiet. His choices were between righteous indignation with threats or flattery and cooperation—the rational alternative to her mad woman covered in mud and detritus. He could still discredit her if Leah died or had amnesia due to the head injury.

'Certainly, Senior Sergeant Windsor. Any assistance I can offer is at your service. This woman has serious psychiatric problems although she can appear to be rational at times. She's currently under investigation by the Medical Council of NSW for her paranoid accusations about other doctors. Her psychiatrist is Professor Jamison. I might be able to get in touch with him for you. I've been trying to help her—I know the history if that's any use to you.'

He'd decided on rational. Dee was tempted to point two fingers at her mouth and mime vomiting. No, she couldn't give them any excuse to sedate her. The sergeant let Adam talk on; his face neutral as he waited for Adam to conclude. Adam had no idea how to talk to people without pompous authority. It usually worked. The sergeant was old school, probably from a farming family; pomposity was the wrong approach.

'Thank you, Professor, will you wait with Constable Martin?' He pointed to the car. 'Over there, please.'

'Don't let him get the near the phone,' Dee blurted. 'My phone, I mean. I recorded the attack.'

'First, your name?' the sergeant asked.

'I'm Dee Flanary. I'm a GP in Sydney.' Dee tried to keep her voice calm as Adam and the constable got closer to the police paddy wagon. 'Please, the phone is the only evidence. It's in your car.'

Sergeant Wilson sighed and called out to his young colleague. 'Where's this phone?'

'In the wagon. In an evidence bag.'

'Okay, wait there and keep the car locked.'

The constable reached his hand towards the door handle.

'With you and the professor on the outside,' he said with raised eyebrows and a muttered last word that could have been 'idiot'.

When he was satisfied the constable understood, he turned back to Dee. 'Dr Flanary, can you tell me what's happened here?'

'It's a complicated story.' Dee paused to collect her thoughts. She had to get them to look at the video. 'The main thing is that Adam Fairborn attacked and abducted Leah Dragic and I have a video of it on my phone. If you look at that it will all be clear.'

'Come on then, let's look at the video.'

The sergeant took her elbow as they walked to the paddy wagon. Dee resisted the urge to shake his hand off her arm. He meant it kindly but it felt like a restraint.

'Take him back and get his things out of the car,' he said to the constable. 'And you keep them, not him. Professor, in this situation the protocol is to treat you both as suspects. You'll understand the need for proper procedure.'

A moment of calculation flickered across Adam's face before he said, 'Of course, that's what I'd expect.'

The constable walked down the track. Adam stayed where he was. The sergeant gave him a quizzical look. 'I'm happy to wait here while he gets the things from the car.'

'I'll ask you to go with the constable, sir.' The sergeant's voice was polite but there was steel underneath.

Dee started to hope.

In the car, Dee sat next to the sergeant as he pulled on gloves and removed the phone from its moist clip-lock bag. He pressed the bottom button. There was no response.

'Try the restart button.' Dee's heart was racing. She tried to sound calm, rational. 'The battery was low. Sometimes it turns itself off.'

The blank black screen persisted. The phone could be flat or dead from moisture. Hopefully the video had gone to Raj's email. Adam could still get out of this and Dee could be in prison for murder.

'Please, it is there. I sent a copy to a friend, you can ring him—' She stopped. '—when we get to somewhere with reception.'

She knew how pathetic she must sound. The policeman just sat there. Adam was on his way back in his perfect black shoes. His legs must be wet but somehow he looked dry. The constable was sopping wet to the knees.

Dee shivered. There were only two seats in the front of the car. Where were they going to ride? They couldn't put her in the back of the van with Adam for the ride back to Moruya. She would be dead by the time they arrived.

'You can't let him near me.' She shivered involuntarily and felt tears well up in her eyes.

The adrenaline was gone and she thought about all that had happened. What had she done? Leah was unconscious, possibly fatally injured or permanently brain damaged. Dee was terrified of what Adam could do if they were together in the back of the paddy wagon.

The older policeman looked at her and put his hand over hers on her knee. 'It's okay, you can ride up here. Until we get this sorted out, though, both of you will have to be in handcuffs.'

'That's good,' Dee said with relief. 'Adam is ruthless and now he's in a corner, more dangerous than you can imagine. Please, I need to know. Is Leah okay?'

'The paramedics have stabilised her. She's not conscious at the moment. They're worried about internal injuries.'

'Tell them she's had punches to the ribs over both her spleen and her liver and a major blow to the head.'

She wanted to tell him the story of multiple suspicious deaths—there was no doubt in her mind that they were murders—in Adam's past but she couldn't afford to come across as a crazy with paranoid obsessions about Adam. Better to stick to the current situation.

Adam and the constable were a couple of metres from the police wagon. Dee shivered more; her teeth chattered. Was it possible to be retrospectively traumatised? This man, this serial killer, had once been her lover. To be near him was to be in a twisted parallel universe where horror came with a smile and perfect white teeth.

'Where will the constable ride? You can't put him in with Adam, please—if he got the gun or got the handcuffs around his neck.' Dee knew her voice was shaky and that was fine. It got the message across.

'Dr Flanary, I think you've been watching too many movies.' Dee started to protest but he held up a hand. 'Stay calm, there's a squad car coming from Batemans Bay. They'll be here soon. You can ride with them and the professor will be in the back, on his own, with us.'

'And the video?'

'When I have everyone safe and secure.'

65.

The paramedics overtook the two police vehicles with the ambulance's siren blazing not far from the last gate.

'Don't die.' Dee prayed. She was a non-believer but when the universe threw too much all at once she indulged her need to believe there was an omnipotent being in charge. But if there was someone in charge why hadn't He helped Tom? The force of good wishes wouldn't save Tom's girlfriend either. Leah was tough. That and chance were all that worked. Dee would bet on Leah's survival.

The police station at Moruya was an original stone house from the 1800s surrounded by wide verandas. Inside it was a hodgepodge of small rooms painted institutional colours. Most of the walls were covered with notices, faded and curled with age.

The constable gave her a blanket and sat her in a window-less room on her own. There were three chairs, a table and a plastic bottle of water. The door was locked. She was still filthy. No shower was allowed till the crime scene investigation officers from Batemans Bay arrived to deal with her.

Dee was exhausted and lay her head on the table in front of her. It seemed a short time till the door opened. She might have fallen asleep.

The sergeant came in and sat opposite her at the table. 'Good news, Dr Flanary. We have the video. Professor Fairborn is under arrest.'

Dee's relief was quickly followed by fear. Why hadn't he mentioned Leah? Did that mean there was no good news about her?

'And Leah?' Dee held her breath for the answer.

'I understand she's partially conscious.'

'Ahhh' the sound was involuntary. Tears started to gather in her eyes. The sergeant looked down at Dee's hands. They were trembling.

'It's okay, you're safe now. Can we get you a tea? Milk?' Dee nodded. 'Sugar?' Dee shook her head for no.

A young policewoman she hadn't seen before came in with tea and a sliced egg sandwich on white bread. It was the most delicious thing Dee had ever eaten.

Sergeant Wilson took her statement of what happened. The crime scene investigators took specimens of her DNA, photographs of numerous cuts and scratches and then gave her paper overalls to put on when, eventually, they said she could have a shower.

Dee stood up and had to grab onto the table until she stabilised her legs.

'This way,' the female officer said and took her elbow.

The station was bigger than Dee had realised. The main room had an observation desk opposite a row of three reinforced-glass cubicles with blue steel frames and heavy-duty bolt and padlock closures.

The middle one held Adam. He sat upright on a stainless steel bench. His eyes stared into the middle distance as though he were deep in important thoughts. He ignored Dee's presence.

Dee moved her arm away from the officer and stood up straight. She paused to look at Adam as a prisoner. He was still dressed in black and somehow his clothes were largely free of dirt. His nose was grossly swollen and a square of gauze was stuck to his chin with dried blood.

'What's happening with him?' Dee asked.

'Nothing, until his solicitor flies in from Sydney—by helicopter apparently.'

'What about his face, doesn't he need treatment?'

'Said he "doesn't want amateurs" to touch him. Says he'll wait until he's back in Sydney for a plastic surgeon. We've explained that could be a long time. I don't think the reality of his situation has sunk in.'

Dee was aware the strength had come back to her legs. Her hands were steady again. The image of Adam's broken face, the tiny cell and his ridiculous attempt at dignity would keep her strong.

66.

Dee was woken by a knock. It was daylight. Half asleep, she wrapped herself in a towel and opened the door to see Rob and a scrum of media, cameras and microphones. Shouts of 'Dee' and 'Doctor', 'over here' and 'how are you' drowned out Rob. She pulled him inside.

'Oh Dee, Dee, how are you?' Rob said as he put his arms around her. 'Everyone's been frantic, you could have been killed.'

She shrugged him off. 'Any chance of a coffee? I need to pee.'

She emerged from the bathroom dressed in the paper jumpsuit to an instant coffee and a worried-looking Rob.

'How did you know?'

'You're the top news story everywhere.'

He turned on the TV to show a photo of her in filthy, torn clothes and hair full of mud and twigs from outside the police station. The photo was blurry and fortunately didn't show her face clearly. A second later they saw Rob knocking on the door then Dee, dressed only in a towel, pull him inside. Some reporter was 'Live from Moruya' outside the motel.

Dee switched off the TV. Rob put the *Daily Telegraph* on the coffee table. The whole front page was occupied by the headline 'Plucky Mum of Three Fights Off Gene Genius' and the awful photo of her.

'Put that away. Let's get out of here. Did you bring clothes?'

This needed to be over. The rest of her life was waiting.

*

Joe drove them back to Dee's hire car at the pub. He managed to lose the press.

Dee ignored Rob's protests and drove them home. He was a hopeless driver. It was sweet of him to come down but his concern, his attempts to protect her, were oppressive.

It was good to have time alone together to talk though. There was an idea she had been mulling over for some time. The drive home was the perfect opportunity to put the proposal to him. He said he'd have to ask Stephanie but it was an ideal solution for all of them. She knew they would agree.

67.

Once Adam's bail was formally refused, the reporters decamped from outside the Glasshouse and the surgery. Dee's life was normal again. Normal apart from spending part of every consultation on her adventure. Dee's hero status and the terrible photo of her outside Moruya police station were revived each time the case came up for mention in the courts.

Leah was in long-term rehab for her damaged legs. Her brain had escaped major injury.

Skye avoided any mention of Tom or what had happened to Leah, and Dee couldn't bring herself to ask how she was coping. At least she was kept busy with Charlie.

Glen was Glen. He had apologised and thanked Dee for not having him charged. His promise to 'stay away from the heavy stuff' sounded as though he would try. He appeared to care for Skye, and was able to tolerate Charlie. Those things were important. Perhaps when the insurance money came through life would be easier for them.

Marlena kept Dee updated about the legal processes. Adam's legal team had organised a plea bargain. There was to be no further investigation of the other deaths. According to Marlena, any connection to Adam was circumstantial and many of the cases were too old or happened outside Australian jurisdiction.

Dee tried to argue for police to examine practices at GenSafe IVF.

'It's not going to happen.' Marlena was emphatic. 'Nothing you've told us about is even recognised in the law—it can't be illegal if it's not recognised. We want to get this guy but if we go after everything we could lose out completely. This way he gets six to eight years jail time, his reputation is trashed and his career is over. It's the best we've got.'

A week after Adam was remanded in custody another of the scary brown letters 'To be opened by the addressee only' was there on the hall table.

> *The Medical Board has postponed its enquiry into the complaint against Dr Dee Flanary until a related matter in the criminal court is resolved. Her right to practice is currently unrestricted.*

Her case had been put on hold till the outcome of the case against Adam. There was no apology, no mention of Adam as the person who had criminal charges against him. A naive reader of the letter could reasonably interpret that the criminal matter was against Dee. The phrase 'currently unrestricted' was hardly reassuring. The qualification suggested the imminent possibility of a restriction.

At first, she was relieved. No one knew and no one had to know. But she had done nothing wrong. Why didn't she want them to know? Why was she ashamed?

Raj was back. Dee hadn't seen him. Tonight he was bringing pizza. Thanks goodness for Raj.

She should tell him. Of everyone, he was the most likely to understand. She knew though that she wouldn't.

68.

Wednesday afternoon was now Dee's afternoon off. A regular afternoon off was the first change she'd made since 'the incident'. The second was the one she was about to reveal to the children now.

She parked in the street parallel to the 'surprise'. She wanted them to come upon the house on foot. Once they were out of the car Beatrice, Oliver and Eleanor kept up a chant of 'Is it this one?' and 'Oh no, not that' with twisted faces and disapproving voices.

The streets of this part of Glebe were wide and quiet, lined with untidy peppercorn trees with their fine, soft green leaves and aromatic pink berries. The berries crunched underfoot on the white gravel pavements. The area felt like a country town with streets of single-storey terrace houses all painted the same heritage colours of cream and oxblood. A big parcel of the suburb had been an estate owned by the Anglican church so the houses from the early days of the colony of New South Wales were preserved essentially unchanged.

Around the block they saw a sold sign on the front of the corner house. It was basically the same as all the others in the street but the corner position meant more windows and light.

'Blah, it's this one,' the three of them said together, still with negativity in their voices.

Their father had let the cat out of the bag a couple of weeks ago about buying back the Glasshouse. So far Dee had resisted pressure to say where they would be moving to. The three children had wildly different views about what they wanted. Dee knew there was no resolution that would keep all of them happy so she made the decision herself. This way no one got their own way and Dee wasn't siding with one against the others. They could move in with Rob and Stephanie if they wanted. They'd be grown up soon, it was time to think of what she wanted once they were gone.

There was a small front garden with weeds, an old lemon tree and a broken terrazzo front veranda. She got through the two locks on the front door and opened it onto a long dark hall. It was about ten degrees cooler inside and smelt of damp with a whiff of tomcat. Ollie went straight through to the end where the hall opened into a large combined kitchen, dining room and lounge. Big French doors opened onto an overgrown garden that sloped down gently to reveal the tips of the city skyline in the distance.

Beatrice and Eleanor came down the hallway with glowering looks. Eleanor had the beginnings of tears in her eyes and stayed quiet but Beatrice gave Dee a blast.

'There's only two bedrooms! In case you haven't noticed you've got three children.'

Oliver ran back along the hall. 'Yeah, Mum, two bedrooms. Is there a hidden dungeon?' He sounded resentful.

Dee felt guilty. She thought the surprise might minimise their distress but knew there was no way she could sell it to them without provoking some conflict.

'Everybody calm down. There's more!' She took Ellie by the hand and put her arm around her shoulder. 'Follow me.'

Dee went out into the garden and unlocked a partly over-grown gate in the fence. They ducked under the morning glory vine into next door. This house was original and unrenovated with rough brick paving and a short passage past a laundry and shower/toilet to a coloured glass back door. Dee unlocked the door with a big old-fashioned key.

The kitchen had a green enamel stove and floral linoleum that looked unchanged from the 1940s. Ollie pushed past them all through to the hallway.

'Yep, three bedrooms. No bathroom though and it's freezing cold. You can hardly see in here.'

Once they had all looked over the place, Dee took charge and herded them back to the first house. Out of the dark and in the warmth of the sun, she sat them down in a line on the edge of the terrace as it stepped down to the garden. She squeezed in between Ollie and Eleanor.

'You want me to explain?' Dee asked.

They hadn't forgiven her yet but Ellie, with her knee pressed up against Dee's, whispered, 'Yes.' The others nodded.

'I'm sorry, I thought it would be a nice surprise.' That wasn't entirely true but Dee couldn't think of another way to tell them. 'Anyway, you must have worked it out. I've bought both houses, and with the money left over we can afford to fix up next door for the three of you to have as your own.' Dee paused to look at her children.

Beatrice looked puzzled; unable to decide if this was to her advantage or not. Eleanor had snuggled closer so Dee couldn't see her face. Oliver was non-committal.

'There's no bathroom and it's all old?' Ollie said but without the earlier resentment and in the tone of a question.

'With the money for the Glasshouse there's plenty left over to renovate. We can open out the back like here and put in a new kitchen. The bathroom will be off the kitchen so you'll still have a bedroom each.'

Ellie squirmed against Dee. 'Does that mean we won't live with you anymore?' she said in a small voice.

'Oh, darling, no, of course not. We're going to put in a door in the hallway and another big opening between the kitchens. It'll be just one big house.'

The three of them were smiling now, considering the possibilities.

'There's another surprise too,' said Dee.

'Raj is moving in,' Beatrice burst out.

Dee laughed, surprised they were still concerned that they would lose her.

'No, Raj is my friend. That's enough. My life has enough complications and so does his.'

Dee reached to put her arms around the three of them but the older two didn't cooperate.

'What's the surprise then?' Ollie was suspicious still.

'I'm not sure I want any more surprises today,' Beatrice chipped in.

Eleanor snuggled closer.

'This is a nice one. Next door is in your names. It belongs to the three of you so when you're older it's an investment. You can rent it out or maybe sell it and have money for a good deposit for your own homes.'

Bea and Ollie looked uncertain about what it meant but pleased. Eleanor still had her face hidden.

She sat up and gave Dee a pleading look, her eyes still damp. 'But I don't want to leave you.'

'Not for a long time and then you all have to approve. Maybe you'll all want to stay there forever so you can look after me when I'm old and can't take myself to the toilet.'

Ollie turned up his nose.

Beatrice said, 'There's services for that.'

'I'll stay with you forever,' Eleanor said.

69.

The lounge room was full of packing crates, piled two high along the glass outer wall. Ollie stood ready with another box.

'No, not on top, they're not strong enough,' Dee called out to him from the hall. 'Start another row on the floor.'

She came in and squinted at the box he was carrying.

'Is that labelled? The removalists need to know where to put things when we get there.'

'It's easy: anything unlabelled goes in my room,' Ollie said with a grin of victory.

'Oliver, you're supposed to be here to help. Please don't make this any more difficult, just do it.'

She handed him a marker pen.

Beatrice and Eleanor had the car packed to drive over to Glebe with some of the smaller things and an esky with the contents of the fridge. They at least were excited to be moving to the inner city. Next year Beatrice would be at Sydney University and Eleanor wanted to transfer to the Performing Arts High School at Newtown. Oliver was reluctant. All his friends and school were nearby. Public transport from Glebe to his school would be a nightmare. For the rest of this year Beatrice would give him a lift in the car Dee had bought her. Transport of siblings was a key promise in return for the present of a car.

'If I want I can live with Dad and keep my own room so why move my stuff?'

Oliver was intransigent. Dee hadn't heard him like this before.

'That's between you and your father. If it's okay with him it's okay with me,' Dee said through clenched teeth.

She was too busy to deal with the fractious teenager Ollie had morphed into since the move was suggested. Maybe you should ask Stephanie, Dee thought but didn't say.

She left him, walked back to the kitchen and continued to pack. The designer corkscrew that never worked and the elaborate wine storage racks that matched the kitchen fittings but just took up bench space could stay. Dee bought wine when she wanted to drink it; who stored wine these days?

Now that she could leave it all behind it hit her—how oppressed she'd been by the furniture and accessories Rob had designed. His masterpiece was in charge of her daily life: of how she sat in the evenings. The leather and chrome lounge suite that was too wide in the seat looked perfect in the sleek glass room but it was impossible to sit on. You could lie right down or perch upright on the front edge.

Whether she wore clothes as she walked from room to room was determined by Rob. She'd been an exhibit in a museum of their failed marriage. From now on she would have privacy to be how she wanted. The first thing she bought for the Glebe house was a comfortable lounge.

Ollie was speaking on his phone and his voice rose to a tone of wheedling, escalating to anger. Then silence. He must have hung up. She gave him a few minutes and went into his room where he sat on the floor in the middle of a mess of newspaper and packing cases.

'No luck?' She waited, Ollie didn't look up but gave a tiny shake of his head.

'You have to give him time and then time to sell the idea to Steph. She has to feel like this is her place too. You'll still be coming for your regular weekends. I reckon next year once Bea is at uni we can work something out so you can stay here for term time.'

'But I want you too.' Ollie put both arms around her legs, like a toddler.

Dee resisted the urge to sit down, to cuddle and reassure him. 'You know you'll be off at uni in a year and a half. You're starting to have your own life … I have to have mine too.'

'I know; but can't I be a baby sometimes?'

She patted him on the head. 'Not now. Now I need you to be a grown-up. The case is coming up in court again next week. If we get everything done maybe we won't have the blitzkrieg of media outside our house every day. I need help with all this.'

'Oh, so the famous warrior doctor hero needs help, eh?' He stood up and beat his chest like a gorilla. 'Son of warrior hero to the rescue!'

Now she was willing to cuddle him. But he didn't need it anymore.

'You know Dad is putting up curtains?' Eleanor interrupted them. 'They got them measured up last week.'

Dee stood with her mouth open. After all her years oppressed by no privacy she was flabbergasted.

'Stephanie said she wouldn't move in unless Dad did it.'

So the domination of Rob's aesthetic over the lives of his family had been tamed. Good on Stephanie.

70.

The steamed dumpling trolley was around again. Dee tried to wave it away but Raj pointed to a basket of the scallop and garlic chive ones. They were her favourite. If she helped him to eat them the risk was she'd be too full for an egg tart.

The Marigold Restaurant in Chinatown was one of the few left in the city with proper yum cha. That meant a huge room where steamy stainless steel trolleys laden with bite-sized, savoury, salty, spicy and sweet snacks snaked between the tables to tempt and tantalise. On Sunday morning it was crowded with Chinese families, from babies and toddlers to elderly grandmothers.

This week it was her treat. Payback for the times Raj shouted her to the $100-plus per person places.

'Enough, please, you need to save room for dessert,' Dee said. 'The secret is to pace yourself so you can have the things that don't come around so often.'

'What have we missed?' Raj said, scanning the room.

'That's not what I meant. You can't always have what you want, at least not all the time.'

Dee knew she was on shaky ground. He was permanently slim and always ate whatever he wanted. The glass-enclosed dessert trolley arrived. It was best to get the egg tarts now in case they didn't come back for a while. Two yellow moons of rich egg custard enclosed in meltingly delicious flaky suet pastry were put on their table.

'It's all so delicious. I want to try everything. Why haven't I been here before?' His voice dropped and he turned the force of his beautiful eyes on her. 'Anyway, why can't I have what I want?'

He put his hand on hers.

'Because you'll burst.'

Raj continued to gaze at her like a puppy. She didn't want to acknowledge what he meant. The move from the Glasshouse meant she was finally out of Rob's oppressive everyday presence. It was time to make her own decisions, be in control of her own life.

To be honest with herself, she wasn't sure of her post-menopausal body as a piece of sexual equipment. It hadn't been tested with another person since Rob and that was before full menopause. Her sexual interest in him had waned in her late forties. Dee wasn't totally surprised by his discovery of himself again with Stephanie.

Did her changed body have the capacity to give or receive pleasure? It was like being a sexually naive teen. She didn't know how to manage the physical transaction with her post-hormonal body.

Other people managed those things. Why couldn't she? Maybe she wasn't scared but wanted to stay in charge, not allow someone else's judgement to be important. All of this had gone through her mind on the morning after their narrow escape from falling into bed in Orange. Since then, each time she was in the physical presence of the gorgeous Raj she tortured herself with the possibilities. Especially when he held her hand and looked at her with those cow-like eyes.

Dee extracted her hand. The teapot was empty. She flipped the lid to indicate empty and caught the eye of a waiter to refill it. She gave him the stamped card so she could pay the bill.

'Now we can eat the egg tarts. They're good with the tea. It cuts the richness of the pastry.'

Raj gave in, turned his eyes to the tarts. Dee refilled their teacups. Two blissful mouthfuls and the tarts were gone.

The place was busy and their bill hadn't come back yet.

'Delicious. The pastry is stunning. Thanks for bringing me,' said Raj.

He took advantage of the delay to put his hand back over hers. She liked the feeling of safety, of comfort and connection. Here in a restaurant there was no threat it could lead to anything more. She left her hand there.

'What about I find us a place down the coast for the weekend after the case? An apartment or rooms at a hotel?'

'Raj, I'm going for Leah. This is the first time she'll have to see Adam in the flesh since the attack. She needs support. I need to be able to pay attention just to her. It's easier if you stay at home. The press will be worked up to a frenzy. I don't want front-page photos of me "escorted by a glamorous Indian playboy".'

'That's ridiculous. I'm not a playboy.'

'Stop being so literal. You know what it was like after Moruya. The press will grab any angle for a story.'

Raj persisted. The trip to Wollongong for Adam's sentencing was an occasion and, for Raj, occasions were to be respected and celebrated. He booked rooms at a hotel right on the beach at Austinmer for the weekend.

*

When Dee broached the idea with the kids they were happy. It wasn't a Rob weekend and she allowed them to spend the weekend on their own for the first time. She warned them no parties, and no noise beyond 10 pm—nothing to alienate the neighbours who they hardly knew yet. Being alone seemed more significant to them than the idea that she would be away with Raj.

They'd been away together before, to Orange. The pressure of his body against hers outside her room at the hotel was one of her treasured memories. They still saw each other regularly and spoke on the phone often—so no big deal. And it was rooms, plural.

He was determined to be at the courtroom too. There was nothing Dee could do. He had a right to attend.

'No one will know who I am. They won't even notice me.'

'Okay, but you have to wear the clothes from Target; you know the ones we bought in Orange.'

'But I threw them out. I didn't even bring them back to Sydney. Who'd look like that voluntarily?'

Sometimes he made her want to tear her hair out. She held her breath and counted to ten.

'Okay, well go and get some more. The same: navy T-shirt, synthetic pants in brown and sneakers that cost less than forty dollars. You can get a jumper in navy too but only if it's acrylic. And don't look at me when we're there, not even outside the court. I'll ring when I've finished with Leah and meet you.'

Her last words to him were 'I really wish you would stay away'. She knew he wouldn't and was glad. It was rooms—plural.

71.

Five months from the incident, Dee slowed the car and pulled off the expressway into the car park at Bulli Pass lookout. The steep drive from the Sydney plateau down the escarpment to Wollongong was notorious for fog on these cold winter mornings but there was a crisp clear blue sky. From inside the car it looked like summer.

Adam's sentencing hearing was in the District Court in Wollongong. She had allowed an extra hour and a half for the hundred-kilometre drive so she could miss the Sydney peak-hour traffic, and in case of fog.

The realisation that she would be in the same room as Adam in a couple of hours chilled her. She almost wished she'd let Raj come with her. She thought about coffee but her stomach said that wasn't a good idea.

It was a gorgeous day. After a few minutes she got out of the car and walked to the fence at the top of the cliff. The air was crisp but still. The cliffs and ocean stretched far away to the south. Tom would never again experience the ocean's deep blue fading to transparent green near the shore. To be alive was the most wondrous good fortune. It seemed her duty to the dead to take advantage of it.

*

At the court Dee sat on a wooden bench outside the doors to the hearing room. Leah got out of the lift and walked jerkily along the corridor towards her. Her dreads were gone and her hair was a close-cropped cap of gentle sandy brown curls. Five months on from the injury she still needed crutches. They were most effective for someone with only one injured leg but Leah had two. Her muscles were crushed so badly at the mid-thigh level on both sides when Adam slammed the car doors on them that Leah had been at risk of kidney failure from the breakdown products of the dead tissue. That part of the danger was over.

She walked slowly, her facial muscles fixed in concentration, and her complexion grey. For Dee, the combination said pain filtered through relentless determination.

Unaided, Leah could only stand for a few moments. Intellectually, she had no lasting impairment.

Dee hadn't seen as much of the girl as she wanted to but Leah was independent and determined. Perhaps Dee's instinct to protect her was too much. Dee had visited her several times on weekends at the rehab facility outside Wollongong. They had met at the committal hearing where Adam had appeared only by video link from the remand centre in Sydney. Today he would be present in person. It was good to be with someone who knew his true evil.

As she came close, Leah gave Dee a nervous smile and propped against the wall next to her.

'Hello, Doc. How's it going?'

Doc was Tom's name for Dee. It jolted her back to the times she saw his black curls in the waiting room. He was always first up, a happy start to the day. The intensity of the pain shocked her. The gnawing ache was worse than when she had first seen his body. She tried to turn the memories into ones of the living Tom: the happiness she felt when she saw his name on the appointments list, his foal-like limbs as he arranged them in the chair opposite, how he pushed his fingers through his hair to get it off his forehead, the shy pride he'd shown the day he brought Leah in to talk about having a baby. The sadness of missed pleasure was easier to bear than the unresolved circumstances of his death.

It was complete nonsense to think she had any control over how the grief took hold of her. Now and forever the great gaping hole of Tom's absence was a permanent feature of her psyche. The pain was always there ready to grab her if she went near it. How much useless comfort had she offered the bereaved in the past? She shook herself away from it. Leah was here, now.

'I'm the one who should be asking how you're going. How's rehab?'

'Getting better. They reckon I'll eventually get off the crutches. Another few months and a couple of operations and I can toss these sticks.' Leah balanced on her own legs to wave the grey aluminium poles.

'That's great. You've done well.' Seeing Leah made Dee feel more apprehensive about what was to come. She tried not to show it. This was the first time either of them had seen Adam since the attack. Leah must be feeling it too.

'How are you feeling about seeing him?'

'Pleased.' Leah gave a defiant toss of her head. 'He's in jail, and we're alive. We won.'

Dee was surprised by Leah's vehemence. What she said was true. Since she'd found out about the plea bargain, Dee had been furious that the justice system would not, could not, reopen Tom's case or investigate the deaths that hovered around Adam like flies around a rotting carcass.

The evidence about the other deaths was all circumstantial. An extraordinary series of deaths clustering around one person but none of them provable as murder. Marlena told Dee that since the Department of Public Prosecutions had come to a deal with Adam's legal team the sentencing hearing today would mostly be a formality. The sentence was a foregone conclusion, hammered out in negotiations in private.

The prosecution accepted Adam's plea of 'recklessly inflict grievous bodily harm' on Leah. 'Recklessly' meant the injury was not deliberate; a chance consequence of a heat-of-the-moment action. The same injury without the intent had a lesser sentence and could be heard in the District Court where sentences were generally less. A further discount to the sentence came because of the guilty plea.

The state saved time and money by accepting a plea to a lesser charge. It also meant Leah and Dee didn't have to endure a cross-examination questioning their veracity, their motivations or, in Dee's case, their sanity. She was grateful the assault did not have to be raked over in minutest detail. And no one had to sit through the violence being recounted in court.

The charge should have been 'attempted murder' and 'kidnapping' at a minimum, but the prosecution feared Dee's video of the attack might be excluded by a clever defence barrister. Dee's phone wasn't readable due to water damage so the evidence came via Raj's phone. The defence could argue that the video was fabricated or edited to leave out parts that showed Adam's actions were rational attempts to save Leah.

The barrister for the prosecution told Dee, 'If we put you on the stand the defence will be able to question you about your past with Adam and the medical board enquiry. Nothing about the death of Tom will be admissible. Your enquiries about the professor would be made to sound like a rejected lover seeking revenge—a divorced and menopausal woman with a grudge. If the video is rejected, which it could be, that might be enough to convince a jury Adam is innocent.'

It was nature's small mercy that Leah did not to have to relive the terror. She had forgotten most of it, although snatches of the dreadful day had returned gradually. There was still a hole though, from the time Adam had tied her to the fence, until she woke up in hospital a week later. That could explain how she was so strong while Dee was sitting at her side trembling with fury and fear at what they had to face inside.

The problem with the amnesia from the head injury was that Leah's evidence would not stand up to cross-examination either. A plea bargain had been the only option.

72.

The prosecution legal team arrived, a phalanx of dark suits with trolleys of documents. The barrister spoke to Leah. She and Dee walked inside with them to sit behind their table, separate from the public gallery. Dee stole a glance around. The courtroom was full. At the back, in the public gallery with a scrum of press, a black head bobbed above all the others. Raj had arrived early enough to score a seat.

As instructed, he was dressed unobtrusively. Relief and comfort welled up as soon as she saw him. His deep brown trustworthy eyes studiously avoided her. She was glad he'd ignored her instructions to stay away.

Adam was brought up stairs directly into the dock from the cells below. The two guards by his side appeared first, then the top of his head. His hair was less brown, less styled, and flecked with grey. He must have dyed it in the past. Dee felt a frisson of satisfaction. It wasn't the grey, it was that it bothered him enough to dye it. His perfectly confident facade was flawed.

There was something different about his face. A pink scar peeped out from under his chin. It must be from when Leah had rammed her head up into his jaw. It had been his blood Dee had seen. Good. But there was something else wrong with his face that she could not place.

Everyone stood as the judge entered from a door to the left of the bench.

Adam had on an expensive grey suit with an impeccable white shirt and navy silk tie. The tie had some sort of crest, probably from the same private school as the judge, or from some exclusive club where they were both members. Adam presented as sober, respectful, patrician, an officer of the court rather than a criminal, but there was something out of sync with the image.

The facts of the offence had been agreed. Adam wasn't allowed to dispute them or claim innocence. Senior medical figures were called as witnesses to Professor Fairborn's excellent character and his achievements; his service to medicine and to genetics were heard. Adam chose to make a statement to the court to express remorse for his actions.

As he was about to stand to speak, Adam put his right hand to his face. His thumb and forefinger palpated the middle of his nose. He glanced at Dee, saw she had observed him and put his hand back down. Dee realised her fear of him was gone.

Adam faced Leah during his claim to be remorseful. From that angle, Dee could see an irregular bump in the previously perfect smooth line from the bridge of his nose to its tip. The evidence of her kick, of his defeat and of her victory, were written there plain as the nose on his face.

Leah held his gaze defiantly. He lowered his head as if ashamed. Clever. Had the defence employed an acting coach?

The judge summed up in the afternoon. Leah and Dee didn't know yet what the sentence was and the judge was painfully slow in getting to the point.

'As you know I can't go behind the facts as agreed by the prosecution and the defence and so cannot sentence him for the more serious offence. The court is not entirely happy with this agreement. In another court, the same injuries could merit a much more serious charge.

'On the balance however, the considerations of a long and expensive trial, the loss to the defendant of his career, business and reputation and the prevention of retraumatising the victims, the court has accepted a guilty plea to the lesser charge of recklessly causing grievous bodily harm. Taking into account the accused's previous impeccable character as well as the seriousness of the wounds inflicted and noting that the penalty for intentionally committing that offence are much greater, the court imposes a sentence of six years imprisonment with a non-parole period of four and a half years.'

It wasn't nearly enough. It left Tom unavenged. Dee looked at Leah. The girl hadn't changed her expression of defiance. Her eyes were on Adam as he was led down the stairs to the cells below the court.

He was out of the way for now. His medical career was over. Now that he had a record of violent crime any future suspicious deaths would be investigated.

She and Leah were alive.

73.

Leah sat near the entrance to the court with the prosecution lawyers to shield her from the press while Dee brought her car to the bottom of the disabled ramp at the entrance. Leah's sticks occupied the full width of the ramp to block anyone trying to get her attention. Once they were both safely in the car, Dee drove till she was sure no press were on their trail and parked in the railway station car park.

She moved the gear stick to park, turned off the engine and pulled on the handbrake. In the close confines of the car there was a connection that didn't need words. They both sat still, not ready for the next step.

To say goodbye to Leah felt like a goodbye to Tom. Dee didn't want to let her go.

After a minute, Dee undid her seatbelt and said, 'I'll walk you to the platform.'

Leah looked pleased.

'Thanks. My train's not for half an hour. Maybe we can sit together for a while.'

Dee thought she was about to say more. So much was unresolved. She waited but Leah opened her door and got out. She hobbled to the platform.

The sky had clouded over and a sharp wind from the south pierced their clothes. They retreated to the Railway Refreshment Rooms, a remnant of the nineteenth-century grand days of rail travel.

Leah said she wasn't hungry but Dee bought them hot chocolate and pastries. She wanted to nourish Tom's girlfriend, to see her eat, to see her partake of the pleasures of the world.

They sat in a wooden booth in the once grand space. Leah was quiet, eyes down as she sipped the hot chocolate. After a while she broke off a piece of the sultana snail and nibbled it. They talked about rehab and what Leah planned to do when she was more mobile. As she spoke, Leah was restrained, her answers about the future lacked detail.

'This is good, thanks.' Leah broke off more of the pastry.

Bit by bit she ate the whole thing. A brown flake of the pastry was caught on her pale pink lower lip. Dee's eyes were captured by the brown and pink set against her perfect olive skin. It was as if she saw through Tom's eyes—all the beauty and the unmovable determination that Tom fell in love with. He would be happy to see her take pleasure in the world. Dee was glad she had tempted her to eat.

It was harder to tempt her to speak. Dee's conversational advances got short answers. It seemed the girl was holding something back.

The train was due in ten minutes. Dee addressed the problem head on.

'Are you okay, Leah? You seem quiet.'

Leah looked up over the rim of her mug and grinned. It wasn't the reaction Dee expected.

'Yes, I'm good. It's just … I've got some news and I don't know how to say it.'

Dee wanted to reach across to hold her hand but knew that was likely to push the tentative foray into communication back into hiding.

'Just tell me. After what we've been through nothing can be too bad.'

'It's not bad, it's good. I'm pregnant.' Leah smiled as she dropped her bombshell.

'Wow, that is big news,' Dee said to cover her instant thoughts of—that was quick, and while you're in rehab too. I hope it's not Joe's!

Leah must have read her face, 'No, you don't understand. It's Tom's. From the sperm at GenSafe.'

At first Dee didn't comprehend. She forced herself to go over Leah's words.

'You're going to have a baby from Tom's sperm?'

Leah nodded, wide eyes examining Dee's face for a reaction.

Dee smiled. 'You're going to have Tom's baby—oh Leah, that's lovely.'

74.

A picture of her potential lover waiting for her at the hotel sprang fully formed into Dee's mind as she drove north along the coast towards Austinmer—a drone's-eye view of Raj's two-metre frame sprawled diagonally across a bed, arms akimbo, knees together and twisted over to the left. The bedclothes were acid bright, lime green and yellow, twisted and tousled as though he had been rolling in them like a dog after a swim. The floor was white ceramic tiles. The only colours were the greens of the bedding with the dense blacks and browns of a naked Raj slashed across the picture like Japanese calligraphy. The tantalising mirage stayed just out of reach as she drove towards him.

It was perfect—could have been a fashion spread in *Vogue*. Where did she fit in the picture? Where did messy things like children, his and hers, fit into the arty image?

They didn't.

A sign indicated 'Sydney via Bulli Pass left lane, 1 km.' She could ring Raj, claim to be exhausted after the trial. Go home to the children. But the kids had planned their first weekend on their own. Mum would cramp their style. It wasn't fair to them or

Raj. He had saved her life and Leah's. And who knew if he even wanted more than a weekend by the sea with a friend?

She moved to the left lane to keep the options open. Fashion shoots weren't reality; even the terminally beautiful were carefully staged and air brushed, only pictures in magazines, or in this case, in her head. The world was more complex and incorporated all sorts of messiness. To confront the complexity was almost the point of a relationship—one of its major pleasures.

The next sign was a 500 metre warning. Quickly she was at 'Sydney via Bulli left lanes'. The arrows in her lane gave left or straight ahead options. She stayed straight. The turnoff passed by on her left.

Along the coast road the sun was gone. It disappeared early behind the escarpment that extended from Wollongong to the Sydney plateau. The sky to the east was pale pink fading to just barely blue. The higher clouds were still in sunlight and reflected bruised pinks from the western sky. Down near the edge of the ocean were clouds in thousands of shades of bright white to silver.

Their suite overlooked the beach. It was seaside modern from ten years ago. Cream walls with hard ceramic tiles in imitation terracotta. Bulky cane furniture with cushions in sand and blues. There were small prints of the beach by local artists on the walls—nothing like her fantasy.

Raj was still in his let's-not-be-noticeable outfit. The pants were synthetic brown as Dee ordered but had stovepipe legs that clung to his long slim legs. The plain navy T-shirt skimmed his nipples in a way that took Dee back to him naked.

'These don't look too bad on you,' she said and immediately regretted putting his physical being out there between them.

'It's interesting to not be noticed,' he said. 'I don't know if I like it or not.'

I'll always notice you, she thought. She wanted to put her hand on his chest.

Instead she said, 'I'm hungry, how about fish and chips? Takeaway? I don't want to be anywhere but here.'

Raj pulled a champagne cork opener and two glasses out of the picnic basket. From the fridge he produced a bottle of her favourite bubbles, a Stefano Lubiana sparkling from Tasmania. He must have brought it from Sydney.

They drank a glass together on the balcony. The ocean breeze was chilly. Raj brought her a wrap from the bed.

'You relax. I'll go do hunter–gatherer duty. There's a good place just down the block,' he said.

Once he was out the door she looked around. The wicker picnic basket he'd taken to Orange sat on the kitchen bench. Raj's suitcase was in the smaller of the two bedrooms. He had taken hers from her at the door. It was in the room with the full-length windows opening onto the balcony and an unobstructed view of the Pacific Ocean.

It was still chilly but she went back outside with her glass. The view would soon be gone. The unending sound of the surf, of long waves rolling and booming against the shore from across the vast ocean reminded Dee that there was more in the world than Adam.

There was a knock at the door. It was two hotel staff with an outdoor heater.

'This is the heater your husband asked for. Should we set it up?'

Dee took them through to the balcony with her head averted so they wouldn't see the flush at the base of her neck.

Raj came back with far too many parcels for just fish and chips. He set out china, cutlery and napkins from the picnic basket. There were a dozen oysters to share first. The heater roasted them on one side as the salt tang of the ocean chilled their faces.

'Can we eat the fish and chips out of the paper—it stays warmer?' Dee asked.

The real reason was to go back to the easy meals of summer holidays and childhood. Her first taste of a Sydney rock oyster was one of her few memories of her father. At low tide they walked around the rocks to 'his secret spot'. The water reached up to Dee's knees. He was tall and strong. He had a short knife to prise the shells off the rocks. He ate several till she felt left out and wanted one too. He tipped the strange thing directly into her mouth. It was salty, soft and slippery. When she squished it with her tongue there was an explosion of flavour, all the scent of an ocean distilled into a mouthful.

Her father was dead. Dada, she still called him. Dead Dada, dead like Tom, like all the others whose lives were cut short by Adam.

The empty paper and uneaten salad on the table between them took Dee back to the summer holidays she and her mum spent here at the caravan park. Any open space was now long gone for expensive apartments but the smell and sounds were the same. There were even traces of sand underfoot. All that was missing were the sunburnt shoulders to be soothed with the cool wetness of slices of tomato or cucumber.

She hoped her kids had similar memories. And Raj, what of Raj? He was only starting to be able to build memories with his girls. Her decision was made.

'You're quiet. Are you okay?' Raj asked.

Dee considered how to pass on the jumbled memories and thoughts about parents and lives cut short but it was too hard, too soppy.

'I was thinking about the past, people who are gone. But it's the living, our children, yours and mine, who we need to think about now.'

Raj moved his chair closer. He slid down so she was higher than him and took her arm and put it over his shoulders. 'You don't have to say it. I know.'

'It's not forever, just till they're older, till they know you and till you know what's going on with them.'

Raj didn't say anything for a long time. Dee turned to snuggle closer. She put her hand on his chest. The T-shirt was soft and silky. Not from Target—probably a designer label. He looked good. She let it go.

'What if I run off with another woman?' Raj said.

'That's up to you.'

There'd been too many momentous moments for one day. She wasn't willing to get involved in another one.

'Sorry,' he said, 'that's not going to happen. You won't get away that easily. I'll keep hanging around till you can't do without me. And, anyway, aren't you supposed to be compassionate and caring for the lost and lonely?'

I already can't do without him. I'd be dead without Raj. It's Friday, no one wants or needs me except Raj. This is for me.

Dee stood up and took his arm. She pulled him up out of the chair. 'Let's go inside and see what we can do about the lonely bit.'